"Fast-paced! Riveting! Emotional! Suspenseful! Compelling! Complex! This book brings it ALL!"

"It is also not the novel to start reading in the evening or the reader will find themselves losing sleep in your desire to learn what happens next."

"*The Girl They Took* by Leslie Wolfe is so good I can't find the words to describe how good it is. Definitely it is the best Tess Winnett book yet and maybe the best book Leslie Wolfe has written."

"The ending is so astonishing I truly believe no one can predict it."

"Plenty of twists and turns lead the reader to a satisfying conclusion."

"I've read most of this author's books and enjoyed each one, but this one ranks right up at the top, it's just that good." -- PWA Allen

PRAISE FOR LESLIE WOLFE

"The queen of suspense is back with another gripping installment in the Tess Winnett series."

"Leslie Wolfe has written another great mystery. Thank you for a great plot and outstanding characters."

Powerful! "Leslie Wolfe weaves a compelling story of an FBI agent who looks beyond the rule book in her quest to recover a kidnapped child."

THE
GIRL
YOU
KILLED

BOOKS BY LESLIE WOLFE

TESS WINNETT SERIES

Dawn Girl
The Watson Girl
Glimpse of Death
Taker of Lives
Not Really Dead
Girl With A Rose
Mile High Death
The Girl They Took
The Girl Hunter

STANDALONE TITLES

The Surgeon
The Girl You Killed
Stories Untold
Love, Lies and Murder

DETECTIVE KAY SHARP SERIES

The Girl From Silent Lake
Beneath Blackwater River
The Angel Creek Girls
The Girl on Wildfire Ridge
Missing Girl at Frozen Falls

BAXTER & HOLT SERIES

Las Vegas Girl
Casino Girl
Las Vegas Crime

ALEX HOFFMANN SERIES

Executive
Devil's Move
The Backup Asset
The Ghost Pattern
Operation Sunset

For the complete list of books in all available formats, visit:

Amazon.com/LeslieWolfe

THE
GIRL
YOU
KILLED

LESLIE WOLFE

ITALICS PUBLISHING

$\varUpsilon\!\varUpsilon$ **ITALICS**

Italics Publishing Inc.
ISBN: 978-1-945302-72-5
Edited by Joni Wilson.
Cover and interior design by Sam Roman.

ACKNOWLEDGMENT

A special thank you to Mark Freyberg, my New York City authority for all matters legal. Mark's command of the law and passion for deciphering its intricacies translates into zero unanswered questions for this author. He's a true legal oracle and a wonderful friend.

ACKNOWLEDGEMENT

For Astrid

1

A LETTER

They'd taken everything from him.

In a matter of days, Craig Brafford's entire world had been torn apart, pulled inside out, shredded to unrecognizable bits colored in hues of nightmare.

About half a dozen cops had rummaged through his house looking for who knows what, sparing nothing and breaking stuff out of spite; he'd seen the photos. Now the place was empty, front door unlocked, an invitation for local thugs to loot and occupy as soon as his arrest hit the evening news. He'd begged his lawyer, the widely successful Lamar Goodridge, to swing by and lock it, maybe turn on the alarm system.

"Not my job," the man had answered calmly, his voice low, frozen, loaded with contempt. "You can barely afford my services as it is," he'd added, glancing at the gold watch adorning his wrist. The man charged $900 per hour, and Craig would've gladly paid for his time, but Mr. Goodridge couldn't let himself be caught giving a crap about one of his clients or running errands for them.

Humiliated, he'd lowered his head and never mentioned it again, cringing powerlessly at the thought of his beautiful home overtaken by hordes of street filth. Goodridge had taken his case on a hefty retainer that had cleaned Craig's accounts. Regardless, Goodridge still frowned when he looked at him, as if the sight of the inmate clad in an orange jumpsuit was offensive somehow, as if he'd never seen inmates before. Maybe Goodridge was wondering if Craig could pay his legal bills once the ordeal was over. Or perhaps he was trying to guess if his client had done it or not, although Goodridge himself had started their first meeting by saying, "I don't care if you're innocent. Either way, you deserve the best defense money can buy. *Your* money that is. Otherwise . . ." He let the word trail into silence, accompanied by a shrug and a hand gesture conveying his indifference for all the potentially innocent people who couldn't afford decent legal representation and would lose their freedom for only that reason: not being rich enough. Even if they were innocent.

He was smug, his lawyer. He rarely worked pro bono cases, and when he did, he only represented defendants from Sunnyside, the neighborhood where he'd been born and raised in dire destitution. He called his unofficial preference "a tribute to his ancestry." Either pro bono or full-paying client, his inquisitive eyes drilled into the very fabric of whoever sat across from him, and there was little he didn't see. That was probably why he could charge that much or why he rarely lost a case.

His retainer had left no bail money to be posted; Craig was tapped out, cash and credit. The five-hundred-thousand-dollar bail could've just as well been five million. Too proud and too ashamed to ask for help from affluent people he knew, he braced himself for weeks of confinement. With a swift drop of the judge's gavel, he'd been remanded, his attorney shrugging off his concerns about the time he'd have to spend behind bars awaiting trial.

Then he was hauled over to the Houston Southeast Jail, where he was locked up with the general population.

He'd assumed *innocent until proven guilty* would somehow apply to his time in lockup. He'd been sorely wrong. With the expedience and efficiency of a soulless conveyor belt, the system had stripped him of his remaining dignity, prodding and probing, inflicting physical pain whenever he didn't toe the line, and slapping a number on him without wasting a moment's consideration on his presumed innocence.

He was now prisoner number five-three-three-seven-one-nine.

The number resonated in his mind, the obsessive chorus of an unwritten song he couldn't rid his mind of, the epitome of his lost dignity, of his disappearing identity and his foreclosed freedom. Pale and feeling his insides tied up in a permanent knot of anguish and fear, he'd held his head down and had endured, day after day, waiting, hoping, reciting the unwilling mantra that had ensnared his rebellious brain.

Five-three-three-seven-one-nine.

That's who he was now. He'd unwillingly *become* five-three-three-seven-one-nine, quickly realizing it was far better than fighting back, than rejecting his new reality and its many insults and injuries, all in the name of a precept that only seemed to carry value in movies. There was no innocent until proven guilty. In prison, he was guilty. Nothing else. No one cared while he festered in that hellhole, forgotten by everyone, choking on his anger and shame.

Him, being there . . . it wasn't supposed to happen. Not to him. Not ever.

He wasn't built for it. His athletic yet slender five-nine frame wasn't a testimony to hours spent pumping iron in the gym, like most of his fellow inmates were. His hands, fine, nervous, with long fingers and clean nails attested to the white-collar status he'd worked so hard to achieve. His tall forehead and pushed-up hair, his fine features and deep hazel eyes portrayed him as a charismatic and attractive man, a quality he'd always valued about himself but had started fearing since the day he set foot in Houston Southeast Jail.

In there, the common denominator of everything was fear. Primal, animalistic, incessant fear.

Yet three weeks had somehow passed, unnervingly slowly, while he learned to respond when called "seven-one-nine" or "inmate." He found that some of the wardens were just ordinary people making a living, while others thrived on inflicting pain on the prisoners under their control. Like E. Mellor, the six-foot-four, three-hundred-pound corrections officer with a sadistic glint in his eyes and a grin that stretched his lips over his grinding teeth like a predator's snarl. Mellor sometimes ran his hand over the tip of his rubber stick in an obscene gesture promising nothing good to the inmate who didn't keep his eyes lowered and didn't pay him off. Officer E. Mellor—who knows what the E stood for on his name tag—had taken the last few dollars Craig had on him the day he was remanded and had kept demanding more from the fountain that had already run dry.

That night, at least Mellor was out of sight, the guard pacing the hallways an older Latino, N. Chavez by nametag. His skin was darkened by years of smoking the cheapest stuff available, and his potbelly, stretching the buttons of his shirt to the point of snapping off like spat watermelon seeds, spoke of cirrhosis at some point in the man's near future. Dark circles under his eyes and a stained, grayed-out mustache completed the portrait of the only guard who had not laid a hand on him yet, since he'd been locked up in there. The others, Mellor more than any of them, had at least shoved him against the wall or took their rubber sticks to his kidneys in passing, just to show him how things worked. Just for the heck of it.

Garbled radio transmission came from Chavez's lapel, and he quickly responded with a numeric code, then headed straight to Craig's cell with a groan and an expression of frustration on his face.

Craig stood and approached the bars, clutching them with cold, sweaty, trembling fingers.

"Hands," Chavez said, waiting for him to turn around and put his hands through an opening in the bars. Then he slapped a pair of handcuffs on Craig's wrists, the touch of cold metal sending shivers down his spine. "Your lawyer's here to see you," Chavez added.

Craig's eyebrows shot up. "Now?" Goodridge had been there that morning, preparing him for tomorrow's day in court, the third in his trial.

Chavez shrugged. Grabbing his arm, he led him out of the cell and down the hallway toward one of the interview rooms. "What are you in for?"

"I didn't do anything, I swear," he replied, his voice sad, defeated.

A roar of laughter erupted from the cell they were just passing by. "Another innocent man thrown in jail," a guttural voice with a thick Guatemalan accent announced loudly, and soon the entire section was hollering, shouting obscenities, and laughing at his expense.

"No one in here is guilty of anything," Chavez said, sarcasm layered heavy in his voice. "Not even the ones who take plea deals." He shot him a quick look, then shrugged as if deciding not to give a crap about him anymore.

"Murder," he said, lowering his voice. "They're saying I killed—"

"Okay, go in there," Chavez said, shoving him gently into the room. The door buzzed and locked as it closed behind them.

A man in a tailored suit and expensive shoes stood quickly when he entered.

Craig turned to Chavez. "This isn't my lawyer." Chavez gawked at him, then grabbed his radio.

The attorney held his hand up. "This is no mistake. Arthur Flanagan, estate attorney," he said, extracting a business card from a holder and handing it to him. Then he popped the locks on his briefcase and opened it. "I have a letter for you." He took out a thick, bubble-lined envelope and handed it over to Craig.

Chavez took it instead, his gesture quick, determined. "I have to check this before you can see it. Procedure."

The attorney waited, standing impatiently, a fresh smell of pricey aftershave regaling Craig's nostrils, reminding him of what he used to have and had lost. Estate attorney? What estate? Had one of his parents died?

Chavez pulled the tab and unsealed the envelope.

"Who's this from?" the inmate asked.

The lawyer's eyes darted toward his open briefcase. Maybe he kept a notepad in there. "It's from Andrea Wilmore Brafford," he replied calmly. "It was to be given to you in the event of her death."

His breath caught. He tried to speak, to ask when she had given him that letter, but his throat was parched dry, and only a strangled, raspy whimper came out. He took a step forward and reached for the attorney's arm, but the man stepped back. Chavez grabbed his elbow, and he stopped, frozen in place, feeling the blood draining from his face.

"Take it easy, all right?" Chavez let go of his arm and pulled out a few folded, neatly typed pages from the envelope. He inspected them quickly, then handed the letter over to him. Before Craig could start reading, the guard looked inside the envelope. "There's something else in here," Chavez said, turning the envelope upside down above his hand and shaking it gently.

A pendant on a silver chain clinked quietly as it fell from the envelope and settled in the guard's hand. When Craig recognized the blue stones, a wave of nausea hit him hard in the pit of his stomach as the room started to spin with him. *No. This wasn't happening,* his thoughts raced. *It couldn't happen. I still remember what I did. I know what I didn't do.*

"Nice," the guard said, closing his fist around the pendant. "But you can't have this; you know the rules."

"No . . . no . . . please, let me touch it for a moment," he pleaded, stuttering, tears streaking his cheeks. "Let me make sure it's—"

"Okay, for one moment, and that's it," Chavez said, reluctantly opening his palm and letting out a heavy sigh tainted with mustard and onion and cheap tobacco.

Transfixed, he touched the chain with trembling fingers, the torn clasp, then ran his thumb over the center stone of the pendant, like he'd done so many times in the past. He swallowed hard, still staring at the small object curled in the guard's chubby palm. It was real. The nightmare was real.

Sweat broke at the roots of his hair and started trickling down his forehead. He raised his handcuffed hands to wipe his brow and noticed the letter he was still holding absentmindedly.

Breath caught inside his chest, he scanned the pages, looking for something that would make sense of it all, that would answer his questions. There was nothing, not until the last page, where the ending paragraph clarified everything for him with a few simple, paralyzing words.

The girl you killed is watching over you from paradise, lounging on cloud number nine with a Margarita in her hand, hoping you'll have everything you deserve in this life after she's gone. Goodbye, my love. You were the one.

Blood rushed to his head in a wave of rage, his heart pounding, his fists clenched so hard his knuckles cracked, the last page of the letter crumpled and stained by his sweat as it fell to the ground. "No, Andi . . . no . . . you didn't do this to me . . ." he whispered. Eyes staring into emptiness like a wounded, panicked animal, he rushed to the barred door and started pounding against the dirty, wired glass with both fists, the steel handcuffs cutting into his flesh.

"Let me out of here," he shouted. "I didn't kill my wife; I swear I didn't . . ." He repeated the phrase over and over, his voice breaking, threatened by tears of rage and powerlessness and despair. The only response he got was from other inmates banging against steel bars in rhythmic, surreal resonance muffled by the closed door.

"Hey, cut it out," Chavez shouted, but Craig didn't hear him. He kept pounding against the door, kicking at it, bloodying his knuckles against the scratched metal, pleading and calling for help. Unable to think clearly, he didn't notice the tears streaming down his stained face.

Chavez touched the radio button at his chest. "Need some help in here." Then he collected the pages of the letter scattered on the floor, slid them back into the envelope, and slid the pendant in there before folding the envelope and tucking it inside his chest pocket. "The DA will need to see this. It's evidence."

The guard's words hit him in the chest like a fist, but he kept banging against the door with all his strength under Chavez's disappointed look and the attorney's disgusted glare until he fell to his knees, drained, sobbing so hard he couldn't breathe. "I didn't kill her, I swear," he faltered, choked, gasping for air. "I didn't . . ."

Chavez walked over to him and grabbed his arm. "Get it together, already. You have court tomorrow."

He looked at the guard through the blur of tears. "You don't understand," he pleaded, grabbing at the man's sleeve. "The pendant, she—" He stopped in time, realizing what he was about to say.

The door buzzed open, and Officer Mellor stepped inside with a glint of excited anticipation in his eyes. "Seven-one-nine, you're coming with me."

Several Months Earlier

2

INTERVIEW

The dolphin twisted playfully in the air then fell into the water with a splash, seeding salty droplets on Andi's navy blue pantsuit and matching pumps. She stepped back, her heels clicking out of place on the smooth, wet concrete surrounding the pool.

Grinning widely, she threw the place a loving look, wondering why she'd stayed away after graduation. Texas A&M University was her alma mater, and the marine biology research facility in Galveston was her favorite place in the world. As a student, she'd spent every available moment in that pool, swimming with dolphins and stingrays, getting ready for a day such as today, when she'd be able to join the marine research team not as a student but as a junior research scientist. One day, soon maybe, she'd be able to lead her own team, but that journey she'd been planning for years started right there, by the poolside, with an in-person interview she absolutely had to pass.

Earlier that morning, she'd spent hours pacing the bedroom floor in her underwear, unable to decide what to put on. Should she wear formal interview attire, showing the organization the respect it deserved? Or should she fall back into old habits, wearing shorts and a T-shirt over her bikini, secretly hoping the interviewer was just as passionate about the sea and its inhabitants as she was, enough not to care about dress code?

"You only have one opportunity to make a good first impression," her dad had offered advice, immediately tilting the balance in favor of the business suit she never got to wear otherwise. It looked impossibly good on her slender body, bringing out the blue in her eyes and the sun-bleached highlights in her short, tousled hair.

Now she looked like she didn't belong in the place that felt so much like home. She checked the time, then glanced toward the main building, wondering if she'd misunderstood where the interview was supposed to take place.

"You must be Andrea," a young woman said in a cheerful voice, after having crossed the pool with a few freestyle strokes, moving smoothly through the water. She rested her elbows on the edge of the pool and wiped droplets off her face with a quick, unpretentious hand gesture. "I'm Marjorie," she added, "the program lead."

Andrea crouched by the poolside and shook the woman's dripping hand. "Call me Andi, please."

"Andi, sure." She had a pleasant, open smile that touched her brown eyes. "You can call me Marj."

Andi's smile widened. She liked her already.

"All right then, let's chat for a few moments," Marj said, putting her palms on the side of the pool as if getting ready to pull herself out but stopped short of it. "We can do this in an office or in here, with the dolphins." She tilted her head, amused. "You wouldn't happen to have a swimsuit—"

Andi was already unbuttoning her suit jacket, grinning widely. A few moments later, her formal clothing abandoned on a bench in a neatly folded stack, she joined Marj in the pool, welcoming the refreshing feel of saltwater on her heated skin as she took a perfect plunge. "I'm ready," she said as soon as she resurfaced.

"Let me tell you a little bit about the program," Marj said. "Looking at your academic achievement, you'd be an excellent fit for it. The study is budgeted for two years, and it measures the effect of climate change on dolphin migration patterns and population growth."

"Excellent," Andi said, the excitement in her voice unmistakable. "This is right up my alley."

"I've seen that, yes, although you chose to run a different study for your final project. Sea lions, huh? There aren't any sea lions here, in the Gulf." Andi could've sworn she heard a tinge of regret in Marj's voice. She'd found a kindred spirit, someone who shared her passion for marine life.

"I was part of a student exchange program with the University of California San Diego—"

"Scripps?"

Andi nodded. "Scripps Oceanography, yes."

"Wasn't this a divergence from your earlier studies?"

"I didn't see it as such. The first three years I dedicated myself to marine life, while the final year I welcomed the opportunity to study its environment in detail, specifically the delicate balance that ensures earth's rich marine fauna continues to exist."

"So, tell me about your sea lions project. I heard it was peer-reviewed and published. Congratulations!"

"Thank you," she replied, a little surprised. Marj had done her homework. She chuckled quietly. "It started from a sea lion pup I found dead on the coast one day. It was almost fully grown and had been killed by a propeller. We were studying pollution patterns that semester, and I thought I'd study the vibrissae. I wanted to see if I could measure the levels of metabolized ocean toxicants in the whiskers." She smiled shyly, looking at the water sloshing against the wall for a short moment. "Sea lions don't shed, so unlike human hair, their whiskers keep growing throughout their entire life, mapping the story of their environment." She stopped talking for a moment, remembering who Marj was. "But you already know this."

"Who processed the whiskers for toxins?" she asked, interest sparking in her eyes.

"A private lab that does work for private pharmaceutical clients and law enforcement forensics teams. I know someone," she added, feeling her cheeks catch fire. It felt as if her study was less valuable because she had help finding the lab to run the tests. "Dr. Ellefson, the chief medical examiner for Harris County, is a friend of the family. He pointed me in the right direction."

Marj's interest remained strong, her enthusiasm as strong as Andi's. "What did you find?"

"The sea lion pup had been exposed to several heavy metals, hydrocarbons, plastics, just to name a few. The study stood out," she added, feeling her face flush as it did every time she talked about her achievements, "because we had a piece of documented history of water pollution in the sea lions' habitat spanning about two years, timelined in the whisker as the pup grew to near maturity. Like circles in a tree trunk if you'd like, only sequential, not concentrical."

Marj gave her a long, appreciative stare. "This is incredible. This is exactly the kind of thinking we need to bring on our team."

Andi smiled the entire time she drove home from Galveston in her red, convertible Beetle, singing along with the radio, at times stopping to call Craig, but he wasn't picking up. She ached to share the good news with her husband, but that would have to wait. He must've been with a client, showing a property or signing papers. Those were the only times when he didn't take her calls, or anyone else's for that matter.

Her father wasn't picking up either, and she left him an excited message before returning to vocalize alongside Maroon 5 and its "Beautiful Mistakes." She blushed as she let her imagination carry her to how she planned to celebrate her future career, with Craig, in bed, just like the song suggested.

With champagne, chilled to perfection and served in tall flute glasses, although, for her, a Coke or beer would work just as well, drunk straight from the sweaty bottle.

Andi had not been formally offered the research scientist job, not yet. But Marj had said she was the most promising candidate, her academic background a perfect fit, and her passion a passport for the team she wanted to join. The rest of the steps were a formality. Another interview with an associate professor, most likely with Mr. Cesar, *The Cesar*, as the students had dubbed the tall and imposing man. She'd taken his Comparative Animal Physiology, and he'd written her the recommendation that had opened the doors for her year in San Diego, calling her "his most promising student yet." She wasn't worried about passing the interview with The Cesar. It would probably be nothing more than a casual conversation between teacher and former student, with a side of advice on how to navigate the perils of an academic career.

Then she'd have to pass a background check, but she had nothing to hide and nothing to fear. Fill out some forms to allow them to pull her credit and criminal history. Nothing to it. Yup, she could celebrate tonight with champagne because that made Craig happy, and if he was smiling, her world was turning just the right way.

The song ended a couple of seconds before she turned the corner onto her street. She and Craig had shared his apartment since she'd moved in right after college. It was a two bedroom on the seventeenth floor of an expensive condo on Caroline Street. It had its charms, its close proximity to Discovery Green park and the Toyota Center, making it easy for them to take a walk or watch a ball game without having to drive and worry about downtown parking.

Andi loved that apartment. It represented her transition into an adult lifestyle she deeply enjoyed, from college student to young wife, madly in love, thrilled and excited for every day she was given to live. It was a good distance from her future job, taking her about an hour to drive without counting any rush hour traffic. So maybe Craig's idea to sell the apartment and move to the suburbs, halving that distance, was a good one.

The first notes of Kelly Clarkson's "Stronger" hit the air as Andi turned onto Caroline Street, but she slowed down and pressed a button to silence the radio. The street was filled with police cars with red-and-blue flashers, so bright they were visible from a distance even against the dazzling sunlight. A section of the sidewalk was cordoned off with yellow *Do Not Cross* tape right before her building's garage entrance.

A chill traveled through her veins as she came to a complete stop. They had cordoned off *her* building. The thought of Craig's phone going straight to voicemail raised alarm bells in her mind, although it was the middle of a Tuesday, and he was at work. He was okay . . . he had to be. Not everything that happened in the world was about him.

Yet the sight of the medical examiner's van rattled her body with another chill. Someone had died . . . someone in her building, someone she maybe knew. Driving slowly, she approached the building until a cop put his hand up and stopped her, then walked over to her side with a scowl on his round, sweaty face.

"We're closed for traffic. Go around the block."

"I live here," she replied, pointing at the high rise towering above their heads. "That's my home."

The cop pressed his lips together for a brief moment. "I'll need to see your driver's license."

Andi handed over the piece of plastic while she searched for a familiar figure among the many crime scene investigators rushing in and out of the building. Its entrance doors, bluish, thick glass, had been propped open with straps. Crime scene technicians, wearing white coveralls, carried several totes with evidence bags to their vans. Unable to see what was being taken away, she turned her attention to the people coming out of the building.

"What happened?" she asked, afraid to hear the answer.

The cop shook his head. "Sorry, ma'am, we can't disclose details to the public. You'll have to hear about it on the news."

"Wh—was it my apartment?" she stammered, the frozen claw of fear still cold and tight around her chest. "I'm in seventeen eleven."

"No, ma'am," he replied quickly, handing her back the driver's license. An intense wave of relief brought tears to her eyes. "Park across the street if there's room, or in the back, and use the side service entrance. Go straight up to your apartment, all right? Don't go on a fact-finding mission for your social media friends. That would be obstruction of justice—"

"Yeah, I know that," she replied, eager to get out of there.

The officer lifted his fingers to his temple then waved her on. She drove slowly, still staring at the building's main entrance. Two techs were rolling a body on a stretcher, wrapped in a black, zippered bag. The silhouette seemed frail and tiny, taking little space on the stretcher. Maybe a woman, someone thin and petite.

Through some touch of favorable karma, a parking spot opened across the street right as she was driving by, and she quickly maneuvered her Beetle to take the space before anyone else could claim it. She put the roof up and locked it with the remote as she crossed the street, making her way to the side entrance.

As the two technicians loaded the stretcher into the van, she recognized the third man coming out of the building. She approached the yellow tape and waved. The man waved back and walked toward her briskly, a hint of a smile on his pale, thin lips.

"Dr. Ellefson," she greeted him with warmth in her voice.

The man lifted his gloved hands in an unspoken apology. "Andi," he said, giving her an appreciative look. "You look stunning. The university interview, was that today?"

"Yes, it was," she replied cheerfully, forgetting for a moment they were standing at the edge of a crime scene. "It went really well. I believe I nailed it."

"Of course, you did," the man replied proudly. "I'd give you the hug you deserve, but—" He gestured with his gloved hands. "I've touched things."

"No worries," she replied, her smile now gone. "When you're done, if you have the time, come up for a cup of coffee. I'm in seventeen eleven." As she voiced the invite, she realized he wasn't going to be able to stop by. He had an autopsy to perform.

"I thought I recognized your building," he replied in a soft tone that carried the memory of concern, or maybe Andi only imagined that. It wasn't that far-fetched to think Dr. Ellefson might've had a moment's worry knowing he was responding to a suspicious death in her building. "Thing is, it's Rebecca who knows all the addresses by heart. I'd be lost without her."

"So would I," she whispered, smiling shyly, "albeit for different reasons." Silently, they shared the briefest moment of friendship and warmth, standing on different sides of the yellow police tape. Then Andi asked, just as Dr. Ellefson was getting ready to leave. "What happened here?"

He looked left and right, then spoke in a low, quiet voice. "A girl's been found dead. Second floor."

"OD?" Andi asked, knowing her neighborhood's crime statistics.

He nodded, his head movement barely noticeable. "You know I can't discuss an open case, sweetie. But once the case is closed, you can ask me again, maybe next time we meet at your dad's for poker night." A glimmer lit his eyes. She knew he loved their card game nights just as much as she did.

"That's a promise." Andi loved talking old cases with the medical examiner, although sometimes the details of such conversations were less than welcome at the card table. One time, the doctor's wife, Rebecca, a Texas A&M English lit professor, jokingly said they were using their conversation about autopsies and forensics as a way to distract other players and win. Of course, it wasn't true.

Dr. Ellefson nodded in her direction and smiled one more time, his wrinkled face and kind eyes turning steeled and professional as he walked toward the van. His thinning, shoulder-length hair, almost entirely white with too few strands of blond remaining, waved in the afternoon breeze as he climbed into the back, followed closely by one of his assistants.

Andi entered the air-conditioned lobby of her building with hesitant steps. Waiting for the elevator, she felt a pang of guilt over how relieved she was that the body hauled in the black plastic bag wasn't Craig's. A chill traveled down her spine realizing that someone had taken her last breath only a few stories below the apartment where she and Craig were enjoying a blissful life, completely insulated from other people's battles. Maybe that girl had cried for help, and no one heard her. Or maybe she'd died quietly in her sleep, unaware she'd never wake again.

While the elevator hummed and lifted her to the seventeenth floor, she realized she didn't know any of her second-floor neighbors. No matter how hard she tried, she couldn't put a face to the shape strapped to the stretcher, although she had to have crossed paths with that girl at least once. But they probably locked eyes for less than a second, nodded and smiled, then looked promptly away in the unspoken gesture of indifference. People didn't care about people anymore. They lived insulated in their own bubbles, intoxicated and overwhelmed by too much of everything going on, rarely letting anyone new in.

Or maybe Craig was right. The neighborhood was becoming too dangerous, unpalatable, not the right place to raise a family. Not when all sorts of shady characters bought their way into what used to be decent buildings with their ill-gotten gains. She loved that apartment, the first home Craig and she had shared, but soon, in only a few days, they were moving to the suburbs, leaving all that behind.

She might never get to know who her second floor neighbor was.

Defense Attorney Goodridge: What was Andrea's state of mind at that time?

Janelle Larimer: She seemed fine, but that was before—

Defense Attorney Goodridge: Thank you. No more questions for this witness, Your Honor.

3

A CLIENT

The client, a middle-age heap of entitled arrogance by the name of Solomon Donati Jr., wore a permanent scowl on his face. His thick, dark eyebrows converged above his nose, seeding firm ridges across his brow. He'd opened the door to his million-dollar Uptown colonial with a hint of a welcoming smile on his tense lips. That smile instantly died when he saw Craig Brafford on his doorstep.

"Now, why the hell would I list my home with someone as green as you?" he asked, crossing his arms at his chest and barring the entrance with his well-built body.

In painful contrast, Craig's slender body, clad in a charcoal suit and white shirt, came up short in more ways than one. The maritime shipping entrepreneur towered at least seven inches over the young Realtor. Craig had always found height to work to the advantage of those who enjoyed the view from the stratosphere. Maybe they were closer to the angels, like an old woman once told him. He didn't really believe that, but either way, taller men had no issue asserting themselves faster and with less effort than shorter ones. Than him.

He'd done everything he could think of to gain an inch or two while it was still possible. He'd spent all his high school and college years on the basketball court, where he was barely tolerated because of his height. He'd seen pro players and had envied their stature, convinced that hoops had something to do with it. Believing he could maybe override his genetics and squeeze a little more elevation from his growing bones, he spared no effort. He ended up almost three inches taller than his father, which meant his efforts had probably paid off some, but he was no Michael Jordan.

That, even more than his twenty-nine years of age, couldn't be helped. Everything else was game.

He'd brushed up his hair and learned how to use a flexible spray on his quiff to shape his brown hair, going for the perception of another inch if he didn't really have it in actual height. He'd avidly learned how to make himself accepted and appreciated in society, figuring out how to make himself indispensable to people, regardless of prominence or place on the human food chain. He understood the power of a warm, sincere smile, and he wielded it like a gilded broadsword.

Intelligent and creative, having finished cum laude with a business degree, Craig found the most effective weapon in his arsenal was other people's feelings. Those dictated people's behaviors more often than their intellect had a say in things. He soon became a virtuoso at playing the strings of the hearts of many, from clients to business partners to everyone really. Only five years after graduation and the youngest team member, he was aching to become the top-performing Realtor at his firm. Yet his digital Rolodex had few client names that could make that possible, his youth getting in the way. His boss assigned him the cheapest deals, saving the big bucks for more senior team members. Craig was there to assist with Tanglewood apartment sales and Chinatown showings no one else wanted.

The man considering whether to slam the door in Craig's face wasn't a lead that had come from the office. He was the result of countless hours of research reading through thousands of mindless social media posts from affluent women with nothing better to do than yap about their new homes. And new homes meant the old ones were about to hit the market. The annoyingly tall and unforgiving Solomon Donati Jr. was a lead he'd burned endless hours locating, someone he couldn't afford to lose.

Craig swallowed, feeling his throat tighten.

"Because I can sell it faster and get you more money than anyone else," he replied, his voice loaded with self-confidence, his lips stretched into a reassuring, warm smile, carefully not overdone. Lips barely showing perfectly white teeth, not the grin of an eager idiot.

"Is that so?"

Craig held the client's gaze openly, unflinching, while sweat beads formed at the roots of his hair. He really needed a big client. If he reeled in someone like Donati, maybe then his boss would show him a little respect.

Slowly, the client extended his hand and gave Craig's a firm, weighing shake, then stepped out of the way, inviting him in. The house was a large, two-story building, relatively new, that would probably take a while to unload, especially if the client knew the market values and wanted it sold at a premium.

The interior, with its large windows and gleaming hardwood floors, was presentable. The charming pool in the backyard—complete with tiki umbrellas and a bar—definitely an element that could lure some rich retirees from California or New York. The kitchen, equipped with expensive, modern appliances, had been decorated by someone with a dubious sense of taste. Some of the cabinets were blue, while others were cream. Craig caught himself staring in disbelief, wondering why someone would do something like that to an otherwise lovely, classy piece of real estate. Maybe the buyer wouldn't care too much about it. Perhaps it could be sold as the new posh kitchen cabinet design or something. Didn't matter. Whatever the challenge, he could pull it off.

Craig turned to the client with a smile. "You have a wonderful investment here, Mr. Donati."

The client's frown deepened for a brief moment, then faded somewhat. "Call me Sol."

Craig nodded. "Well, Sol, I can make you a lot of money on this house. How much did you pay for it?" He already knew when the client had acquired the 3,200-square-foot mansion and for how much. He'd done his homework. But every trap had to be adequately baited, and that took time and patience.

"We bought it four years ago, for about seven hundred." The client was truthful. Usually, his clients tended to lie just a little bit, either playing it lower to show how smart they were or higher to indicate the house had more value. But Sol, he was a tough one to read. "The market is a different animal today."

"Exactly," Craig replied, the excitement in his voice genuine. "You're looking at about one million dollars, and that's only if you're in a big rush."

"I'm in no rush," the client replied, drilling his eyes into Craig's. Not a hint of emotion washed over Donati's face. "Don't want this piece of business pending for too long either."

"Understood," Craig replied calmly. He paced the living room floor a little longer, studying the layout in detail, letting his client's curiosity build up. "When will this be ready to show?"

"In about three weeks. The new house is ready. People are coming on Monday to get everything moved."

Craig stared at the walls for another long moment, rubbing his clean-shaven jaw with his cold fingers. He didn't take too long; the client was growing impatient. "I'll be entirely honest with you, Sol, even if that goes somewhat against our normal business practices when it comes to managing clients' expectations."

He paused, and the client invited him to continue with a head nod and a hand gesture, a little impatient. He'd pushed it as far as it would go without breaking.

"If I have time, I'm confident I can get you one-point-one for this house." A flicker of excitement lit Donati's dark eyes. "But, if you'll give me an exclusive contract for, say, one month, I'll do anything and everything in my power to get you one-point-two."

First to break eye contact, Donati shoved his hands into his pants pockets. He wore blue slacks and a white Brioni golf shirt, both pristinely laundered and pressed, the unmistakable mark of old money. Not ridiculously rich old money, but enough to have been raised a certain way. He walked toward the window facing the backyard pool and looked outside for a long, loaded moment of silence.

"Two weeks," Donati eventually replied. "You have two weeks, and you'll shave one percent off your commission."

Craig frowned and pretended to consider the offer. He'd come prepared to slash two points and accept a week exclusivity. "All right," he eventually said, his words carried on a poorly disguised sigh. "You drive a hard bargain. I'll do the papers for an exclusive listing for two weeks, nonexclusive after that, one percent off during my exclusive time."

"During all of it," Donati added, his tone firm. "And you'll have three months to sell it, or the deal's off and I hire someone else to do it."

Craig nodded pensively. "All right. But what if I get you more than one-point-two?" Donati's eyes glimmered again. "Would you consider paying an extra five percent for anything I get you over one-point-two?"

Donati sized him up again, just like he'd done on his front doorstep. Then he extended his hand. "Hell, yeah. You bring that cash in, and I'll make you one happy cowboy, son."

Craig shook the man's hand with enthusiasm. "We won't be putting that last five percent arrangement in the contract; I hope you understand."

A lopsided grin blooming on Donati's lips sealed the deal. Craig quickly pulled a contract form from his briefcase and started filling it out while Donati checked his watch impatiently.

"What are you planning to do to push this house above one-two?" he asked, stopping his pacing by the dining room table Craig was using for a desk.

Craig lifted his eyes from the paperwork with a quick grin. "I have a few tricks up my sleeve," he replied. "My secret sauce, if you will." He resumed filling in the particulars of the deal with hasty caps. "Need not worry. Once I've earned the privilege of assisting you in the sale of your first property, I will always be there for you."

"Ha," Donati laughed, "of course you will." He resumed pacing and didn't speak for a while. Only the sound of shuffled papers and distant chirping coming from the backyard invaded the tense silence. "I like to isolate, alienate, and drain resources," he added, his voice unexpectedly mellow, like a father teaching a son. "That's how I hunt. My clients buy what I'm selling thinking I'm their last resource, nothing short of their salvation."

Craig watched him intently, transfixed, for what seemed like a long moment. His short sentence answered the big question that was keeping Craig up at night. Isolate, alienate, drain resources. Brilliant.

"I'm nowhere near that sophisticated," he reciprocated gratefully. "I just know the market really well and I think globally, not locally. Chances are your buyer won't be a Texan. I hope you don't mind."

Donati chuckled and didn't hesitate when Craig pushed the paperwork over to him. Taking Craig's pen, he signed vigorously, a complicated, illegible signature with a bit of an upward slant, the trademark of a confident overachiever. "When you get tired of real estate, come work for me." He set Craig's pen on the contract and pushed the papers across the table. "After you sell my house, son, not before." He patted Craig on the back rather forcefully and cackled, his breath smelling of cigar smoke.

Craig allowed himself a quiet laugh. "Understood, yes sir. Thank you." He grabbed his briefcase after shaking the client's hand once more, then headed for the door. "By the way," he said as he was about to grab the handle, an unfinished thought prodding him to take advantage of the unique opportunity presented by the businessman's good mood. "The last Thursday of this month, my wife and I are hosting a little get-together for local business leaders and VIP clients. If you and the missus should find the time—"

"Send me the details," Donati replied, nodding slightly, his smile gone, his frown still there. "It will be interesting to watch you work a room."

He thanked him and left, careful to not show too much spring in his step on the way out. As soon as he started the diesel engine on his black Mercedes SUV, and the door to the million-dollar home was closed, he breathed deeply, his smile vanished, replaced by a tension in his jaw that made his muscles ache and knot under his skin.

He had less than twenty days to move into the new house he'd just bought, get it ready for the party, and find about nine other prominent businesspeople willing to attend.

District Attorney Buscher: As a partner in the firm and the defendant's supervisor, what was your opinion about Craig Brafford from a professional standpoint?

Jeremy Hughes: Our firm thrived with him onboard. He was intelligent, dedicated, a hard worker. Immensely ambitious.

District Attorney Buscher: The kind of ambition that pushes people to break the law?

Jeremy Hughes: The kind of ambition that gets the job done. You should know, Mr. District Attorney. I'm willing to bet this is exactly how you got where you are today.

4

LUNCH

Andi loved Italian food.

Mille Ponti Restaurant brought Italian cuisine to the downtown Houston area with mouthwatering flavors that lured with the promise of rich Parmesan cheese and unctuous Alfredo sauce dripping from every piece of fettuccine. No matter how many times she'd promised herself to try someplace new, she always ended up on Commerce Street again, staring at the red, white, and green logo representing a gondola on a Venetian canal. The place felt like home.

This time, she hoped the familiar place would help her dissipate the dark gloom that had tightened an iron fist around her heart. It was as if she was submerged in a sea of impending doom, of an inexplicable terror about to strike her down, unable to breathe, paralyzed.

Lunch rush hour was finally receding, leaving a few patio tables open. Andi loved dining outside and believed no other way was better suited to enjoy an Italian meal than eat it the way Italians, the inventors of al fresco dining, had intended. Maybe sunshine and blue sky were all she needed to scare the shadows away.

She was a few minutes late meeting Janelle Larimer for lunch. Janelle was her best friend and had been since they were eight-year-olds, and Andi's father had bought a house next door to the Larimers. A bittersweet memory for Andi.

Although she was young at the time, she still recalled her mother's unexpected death and the devastation her absence had brought to her father, to her own broken heart. For weeks, they both cried themselves to sleep yet hid from each other as if grieving was a sin. As if it was a shameful act meant to be carried out in darkness and seclusion, under threat of heavy punishment if somehow exposed to the light of day or the presence of others.

During the day, they rarely spoke, as if disturbing the heavy silence engulfing the empty house would somehow jeopardize the cherished memory of her mother. Andi still went to school. Her father made breakfast, packed her lunch, and fixed dinner for the both of them. Silently, with an unconvincing smile and a quick tousling of her hair after placing a plate in front of her and wishing her bon appétit, the way he always did before taking his seat at the table. But he wasn't there anymore. His eyes were almost always staring into emptiness as if searching for something that wasn't there. He rarely spoke. Whenever he tried, tears strangled his voice, and he'd turn his head away from Andi, hiding his sorrow. She endured the silence and the loss, too young to know which one was worse or how to find her bearings in a world turned upside down.

"How could I have not seen it coming?" was the one phrase he kept saying, over and over, his face scrunched in a desperate attempt to hold back tears, the wail that must've filled his chest urging to come out. "The signs were there, all of them," he'd added one night, still seated at the dining table among half-full plates pushed aside, leaning into his elbows. He rubbed his forehead angrily as if trying to get to something buried in there beyond skin and bone and rip it out. She'd reached across the table that night and touched her father's arm, but he didn't seem to sense her closeness. He was miles away, probably clawing at the already fading memory of his wife, trying to hold on to what he'd lost.

Then, one night, when she dreaded turning off the light in her bedroom, knowing tears would soon follow where her mother's tuck-in kiss had left a chasm, her father had stumbled into her room, falling to his knees and opening his arms wide.

"Forgive me, my sweet girl," he sobbed. "I—I wasn't there for you when you needed me the most . . . I was too damn busy blaming myself for not seeing your mother's illness until . . . Will you forgive me?" She still recalled rushing into his arms and curling up against his tear-streaked chest, hearing his strong heartbeat pounding. They sobbed in each other's arms for what seemed like hours, but once the light of dawn cast away the shadows of the longest night in her entire existence, they had a plan. They were moving.

Her father, Dr. Hunter Wilmore, a known and respected veterinarian, chose a brick single-story house within walking distance of Clear Creek and Walter Hall Park. It had large windows to invite the sunlight in to warm their battered hearts, and a large lot with mature trees to hang swings and hammocks from. It happened to be next door to a scrawny little girl, Andi's age, a spirited adventurous girl with unruly curls and fire in her blood.

Janelle didn't believe it, but both father and daughter credited her with bringing them back to life that fall. She was always in trouble, the little firecracker. One time, she'd climbed so far up a live oak tree in the Wilmore backyard, they had to call the fire department. Another time, she talked Dr. Wilmore into helping her keep a puppy she'd claimed she'd received as a gift from a neighbor. The vet talked the Larimers into adopting the pup, only to realize a few weeks later he'd been duped by the clever little girl. It took two hours of questioning until Janelle confessed that she'd come across a litter of coyote pups in the woods behind the park and had swiped one from the den.

The girls started third grade together that fall. They entered the schoolyard holding hands. A shy and hesitant Andi walked just half a step behind Janelle, who wouldn't let go of her hand. Since that day, they'd been inseparable. Until college.

Andi had chosen to follow in her father's footsteps, and Dr. Wilmore not so secretly dreamed of putting his well-established veterinary practice into his daughter's hands at some point when it was time to retire. But Andi's passion wasn't in seeing furry patients one after the next.

She loved the ocean.

No, it went far beyond that. Andrea Wilmore was in love with the ocean, with all its creatures, large and small. Locking her into an office for days on end would be a sin, or so Dr. Wilmore believed.

Andi had tried to talk Janelle into taking marine biology with her, but her bestie had stayed firm, although her eyes occasionally teared up. "Nope, no way, girl. It ain't for me. I've seen you sitting on your ass in those tide pools filled with who knows what creepy crawlies, having a blast. But have you seen me? In the water, I mean. If a tiny little fish swims by and I feel the water moving against my leg, I run for my life. And I scream."

Janelle screamed like no one else, a piercing sound that seeded instant panic in anyone who still drew breath thinking the sky had to be falling. Sadly, she wasn't a fit for marine biology or any such field of study. Instead, Janelle had opted for a management degree and thrived, zooming through classes with straight As and finishing her degree in record time.

They'd stayed in touch throughout their college years, went to parties together in both worlds, double-dated, chatted almost every night, talked almost every day on their drive to school. They shared the same old hammock behind the Wilmore house to watch the sunset, sometimes drinking iced tea or, as seniors, cold beer straight from the bottle. Their friendship, forged over the years, grew stronger than ever. Janelle's job had taken a toll on her free time, as did Andi's relationship with Craig, but they still managed to squeeze in a couple of lunches each month, a dinner or two, and several calls.

Her mouth watered as she picked up the scent of chicken Parmesan, Andi stopped by the patio fence, looking for Janelle. She was easy to spot, her black, curly mane a dead giveaway in any crowd. She spotted her across the patio, seated at a table by the railing, facing Buffalo Bayou.

Approaching silently on her toes, Andi wrapped her arms around Janelle's shoulders and planted a loud smooch on her cheek. Janelle squealed, then returned the kiss.

"Ooh, what is that?" Andi asked. "New makeup? New hair? Anybody I know?"

"Damn, you're perceptive," Janelle replied. "Yes, new makeup brand. I went top shelf this time."

"Good for you. It shows." Andi took a seat across from Janelle and dragged her wrought iron chair closer to the table, its legs grating loudly against the concrete. "And the hair?"

"What? This?" Janelle replied, tugging at a couple of beaded braids that emerged from the left side of her part. "This is just a nice try," she laughed. "I don't have it in me to spend a gazillion hours braiding my hair, so this is as braided as it's ever going to get."

"All right, but you're deflecting, woman." Andi picked up the menu and pretended to parse it, although she knew what she wanted.

Janelle lowered her eyes and smiled, playing with the hem of her white napkin, her manicured fingernails following the thread up to the corner and then back to where it disappeared into the fold. "I met a guy."

"Aha," Andi replied, smiling widely. She leaned back against the chair's wiry backrest. "Let's hear it all. Details please . . . all of them. We're adults here," she chuckled.

"Well, he's—"

"What can I get you, ladies?" The server was tall and skinny, not a day older than twenty-two, and he was shamelessly sizing them up with a lustful grin on his pale lips.

Through the mesh metal table, he stared at Janelle's legs, then at Andi's. Janelle wore a short skirt and a sleeveless blouse, while Andi had on jeans and a tank top. The server's attention returned to Janelle's exposed skin while he pretended to take notes.

The two girls looked at each other and chuckled.

"We'll have the bruschetta to share and a tossed salad for me," Andi said.

"You turned vegetarian, girl?" Janelle shifted her eyes to the server and batted her eyelashes, mock-flirting with him. "Let's add a carpaccio and some chicken Marsala."

The server managed to peel himself away from the table and disappear.

"You are shameless," Andi laughed.

"He's going to spill the food, you think?" Janelle batted her eyelashes again and bit her lip provocatively. "If I give him the high-altitude joyride?" She winked, and they both burst into laughter.

"Oh, cut it out. You were about to tell me about your new mystery man."

"Ah." Janelle turned serious for a moment, then a different kind of smile bloomed on her lips. "He's, um, not who I would've expected to date." She lowered her eyes for a moment. "His name is Troy. He's a project manager for a construction company."

Andi frowned a little. "And what's wrong with Troy? How does this poor man fail to meet the goddess's expectations?"

Janelle locked eyes with Andi for a moment, then blurted, "He's divorced, and has a kid. Ugh."

"That's okay," Andi replied, reaching out across the table and giving Janelle's hand a squeeze. "Marriages fail all the time, and people deserve second chances. Hey," she called, seeing Janelle didn't lift her eyes from the napkin she was busy studying. "As long as you're happy, everything's fine."

When Janelle looked at Andi again, her smile was gone. "When did you know Craig was the one?"

Andi breathed; her lungs starved for air for some reason. Janelle's question brought a swirl of thoughts and doubts, of questions about herself and her future with Craig.

The young woman sitting across from her was just about to stick her fork into a fresh piece of raw beef covered in capers and finely chopped red onion. She was her best friend, and still, there were things she didn't dare to say out loud, to share with her. Things so profoundly personal, so twisted that not even Janelle could understand.

Craig was like a drug to her . . . pure cocaine, shot straight in the arm, uncut. She ached for his touch, trembled for it, would've done anything to see him smile, to know he kept loving her more and more just as she did him. She barely remembered anything from her past twelve months since she'd met him, all swept into oblivion by a whirlwind of emotion so intense it had wiped everything else from existence, from physical memory.

The times they made love left her spent and weak, craving more, never getting enough of him. What always started as a waltz of equals in foreplay ended with him taking her as he desired, somehow turning dominant while she turned submissive, aching, wanting, yearning. He was the one . . . the only one for her.

"Wow, I shut you up good, didn't I?" Janelle laughed, then stabbed another piece of meat and rolled it expertly with her fork before biting into it.

She managed a light chuckle. "How did I know he was the one? . . . Well, I guess when I acknowledged I couldn't see myself with anyone else. I didn't even realize when and how, but I had become obsessive about him. He was all I could think about."

"Yeah . . ." Janelle replied. "Funny how that works, huh?" There was a sadness in her voice, an unspoken sense of loss.

"Why the long face?" Andi bit into a piece of crunchy bruschetta. The taste of garlic and fresh basil filled her mouth.

"I'd thought I'd stay free, unattached, remember?" She set the fork down and took a sip of cold, sparkling water.

"Unmarried and childless. An independent woman. My own person."

"And now? Did that change?"

"It's changing." She sighed, then pushed the plate aside, half-eaten. "The worst part of it all, I don't seem to care much about any of that independence crap anymore." She stared at Andi intently, as if asking for help. "I'm changing. And it's petrifying."

Andi took another bite, then chewed it quickly. "It's okay, you know. You might discover the person you're changing into is better than the old you. Who knows, you might actually enjoy the new you a whole lot better."

Janelle smiled, an unspoken thank you in her eyes. "Are you happy? I mean, really happy, deep inside?"

Her question drove a sharp icicle through Andi's heart. There was a sense of foreboding in that simple, uncompromising question, no reason for that chill spreading through her veins whatsoever.

"Yes, I am," she replied honestly, although she felt as if she were lying. She felt guilty somehow. "I wouldn't have it any other way. I can't imagine a life without Craig." That part felt true.

"Don't tell me, he takes out the trash every night?" Janelle's right eyebrow was raised, but her earlier spark of laughter had vanished.

Andi nodded. She felt bad flaunting her happiness like that, but Craig deserved recognition. "Every night, like clockwork."

Janelle chuckled quietly, but her eyes remained serious, grim. "Good. Then there's hope for good ol' me." She pulled aside, making room for the server to unload their entrees, then pushed the chicken Marsala plate closer to Andi. "Wanna share?"

"Uh-uh." That unnerving sense of foreboding was back, gnawing at her insides relentlessly. She put her fork down on her untouched salad plate and leaned back into her chair, lost in thought, miles away from the sun-filled patio of her favorite restaurant.

"My turn to ask," Janelle said. "Why the long face?"

Andi struggled to pull herself back to reality. One of her fears was real, menacing. "I haven't heard back from the university yet." Her hands felt cold, and she clasped them together tightly. "I thought I had the job, but then . . . crickets."

Janelle's brow furrowed for a brief moment. "These things take time. I'm sure they're just slow with their paper pushing. Did you send them a thank you note?"

"Yes, as soon as I got back home. But that was almost a week ago."

Janelle chewed silently for a while. Usually, that was a bad sign.

She worked for the Department of Labor and had insider's knowledge into human resource practices and statistics. The résumé Andi had sent to the university when she'd applied for the research position had been vetted by Janelle, her cover letter too. Janelle had trained her with mock interview questions, taught her what to say and how to act.

"I'm sure they'll be in touch soon with next steps." She seemed serious. "Just in case, have you ever googled yourself?"

Andi nodded. "Squeaky clean."

"Good." Janelle's smile returned. She cut a piece of chicken and put it in her mouth, then half-closed her eyes while chewing it. "I don't care how many calories I've gone through today. It was worth it." She patted her lips gently with the napkin, careful not to smudge her lip gloss. "Oh, almost forgot to tell you. We saw Craig the other night."

"We?"

"Troy and me." Janelle's cheeks flushed a little. "He was at Game Nite, downing drinks with that guy, um—"

"Who?"

Janelle pressed her lips together, frustrated. "Can't remember his name. Tall, sexy, with a short beard. He was best man at your wedding."

"Ah, Jude." Andi took a sip of water. "He's Craig's closest friend."

Janelle shot Andi a quick, inquisitive glance then looked away.

"What?" Andi asked. A bit of the earlier chill returned.

"Nothing," Janelle said, shaking her head. "Really, it's nothing."

"Oh, come on," Andi insisted, hoping the slight tremble in her voice was imperceptible. "Whatever it is, out with it already." Janelle just stared at her. "It's me, remember? You can tell me anything."

"Okay," she replied, looking sideways for a moment. "Listen, if I didn't know Craig so well and his relationship with you, I'd say he's gay."

"What?" Andi laughed out loud, turning a few heads on the patio. "No way. Jude's his best friend, nothing more."

"They were sitting very close together, their heads almost touching, whispering. Craig didn't even notice me, and I was standing right there, by their table."

"That's Craig when he's talking business with Jude." She chuckled, relieved. "They never talk about anything else, not even sports."

"If you say so."

"Janelle," Andi reached over the table and took her friend's hands into hers. "Craig isn't gay. Don't you think I'd know? You and I, we're sitting close together, holding hands right now. Are we sleeping together?"

Janelle grinned widely, a mischievous glimmer in her eyes. "Nope. But I often wondered—"

"Get out of here." Andi threw her napkin at Janelle. It landed on her head, and they both roared with laughter.

They walked together to their cars and parted with a long hug. And yet, somewhere beneath all that good spirit lurked a merciless chill, coiled like a venomous snake inside Andi's gut was a sense of dread she just couldn't shake.

District Attorney Buscher: What can you tell us about Andrea Wilmore Brafford's demeanor after that job interview?

Jude Drennon: The one at the university? Andi seemed all right to me; but let me tell you this. I don't believe any of this mess would've happened if it weren't for that friend of hers, Janelle. That busybody should be outlawed. Always meddling in people's lives, digging, prodding, nagging, seeding suspicion, all under the guise of helping a friend.

District Attorney Buscher: What suspicion?

5

INVESTIGATION

The new house was a dream.

Craig must've had access to some information, maybe a distressed seller or some other way he took advantage of his role as Realtor. No other way he could've managed to get them the sprawling 3,400-square-foot property sitting on one acre of perfectly manicured landscaping. It was way above what they could afford.

A few days before, he'd surprised Andi with a phone call and an invitation to see the house. She'd expected a showing, but he was waiting with a keychain engraved with her initials instead, holding it with two fingers in the air, ready to drop it in the palm of her hand. The surprise was overwhelming, the house absolutely perfect. Yet she felt a tinge of sorrow for having been excluded from the entire journey of finding it together, of discussing the purchase and making the offer, of all that which made buying a house together the cornerstone of married life.

He'd apologized profusely and explained he'd had only two minutes to sneak in an offer. The property was going to hit the market way below its real value and all he could do was hold back the listing until he filled out an offer form and submitted it, hoping the seller would sign the deal quickly. Jude had helped get him the mortgage on the fly. "Welcome home, sweetheart," he'd whispered in her ear as he scooped her in his arms and crossed the threshold.

He set her down on the gleaming white marble floor of a breathtaking foyer that opened up into a vast living room with vaulted ceilings. Taking her hand, he walked her through the entire house, presenting it in typical overzealous Realtor style, in a pretend game where she was a picky buyer, and he was selling the home to her.

"For those rainy nights when you feel like spending the evening with loved ones watching a blockbuster, this screening room has been designed with entertainment and luxury in mind. The sconce lights on a remote-controlled dimmer; the dark-colored walls; the built-in, five-point-one surround system; and the rich, sound-absorbing velvet draperies will confer a unique viewing experience. Add a few comfortable armchairs and a screen to suit your preference, and you're ready to make out in your very own movie theater."

She smiled, enchanted, a little dizzy, still unable to believe that the fantastic property was now theirs.

"Crown molding," he continued, his voice loaded with pride and the thrill of achievement, "premium custom framing around windows and doors, upgraded granite in the kitchen and baths—"

"All right," she said, wrapping her arms around his neck and sealing his mouth with a kiss. "I'll buy it," she whispered out of breath when he let her go.

"You won't regret our tiny apartment?" he asked with mock worry in his voice.

"Let me think," she played along. "N—no, I don't think so." They burst into an echoing roar of laughter that ended in a torrid kiss and breathless, rushed lovemaking on the upgraded granite of the kitchen island.

That had happened a few days ago, but her cheeks still burned when she recalled the details of that afternoon, the way her entire being had come alive under his touch. Like warm clay, ready to be molded into whatever he wished her to be.

Aching to be spun into the shape of his fantasies, completely filling his hands, her body a perfect fit for his.

Now she stood among piles of neatly packed cardboard boxes in the old apartment, almost ready to call the job done. Kitchen cabinets with their doors gaping open, stood empty, barren, ready for the cleaning crew to render them spotless and irresistible to any interested buyers. Ripping a new section of paper towel, she grabbed a bottle of Windex fitted with a sprayer and wiped the Formica counters one more time, not leaving much for the cleaners. She was a little afraid to be still and unoccupied with her thoughts; somewhere underneath all the excitement of the new house and the move, that unspoken fear wrapped frozen fingers around her heart.

Craig's voice carried through the thin walls from his study. He was still making phone calls for work, although it was almost seven in the evening, and they hadn't had dinner yet. The following morning, the movers were scheduled to show up early. She felt a sense of excitement at the thought of living in their new house, closer to the university, closer to her father's house. For a few moments, that rekindled elation drowned the angst coiled in her gut, silencing it. If she didn't think about it for a while, it would disappear into the nothingness it had come from, because it was entirely baseless. It had to be. Everything was perfect and there was absolutely nothing to be afraid of.

The doorbell rang, startling her. She wasn't expecting anyone in particular, but people had come and gone incessantly over the past few days, as Craig had repairs done to the apartment before putting it on the market. She didn't check through the peephole; she just opened the door. Then froze.

She was staring at a police badge, held in front of her face by a bleached blonde with dark shades and tight lines flanking the downward-pointing corners of her mouth.

"Detective Otwell, Houston PD," the woman said. She spoke with an authoritative, harsh voice. "I have a few questions about Nikki Edwards. May we take this inside?" She gestured toward Andi's apartment with her left hand, holding a notepad and an envelope.

Andi frowned, then threw a quick look over her shoulder at the piles of boxes lining the living room walls. "I don't know any Nikki, um—"

"Edwards."

"Okay, sure, come in." She stepped aside, invited the cop to enter with a hand gesture, and closed the door behind her. "We're moving; pardon the mess."

The cop shrugged while she scanned the room thoroughly as if she was investigating Andi and Craig, not some unknown woman. As if they were suspects in who knows what crime.

"When are you moving?" she asked, her dark shades still on her face. Andi wondered if that was a technique to hide her eyes during interviews, or if light really bothered her that much.

"Tomorrow," Andi replied calmly. "Tell me, what can I do for you, Detective?"

Craig's voice carried through the walls as he started another phone call.

"Who's that?"

"My husband. He's working." Andi stared at the dark, reflective lenses intently, not hiding her annoyance. "I'm sorry, Detective, but we're busy with the move and everything. If I can answer anything for you, I'd be happy to. If not, please excuse—"

"Nikki Edwards," the woman said, speaking slowly. "Do you or your husband know her?"

"No. Who is she?"

"Was . . ." The cop allowed for a loaded, almost scary moment of silence. "She was your neighbor on the second floor."

"Oh, the overdose from last week?"

"How did you know she overdosed?" Andi bit her lip for a brief moment. With cops, she had to be careful what she said. They could twist her words around in their rush to make arrests, warranted or not.

Otwell took the tip of her pen to the notepad, ready to scribble.

"We didn't. It's building gossip and a safe guess considering we're in downtown Houston, right?"

A beat of silence. "Right." The detective stared at her again, but Andi held her gaze unperturbed. "And you didn't know her?"

"I already told you, no, I didn't."

"How about your husband? I'll need to speak with him too."

"He didn't know her either. We discussed it after we heard of her death. I was coming home from the university when they were taking her body away. Terrible . . ."

"Yes, these things usually are." Otwell flipped the cover of her notepad to close it with one quick hand gesture. "I was thinking, she was about your age . . . maybe you knew her, at least in passing."

Andi shook her head and kept her lips pressed tightly together. How many times would she have to say she didn't know that poor girl? "I'm actually surprised it took you so long to get to us. She wasn't a priority for the department, I guess?"

That statement brought lines of tension around the cop's mouth. "Nothing could be further from the truth." The woman propped her right hand on her hip. "What you see in movies doesn't match reality. Things take time."

"What is the reality?" Andi asked sweetly, smiling. "I bet you guys are overworked to the bone."

"Uh-huh, damn right we are. Since the beginning of the year, we've had over three hundred murders in this city. An accidental overdose rarely justifies the hours to run follow-up interviews."

Andi waited for her to continue, but that didn't happen. Otwell flipped open her notepad and asked, "Where are you moving to? In case I have more questions."

"Brookhaven, just off Bellfort Avenue." Andi gave the exact address, and the cop wrote it down.

"Nice," she commented with discernible envy. "Way better neighborhood than this one. Congratulations." She turned to leave but then turned around and handed her the envelope she'd been holding under her notepad. "I found this in the hallway, in front of your door."

Andi took it and recognized the Texas A&M University logo. She felt the blood draining from her face as the room started spinning. It couldn't be . . . They'd rejected her. Only rejections were done by mail; everything else was handled by email or phone call. Her dream job, the career she'd been preparing for her entire life, wasn't going to happen.

"Are you okay?" the cop asked, grabbing her arm as if to support her.

She nodded as vigorously as she could, eager to be rid of the cop and open the letter in peace. Maybe there was a reason why they didn't extend the job offer, something she could fix. Perhaps there was some hope left.

District Attorney Buscher: Did you meet Andrea Wilmore Brafford in person while investigating Nikki Edwards's death?

Detective Barbara Otwell: Yes, I did.

District Attorney Buscher: At that time or during subsequent investigations, did you establish any connection between Andrea Wilmore Brafford and Nikki Edwards?

Detective Barbara Otwell: No. The cases are completely unrelated.

District Attorney Buscher: During your interview, how did Andrea Wilmore Brafford seem to you?

Detective Barbara Otwell: Happy. I remember thinking, they must be newlyweds because she was beaming. Then she saw the letter.

6

THE FATHER

Dr. Wilmore didn't work Monday mornings.

Since his veterinary practice had started doing better than he'd ever anticipated, he worked long days all week, and that included a full day on Saturdays and a half-day on Sundays. He deserved to sleep in on Monday mornings, but Andi knew he'd already be up on his feet at eight or so, sipping his first cup of java and ignoring the slice of toast he always made for himself just like Andi's mother used to.

Only he never touched it.

Later in the evening, in a silent homage, he'd feed it to the fish in Clear Lake, only if the ducks didn't get to the fast-sinking pieces first.

Andi pulled her Beetle into the driveway after the short drive from her new house, only minutes away. The perfect spring morning with incredible azure skies and a touch of breeze went unnoticed; her mind was elsewhere, stuck in an interior debate over what she was about to do.

Her father opened the door before she could put her key in the lock.

"Andi, what a nice surprise." He wrapped his arms around her and placed a smooch on her cheek, then rested his face against hers for a moment she relished. Her father's strength and warmth were what she needed. Still, it made her sad somehow. "What brings you here so early? And all dressed up?" He led the way inside the house that used to be her home until about eighteen months ago. It already seemed a touch foreign, yet so familiar. The scent of toast and fresh coffee, lavender dryer sheets, and apple-scented candles.

"On my way to a job interview."

"Ah," he replied as he poured her a cup of coffee from the pot. He replaced the pot in the coffee maker and sat at the kitchen table, hands clasped neatly in front of him, ready to listen.

Silence filled the room with unspoken words, yet Andi's thoughts swirled, unsure what to say. "I wanted to invite you to a little get-together we're having with some friends. It's our six-month wedding anniversary." Her voice was choked. She sounded off as if she were still a little girl and she was telling a lie. She wasn't, but the invite wasn't the only reason she'd stopped by.

A cloud washed over her father's eyes. He suddenly seemed tired, details Andi hadn't noticed standing out. The veins on his temples. The myriad wrinkles around his eyes. The slightly swollen joints on his hands. The sadness he was trying to hide when he smiled and lifted his eyes to meet hers.

"I'm grateful and honored, my sweet girl, but I don't believe I'd be truly welcome there. The other guests are probably your age, right?" She nodded. "See? I wouldn't be a fit. Everyone would probably wait for me to leave to start with whatever it is young people do these days, dance to loud music, tell dirty jokes, smoke pot." He chuckled, but his voice was riddled with sadness. "I'm sure your husband will appreciate my choice to wish you both a happy anniversary from a distance." He reached across the table and touched her face with warm fingers, caressing her cheek as he used to do when she was sad or had scraped a knee, encouraging her. "I will send something nice. A bottle of—what was that wine Craig liked, Dom Perignon, wasn't it?"

Andi blinked back unwelcome tears but leaned into his hand. "You're wrong about him. He'd love to have you there." As she spoke the words, her eyes veered sideways. His hand withdrew.

"You know that's not true, Andi, and it's okay. I'm your past. This man is your future. I—" he choked and cleared his throat quietly before continuing, "I hope you chose well, and I was wrong. I'd never be happier to be proven wrong about anything else in my entire existence, you know that, don't you?"

She nodded. Her father never liked Craig, and nothing she'd say would make a difference. Over the almost one year they'd been together, she'd said it all and still failed to convince him. There was nothing concrete he didn't like about Craig, nothing that could be named. "Just a father's instinct," he'd said on occasions before she got married. Then, after having reluctantly walked her down the aisle, he'd stopped bringing it up, respecting the sanctity of her marriage. But the problem was there, barely buried beneath the surface, poking its ugly head whenever she tried to bring the two most important people in her life together.

"Let me ask you something else," she said, her voice clearer, although still loaded with the tremble of threatening tears. "Are you still looking for a vet technician to bring onboard?"

Her dad's face lit up. "Yes! We're desperately short-staffed since we extended office hours. Do you have someone you can recommend?"

She stood and executed a mock curtsy accompanied by a shy smile. "Me."

His jaw dropped as silence fell heavy in the room. Outside, through the sun-filled window, Andi could see a blue jay on a live oak branch. For some reason, her mind grasped at the soothing image of the bird just as she would've grabbed a lifesaver in stormy seas.

"Andi, why?" Dr. Wilmore asked, his voice a stunned whisper. His ruffled, white eyebrows were raised, ridging his tall forehead with parallel lines. He ran his hand through his short hair a couple of times in a gesture that conveyed his bewilderment.

She lowered her eyes and took her seat at the table. "I could shift careers in mid-flight, Dad. It would be nice for us to work together, wouldn't it? I have many of the credits needed for the license. I only need the hands-on training, and I could do part of that in your office, helping you out. Then, I could go back to school and shift doctoral programs to become a DVM instead of earning a PhD in marine biology. I could grow and learn under your wing." She smiled, but her eyes burned. "Learn from the best."

He let a long breath of air come out of his lungs and reached across the table to squeeze her hand. A tear rolled down her cheek. She shifted her attention to the blue jay outside, willing it to sing.

"There's nothing I'd like more than to spend my days with you, dear child. But we've been through this. Your passion is not in giving pets their shots or trimming their nails." He inhaled loudly, his breath shaky, shallow. "You belong out there at sea, in the sun, like Cousteau on his Calypso. Didn't he used to be your role model, your hero?" He leaned more over the table, taking both her hands in his. "Didn't we watch all his documentaries together?"

She stared at his hands, speechless, unable to lift her gaze to meet his.

"What's going on, really?" he asked, his voice warm, patient. "Tell me. Whatever it is, we'll find a way to fix it, you and me."

She shook her head and stopped fighting back tears. "I—no one wants me, Dad. They turned me down everywhere. The university was the first; they sent me a letter, no explanation, nothing. Just no, thanks." She sniffled and shot him a quick glance before lowering her eyes again. "There aren't that many jobs in biology research to begin with. I burned through all of them in two weeks. I got nothing . . . seems I'll never be a marine researcher. That dream's gone."

"And today's interview?"

She pressed her lips tightly for a moment. "Office manager at a dental clinic," she whispered.

"Andi . . ." He stood and walked over to her, then crouched by her chair. She buried her face against his chest and sobbed while he caressed her hair silently. "We'll find something, you'll see," he said after a while. "Chin up, young lady. The world is yours to conquer. You cannot possibly call defeat after three attempts."

She sniffled, then reached for a tissue to wipe her eyes. "Now you see? I'd rather work with you in your practice than be the office manager for some dentist. Sorry, but I can't find meaning in life if all I'm supposed to do is make appointments and overbill people."

He stood and started pacing the room slowly, his hands clasped behind his back, the way he always did when he was thinking intensely. "You gave biology seven years already. You're halfway through your doctoral program. You can't quit. Not now. Not ever."

"But what if there's no future for me in biology? I need to make my own money, Dad. I need my life to mean something."

"Yes, yes," he replied quickly. "But I don't believe working as a vet tech gets you there. You'd waste a good year of your life getting licensed."

"Just for a while," she insisted. "Then I'll figure out if I like it, and if I do, I'll take any DVM credits I'm missing and join you in your practice."

He shook his head, then cupped his mouth with his hand as if trying to keep words sealed in before they could come out. "Nothing would make me happier than to have you near me every day. At the same time, it would break your heart, and mine along with yours, because it's not what you really want." He looked at her intently. "Let's give this some more thought. Don't waste all you've built over a couple of rejection letters.

Wait it out. New opportunities will come. Marine biology is your passion, kiddo. It's worth fighting for," he added, making a fist and punching the air. "Fight for it. Tooth and nail."

"Tiger nail?" she quipped, playing an old game they used to play together when she was little.

"Tiger claw," he laughed. "Yes, exactly. Sabertooth and tiger claw." The sounds of laughter died, leaving room for loaded silence. "I thought you were busy moving into this new house."

She made a dismissive hand gesture. "Craig's company offered him white-glove moving service. They did everything. I didn't have to lift a finger. You have to come see it one day soon. It's incredible."

Dr. Wilmore frowned and ran his hand through his hair again. Sometime in the past year, every strand on his head had turned bright white. "How do you imagine he can afford all this? A house bigger than mine, white-glove moving service? Are you sure you know everything that's going on, Andi?"

"Argh, please, Dad, enough with your suspicions, I'm begging you." She stood and started pacing the room angrily, touching familiar objects in passing as if to soothe herself. The shiny surface of the lacquered cabinets. The stainless-steel housing of the toaster, still warm. The buttons on the coffee maker. "You're not there, to see him working every day until ten, weekends too. He's ambitious and dedicated, a good husband and provider. He's just like you."

"He's nothing like me." His words came out cutting like razor blades. He closed his eyes for a moment, probably regretting his outburst.

"He's kind and loving, hard-working, and makes me happy. I love my life, Dad. The only thing is my career . . . that breaks my heart. It's like the stars are aligned against me, against fulfilling my dream. All I do all day is look for work, interview, write cover letters. And wait for Craig to come home."

His brow ruffled again, while his hand found and cupped his mouth once more. When he spoke, his voice had recovered his usual warmth. "Come on over for poker night next Thursday."

She lowered her gaze with sadness. "I may be really late, Dad. We have a party at our house for Craig's business clients."

He bit his lip, before he could make a comment about Craig's work. She knew his opinion and didn't care to hear it again. She knew his opinion of them and didn't care to hear it again. Just like her dad had done in his time, Craig was doing everything he could for his family, for their future together.

Grateful he'd decided to not say anything else against her husband, she placed a kiss on his cheek and rushed out. She was already running late for her job interview.

District Attorney Buscher: What were the circumstances of your interaction with Andrea Wilmore Brafford?

Dr. Marjorie Hitchens: I interviewed her for the role of research scientist at the Texas A&M University, Department of Marine Biology.

District Attorney Buscher: What was your opinion of Andrea Wilmore Brafford's qualifications?

Dr. Marjorie Hitchens: She was one year from earning her doctoral degree in our specialty, and she demonstrated the mindset and the passion required to achieve success in our line of work. She was the ideal candidate.

7

JUDE

Game Nite Bar and Grill was packed at that time in the evening, a little after seven. A loud and rowdy sports bar on its quiet nights, that night it was almost unbearable, although Craig enjoyed a good crowd. The place smelled of greasy grills and sizzling bacon, of burgers covered in molten cheddar and washed down with copious amounts of beer. Some of that occasionally landed on the floor or spilled on the tacky tables, but that was part of the rebellious charm of the place.

Jude was running late, and Craig passed the time munching on the house peanuts he cracked expertly between his teeth before shelling them and chewing with an unsatiable craving for their saltiness. Staring at one of the TV screens mounted above the bar, he nursed a sweaty Heineken, occasionally cheering for the Rockets when they scored points.

A tall blonde in ripped Daisy Dukes and a sleeveless top sauntered by, probably headed for the can. She swayed her hips as she made her way through the drunks in her path, ignoring their lewd comments and wolf whistles. As she approached Craig's table, she made eye contact and slowed her roll just a tad, letting her fingers trail on the table's scratched surface. He smiled, flattered by her attention. She could've taken anyone from that joint home with her that night, yet she was eyeballing him. That felt good.

"Dude, you're unbelievable," Jude said behind him in passing, before taking a seat at the table. He patted Craig's shoulder twice, his usual greeting. "You've got a fantastic wife back home, a girl to die for, and you're gawking at pub trash? What the hell, man?"

His smile waned, and the eye contact with the blonde broke. When he looked up again, the girl was gone. At his side, Jude grinned, showing two rows of impeccably white teeth. That smile earned him instant attention from the bartender, a redhead with long, silky curls that would've made Cher jealous. Her plunging neckline didn't disappoint either, and she knew just how far down to lean when taking Jude's order or just how slowly to bite her glossy lip. Although not the object of her interest, Craig enjoyed the show just as well.

"Just killing time until you got here," he eventually replied after taking a thirsty swig from the almost empty bottle of beer. "Looking, not touching. That's allowed." He put the bottle down on the coaster, and it was instantly replaced with a full one, cap off.

The redheaded Cher dropped a Bud Light in front of Jude, then added, "Anything else you want I can get you real quick. All right, honey?"

Craig laughed. He couldn't understand why Jude wasn't sandwiched between the redhead and the slick-haired brunette at the bar who had been eyeing him since he'd entered the bar, having epic sex until he couldn't draw breath anymore, instead of killing time with him. "Just admit you were jealous," he quipped.

"Jealous? Of what?" Their bottles clinked, and they downed a few gulps. Jude wiped his mouth with the back of his hand in a quick gesture that still left behind droplets of foam clinging to his neatly trimmed beard. "She was eyeing your car keys, dude. She was after your Benz, not your . . . charming personality."

"The hell she was," Craig pushed back, roaring with laughter. "You're becoming the green-eyed monster. I'm gonna call you Mr. Jellz from now on."

"Yeah? Then explain to me why you always leave your car keys on the table when we go out, when you've got plenty of pockets, like the rest of us decent people who don't feel the need to rub the three-pointed star in people's faces."

That comment put a bit of slack in his jaw as his cheeks reddened. He was doing it on purpose. He liked how he felt when people noticed it and shot him quick glances filled with envy or, for women, materially fueled sexual interest. There was a sense of validation in that, of self-worth, that swelled with every place he went and conveniently forgot his keys on the table, the remote carefully placed with the logo facing up. The servers moved faster. His meat servings were better cuts, larger, juicier. His beer was colder. His peanuts fresher. His tips had to follow suit and be bigger than the average, at least thirty percent, but it was well worth it. Maybe one day he could send redheaded Cher home with a thousand-dollar tip. One day. He could easily imagine how she'd stare at the check, then ask if he was sure, then burst into tears and look at him with respect. A lot of respect.

He hadn't expected Jude to have paid attention to what he did with his keys. For the affluent, better-educated man coming from a far-better family than his, such tricks weren't necessary to get the attention he craved. Or maybe he didn't desire the type of attention Craig did, the kind he couldn't live without. But Jude was his friend; he'd seen him at his lowest and at his best. Surely, he didn't really mind his innocent car key trick.

"Well, if my car key is a problem for you in bars and such establishments, I'll make sure I pocket it accordingly." He took a swig and savored the cold, tasty fluid. "I don't want to rob you of your chances to score. After all, like you said, I'm a happily married man."

Jude laughed and mock-punched him in the side. "Are you serious right now? You really think that matters to people?"

He laughed along, but there was a touch of seriousness buried underneath that laughter. "Sure, and you just implied it did. Let me demonstrate. Your car keys, please." He held out his hand until Jude, staring at him as if he'd just seen him dance naked under the full moon, extracted his car key and placed it firmly in Craig's hand.

The Audi logo, four intersecting rings, was just as familiar to everyone as the three-pointed star on his fob. He set the two keys side by side, then beckoned the bartender with a finger-snapping hand gesture. She quickly obliged.

"What can I get you, hon?"

"Just your opinion, for now," Craig said, smiling. "Please help us settle an amicable dispute." She seemed worried for a minute. "Nothing to be concerned about, I promise."

"Okay, shoot." She slid her notepad inside her apron pocket and propped her hand on her hip.

"Looking at these two keys, which car owner would be likely to leave a bigger tip?"

The redhead placed a long acrylic fingernail next to the Mercedes key and tapped twice.

"Ah," Craig reacted, "I knew it. Told you so. But you already knew that, didn't you, Mr. Jellz?"

"Oh, fuck," Jude cackled, then touched the bartender's forearm while his face turned serious. "Do you know anyone who wants to buy an Audi TT?" His voice was grim, but his eyes glimmered with laughter. "The seller's motivated."

The redhead shook her head, then stared at each of them for a short moment before disappearing, probably doubting their sanity.

"Yup, I stand defeated at my own challenge," Jude said somberly. "Next thing you're going to say is I told you so."

"Nope, I already said that," Craig replied. His chest swelled. He loved Jude's camaraderie, the games they often played, the time they spent together. "Next thing I'm going to sell you on is this year's roadster from Mercedes-Benz. You can afford it. I can't. I had to settle for a used crossover." He did his best to look humble for a moment. "But I still kicked your ass."

Jude gulped the rest of his beer, then summoned the redhead for another round. He touched Craig's arm to get his attention. Laughter was gone from his face. "Speaking of affordability, I have something to discuss with you." He paused for a moment while the bartender placed two new bottles in front of them and cleaned the table of peanut shells. "The mortgage I got for you—"

"Yes, thank you a million times, buddy. You made my new house happen. I don't know how, but—"

"Yeah, okay, you thanked me before," Jude replied. "It's not what I mean. The company I work for, they're mortgage originators, right? The actual mortgages come from various lenders. I work for the brokerage that facilitates a large number of such loans."

"Yeah, I know that. What's your point?" Craig fished a peanut and cracked open its shell, then started munching on the two tiny peanuts that escaped in his hand. A bit of anxiety brought a crease on his forehead. Was something wrong with his mortgage? Was he going to lose the house?

"The point is, we have a really fabulous plan for employees, their friends and families. I used it for your loan. It's almost one percentage point below market. I can shop around without running the credit for each lender, and the paperwork is done on . . . you know. On the skinny." His voice trailed off to a whisper Craig could barely hear.

He frowned. "Meaning?"

"Meaning no one really has to check it, if you catch my drift. It's based on my word, my guarantee, so to speak. If I say you qualify, then you qualify."

"Oh," Craig said, while the wheels started turning in his mind faster and faster. "That explains a few things. Any limits to this friends and family thing?"

"None whatsoever."

"Can you get in trouble?"

"Not unless I sign off on a loan and it defaults. That's when they pull the original documentation, and if they find I broke some rules or the file folder is empty, then yeah. Trouble."

"Then we won't default on anything," Craig said, while a smile bloomed on his face. "I can get us access to undervalued homes, just like the one I bought for myself. Even fixer-uppers, anything like that. We'll slap a coat of paint on it, or whatever, and resell like only I know how to resell."

Jude held his beer in the air. Craig met it with his bottle in an enthusiastic, loud clink. "We're going to make millions."

"Yup," Jude agreed. "Starting tomorrow. Then I'll be able to afford the damn roadster."

Craig's smile turned mellow as he daydreamed of a future where he and Jude worked together raking in boatloads of money, traveling, buying stuff, living large. That future, a cherished dream of his, was finally coming true.

Life was good.

8

PLANS

"We need something for this mantle," Craig said. His voice echoed strangely in the sparsely furnished, vaulted ceiling room. "An attention grabber. A conversation starter."

He'd come back from his dinner with Jude in a frenzy like she'd never seen him before. Exhilarated, so high on his own adrenaline, he was restless, effervescent. Sometimes she hated the pull Jude had on her husband. With only a few words, that man brought changes in their marriage, direction, and goals. Craig barely consulted with her before making up his mind and starting to act. He had the drive of a thoroughbred racehorse, more unstoppable than a speeding freight train.

It was almost midnight on a Monday, but Craig showed no signs of slowing down. She stood in the middle of the room, shifting her weight from one foot to the other, wondering what was coming next. Where was Jude reeling Craig this time, and how badly was her man hooked?

"One of those geodes would be nice, but a large one, like an amethyst cathedral or something like that," he added, running his hands on the mantle as if dusting it off. It was perfectly clean; she had the entire house spotless in preparation for Thursday night's dinner party, the source of Craig's anxiety. Maybe Jude didn't have anything to do with it after all.

Craig liked to play it cool about those parties, but she knew better. The days before one, he was tense, wound-up like a spring ready to burst out of its box, fretting over every little detail. He'd done these types of parties twice already. The first time was tough; only four of the guests had shown up, embarrassing him. Thankfully, the attendee list included one of his most recent high-profile clients, Sol Donati and his trophy wife, a supermodel less than half his age. Donati, whom she didn't much care for otherwise, had saved the evening, entertaining the very few guests side by side with Craig, helping him save face.

Word of that must've gone out because the second party had ten guests on the list, and they all showed up. By the end of the tiresome soiree, three had made verbal commitments to list their properties with Craig. He'd called that evening a decent success.

For the coming Thursday, they had a dozen RSVPs, including Donati.

Craig was feeling the pressure and freaking out. There wasn't enough furniture in the house, but there wasn't enough money to buy more. He'd rush applied for another credit card and was about to max that out too, only he couldn't bring himself to decide on what.

"Those people know, Andi," he'd said at least three times already. "They'll see through cheap shit like you and I see through glass. We have to make an impression. We have to behave like we've already earned business the size of the whales they can bring to our doorstep."

She'd offered to borrow some things from her dad's house, but he'd crinkled his nose. "No offense, Andi, but your old man is not that classy. He's practical, sure, but he doesn't really care about material things, does he?"

That was true. Dr. Wilmore had never turned away a pet owner from his clinic because of money, and that made his daughter proud, not ashamed. It was the wrong time to say anything about that to Craig, although the contemptuous tone of his voice had cut through her heart like a switchblade.

"Can you at least get me something for this fucking mantle? It's the size of a football field, and we can't have it empty again. Last two times we got away with it . . . it can't happen again. People notice these things." He paced the floor angrily in front of the fireplace. "How about one of those big coral things?" He gestured with his hands. "A rare one, not something you can buy at Alvin's Island."

"That would work," Andi replied, breathing slowly. She needed to stay calm. She'd seen Craig like this before. It could very well be four in the morning before he'd run out of gas.

"Well?" he asked, turning toward her and propping his hands on his hips. His tie was loosened, and his shirt's top two buttons undone, but he was still sweating. "Can you get it?"

Andi's brow furrowed. She wasn't sure she understood. "How, exactly? Order one online?"

"No, I mean, from your . . . whatever it is you do for your PhD. It's marine biology, right? They must have some weird shit in those labs, right?"

Her eyebrows shot up. "You want me to steal one from the university?"

He scoffed. "Not steal. Borrow. Draw paperwork with them, I don't care, only see what you can do for this—" he gestured angrily toward the offending mantle, keeping his lips pressed tightly together, probably to keep profanities from pouring out. She hated those.

"All right," she sighed. She had no intention of doing that, but she hoped she could make a call to a friend who collected rare coral. Or maybe she could dig through the local gift shop offerings and pick something up, something that showed promise if treated with some bleach or white spray paint. Red would work. Dark gray also.

"You're smiling," Craig said, then took her in his arms, lifting her up just a little. "You have an idea. I love you, my sweet wife." He kissed her lips then set her down. "Let's talk furniture. I have a few concepts."

Her frown returned. The leather sofa set in their living room was a loaner from Jude. He would've let them keep it a while longer, but Craig wanted something better. As usual, he wasn't asking her what she wanted to have in her new home. It was all about the dinner guests, his business partners, his ability to make more and more money. And still, she didn't much care because whenever she let him drive, he ended up surprising her in a good way, impressing her, exceeding her wildest dreams, like he'd done with the house.

"Craig, we don't have money." The statement brought tears to her eyes. "Maybe when I get a job, it will be better, easier for you to do everything you have your mind set to do. But for now—"

"That's what I'm working for," he replied, raising his voice a little. He grabbed the knot of his tie and pulled at it forcefully until he could take it off, then threw it on the sofa. "That's what all this is about, making money. Not having to worry about money again." He stared at her as if daring her to say something. She didn't. She could see it was the wrong time to say anything. Maybe tomorrow, after he'd cooled off a little.

She crossed her arms at her chest and waited, holding his gaze but refusing to speak.

"Great," he cheered as if she'd agreed with everything. Pacing the room, he gestured with his hands, pointing at various sections. "They won't have access everywhere, right? We just need the kitchen, dining, living room, and that bathroom over there. I want new towel sets, aligned, arranged, color matching the bathroom marble. A vase with dry herbs in it, classy. Look it up online to see how it's done. Needs to spell out mucho dinero."

She shook her head quietly. He was repeating himself over and over, almost obsessively, as if reminding himself what mattered. For him, it was as if he was dreaming awake and aloud. She loved Craig's ambition, the fire that raged inside his soul, but sometimes it was burning too intensely. On days like that, it got scary, even if just a little, even if without reason. Her frenzied husband, foaming at the mouth about furniture and towels and dry rose petals, would cancel all the invites if she so much as broke a fingernail.

He stopped in front of Jude's sofa. "This crappy thing's gotta go. I'll arrange with Jude to take it back, or I can put it in one of the bedrooms until the party's over. But here, we'll need one of those oriental rugs, a large one." He froze in place for a moment, staring at the gleaming maple hardwood floor. "Let's go with modern," he added, speaking slowly, hesitantly. "I'll never be able to compete with these guys in 'old money.'" He made air quotation marks with his fingers. "They'll own me before I even try. But modern? I can show them a few things. I'll give you some study material for tomorrow, then you'll have to make a shortlist of rugs, something that would work." He turned toward the far end of the living room. "Over there, I have an idea that would cost us very little money."

He walked closer to the window, probably envisioning what he was planning to do. She followed, intrigued, contaminated by his excitement.

"We'll get a new leather sectional, but there, my lovely wife, we'll put our bed."

"What?" Maybe he'd finally lost his mind under pressure. "Are you crazy? We can't put our bed there."

"Yes, we can. I've seen it done. Strip it of bedsheets and stuff. Leave the mattress protector in case someone spills their drink. Cover it with a luxurious throw and a bunch of fancy pillows in colors that will match the rug. People will lounge on it, you'll see. It's a thing now. To make it look like a lounge bar or something. But we need small, modern tables scattered in various places. Then we'll bring a few of those huge bean pillows. You know, the ones that are large enough to be a bed? They make comfy armchairs or impromptu love seats." His shoulders relaxed a bit as he grinned widely. "We're gonna look sexier than Google, you'll see. We just have to make it all fit in five grand. That's how much credit I was able to score this time around."

A long breath. As always, he was about to pull something off that would be astounding. "All right, you got it." All she had to do was go along with it.

He rushed over to her and kissed her lips quickly. "You have everything you need to do tomorrow?"

Counting on her fingers, she recited, "Homework and shortlist on modern rugs, new towel sets, art for the bathroom—"

"Argh," he shouted, slapping his forehead with his palm. "I forgot the damn art. Our walls are empty. We got nothing."

A mischievous smile bloomed on her lips. About forty bucks in spray paint and some acrylic would take care of the wall art. "Just pick the rug, okay? Once I have the colors, I'll make something happen. Modern art is easy." A pang of self-doubt deflated her a notch. "Well, for these folks, anyway. They don't seem like modern art aficionados."

He looked at her for a long moment, his eyes intense, searing. "You don't even know how marvelous you are."

Her cheeks caught fire. "I just want to make your dreams come true, that's all. I wish I could make mine happen at the same time." She let a bitter sigh leave her lungs. "If I could make money too, that would help. I thought that, by now, I'd be earning my keep. But no one wants me." With those simple words, tears returned in full force. Her shoulders heaved.

Wrapping his arms around her, he swayed slowly from side to side as if she were a baby in need of soothing. "Shh . . . It will be fine. I know it will." He caressed her hair while her face stayed buried on his shoulder. "Why don't I make some calls? Open some doors for you?"

She pulled away, sniffling. "No . . . not yet. I'd rather succeed on my own. Or at least try."

He bent his knees a little, seeking her eyes. "Let me know if you change your mind, all right? I've been sucking up to these people long enough to ask for favors, you know? Maybe I can make things happen for you like you're making them happen for me. Huh? What do you say?"

She nodded, wiping her eyes with the back of her hands. "I'll tell you. Too bad you don't know anyone in my field."

But his attention was gone. His eyes stared into thin air with that intense expression she'd learned to recognize. "What can you make us to eat that will stand out?"

She didn't have an answer. Cooking wasn't her strength. The last two times, she'd managed with cheese trays and a collection of fine wines.

"Can you make something fancy, like salmon mousse?"

Oh, crap. "I have no idea," Andi replied, undertones of exasperation coloring her voice. She was supposed to help furnish the place, get corals for the mantle, make art for the walls, and cook fancy stuff in three days? Then, what else? She had an interview on Wednesday morning, and she wanted to keep looking for work. That had to be more important than a stupid, snobby hors d'oeuvre. "I've never even had salmon mousse."

"I'm sure there's a recipe online you could find." He was smiling, approaching her while slowly unbuttoning his shirt, his fixed gaze loaded with desire.

"Craig," she protested softly, pushing him away weakly. "I'm tired."

"And we'll get you to bed," he whispered as she melted into his arms.

That night, after he'd fallen asleep, she stared at the ceiling with eyes wide open until the light of day started casting shadows on the barren walls.

9

THE BOSS

It wasn't too hot outside, but Craig could barely breathe. He'd struggled all the way back from the showing, despite the frozen airflow coming from the dashboard vents. He lowered the windows at times because he wanted to be rid of the smell of that nasty place. The stench had clung to his nostrils, his hands, his clothes, taking him back to memories he wished he never had. Poverty had the same foul odor, no matter the ZIP Code.

He'd shown a shithole of a place in East Houston, so grimy he didn't want to touch the door handles or set his briefcase on the stained counter. The kitchen reeked of odd-smelling spices and stale vomit. He would bet good money one of the walls had been peed on without as much as a shred of effort to clean that mess up. It should've been an easy sale; it was a pre-foreclosure, heavily discounted. But the client, a single mother of three with a thick South American accent, had taken the longest time in real estate history to make up her mind.

A few endless hours later, the offer was submitted, and the seller had quickly accepted it, the confirmation email finding him before he'd had the chance to be rid of the client. Too bad her mortgage would probably fall through; with people like her, paperwork almost always went sideways.

That colossal waste of time of a showing had been bestowed on him by none other than his boss, Jeremy Hughes, a fifty-something dinosaur with dismal ambition and the mindset of a galley rower. He'd been happy to run that realty office for someone else his entire career, never wanting more, never opening his own shop. Spineless. Stubborn. Idiot.

Pulling his black Benz at the curb in front of the office, Craig gave the office a critical look. Grabbing his briefcase and the jacket he'd discarded on the passenger seat, he rushed inside.

The door whooshed to a close behind him when he heard Hughes's voice.

"Brafford," he called, anger clear in his voice. "In here."

Craig muttered a curse while giving the ceiling a long stare as if the water stains on the once-white panels held an answer to his questions. Many times, he'd thought of resigning his job and starting his own office, but he wasn't ready to make that move yet. He didn't have enough cash flow and, most important, had no access to new listings he could grab before anyone else did. For that, he needed to stay enrolled behind a good, established name like Parker Jones Realty. They gave their agents access to their nationwide system, where listings were prepared before being pushed out on the internet for buyers to see. He needed that access, which was the main reason he couldn't tell Hughes to take a long walk on a very short pier.

He knocked on the open door just to get Hughes's attention. His boss was browsing through a thick report bound with heavy-duty staples. Colorful stickers marked pages where he'd made notes in illegible cursive or highlighted entries with yellow or green.

"Wanted to see me?"

Hughes pointed at the chair in front of his scratched, cluttered desk without lifting his bloodshot eyes from the report. A thinning tuft of hair exposed his shiny scalp, despite his efforts to comb it back and load it with gel to stay put. A thick vein pulsed on his temple like a living creature writhing under his pale skin.

Hughes closed the report with a loud, frustrated sigh.

"How did it go?" he asked. A menacing smile flickered on his mouth.

Craig shrugged, struggling to hide his disappointment with how he'd spent the better part of the day. "Offer's been accepted. Now we wait for the close."

"Do you know why I called you in here?" He rapped his fingers against the thick report in a rhythm only he understood.

Craig shook his head and crossed his legs, projecting a relaxed demeanor. "No idea. You have another lead for me?"

"No. We'll discuss your performance and the two code of conduct violations you managed to score in the past month."

His eyebrows shot up. That he didn't expect. "Oh?"

"Congratulations on your new house," Hughes said, his voice low, loaded with frustration.

So that's what's crawling up his ass. Good old envy. Craig bowed his head for a brief moment. "Thank you, sir."

"You are not supposed to put a personal offer on a property before it's listed on the market."

Craig stared at Hughes with eyes open wide. "I'm so sorry—"

"You mean to tell me you didn't know? How is it possible? You signed a document outlining your responsibilities when you took this job. All properties purchased by our employees have to be previously approved by a senior manager."

Craig leaned forward and put his hands out in a gesture of appeasement. "I—I'm speechless. I can't believe I didn't remember that. It's been more than five years since I signed that paperwork, but you're right. I should've asked you before making an offer."

"And I would've denied your request." He'd raised his voice and punctuated it by slamming his hand on the report.

The bastard. Of course, he would've denied it, only to buy it for himself. "Please, let me know where I made the wrong call, other than not seeking your approval first."

"The same document you conveniently forgot you signed specifies clearly that no Realtor can purchase a home before it has been listed on the market for at least thirty days." Another rap against the report. "We're in the business of making money for our clients and, through the commissions we earn, for our company. Not for ourselves. You snatched that house off the market before it was listed. You knew it was undervalued, and instead of letting buyers bid for it, you made a lowball offer and ran with it."

"Oh, I see," Craig whispered. Anxiety swirled in his gut. "Please, sir, tell me how to make this right."

Hughes stared at him with nostrils flaring, the look of contempt on his face unmistakable. "I'm tempted to have your Realtor license revoked just because I can. You gave me enough reasons."

Craig's jaw slacked. For the first time since he'd bought that house, he felt fear strangling him. He swallowed hard, his throat dry, his breath caught in his lungs. The sack of envious shit seated across from him could crush him and his dreams like a bug.

"I won't, though," Hughes added, lowering his gaze and breathing loudly, not even bothering to hide his frustration. "If I did that, I'd open us up to liability from the client. Head office has instructed me to write you up for insubordination, put you on a performance plan for ninety days, and fire you for cause the moment you don't toe the line."

Craig breathed. "Thank you, sir. I appreciate the second chance you're giving me. I swear, it was an oversight—"

"Don't you dare fucking insult me." His slamming hand rattled the coffee cup and the pen holder. "You know exactly what you did and why."

Craig leaned away from the desk, instinctively putting distance between the enraged man and himself as if Hughes was going to pounce and beat him to a pulp. "Once again, I'm sorry," he whispered, feeling the bitter taste of rising bile in his throat. Apologizing to that son of a bitch took every ounce of willpower he could muster. "I'll make it up to you. That's a promise."

"I'm not done with you yet." Hughes opened the report where a green sticky note marked the page. "I discovered there was white-glove move-in service charged to your new address. Almost five thousand dollars' worth of labor hours you stole from us."

"Oh, no, sir, I didn't." He sprung to his feet and grabbed his briefcase, opening it on the chair where he'd been sitting. "I have the check right here. I was gone to showings all day long, every day since Mary gave me the final amount last week. She said to bring a check next time I'm in the office during business hours." He extracted the check, already filled out, and slid it over the desk until Hughes could take it without reaching.

"Mary knew about this?"

He nodded vigorously. "Absolutely. She booked it for me."

Hughes pressed his lips together, staring at Craig with scrutinizing, doubt-filled eyes. "Let's say I buy that," he muttered. "Then there's the issue of your performance. You didn't close much this month, and, except for the Donati property, you didn't bring in any new clients." He smiled, more like wickedly showed his teeth, the crease in his upper lip a telling sign of how much he wanted to be rid of Craig, to cause him pain.

"I've been working some exciting new leads," Craig replied, closing his briefcase and setting it on the floor. He remained standing, his shoulders hunched forward just a little.

"That's your problem, Brafford. You chase the big ones; you can't be bothered to do the hard work like the rest of us. One day, this ambition of yours will—"

"Make us both rich," Craig said, looking into Hughes's eyes with confidence. Now he knew what his boss's problem was. Envy. Lack of drive. The man was limper than an eighty-year-old's dick before the invention of Viagra. He liked money, envied people who had it, but he didn't know how to get it for himself. That stinking dog couldn't hunt. But he could still be lured to make nice for the occasional slice of bacon and learn to lick the hand that held it. "This Thursday, my wife and I are hosting a dinner party for prospective clients at our new house. We'd like you to join us and meet those clients for yourself. They're all whales the size of Donati or bigger. Leads I've been nurturing."

Hughes stood and leaned forward, his palms flat on the desk. All contempt had vanished from his face, the glimmer of interest lighting up his eyes. "You were going to ask me all along?"

"Yes, sir. I just waited to see that there were enough RSVPs before wasting your time. Mrs. Hughes is also welcome; my wife would love to meet her. I'll send you the address."

"I have the damn address," he said, tapping his fingernail against the report cover again.

"Yeah. Right."

The man straightened his back, staring at Craig the entire time. The coldness in his eyes had tapered. "Maybe you and I could work together to get us some big clients. Seems to me you have connections. You definitely have the money to afford a place like the one you snatched, and the movers, the whole shebang."

Craig nodded, not trusting his voice to lie convincingly about his means. The check he'd just given his boss was going to bounce unless he somehow managed to come up with five grand before the banks closed that night. Fuck.

"I would love the opportunity to learn from you how to close the big fish. You could watch me work the room on Thursday and coach me afterward."

Hughes extended his sweaty hand, and Craig took it. "I'd love to do that, son."

This time, the man's smile was sincere. Oily though. He was probably spending the big commissions in his mind, the ones that should've been Craig's and only Craig's, but what the hell. Sometimes the piper had to be paid, or else he could ruin the entire damn party.

Hughes picked up a listing sheet and showed it to Craig without letting it go. The address was another hellhole in East Houston.

"Then I'll give this to Patterson instead," Hughes said. "Go work on the big leads, son."

District Attorney Buscher: There was a write-up in Craig Brafford's human resource file bearing your signature. What was that for?

Jeremy Hughes: Insubordination, with a ninety-day probation.

District Attorney Buscher: Is it your opinion that the defendant didn't show much respect for the rules governing his profession?

Jeremy Hughes: Craig messed up some paperwork, that's all. He made a mistake. I didn't want to write the kid up, but we have rules we have to follow.

District Attorney Buscher: Is it your testimony then that Craig Brafford is an honest, law-abiding man?

Jeremy Hughes: As far as I know, yes.

District Attorney Buscher: Mr. Hughes, may I remind you that you're under oath?

10

Hold 'Em

The mantle had a centerpiece that would definitely start conversations, hopefully not the wrong ones. Andi had built it from several pieces of coral she'd bought at the local gift store, carefully superglued together, the join lines filed and painted the brightest white she could find.

What she'd created was biologically impossible, but only to the expert eye. If such an eye were to surprisingly attend the dinner, she'd be happy to make the acquaintance of a kindred spirit and then share a giggle at her own expense. Otherwise, Craig would be thrilled, his guests in awe of the eye-catching grouping of Merulina coral, no one the wiser.

The massive, white centerpiece was flanked by a cluster of Blue Ridge coral to the left and a clump of Red Pipe Organ coral to the right. She'd snatched both items in their original, unaltered state, for under $10 apiece from a tiny store in Galveston she knew well. They imported exotic species by the crate and sold them at a bargain. Craig would probably never set foot in that kind of store.

Throwing the mantle a satisfied look, she checked the time and rushed out the door. It was getting late.

She drove the short distance to her father's with the top up, ignoring the setting sun that splashed the landscape with bright oranges and reds. Her thoughts swirled anxiously, mulling over Janelle's offer. Earlier that day, she'd called and suggested she pull all the facilities that employed marine biologists to build her a list of nationwide job prospects. Then she'd asked, "Would Craig be willing to move to California or Florida for your career?"

She remembered the pained silence that had taken over their lively call for an endless moment. Her dream of working in her chosen profession, for which she had trained and studied for almost eight years, was falling apart like windblown gossamer. She would've traveled to the ends of the earth for a chance to fulfill that dream. But Craig, moving out of Houston?

He'd rather die.

The call ended before Janelle could hear the tears in her voice. Moments later, the list of prospects she'd promised hit her inbox. She didn't even open it; instead, she chose an area rug that looked just right, shopped online for throw pillows in matching colors with local store pickup, and found a recipe for salmon mousse.

Now, driving to her dad's for the pushed forward poker night, she kept wondering why she hadn't even opened that file. How many prospects were in there? Three? Or thirty? Should she completely give it up and resign herself to being Craig's wife, the mother of his children?

Instinctively, she touched her abdomen with her right hand while she wondered if a new life was growing inside her. Her body felt different. She'd been off her birth control for a while and hadn't even mentioned it to Craig. Maybe it was time to tell him; he might not like that kind of surprise, even though he wanted children just as much as she did.

Moments later, her unfinished thoughts stashed in a safe recess of her mind, she entered the screened porch where everyone was gathered. They had waited for her; the cards were stacked in a deck by her father's side, untouched.

"Hey, you guys," she greeted them cheerfully. "Are you ready to lose some money tonight?"

Her father stood and wrapped her in a warm hug, followed by a loud kiss on her cheek. "You look good today. I missed you."

The seat at her dad's right was empty, reserved for her. Then, Dr. Ellefson and his wife, Rebecca, took the next two. She snuck in between them, her arms on their shoulders in a side hug.

"Look at her," Rebecca said, "she's gorgeous." She caressed Andi's cheek, then touched the fabric of her blouse. "Genuine silk?"

Andi chuckled. "Not unless they sell it at Walmart for nine bucks ninety-nine." The fabric was lovely, though. "Love your shoes," she said, admiring Rebecca's kitten-heel pumps. Almost sixty years old, she was classy, elegant, always a head-turner with her manners of fashion, speech, and behavior. A retired English lit professor at Texas A&M University, Rebecca was the only one sitting at the green table who wasn't a medical professional. Except for Andi, of course.

Her husband, Dr. Ellefson, was the county's medical examiner. A little tired, gaunt, his usual warm smile was absent. Staring at the green felt surface, he ran his fingers against it, back and forth, seemingly lost in thought.

Sitting next to Rebecca was Dr. Robert Blass, a retired dentist of fifty-eight. He was a hoot; he always had a joke ready, puns too. He picked on everyone indiscriminately. Andi knew when he was about to turn someone into the butt of a joke by the flicker of amusement that lit his eyes before he spoke. His hands trembled slightly, probably the reason he'd retired so early. His wife, Kim, was a dental hygienist who still worked, just because she loved to get away from Bob at least four days a week, or so she stated. A tall woman with kind eyes and beautiful auburn hair, Kim rarely joined them at the poker table. Poker wasn't her thing; she preferred to cook, and everyone loved her for that. While cards were dealt and money changed hands, she busied herself catering to the cheerful bunch, replenishing drinks and fixing snacks. Sometimes, she surprised them at the end of the game with a mouthwatering appetizer no one saw coming.

The oldest one in the bunch was Freddy DeMaria, sixty-eight, a retired shrink. Aware he somewhat resembled Robert De Niro, he dressed and wore his hair like the star did in real life, long graying hair and a buzz-trimmed beard to go with a white shirt, top buttons undone, and a sporty jacket. He was the preferred target for Bob Blass's humor and took it like the passionate Freud scholar he was, twisting it around and sending it right back. The banter between the two was a show worth buying tickets for. The other attendees, knowing the two needed a little bit of alcohol to get warmed up and start firing, made sure their glasses were always full.

Andi ruffled Freddy's hair and took her seat. The dealer button was next to her pile of chips.

"I deal?"

"You were late," Dr. Blass replied, glancing at her above his reading glasses, "but we're suckers for a pretty face. You shouldn't be rewarded for your tardiness; you should be punished for it."

"Ah," Dr. DeMaria reacted. "Such an intriguing choice of words, my dear friend."

Dr. Blass's cheeks burned. Andi laughed out loud. It was up to Dr. DeMaria to make everything about sex. "Same as usual? Ten-dollar buy-in, maximum raise is a quarter?"

"Yes, my dear," her dad replied.

"That's it," Dr. Ellefson added. "We can't afford to go any higher with you at the table."

She grabbed the deck of cards. "Thank you all for pushing the game forward by one day. I would've hated to miss it." As she spoke the words, they resonated inside her a certain way. Not only were they true, but she realized the aged gathering around the green table, with their off-the-cuff humor and bad bluffing techniques, were the highlight of her week. What did that say about her life?

"Wouldn't be the same without you," her dad said, reaching over and kissing her temple. Then he grabbed a pair of yellow chips and threw it in the center. To his left, Dr. DeMaria threw in one yellow chip. She started dealing.

"I wonder why she's so good at this game," Dr. Blass said, sneaking a quick peek at his cards. A flicker of disgust crinkled his nose. The dentist didn't have much of a poker face.

"She's right here, you know," Rebecca replied calmly, her voice soothing. "You can address her directly."

Andi laughed. "I don't believe I'm as good as you say. I just—well, it's a matter of luck, I guess."

"She's laser-focused," Dr. Ellefson said, staring at his cards as if he had an issue understanding their value. His hand was either incredibly bad or absolutely fantastic. "I noticed," he turned to her, glancing at her quickly, "you keep your eyes on the goal at all times. You don't allow yourself to be swayed by emotion." He cleared his throat quietly, then set the cards down with care. His hand was good, but that could still change. "You don't allow yourself to be."

Smiling at the medical examiner, she burned a card, then set another one on the table, face up.

"No, that's not true," her dad countered. "My little girl makes the same heart-driven mistakes as everyone else." The tone of his voice was touched by bitterness and disappointment.

Rebecca glanced at him quickly and whispered, "Hunter. Stop it."

"No, I know what I'm talking about," he reacted, Rebecca's pacifying attempt having the opposite effect. "Otherwise, she'd see what I see—"

"Dad," Andi said, placing her hand on his forearm and squeezing gently. "Please, don't. Craig is my husband, and I love him. Please, respect that."

He lowered his head as if his thoughts were too heavy for him to support it with a straight spine. He sighed and whispered, "Yes, yes, my dear. I apologize."

"Nothing would make me happier than you accepting your son-in-law like a member of this family. Like a son. You're . . . tearing me apart."

Strangely, neither Dr. Blass nor the shrink had anything humorous to say, leaving silence to weigh heavily at the table. Eventually, the dentist threw a couple of yellow chips on the pile and said, "Call."

"Tell me, how did you two meet?" Rebecca asked. "I'm not sure I heard that story."

11

ONE NIGHT

Andi lit up and smiled. She loved remembering that first day for Craig and her. "Well, I was coming back from school one night in October, the day after my birthday, actually. I remember because the day before, on my birthday, I visited with Dad at the clinic, and they had a cake waiting for me, decorated with a cat face with huge whiskers." She looked at her father with warmth in her eyes.

"Aww, that's sweet," Rebecca said.

"The next day, it was raining bad, and it was dark. On I-45 headed north, crossing the bay bridge, my car started swaying and making an awful sound. I had a flat. I pulled over to the curb, but I was scared to get out of the car to look. The traffic there goes crazy fast."

Rebecca placed her hand on her chest. "That's terrible. What did you do?"

"After a while, I decided to drive slowly and take the first exit off the freeway."

"Did you turn on—" Dr. Blass started to ask.

"Yes, I kept my flashers on, and crawled to Highway 197, then I stopped. It was pitch black. I honestly thought I was going to die that night. I felt it in my bones as if it were real. As if it was already happening." Fascinated, her father listened to the story he'd heard before with unusual intensity in his eyes. Touching his arm again reassuringly, her smile bloomed as she remembered. "I was just about to call Dad to the rescue when a car stopped behind mine. I thought that was it. I'm alone, in the middle of nowhere, and this guy, whoever he is, will kill me. Because why wouldn't he, right? Nobody would know."

"Oh, my goodness," Rebecca whispered, then took a small sip from her beer. "I would've fainted."

"I had mace," Andi said, and her comment ignited a roar of laughter around the table.

"What did I tell you?" Dr. Ellefson said. "No useless feelings, just a practical, cool head, screwed tightly on her shoulders. Atta girl."

"Okay, what happened?" Dr. DeMaria asked. "Don't leave us hanging."

"So, I have the mace in my hand, ready to give him a load of it. I had locked my doors, but I feared he'd break my window or something. Instead, he approached the window in that pouring rain and knocked politely, calmly, as if the rain wasn't coming down so hard. He said, 'Ma'am, you don't need to get out of the car. Just pop the trunk for me, and I'll fix it.' In that soaking downpour, he smiled at me."

"Aww . . ." Rebecca said. "Such a beautiful story."

"Then he drove behind me until I reached the house, just to make sure I was safe." She lowered her gaze and half-closed her eyes, reliving the most cherished of her memories. "Then the next day, I got a dozen pink roses delivered. And that's how it started for Craig and me."

Another moment of silence, then the sound of a chip hitting the pile. "Call," Dr. DeMaria said. "You know, there's an anthropological basis for parents struggling to accept their sons-in-law. The daughter is now possessed by another, younger male—"

"Oh, shut up, already," Dr. Blass said. "Not everyone here is obsessed with sex. I know someone who is, though. Have you checked the mirror lately?"

Soft laughter emerged around the table as the game continued.

"Dad, what's wrong?" Andi asked. The same intense, burning gaze was in her father's eyes, sending shivers down her spine.

"Ah, yes," he eventually said, then broke eye contact and threw his cards on the table. "Fold."

Another moment of silence while Rebecca weighed her chances. "Raise," she eventually said, then threw a couple of green chips on the pile.

"I promised you I'd answer questions about the Edwards case," Dr. Ellefson said, breaking the awkward silence. He was looking at Andi.

Thankful, she turned to him, glad to take her mind off her father's bizarre demeanor for a moment. "Sorry . . . who?"

"The girl who overdosed in your building. Nikki Edwards? Remember her?"

"Ah, yes," Andi replied, feeling a pang of guilt for completely forgetting everything about that poor girl. It was as if her forgetfulness took meaning away from her short life.

Dr. Wilmore leaned over the table to catch Dr. Ellefson's eye. "Nikki Edwards, you say? A twenty-year-old brunette with long hair, tall, beautiful?"

"Yes," the medical examiner replied. "Well, twenty-five, but still. How do you know her?"

"She was a patient of mine some time ago. Her cat died of old age." He ran his hand over his chin, lost in thought. "Or was it diabetes? I can't recall. Haven't seen her since."

"Who? The cat?" the shrink asked. "That's actually a good thing."

The vet mock-punched him, chuckling. "No, you twat, the girl."

"So, it was an overdose after all?" Andi asked.

"Yes," Dr. Ellefson replied. "She wasn't a habitual user, not for too long, anyway. It's usually the new drug users who make such mistakes. They don't know how much their bodies can take." He checked his cards quickly. "Fold." Seemed that his hand wasn't that great after all.

Andi hesitated. Quite a few chips were already in the pot, but her hand was decent. With three of the cards on the board, she had a full house, fours over tens. But it was a tricky situation; all the fours were on the board, which meant anyone holding a pair higher than her tens would take the pot.

"Call," she eventually said, tossing two of her green chips on the table. She hoped the excitement of the game would dissipate the darkness her father's eerie comments had brought to the group atmosphere and her own heart. Why did he have to see the worst in Craig, when he was otherwise such a kind man, seeing only the good in people? The hatred her father seemed to foster for her husband had to end somehow, or she'd be forced to keep her distance. That's what he didn't understand; he was pushing her away, forcing her to take sides.

"She was pregnant, by the way," Dr. Ellefson added.

"Who?" DeMaria asked. "The cat?"

Laughter roared around the table like in the old days when not a single frown clouded her father's brow. Before he'd turned so dark and hateful. Before she'd met Craig.

A couple of hours later, she stood, right after raking in a decent amount of chips amounting to thirty-four dollars or so. "I have to go," she said, and most of the players booed openly, pleading with her to stay longer. Of course, Rebecca didn't make any such plebeian sounds; she was too much of a lady. "Craig has this big party tomorrow night, the reason why we played today instead of tomorrow, and I still have to get things ready."

She circled the table, saying goodbyes and giving hugs to everyone.

"How's the job search going?" Dr. DeMaria asked.

"Argh, I wish you hadn't asked," Andi replied. "It doesn't. No one will have me."

"How about the university?" Dr. Ellefson asked. "You were thrilled after that interview."

She shook her head, saddened. "Nope. They sent me a letter."

Rebecca stared at her, then at her husband, but didn't say a word.

The last one lined up for hugs was her father. Andi hesitated a little before embracing him, a bit upset with his reluctance to accept Craig. Instead of hugging her, he grabbed her hands in his, squeezing them hard.

"What was wrong with the tire?" he asked. "Andi, look at me."

"Huh?"

"The tire," he repeated. "The flat you had the night you met Craig. What was wrong with it?"

She shrugged. "I took it to the shop, and they fixed it."

"Was it pierced?"

She frowned, trying to remember. Why was her father asking such questions? Who cared about the damn tire? "N— no, they said it was just deflated." She reached up and placed a kiss on his stubbly face. "Good night, Dad. I'll call you tomorrow."

He didn't let go of her hands. "What if you were right?" he whispered, staring into her eyes with the same intensity she'd noticed before. "We're animals, nothing more. We still have instincts, powerful instincts that warn us when a predator approaches. Those instincts have kept humans alive for ages in a jungle full of leopards and tigers and wolves. What if you were right that night?"

She tried to free her hand. "Dad, you're scaring me. Right about what?"

"What if that first instinct of yours was real, Andrea?"

"When I thought I was going to die when I had the flat?" Her voice's high pitch sounded scratchy. "Jeez, Dad, you're insane. I was just alone and afraid of the dark. My first flat tire ever, and it had to happen at night, in the rain. Nothing else."

"But what if—"

She pulled her hands out of his grip and pressed her lips together for a moment, not sure what else to say. He looked desperate for some reason; his eyes were filled with unspeakable fear. Maybe she needed to call Dr. DeMaria one of those days and ask for his professional opinion. As far as she knew, that's how symptoms of dementia started, with personality changes and paranoia. Her father was still too young for that, but people get sick all the time. They have ministrokes and transient ischemic events. They lose themselves and become unrecognizable.

Nevertheless, her father should trust her about Craig. If he loved her, he had to find a way to kindle a normal relationship with his son-in-law. Otherwise, how would he be able to love his grandchild?

Without realizing, she touched her belly with a soothing gesture. "This was an excellent evening," she said, sounding colder than she would've wanted. "Until now."

She cried all the way home.

12

HOME

The house was completely dark when Andi arrived, but Craig's Mercedes was in the garage. He must've been asleep, although it was a few minutes shy of one, and he liked burning the midnight oil. Opening the doors carefully to not wake him, she tiptoed through the laundry and the kitchen, and sat on the new sofa, feeling bone tired. She needed a moment before joining him, to wipe her tears and clear her mind.

"How nice of you to join me," Craig said calmly, startling her. He was sitting on an armchair by the wall.

She gasped and sprung to her feet. "You almost gave me a heart attack." A touch of insecure laughter colored her voice. "Why are you sitting in the dark?"

"I'm waiting for you." He didn't get up to kiss her. She started walking toward him but stopped halfway.

"Are you mad at me or something?" She walked briskly to the wall and flipped the light switch on. Squinting, she studied his perfectly immobile face. What the heck was wrong with him?

"Should I be?" he asked just as calmly, unnervingly so. "Why?"

She waited, starting to lose her patience. He must've felt abandoned, the evening before his big party, just because she could hold her own and didn't need to be fretting over every tiny detail. After her dad's unusual behavior that night, all she needed was Craig to go nuts on her. She wanted to scream, scratch something until she broke a fingernail, or maybe break something to pieces.

"After all, tomorrow we have this big party happening, one that could make or break us, and no one's here to take care of things."

Andi's hands quickly found her hips. "What things? Everything's good and ready. Shopping is done. All I have to do tomorrow is pick up a few things and scatter them around. They're paid for, ready for me to show up and load them in the car. Even your precious mantle is done."

A flicker of a smile tugged at Craig's lips. "Saw that, yes. Impressive."

"Yeah, damn right it is. These are priceless items, one of a kind. I signed a document; I have to take everything back on Friday," she blurted, finding herself weaving an elaborate lie without understanding why. She bit her lip, forcing herself to stop with the lies. "I see you moved the bed in here."

"By myself."

She lowered her eyes for a moment, hiding a flash of anger ignited by his comment. "It looks . . . interesting." The bed was placed at an angle, not parallel with the wall, not touching the wall either. At least three feet of empty space on all sides invited people to approach and sit leisurely. She breathed, willing herself to stay calm. "What if I picked up some smaller rugs to go with the large one? To scatter around that bed?"

"You could try."

She felt the sting of tears. "Do you have to be like that?"

"Like what?"

"Monosyllabic. Cold. Pissed off without reason."

He steepled his hands in his lap, keeping his elbows on the armrests, and stared at her. "You call this ready for tomorrow? Do you know who's coming?"

She shook her head again, breathing back the knot in her throat, blinking off tears.

"People who live in million-dollar homes. People who were born rich. You think we can fool them with a bunch of dead marine biology on the damn fireplace mantle?" He spat the words as if his contempt engulfed her background, her entire world. Everything that was important to her.

"Listen, if this is what our life will be like, I want no part of it."

He stood abruptly and paced toward her angrily. "What?"

"If it's making you so anxious, maybe it's not worth it for us. It will ruin our lives."

Frustrated, he lifted his arms in the air, then let them drop. "It's not anxiety, for crying out loud. It's opportunity. It's ambition. It's will to succeed against all odds." He paced back and forth for a moment. "We make friends with these people, then they list their homes with me, and I make double commission. They refer their friends to me, and again, double commission. I don't know about you, but I have no intention to pay for this house for the next thirty years."

She nodded, biting her lip to keep it from quivering. She wanted his arms around her, his breath on her neck, his lips on hers. Not a lesson in real estate economics.

"How much is the mortgage, anyway? You never told me."

He veered his eyes for a moment. "Doesn't matter. You don't need to worry about anything. Just make sure we're set for tomorrow, and let's shine. Let's show these entitled assholes we're just as good as they are."

He took her hands, and she shivered when his frozen fingers touched hers. "You cold?" He started rubbing her arms with his hands to warm her up.

Slowly, she leaned back against his chest, yearning for his love, her anguish starting to dissipate. Maybe he was right to be anxious. He was playing way out of his league and had signed up for significant expenses they couldn't afford, especially with her still unemployed. A big part of what was happening with Craig was her fault.

"Everything will be fine, Craig. Just relax. I have three pieces of art you might like, ready to hang. They're in the small bedroom, drying. Most of the food is done. The rest I'll whip together as soon as I come back from shopping and the interview."

His hands moved off her skin and into his pockets. "What interview?"

She turned to face him. "It's early stages. We'll see if anything works out."

"Who's the employer?"

"A bank." She lowered her eyes under his stare. "It's for a teller job at the local branch."

He stared at her in disbelief. "My wife, a bank teller? Have you lost your mind? Do you know what that will do to me? To us?" His shouting echoed strangely against the tall ceilings and barren walls.

She wrapped her arms around her body, feeling the chill of his anger traveling through her blood like icy shards. "Then don't tell anyone," she tried to quip, but her voice sounded miserable. "I have to start somewhere, Craig, and no one will hire me. I'll keep trying until I get a job, any job, and then start from there."

Slowly, he approached her and gently touched her face. "I'm sorry you didn't tell me, that's all."

"Why?" Tears stained her cheeks, unwanted, unstoppable.

"So that I could coach you, give you some tips. We could research this bank together, find out what they're looking for in an employee, then you'd sell that to them, and they'd fall in love with you."

She stared at the hardwood floor where her teardrops had fallen. The salt in them would probably stain the wood. "Thank you," she whispered.

"This is important for you, isn't it? Earning your own money?" He ran his fingers through her hair and around her ear, tucking a few short strands behind the lobe. She shivered, but this time, it wasn't the chill in his fingers; it was the fire he seeded in her blood. "Because we could be just fine without you having to put up with the daily grind of working."

Reluctantly, she pulled away. "What would that make me, then? A wife? A mother? All great, but I can be so much more, Craig. I need to be."

"You're a fabulous wife," he whispered, kissing her neck.

"And I'll make a fabulous mother. Soon."

His lips stopped in place. "How soon?"

She chuckled and buried her fingers in his hair, tugging gently. "I don't know, just saying."

"Good," he mumbled, his lips resuming their exploration of her neck. "Because we're kinda busy for now." He took her hand and led her to the bed. "We'll need a throw for this bed, by the way. Something expensive."

He was funny. "Yeah, it's on my pickup list for tomorrow."

His hands on her waist, they sat together, side by side. "Who cares about a nothing-per-hour bank teller job when we could do great things together?" His fingers expertly unbuttoned her shirt, slowly, too slowly.

"Like what?" Staying focused on the conversation topic when his hands traveled on her body demanded a lot of effort. She just wanted to let herself fall back on the bed.

"Jude and I will start a business. I'll find the houses, he'll buy them for cheap, then we'll resell them the next year, a fresh coat of paint and whatnot. I need your help to make it happen, Ands." Her blouse, all buttons undone, fell open to the sides. Her chest heaved. "You're my teammate, my partner," he whispered, his lips trailing the edges of her bra. "My strength .. . my core."

The warmth he was injecting into her body rendered her weak, helpless, ready for him. She moaned, relishing every sensation with eyes half-closed.

Then his hands turned to steel as he positioned her, his eyes drilling into hers mercilessly as if trying to pierce her skull open and read her mind. As if trying to control it.

Warmth turned to a sudden chill, freezing her soul. She pushed the feeling away and abandoned herself in Craig's arms, reminding herself how much he loved her. Whatever was wrong was only in her mind. Shunning his unyielding gaze, she closed her eyes and kept them squeezed shut until it was all over.

13

PHONE CALL

The Ellefson residence, a large Craftsman sitting on a quarter-acre lot in a cul-de-sac, was landscaped with colorful flowers that bloomed all summer long. The medical examiner had taken on gardening as a hobby, most likely inclined to bring fresh air, sunshine, and color into his life. His day job kept him locked in a morgue the entire day or visiting crime scenes, neither alternative seeming too healthy, at least in Rebecca's opinion.

She was happy with her husband's recently discovered passion for bulbs and rose blooms. She liked to read on the veranda, stretched out on the swing, her back rested against a couple of pillows, while he busied himself a few yards away.

On summer weekdays, their routine started in the early hours, relished by both enough to warrant waking up with the rising sun. The pillows on the swing still retained some of the overnight moisture that morning. Rebecca remained standing, leaning against the banister and holding a steaming cup of coffee in her hands.

She checked the time, then announced, "It's almost eight."

"Yeah, I should be going." Dr. Ellefson groaned as he stood, then massaged his right knee with expert fingers for about a minute. "Damn thing is aching again."

"Old age is aching again, Aaron, nothing else."

"Don't I know it." He took a potted rose from the deck and set it on the ground, next to the hole he'd dug. Then he walked over to the faucet to turn on the water for the hose. "You should see them opened up."

"Who?"

"Older people. Age shows on the inside much worse than it does on the outside."

"Eww. Thank you very much. I'll pass." She took a sip of coffee, savoring the bitter taste, eager to wash off the image Aaron's comment about opening people up had brought to her vivid imagination. "You're in a dark mood this morning. What's wrong?"

Shaking his head, he crouched by the hole and started filling it with water from the hose. "I don't know. Something about last night's game kept me up for a couple of hours."

"You tossed and turned a little, dearie. I noticed. You move like a rhinoceros, gently and full of grace."

Dr. Ellefson laughed heartily. "It's been a while since you paid me a compliment." He cut a blooming rose and offered it to her. Charmed, she took it and smelled the blossom. The rose fragrance was faint, barely distinguishable.

"Have you ever wondered why American roses don't smell as nice as the ones at our hotel in Greece?" They'd vacationed there a few years back. That Thessaloníki hotel rose garden had seeded the passion for horticulture in her husband. Those blooms were dizzying with their strong scents.

"I don't have to wonder," he replied, shooting her a quick smile. "It's the chemicals they feed the plants here for accelerated growth. Americans have no patience." He walked over to the older rose bushes that bloomed a few feet away. He'd planted those two summers ago. With a quick snip of his pruning shears, he cut a blooming red and offered it to her. "Smell the difference?"

She inhaled. The scent of the rose was intoxicating as if the entire essence of the exquisite flower had entered her body and took residence in her chest. "Thank you," she said, inhaling the fragrance again and again. "I had no idea."

"Yeah," Aaron replied, crouching next to the hole. It was about half-filled with water, perfect for planting the new rose bush. Gently, he set the pot on its side and slid the plant out without damaging the roots. Then, holding the bush carefully with both hands, he put the root into the ground and gave it a few minutes to let the water loosen the roots. "Speaking of no idea, what do you think is going on with Andi? Why didn't they give her that job at the university? I thought alumni are given preference."

She leaned into her elbows, resting them on the wooden banister. "I was wondering the same. I'll make a couple of calls later today. I'm sure I can get a straight answer from someone."

"Do you think it's our place to meddle in this?"

"We're not meddling, Aaron. I'm not pulling strings. Just asking a question. Andi is like our own daughter. It was hurtful to watch her and Hunter last night, by the way."

"That's what kept me up. Can't believe what I saw. Hunter was never like that."

"Like what? Insane?"

"Yeah, you might say that." Aaron shot her a quick, inquisitive glance before gathering the displaced dirt around the rose bush root. He didn't press too firmly. The ground felt soft under his fingers as the water still worked its way to separate the roots and nourish them. "Do you think he's right?"

"What? About Craig?" She frowned for a moment, thinking. She failed to remember a single time when Craig had behaved in a manner that would've justified Hunter's opinion of him. At the same time, she vividly remembered how her own mother had hated Aaron for no reason whatsoever. He turned out to be an excellent husband, but her mother had died unassuaged that her daughter was married to a man who touched the dead. Oh well. Parents could be wrong; they were nothing but people who made mistakes. "I don't think so. Andi seems happy, totally in love with him. Did you notice how her face lit up when she was telling us the story of how they met?"

Satisfied with his work, Dr. Ellefson stood, brushing his hands against his gardening jeans to lose the dirt that still clung to his fingers. "Yeah. She's happy. You'd have to be blind not to notice." He turned off the water and gathered his tools. "Maybe Hunter has difficulties dealing with it. After losing his wife, Andi is all he's got left. Perhaps he's seeing a monster where there isn't one, just because this man took his only child away from him."

"Yeah, that could be true. I heard he's spending all his days at the clinic, twelve-hour days, six days a week, and he goes in on Sundays too."

"He'll burn out." The gardening tools clattered when he dropped them in their crate inside the shed. "And he'll push her away if he keeps on with this madness."

Rebecca looked at him with pleading eyes.

"Okay, I'll talk to him," he conceded with a sigh. "I'll take him fishing, just the two of us and some beer. Maybe he'll tell me what this is all about. Maybe he'll listen to reason."

Grateful, she touched his arm as he passed by on his way to the shower. She followed him inside, where she put the two rose blooms in water in two small, narrow vases. Leaning against the bathroom wall, she chatted with Aaron while he took his shower, mostly about how dreadful it would be if Andi and her father became estranged, about how that poor girl must be hurting, being torn apart like that between father and husband.

But all Rebecca could think about was the call she was about to make to find out what had kept Andi from getting the job she wanted. She'd been brave about it, but Rebecca had noticed the sadness in her eyes when she'd answered Freddy DeMaria's question the night before. Thankfully, she still knew enough faculty members to find out.

As soon as Aaron's car turned the corner and disappeared from view, Rebecca topped off her coffee and took a seat on the sofa, legs crossed, phone in hand. Impatiently waiting for nine o'clock, when faculty came to work, she flipped through her many saved contacts, looking for someone who would know about Andi.

"Ah, The Cesar, he'd know," she mumbled, referring to Professor Cesar.

At precisely 9:01, she made the call. While it rang, she stood and started pacing nervously. Without any particular reason, she felt anxious about making that call, and she wanted it over and done with.

Thankfully, The Cesar picked up and seemed glad to hear from her. They chatted about students, faculty, summer plans, and who else had retired since Rebecca left. Then she said, "I need a big favor. A protégé of mine needs some coaching on how to get the job she studied for. You might know her. Andrea Wilmore?"

Silence fell heavy on the call. It was as if the professor wasn't even breathing.

"Could you please do me an immense favor and find out what went wrong during the interview?"

"I don't need to find out," The Cesar replied, his voice somber. "I already know."

It was Rebecca's turn to hold her breath. She listened to her former colleague's words speechlessly. Then she thanked him with rushed, whispered words.

As soon as the call ended, she dropped the phone on the sofa as if it burned her fingers. "Oh, no," she whispered, "this can't be happening."

She stared at the phone, dreading what she was about to do, but she saw no other choice. With shaky fingers, she grabbed the phone and called Hunter Wilmore. As soon as he picked up, she cut through the pleasantries and said, "There's something disheartening you should know. It's about Andi. About her inability to find a job."

Defense Attorney Goodridge: Where did you meet Andrea Wilmore Brafford?

Holly Hughes: At the Brafford party. My husband is Craig Brafford's boss.

Defense Attorney Goodridge: How did she seem to you?

Holly Hughes: She was perfectly fine. Smiling, greeting people, being a good host.

Defense Attorney Goodridge: Did she seem distraught over this job search issue?

Holly Hughes: No, not at all. And honestly, I don't understand what the big deal is. I've seen some stuff on the news, but is it really that wrong to support one's husband in his business? That's what I've been doing all my life.

14

ZEGNA

Craig was having a rollercoaster of a week.

On Tuesday, he had to fork out a check for almost five thousand dollars he didn't have to cover his moving expenses. Then he had to run as fast as possible to get a title loan from a slimy, fat loan shark named Alf. With 59 percent interest. For the first three months.

Through some miracle, he managed to deposit the cash in his bank right before closing. By the next morning, the moving expenses check had already cleared. That son of a bitch, Hughes, didn't waste any time.

On Wednesday, he had follow-up calls to make to his guests, confirming they had the address, what they liked to drink, and how they liked their backs scratched. Then he had to run and pick up the area rug Andi had ordered and bring it home. He'd laid it down and had to admit his wife had reasonable taste. Struggling to haul the king-size bed into the living room by himself, no one to hold the doors open for him, he eventually managed that part too, then had to rush out again to bring home the new sectional.

Finally, he sat down on one of the new armchairs, sweaty and tired, and waited for Andi to return.

And waited. Then waited some more, almost till midnight, while she was out, playing poker with a bunch of old-timers, not giving a crap about him. He hated her going there beyond words. Especially when he needed her focused.

The woman didn't seem able to care any less about the party he'd been working his ass off to make happen. She had no idea how many times he'd made calls only to get hung up on, sent to hell, or threatened. She seemed restless, unable to settle, self-centered like no one he'd met before. All she cared about was her stupid career and now kids. Seriously. Because everything else was great, and they were bored, with nothing better to do than procreate endlessly and sink sizeable fortunes into the asses of spoiled brats. They said raising a kid set one back by the cost of one brand new Ferrari. So not worth it.

After a crappy start of the week, his luck had changed. On Thursday morning, an offer for the Donati house beeped through the fax machine in his home office while he was still in his jammies. One million, four hundred thousand, with immediate closing, cash deal.

Yes. Finally.

By tomorrow, he could have his Benz title back.

Doing a silent happy dance, he dialed the buyer's number and talked the Chinese national into raising the offer by seventy-five thousand more. He typed the formal offer on the Parker Jones letterhead form and sent it to the buyer for signature. Within minutes, it came back. Signed.

Grinning widely, he called Donati and told him the good news, then faxed him the formal offer. Rushing to make himself a sandwich before hitting the road for a complicated day, he made time to stop by the small bedroom to look at Andi's attempt at wall art.

Three large, stunning canvasses were propped against the walls. He didn't know much about art, but he'd seen enough expensive houses, richly decorated, to know his wife's handiwork would've fit right up there with Jackson Pollock and the sorts. She probably could be a half-decent artist if she tried, but he had other plans for her.

He needed someone he could trust to make his calls for him, send contractors to the houses he and Jude would buy together, make sure the work was done correctly, get the workers paid, and the houses ready to sell. She could stage the homes to have them sell higher, cater the open house showings, fill out paperwork. She would probably need to get her own Realtor license soon. There was no time for any art bullshit, no more than there was for any of her marine biology nonsense. There wasn't any decent money in that. Soon, she'd get over that and start seeing the big picture he wanted her to see.

Crouching down and squinting to read the signature, he let out a loud sigh of relief. She'd had the common sense to sign with a fake name. Good girl. He'd been worried her ego might pop its ugly head, and she'd sign the paintings with her own name. Then everyone would know they couldn't even afford to buy art; they had to make some.

Half a sandwich later, he was on his way out when the fax machine chimed again. From the garage doorstep, he turned on his heels and rushed back inside, just in time to grab the signed Donati offer as it came out of the printer, hot and smelling of fresh burned toner.

His boss would be thrilled, just in time for the party. Craig couldn't wait to see the weasel's face when he showed him the signed deal, almost three hundred thousand above the asking price.

But first, he drove straight to Galleria and parked in front of Neiman Marcus. He rushed to the door but then paced himself as soon as he entered the store. He walked casually, avoided looking at price tags, taking it slowly as if he had an entire day to waste.

Soon, a sales associate with small, beady eyes started fawning over him. He gave into the man's insistences and tried on a Brioni suit after feeling the fabric with the tips of his fingers. The wool linen jacket changed who he was. He seemed taller in it, although the suit was a light, pearly gray. His back seemed straighter, his shoulders wider, his demeanor more imposing. The pants were a little too much on the skinny side for him, taut on his thighs. Once inside the dressing room, he checked the price tag and balked.

"Seven thousand dollars," he whispered with sadness in his voice. He spent a few moments staring at his image in the mirror, wishing he had the money to afford it. Not yet, he didn't, but soon.

"The pant legs are too tight," he told the associate when he came out of the fitting room, his cheeks on fire, betraying him. "I don't know who could wear this and be comfortable. Anything else you can show me?"

The associate nodded and looked at him just a split second too long. Craig swallowed a curse. There was nothing he hated more than poverty, not having enough money. Not being one of the people who could do whatever they wanted.

The associate returned with a navy suit he carried on his extended arms like an offering meant for a god. "This is an Ermenegildo Zegna original. Touch it," he encouraged Craig. "This unbelievable fabric is Zegna's signature wool-silk. No one else makes a suit quite like it."

Craig smiled. He could see himself wearing it. All the hotshots who'd brush against him later tonight would sense the fine fabric as being something they would wear. What was it with Italians and luxury? No one did luxury like the Italians did. It was unbelievable. One small nation, not even twice the size and population of California, and they had it all. Ferrari, Lamborghini, and Maserati drove under the Italian banner. In fashion, the list was even more incredible. Gucci, Armani, Versace, Cavalli, Valentino, Bulgari, and the names went on and on. Must be something in the Italian air. He had to visit, breathe that air in.

The Zegna fit him like a perfect glove. He felt the luxury with every pore of his skin. The pant legs were just right, and the price tag had him swallowing hard, but there was no way he could say no.

"I'll take it," he informed the associate. Then he followed the young man as he helped him pick a silk shirt and a matching tie, also from Zegna. Having difficulty choosing between the many brands he recognized, he ended up with a pair of Ferragamo leather shoes to complete his attire. Sweating profusely, he waited for the associate to hand everything over to the cashier.

"That will be five thousand, three hundred and eighty-seven dollars and twenty-nine cents," the petite blonde at the register informed him in a tiny voice after she finished scanning the labels.

Damn. None of his cards had that much limit left. And that stupid associate wasn't going away. What the heck was he still waiting for?

He took two cards out of his wallet and handed her the blue American Express first. "Charge two thousand on this one, then the rest on the Mastercard."

She hesitated just a split second, then took them both with perfectly manicured fingernails that clicked pleasantly against the plastic. She stared at him a little while she waited for the first charge to go through. Craig held his breath and ground his teeth until the cashier had him sign for everything with a sweet smile. The associate took the items from the cashier, the suit packed in a long bag and everything else in shopping bags with the Neiman Marcus logo, and walked him out.

"I'll take it from here," Craig said, grabbing the bags and the suit. The associate held the door for him with a smile. He was quick to step outside and put distance between him and those beady, insolent eyes.

Halfway to his car, Craig started smiling. Screw them and what they thought about him. Soon enough, he'd buy that Brioni, with credit or cash, whatever. But those two would still be hourly employees catering to his whims. Not the other way around.

He crossed the parking lot with a spring in his step. The day was looking great, and it wasn't even noon yet.

15

OF THE HEART

The soufflé was tricky to make. At any given moment, it threatened to go flat and turn into an unsightly, unsalvageable mush. It was Andi's first attempt at making it. She would've never tried to make it had she not had so much time left until six when the guests were scheduled to arrive. Maybe that wasn't the only reason. She wanted Craig to be happy, to be proud of her making his party a success. Otherwise, she would've spent her time looking for work or studying. Recently, in the wake of everything that was going on in their lives, the new house, Craig's increasing list of business partners they had to entertain, she'd all but abandoned working on her doctoral degree.

That was only a temporary setback, she promised herself every morning when she took to house chores or helping Craig make it through his day. Every morning, she broke the promise she made herself.

Since Craig had left that morning, she'd whipped together everything she needed for the party, neatly arranged the hors d'oeuvres on serving platters, and covered them with shrink-wrap to keep everything fresh. She even took a star-shaped cookie cutter to watermelon slices and set the shaped pieces on a platter, sprinkled with fresh berries and basil leaves. The remaining menu item was the salmon mousse, but she wanted that done right before the party, so the crackers wouldn't draw too much moisture and turn soft.

But the soufflé was a different story. It was as if the thing had a will of its own, holding her hostage, threatening her. If she moved the wrong way, rushed through the process, or even breathed wrong, the thing deflated out of spite. Muttering a curse under her breath, she made a commitment to herself to never try that recipe again, regardless of the day's final results. The smell of strawberries was mouthwatering, though, and she hadn't tasted a soufflé in years.

She almost didn't hear the phone ringing under the sound of the handheld mixer. She wasn't going to pick up; stopping the mixer could deflate the egg whites while she spoke on the phone. Whoever it was could wait for a few minutes. But then she shot a glance at the screen and, recognizing the number as her dad's vet clinic reception desk, she turned off the mixer and let it sink into the peaking foam.

They never called. Her father called her directly from his cell. Something had to be wrong.

"Hello?" Her voice was strangled, shaky. The chilling angst coiled inside her gut started unfurling.

"Andi? This is Gabriella from—"

"Yes, hi, Gabriella, what's up?"

"It's your father. They're taking him to Baylor St. Luke's Medical Center, where there's a large cardiology—"

Her knees gave, and she sat quickly on the edge of a kitchen chair. "What happened?" Tears burned her eyes. Oh, please, God, please let him be okay.

"They're saying it's a heart attack. They'll know more once they investigate."

Finding her strength, she got rid of the apron and put her shoes on while still on the phone.

"Andi, they're taking him to the Texas Heart Institute—"

"Yeah, I got that," she replied, scurrying in a rush through the house in search of her car keys.

"I wanted to say they're taking him there because he already knew people at the institute. A surgeon. Doctors. We had no idea."

She froze in place, a rush of ice streaming through her blood. He knew he was sick and hadn't said one word to her.

"Thanks, Gabrielle. I'm heading there now."

The drive to the hospital was a blur of tears and a struggle to breathe, her chest heavy, her heart numb, petrified with fear. The night before, they had parted with bitter words from her. Those couldn't be the last words she'd get to say to her father. It just couldn't end like that. It couldn't end . . . not now. Oh, God, please.

She stopped with tires screeching against the heated asphalt under the white porte-cochere and dashed inside, leaving the engine running and the keys in the ignition.

"Ma'am?" a security guard called. "You can't park here."

She didn't stop until she reached the reception desk.

"My father, Hunter Wilmore. He was just brought in," she blurted out of breath, leaning over the reception desk as if her proximity would motivate the jaded woman to type faster.

"Woolmore, you said?"

"Wilmore, W-I-L-more."

"Uh-huh," she muttered, correcting her typing incredibly slowly. Her fingernails were so long she had to type with the sides of her fingers, not the tips. "Third floor, Cardiology ICU. Room three-oh-seven."

"Thanks," she threw over her shoulder as she rushed to the elevators. One had started to close its doors, but she slid her hand between and stopped them. Then she apologized to the two men who stared at her with critical eyes and pressed three.

Only then she breathed.

He was still alive, wasn't he? He had to be. Reception didn't give room numbers for deceased patients, did they? Her mind spun in senseless circles while the elevator crawled up to the third floor, then opened its doors with a creak.

The Cardiology Intensive Care Unit was quiet and filled with light, coming from the large windows in several empty rooms and the fluorescent lights overhead. Faint, distant beeping tracked someone's heart rhythm. Frantic, she avoided the empty nurses' station and looked for room numbers and found them marked neatly on small, silver metallic tags affixed to the walls by the sliding doors.

Three-oh-seven. He was there. His heart was still beating.

Pale, his eyes closed, he didn't react when she slowly slid the door open and snuck inside. The room smelled faintly of antibacterial gel and her father's aftershave. Sunshine was piercing through the open blinds. The monitors showed a steady heart rhythm, the beeps the only sound she could hear.

Fresh tears burned her eyes. He was still there. Still alive.

She crouched on the side of the bed and gently took his hand into hers, resting her heated cheek against it.

"I'm so sorry," she whispered. He didn't deserve anything she'd said to him the night before or on other occasions, whenever they'd argued about her husband. They'd never argued about anything else, not as long as she could remember. His only fault was he cared deeply for her and wanted what was best for her.

"Don't cry, sweet girl," he whispered, squeezing her hand just a little. "I'm okay. You know me, tough as nails." He attempted a smile, but it was lopsided and weak. He opened his eyes then immediately closed them. "It's bright in here."

Although tempted to rush and close the blinds, she decided not to. Sunshine was good for the soul. It brought hope and the will to survive.

"What happened?" she asked, blinking away stubborn tears. "What are they saying?"

"They're saying I'll be fine." His voice was weak. He opened his eyes a sliver and looked at her. "Don't worry about me."

"A heart attack gives me the right to worry, Dad," she replied. "How bad was it?"

He turned his head away slightly but then looked at her. "These things are never good, but I'll be okay." He opened his eyes a little wider. "I swear I'll be fine. You can ask the doctors yourself."

"Don't believe I won't," she replied, sniffling. "I don't trust you in these matters."

"Ah," he replied as a wave of sadness washed over his face. "You're talking about your mother. How did I not see she was dying until she dropped on the floor one day?"

"Dad, no . . . I didn't mean that. You've been blaming yourself for her death all these years?" She kissed his hand, then gave it another squeeze. "You shouldn't. No one's to blame."

"Then what? What did you mean?"

"I meant you can't be trusted," she replied, a tiny smile in her voice. "You lied about your health to protect me. You knew this was coming, didn't you? You're burned with me, mister," she quipped the way she always did with him.

"I am, aren't I?" He shifted slightly, turning toward her. "That's why you're welcome to question my doctor when he makes his evening rounds."

She closed her eyes briefly, unwilling to let him see her frustration. The stupid party . . . she couldn't stay long.

"Can you forgive me?" she asked quietly. A fresh tear pooled at the corner of her eye, then dropped on the back of his hand. She wiped it quickly with the tip of her finger.

"For what, dear child?"

"What I said last night. I didn't mean it—" She choked, unable to find her words. "You didn't deserve any of it."

"That . . . It doesn't matter, Andi. Nothing you say or do is beyond forgiving by your old man." He stopped talking for a moment she cherished, her head rested on his hand, holding on, without knowing for how much longer he'd still be there for her to hold on to. "Tell me one thing." His voice sounded a little stronger.

"Anything."

"Are you happy?"

His question shook her, resonating inside her for a long moment. How could a simple question like that have such a complicated answer? And yet, the answer was simple, if she wanted to look past her baseless fears and her selfishness.

"Yes," she replied, lifting her head to meet his eyes. "I'm happy, Dad. He makes me laugh. He's always there for me. He cares for me and always puts me first. I only wish you could see him the way I do." The beeping coming from the monitor increased in frequency as she sensed his body tensing. There would probably be a better time for what she wanted to say to him next. "Maybe one day," she smiled, "who knows. We'll get to be one happy family, all of us."

"Well, if you're happy, I'm happy too," he replied, then closed his eyes.

"Dad, I need to go," she said reluctantly, wishing she could stay, just to watch over him, to keep him company when he was awake, to doze off by his side overnight. She'd called Craig several times on the way to the hospital, but her calls went straight to voicemail. She didn't leave a message . . . it was her husband she needed, not some cold, heartless recording. And she needed him now more than ever.

"It's that party, isn't it?" he whispered. "Go, Andrea. Don't worry about me. I'll still be here tomorrow."

16

PARTY

Craig's Mercedes was in the garage when she pulled in. Frowning, she wondered why she hadn't heard from him if he was home already. Passing in front of his car to reach the door, she touched the black grille of the Benz. It was barely warm. He'd been home a while.

Swallowing her disappointment, she forced some air into her lungs, willing herself to stay calm and survive the party. Then there would be time to ask questions.

The door opened before she could squeeze the handle. Craig, wearing a suit she'd never seen before, stared at her in disbelief.

"Where the hell have you been?" His voice was tinged with frustration, the pitch elevated, grating.

Instead of being her usual, understanding self, Andi snapped. "I tried to call you, I don't know how many times. You never called me back." She threw her purse on the sofa and kicked off her shoes, then entered the kitchen with a frustrated sigh. The place looked like a war zone. There wasn't going to be any soufflé that night.

She poured the flattened egg white mixture into the sink, then rinsed the beaters under a strong flow of water. After wiping them dry, she set them on the counter and looked at the time. "Shit," she mumbled. Less than forty-five minutes until the first guest arrived.

"No, really, where were you?" Craig's voice was low and menacing, his stare almost hateful.

Tears stung her eyes. "Our honeymoon didn't last long," she said matter-of-factly, clearing the counter of the soufflé ingredients and pulling out the smoked salmon and cream cheese. The fridge door was slammed shut with a kick of her left foot. "Did it, Craig?"

"What are you talking about?" He propped his hands on his hips but kept his distance from her as if she was going to throw food at him and stain his new suit.

"They say the honeymoon lasts until the wife cries her first tear. The real honeymoon, not the two-week vacation that we took after the wedding." She wiped her eyes and used a fork to scrape the smoked salmon into the food processor.

He didn't seem to care about anything she'd just said. "You left me here and went who knows where. You don't give a shit, do you? People are coming. Nothing is ready."

"*Everything* is fucking ready," she shouted, angrily throwing the fork into the sink where it rattled against the mixing bowl. He took a step back. "Everything except your precious salmon mousse." Scraping the cream cheese on top of the salmon, she turned the processor on in rapid, short bursts. "Even that will be ready on time if you just get off my back." Another tear brimmed in her eye, then added salt to the mix. She looked at Craig and said coldly, "Leave me alone. I'll call you when it's all done."

He did the exact opposite. He approached her slowly, his hands held out in a reassuring gesture, his eyes understanding. "Babe, this isn't us. You're right. If you hate these parties so much, we won't have them anymore. It's up to you. I just don't want to see you upset."

She pushed him away and restarted the processor, but her anger was subsiding. She was yearning for his arms to wrap around her body and give her the strength she needed. "Dad had a heart attack," she eventually said, her voice loaded with unspent tears.

In an instant, he took her in his arms. "I'm so sorry, Ands," he whispered in her ear. "Is he—"

"He's in the hospital. That's where I was." She wriggled free, although she would've loved to spend a moment in his embrace, feeling safe, loved. "And I came back to finish everything and do the party like I promised."

He was speechless for a brief moment. "I had no idea," he replied. He patted his pockets, feeling for something, then fished his phone out. "This thing was off. I'm so sorry I wasn't there for you when you needed me."

She nodded, staring at the mousse instead of looking into his eyes. It somehow felt safer to avoid his glance for some reason. "New suit?"

"Yes," he replied, the smile in his voice unmistakable. "Like?" He turned around for her, took a few steps back and forth, undid his jacket button, opened the flap, and put his hand in his pants pocket, modeling it like a pro.

It looked good on him. Smiling, she wiped a rebel tear and started putting the mousse on crackers laid out on platters in even, angled rows, like tiny little soldiers wearing pink hats.

"Dare I ask?" she said, a slight frown furrowing her brow for a moment. He'd been spending a lot of money lately, money they didn't have.

"No, please don't ask," he replied quickly, gesturing with his hands so desperately it was hilarious. "The Donati house sold today, and it more than paid for this, and that's only from the extra deal I struck with the man."

"Extra deal, huh?" Craig had a nose for money. He craved it like people crave ice cream or chocolate, like addicts twitch for their next fix, always bigger than the last, never enough. He thrived on cash like others do on coffee. And he had a talent for money, an innate gift to smell it, find it, and earn it. As for spending money, Andi believed it gave Craig more pleasure than sex.

Everything was ready. "Set these platters on the kitchen island, those platters on the dining room table. Ba careful not to stain your new suit." For a beat, he seemed petrified at the thought of ruining his attire. "Never mind, I'll do it." She grabbed two of the platters and took them into the dining room, then returned for more. "You bring napkins and glasses. Bottles too."

"Yes, ma'am," he replied, trotting on the hardwood floor in what seemed like new shoes with a bit of a heel. He looked stunning. Taller, full of self-confidence, beaming. When he smiled, he was irresistible.

In passing, she looked out the living room window and noticed a young man dressed in a white jacket lingering at the end of their driveway. "Craig, who's that?"

"That guy? He's our parking valet for the evening." He laughed, probably when he noticed her gaping mouth and rounded eyes. "He's the next-door neighbor's kid. He won't cost us a dime. Just the tips, and maybe some leftovers if there are any, to send him home with."

"What? And lose the opportunity to eat stale hors d'oeuvres for an entire week?" She laughed and, in passing, touched his face. "Going to get dressed."

It took her about ten minutes to put on the dress she'd chosen for the occasion, a long satin gown in shimmering midnight blue with a generous slit on one leg and a plunging neckline. It went perfectly with the blue chandelier earrings she got from Janelle, and probably none of the guests would notice they were cheap zirconia. Not that she cared what the guests would or wouldn't notice; she just didn't want Craig to be embarrassed with her. She loved the earrings; they made her keep her head up straight and walk with swaying elegance. Otherwise, they bounced around like rattles in the hands of a toddler.

She called out for Craig from the bedroom door, holding two pairs of shoes, one in each hand. "Which ones?"

"The heels, Ands," he grinned. "Always the heels."

She was a couple of inches taller than him in those heels, and the other choice would've been flats, but he didn't seem to mind. Smiling, she slid on the pumps and stood. There was something about heels, the way they made a woman walk with her back straight, especially someone like her who liked to stomp and bounce and prance when she walked. Satisfied with the image smiling back from the mirror, she touched up her lipstick and headed back to the kitchen.

He whistled when he saw her, and she took a mock bow while her heart swelled. Taking her hand to his lips, he said, "Something's missing from your breathtaking attire, Mrs. Brafford. I think I know exactly what. Don't move."

Opening his briefcase, he took out a long box and extracted a blue pendant on a silver chain. It was stunning, albeit a little unusual. The pendant was square, a central blue topaz surrounded by small sapphires. The rolo chain was what a man would wear, not fine and delicate like traditional women's jewelry, but fashion wasn't Andi's strongest suit. All that mattered was the man who was holding it. Squealing with joy, she wrapped her arms around his neck and kissed him breathlessly.

He clasped it on for her, and she touched it, feeling the central stone with the tips of her fingers, then rushed to the bathroom mirror. Craig stood by her side in the reflected image, beaming with pride. The pendant's color matched her earrings to perfection. "Thank you," she whispered, "I wasn't expecting this."

His grin widened. "I'm glad you like it."

"Is it, um, was it expensive? Are these stones real?"

"What do you think?" He looked at her from head to toe and whistled. "Mrs. Brafford, you look unbelievable."

The sound of a car entering their driveway got their attention.

"Let's put our game faces on," Craig said, giving the white Cadillac Escalade a quick look. "It's Donati. Right on time."

She walked toward the entrance, ready to greet the guest and his stunning wife. "By the way, is Jude coming?"

"Nah," Craig replied, lowering his voice to a whisper, probably because Donati was already within earshot. "Jude has enough business functions to last him a lifetime."

Through the etched glass of the front door, she watched the valet take the keys from Donati's hand and sighed. The dreaded party had finally started.

District Attorney Buscher: At the time of the arrest, had you already conducted the search of the residence?

Detective Barbara Otwell: Yes.

District Attorney Buscher: What were your findings?

Detective Barbara Otwell: There were traces of blood on one of the kitchen chairs. Some blood residue was found in the tile grout under the kitchen table, damaged by bleach but still forensically viable. The primary bathroom shower curtain was missing, and there was visible evidence of tearing. A small section of it was still attached to the rings. In my professional experience, shower curtains are often used in forensic countermeasures, such as body disposal.

District Attorney Buscher: Was that shower curtain located?

Detective Barbara Otwell: Yes. It was found at the landfill, stained with blood. The section recovered was a perfect match to the piece still attached to the rings.

17

STARTING FIRES

Craig felt like dancing.

As soon as he closed the door behind the last of his guests, he grabbed Andi's hands and started dancing to the music in his head, a waltz he hummed in her ear, louder and louder.

"Pa rum pum pum pum, pum pum, pum pum," he vocalized and spun with her in his arms until they burst into laughter.

"Oh, please, stop," she said, then pulled away and kicked off her shoes. "I'm bushed." She walked barefoot into the living room, then sank into an armchair.

A quick rap on the door got his attention. It was the neighbor's kid.

"Mr. Brafford? They're all gone, sir," the young man said, then lingered. He probably wanted some more money. Everyone did.

Craig was feeling generous. The evening had been a smashing success. Fishing a hundred-dollar bill from his wallet, he gave it to him, then patted him on the shoulder. "Thanks, buddy."

The kid grinned. "Whenever you need me, sir."

Craig locked the door behind him and leaned against it, catching his breath. It had been a fascinating party.

Donati had shown up first. A man of his word, he immediately handed Craig a thick, yellow envelope. He'd been graceful enough to round up the cash portion of his unofficial commission generously, from fourteen thousand to twenty. Craig was still thanking him when his boss showed up with his wife, Holly.

Mrs. Hughes looked exactly like he'd pictured the wife of the dinosaur. An overly suntanned blonde with short hair blow-dried in a complicated do and sprayed firmly in place, the boss's wife had a permanent smile on her lips, and a know-it-all, in-your-business kind of attitude radiating from every pore of her skin. She was pleasant, though, when she spoke. She said the right things at the right times and was quick to pay Craig compliments about the house and Andi's looks, although when she mentioned the house, she shot Jeremy Hughes an inquisitive glance tinged with disdain. Later she would probably grill him over how one of his younger minions could afford a property that was probably more valuable than theirs. Poor ball-less dinosaur. An idea popped into Craig's mind, seeing Holly Hughes's side glances and her husband's clenched jaw.

While Andi took Donati and his wife, Martine, into the living room, he snuck into his office and took the envelope from his pocket. Taking the bulk of the money out and leaving twenty-five hundred dollars in it, he slid it back, then went to find his boss.

He found Hughes nursing a glass of wine and chatting casually with Andi. Through the living room window, he saw another vehicle approaching. Truman Haskett, a local manufacturing magnate, and his plus one, too young to tell if it was the wife or the daughter. Pressed for time, he got Hughes's attention and took him aside, away from prying eyes and indiscreet ears.

There, he handed him the envelope. "This is for you, sir."

"What's this?" The man's whisper was nothing short of hostile.

"Your half of the off-the-record bonus I got from Donati."

Incredulous, Hughes opened the envelope and whistled quietly. His frown waned but didn't entirely vanish.

"Whatever windfall I catch, we share," Craig added. "That is if you're interested."

Those few words did away with the man's frown. He smiled and patted Craig on his shoulder. "You got the goods, Brafford, that's for sure. Now you go out there and catch them big fish." Then he walked straight to Donati while Craig's breath caught, dreading what Hughes could say. "I hear you're happy with my boy here," he said, raising the glass.

A gentleman, Donati raised his glass also while shooting Craig an amused yet sympathetic look. His boss's comment had been an embarrassment only to Hughes himself, not to Craig, and definitely not to Donati.

"Yes, I am. Mr. Brafford has the class I'm looking for in the Realtor I'll be dealing with from this point forward. No one else will do."

Put in his place, Hughes thankfully shut up, wearing a polite smile on his face for the long moment he took before he wandered away. But then he redeemed himself somewhat, introducing himself to all the guests and talking about Craig's success in getting the Donati home sold for way above market. People were more inclined to hear it from a third party instead of Craig himself.

That was when the men weren't busy undressing Andi with their eyes. Whenever she sashayed through the living room with a tray of hors d'oeuvres or sweaty flute glasses with champagne chilled to perfection, the guests stopped talking and just watched. Women, especially the young trophy wives, were green with envy, shooting her piercing glares that his beautiful, brilliant wife graciously ignored.

The men were an open book to Craig. He'd been in their shoes, eyeing some long-legged stunner, unable to take his eyes off her curves while the sight of her undulating body stirred him, igniting his imagination, leaving him wondering about the color of her panties, whether they were silk or lace. What she smelled like, how she'd tremble if he touched her heated body.

Taking an empty tray back to the kitchen, Andi smiled and winked at him. The party was going well; everyone had shown up, the chatter was engaged and lively, the food was a success, and that was no small feat when the crowd consisted of wealthy, spoiled individuals who didn't want for anything. Albeit reluctantly still, she was becoming his partner. Maybe she needed to taste the rewards of their work before becoming passionate about catering to people like those, before she could look at them and see them for what they really were, nothing but opportunity.

Until then, though, he needed to take her shopping for a new cocktail dress. Something shorter, with a deeper cleavage, maybe backless even. Never in the history of money had skin like Andi's done any damage unless it was covered under unnecessary layers of textile.

Meanwhile, he had to remember the wives. Jealous of Andi's looks, they could become a problem unless he made the evening one to remember for them. The right compliment, a long, deep gaze into their eyes, a casual brush of his hand against a bare shoulder enough to kindle the fire inside; it didn't take more than that to make them smile. Most of them were starved for attention and affection; the people they'd married were power addicts, always busy, always gone from home.

He started his tour with Martine Donati, a brunette with long, silky hair and skin the color of caramel latte. He offered her a new glass of champagne and took the old one from her hand, smiling, his eyes lingering on her full lips, then a bit lower. They chatted briefly about the house that had just sold, then about their future home, a sprawling 6,000-square-foot mansion on two acres of land that was still being built to order.

Donati approached and put his hands on Martine's shoulders possessively, pulling her closer to him. Craig held his cool and continued the conversation.

"I offered this young man the opportunity to come work for me as soon as the house was sold," he said, speaking in a low voice as if only for his wife. "What do you think?"

"You know what's best, Sol," Martine replied, not taking her eyes off Craig. Then she bit her lip in a quick, fire-starting gesture. She would remember him for a while.

"I'm, once again, flattered by your offer," Craig said, shifting his attention to Donati.

"But?"

No salary, no matter how generous, could justify forfeiting the future he and Jude had planned together. He'd be locked inside an office, forced to engage in mind-numbing politics just to survive the day without being backstabbed over meaningless stuff. As for Donati, he was too powerful a man to antagonize. He'd already attended his parties twice, always endorsing him. Had it not been for his support, Craig and Andi would've been home alone that night, wondering how they'd make their next mortgage payment. Truth was the best policy.

"Can I be entirely honest with you, sir?"

"I'd have it no other way." He encouraged him with a hint of a smile and a hand gesture.

"My passion is real estate. My dream is to have my own business in a couple of years, once I get a little capital lined up." Donati was impossible to read, but there was a flicker of interest in his steely eyes. Interest, not anger. "I hope I'm not disappointing you. It's just that I believe one can never truly be successful unless one follows one's passion."

Donati's lips stretched into a smile. "That's what I did thirty years ago. Ships mean to me what houses mean to you."

"Exactly." Craig's voice was loaded with excitement. He'd found more than a sponsor; he'd found a kindred spirit. "I look at a house, I see a story waiting to be told, a family starting on a new leg of their life journey. I see dreams about to come true for both seller and buyer. It's as if I can help shape the future for all these people."

Donati lifted his glass. "When you're ready to raise capital for your future business, give me a call." His comment got Truman Haskett's attention. He sized Craig up as if he hadn't seen him before and scratched his trim, white mustache with his finger, then smoothed it out. The fire was spreading.

He thanked Donati with a bow of his head followed by a raised glass. "To you and all yours."

"And to you, son."

The next stop was Mrs. Hughes, who mindlessly yapped for ten minutes or so about the house furnishings, what she thought would work best instead of what they had. She made endless comments about the bed in the middle of the living room, about the color of the drapes. Thankfully, when he was just about to lose his mind, Andi rescued him, making an apology and saying he was needed in the kitchen.

A few moments later, he continued his tour with Gemma Haskett, then moved on to the next guest, a mid-market oil refinery guy by the name of Bill Parsons, whose pale wife was turning into a withering wallflower by the window.

His guests lingered, staying later than was fashionable for these kinds of things. Hughes worked really hard for the twenty-five hundred he'd paid him, not aware the roles had swiftly changed, and now Hughes was working for Craig in every aspect except on paper. He'd worked the room just as feverishly as Craig had. He didn't think Hughes was a dog who could still hunt. Turned out, it depended on who held the leash.

Hughes and the missus were the last ones to leave. The man thanked him for an excellent evening. As he said the words, he patted the chest pocket of his jacket where Craig had seen him slide the envelope earlier.

He'd smiled graciously and replied, "Always a pleasure. Glad to have you by my side, sir. Something tells me we'll do wonderful things together."

The flicker of greed sparkled in his eyes. "Yes, we will. You can count on it." He licked his lips and lit a thick Cuban before walking out the door. No one had come to take the money.

18

BOMBSHELL

In the silence left behind by the last departing guests, Craig took off his shoes, welcoming the cold sensation of marble flooring of the foyer under his feet. Next, his suit jacket found a hanger in the nearest closet, and the tie was next to follow. Undoing the top two shirt buttons, he joined Andi in the living room and sat on the armrest of her chair, running his fingers up and down her bare arm.

"Thank you," he whispered. The voices that had filled the house with lively chatter still resounded in Craig's mind. "Now it's time for you and me." He leaned over to kiss her, but she pulled back. "What's wrong?"

She showed him the phone she'd cradled in her hands. "This time, they rejected me by email, and they took less than a day to do it."

Ah, the stupid nonsense with the jobs again. Andi was nothing if not relentless when she set her mind on something. That would work great once he got her to focus on the right things.

"I'm so sorry, Ands," he murmured close to her ear. The lie flowed easily; he'd said it so many times before it came out automatically, rolling off his lips with just the right degree of feigned empathy. "Let me make some calls. You've seen these people here tonight. Do you think any of them would hesitate to hire you?"

She shook her head, still avoiding his eyes. "No. I have to do this for myself, Craig. I have to prove to myself I can do this."

"All right," he replied, relieved. He wasn't expecting her to accept his offer. She was too proud and self-reliant for that. Had she accepted his offer, he would've been faced with a real dilemma. Why help her work for someone else when he needed her to partner with him and Jude? But a promise would've been a promise. He would've made those calls. Thankfully, she was still his predictable, trustworthy wife.

"Tell me, aren't there any women entrepreneurs in your world? You only invited men."

"I don't want to make my wife jealous," he replied quickly, stealing a kiss on her cheek.

She smiled and leaned back into the comfortable armchair. She was starting to relax. "You wouldn't make me jealous. I'd understand."

"Is that to say you don't love me anymore, Mrs. Brafford?" he slid off the armrest and crouched at her feet.

"Don't be ridiculous," she replied. Her voice sounded cold, tense, but her fingers tousled his hair before withdrawing into her lap. "I was wondering maybe that's why I'm not getting the jobs. I might be the wrong gender."

"In this day and age? I don't think that's the case."

"Then what?" Her face scrunched as if bile had risen in her throat. She coughed quietly, covering her mouth with her hand.

"Then . . . I don't know. What I do know is how much I need you by my side. Wouldn't you want to work with me?" Her shoulders heaved, and she forced herself to breathe, taking deep breaths. "What's wrong?"

"Nothing . . . maybe I had too much salmon mousse."

"Or too much champagne?"

"I didn't drink—" she started to say, but then covered her mouth with her hand and sprung to her feet. A moment later, she was retching in the sink.

He rushed by her side, feeling a chill tingling his spine. "What's wrong?"

She held a hand in the air for a moment, then rinsed her mouth with cold water. Then she took a bottle of sparkling water from the fridge and removed the cap. After taking a couple of swigs, she finally looked at him.

"Remember the day you showed me the house the first time?" She smiled, a tired, weak smile, but her eyes darted over to the kitchen island where he'd made love to her that day.

"Of course, I remember," he replied, slowly undoing his shirt buttons. But desire wasn't what he read in Andi's eyes. It was something else, a peaceful warmth that sent a shiver through his body.

She touched her belly with her hand. "I got pregnant that day." Her smile widened as his entire world collapsed. "I'm pretty sure it was that day."

Oh, Andi, you had to screw everything up, didn't you?

Thoughts swirled angrily in his mind, dizzying, nauseating. He reached for the counter and grabbed it. "Y— you're pregnant?" he stammered, his lips dry, his throat constricted. Nightmarish images invaded his imagination. A kid, screaming his lungs out every night while he couldn't get a wink of sleep. His beautiful Andi, her body deformed by pregnancy, content to cater to the little invader's whims instead of conquering the world with him. That couldn't be his reality. "Are you sure?"

Her smile had waned, replaced by a grimace of worry and disappointment. "I'm pretty sure, yes." Her eyes glistened. "You're not happy?"

He wrapped his arms around her and held her tight, glad he could hide his eyes. "Just a little surprised, that's all," he managed to say. "I thought we'd decide on this together." He swallowed hard. "You know, when we'd be in a better place financially."

She pulled away. "I'll get a job, you'll see. It won't be that hard." She rubbed her belly again. "I'm sure we'll make great parents."

Stunned, he faltered a few steps back, acutely needing a stiff drink. Walking over to the kitchen, he opened a bottle of Black Label and poured himself a generous quantity of scotch over a handful of ice cubes in a cut crystal glass. Then he gulped it down without giving it time to chill. It burned his throat and spread heat throughout his veins.

When he returned to the living room, he found her standing still, her eyes brimming with tears. She was touching the pendant she still wore, her eyes absently staring into thin air. He grabbed her hands and took them to his lips. "If this is what you want, I'm all in. I just thought we'd have a little bit more time for us, that's all. We could do so much in this life."

She wasn't responding in any way. Not to his touch, nor his words. He took her in his arms again, swaying back and forth the way he did when she was upset.

After a while, she pulled away and asked, staring at the floor, "What are your plans for tomorrow?"

Maybe the storm was over; they were back to discussing practical things. Relieved, he breathed with ease and said, "I'll be busy the entire day tomorrow. I'll follow up with everyone while they can still remember the taste of your fabulous appetizers. Then we'll start building the next list." He put his hands on her waist and drew her close to him. She didn't resist, but the spark wasn't there.

"What next list?"

"The next party." He groaned quietly. "Remember we discussed? That's how you keep the exclusive listings coming. Do you know how much money we made today, the extra deal with Donati I was mentioning?" She shook her head. "Ten thousand dollars. Cash and tax-free."

She looked straight at him. "Congratulations, Craig. I know you worked hard for it."

"We did, Andi. You and me. You earned more helping me out than you would've earned in one month of soul-sucking work at whatever bank."

"How about raising a family, Craig? Is that on your list of priorities? Will it ever be?" There were tears in her voice and something else, a glimmer of the steel mesh that lined Andi's inner core.

"Anything you want, sweetheart." He shrugged and started pacing slowly. "I don't know how many times I have to say this to you. If you don't like the parties, we won't have them anymore. But it would be such a waste of opportunity and income. If you want children, I'm all for it, as long as they're mine," he quipped. Her lips quivered. "I'm taking you seriously," he added quickly. "It also happens to be the truth. No matter what life you decide we should have, I don't want to lose you." He approached her slowly, looking into her eyes intently, passionately. Then he placed a kiss on her throat.

She held firmly, unmoved. Unyielding. What else did he have to do? Drop on his knees and beg? One wrong step, and she could be out the door, and he'd be left with crippling alimony and a divorce he could never afford. Not when his salary barely covered the mortgage payments.

But Andi was, first and foremost, a practical woman.

"How about you? What are your plans for tomorrow?"

She sighed and turned away, then wrapped her arms around her slender body. "First thing, I'm going back to the hospital. I want to talk with Dad's doctors. Then, at two, I have another interview." She shook her head with unspeakable sadness in her eyes. "It's for a receptionist job at a family planning clinic."

"Jeez, Andi, have you no self-esteem left? When will you draw the line and say, this is enough, I won't go any farther down this road?" He'd never shouted at her before, not that he could remember. What was it that kept her from working with him, from doing what he wanted her to do, dammit? Was it ego? Because it definitely wasn't ambition.

"Apparently, I don't," she replied calmly. "I secretly dream of working my way into a biology job, of earning my keep until I get my doctoral degree. Maybe that's why the research labs won't have me." She came close to him and stared straight at him. "I spend my time wondering why no one wants me to work for them. Why I spent almost my entire life training for something that's completely invaluable on the market." She inhaled sharply. "Then I ask, is it me? Am I worse than anyone I know who has a job? Am I really that bad? What am I good for, really?"

"Oh, Andi," he whispered, "I'm so sorry. I'm sure we can find people who would love to have you—"

"Not we, Craig. Me. I have to find it on my own. I can't be someone who got the job just because she's their favorite Realtor's wife. I can't be that; do you understand?" Tears streamed down her face, and quiet sobs shattered her breath, but that didn't stop her. "That's why, when I found out I was pregnant, I thought, finally, something to give me purpose in this life. Something to matter. I can still make a difference." She sniffled and reached for a tissue to wipe her tears. "Sorry for messing up your plans with this pregnancy, but this baby is all I have."

He swallowed a long, detailed oath. Why now? Why did it have to happen to him? She was supposed to be on birth control for crying out loud. The woman just couldn't be trusted . . . she'd set him up. She'd effectively killed every single one of his dreams, scorching the earth in her wake without even knowing it.

Slowly, he reached and touched her face with his fingers, brushing away a tear. "I didn't react the right way, but I'm happy to have as many children as you'd like to have." He lifted her chin up with two fingers. "Cross my heart." Maybe they still performed vasectomies. His insurance might cover it.

Looking at him through a blur of tears, she smiled shyly. "You really mean that?"

Crisis averted. He kissed her lips, lingering just a little. "I absolutely do."

She wrapped her arms around him and rested her head on his shoulder. "I love you. I hope you know how much."

"I do, yes, of course I do," he whispered. "Did you tell anyone else about this?"

"Not yet," she replied, pulling away slightly. "Why?"

"Let's make the announcement the right way," he said while his wheels were turning fast inside his restless mind. "Let's have a party. A real one, for friends and family."

Defense Attorney Goodridge: Based on what you witnessed at the August nineteen party, what was your opinion of the defendant's relationship with his wife?

Jeremy Hughes: They seemed happy. She was well-tamed, if you know what I mean. She knew her place and did everything right to help her husband make money. Real estate is brutal business.

Defense Attorney Goodridge: Did she speak with you that night?

Jeremy Hughes: Just the usual pleasantries. She wasn't bitter or anything. Don't believe everything you hear in the media. I don't think any of it was true.

19

HOUSTON DAWN

Houston at dawn was humid, yet the late August day knew no better moment. The purple sky lighting up with orange and gold hues, the birds chirping loudly in the trees as if they had to quarrel over the last worm in the ground, and the smell of lush greens touched by dew lured Rebecca out on the porch every morning.

Usually, she waited for Aaron to brew their coffee and get ready for the one hour of gardening he squeezed in before leaving for work. That morning, following a sleepless night she'd spent mostly on the living room sofa watching television with the sound turned off while her thoughts wandered, she didn't wait for him to wake up.

At first light, she started the coffee maker, breathing loudly, a sigh of relief that the seemingly endless night was finally over. A couple of minutes and three muted beeps later, she filled a cup to the brim and stepped outside, where the lingering chill awakened her. Inhaling the fresh, scented air, she repressed a shudder and sat on the top step instead of the wicker love seat she usually preferred.

She kept her hands wrapped around the coffee mug, inhaling the bitter vapor lifting from the black liquid and invading her senses with the mouthwatering aroma of French vanilla. Yet, no matter how hard she tried, all she could think about was Hunter.

The screen door behind her squeaked.

"Good morning, sunshine," Aaron said. "Having coffee all by your lonesome?"

She turned her head and smiled at him. He looked tired, more so than usual. Dark circles layered under his eyes, and his eyelids seemed a little swollen. He must've indulged in too much salt last night at dinner. Salty and greasy foods were Aaron's weaknesses, although he knew better than anyone the damage those did to a person's health.

"I'll get you one," she offered.

"Already got it," he replied, raising the mug and clinking hers as if they were drinking wine. "Cheers."

She smiled, but the pervasive sadness wouldn't shake off.

"What's on your mind?" he asked, sitting down next to her with a groan.

"Hunter." Once she said his name out loud, tears came uninvited. "I might've killed him, Aaron."

Aaron put his arm around her shoulders. She wept quietly against his shoulder, letting out all the pain that had nestled in her chest, rendering her sleepless.

"Your heart was in the right place," Aaron said softly. "You did what you thought was best."

She nodded, whimpering. "I gave the man a heart attack, that's what I did."

"No . . . Hunter's genes and lifestyle choices gave him the heart attack." His soothing words made her sob harder. "Shhh . . ." he whispered, squeezing her shoulders. "If not from you, he could've heard it from someone else and it would've had the same effect. Maybe not yesterday, not today, but definitely tomorrow." He rubbed her back with his hand, warming her up. "People die, Becca. Everyone does. That heart attack was a long time coming and had nothing to do with you."

She sniffled and looked at him through a blur of tears. "You've seen too much death, Aaron. You've become immune to its psychological effects. You're so . . . clinical about it."

He scoffed and took a sip of coffee. "Can you imagine what my life would be if I weren't clinical about death? I wouldn't last a week."

"Right." She nodded. "I still believe actions have consequences, and mine almost killed a man. A dear friend. Hunter might never recover, and I'll have to live with that for the rest of my life."

"Let's explore that statement for a moment," Aaron said, setting his coffee on the deck and turning sideways to face her. He spoke in a somber, dispassionate voice as if he were testifying in a court of law. "Let's assume it's true, and the news you shared with Hunter had caused, in fact, his heart attack."

"Okay," she whispered, frowning.

"Were you anything else but the messenger?"

"No, but—"

"So, then, why isn't responsibility owned, or at least shared, between you—the messenger—and whomever or whatever—"

"Ah, I see where you're going with this. That's not really what's happening here."

"No? Argue your point to me. Then we'll dissect what a coronary is, what other causes contribute to one, and how you don't share responsibility with those causes either."

"You mean causes like family history? I remember him saying his mother died of a heart attack . . . or was it a stroke?"

"Either way, it's cardiovascular disease." He smiled, the kindness in his eyes heartwarming. "I'd take the quick win and run with it, but so that you know, cardiovascular disease is the leading cause of death in the United States. You'd have to argue how that's not a factor either and that only you alone carry the blame for Hunter's coronary. He'd be happy to hear that, by the way. It would mean that, if he recovers from this heart attack you caused, he can eat all the burgers he wants and smoke like a chimney, as long as you're not allowed to come near him or address him ever again. He'll never die, because you won't be there to cause it. Lucky bastard."

She looked at him with mock defiance. "I can't win with you, can I?"

"Nope. Not when it comes to death and its many tentacles." A shadow washed over his forehead, wrinkling it. "All day long, I stare at the bastard's handiwork. Don't you think I know death's workings by now?"

She stared at him for a long beat, grateful to have him in her life. Many years ago, when she was still young, she'd feared that age would drive a wedge between them, but with every passing year and new wrinkle on his face, she loved him more.

"Now, about Andi, what do we do?"

He shrugged and picked up the mug, then took a big swill. "You told Hunter what's going on. Let him handle it how he sees fit."

Her eyebrows shot up. "He's on a hospital bed. He can barely handle breathing and peeing, for goodness' sake. We should tell Andi. She's like our own daughter."

He stood, then offered her a hand. She took it and got on her feet, hiding a shot of lumbar pain under a fleeting grimace.

"Yes, Andi is like our own daughter," Aaron said quietly, his voice thoughtful and measured. "But her father just had a coronary. This other deal, no matter how bothersome, shouldn't weigh on her mind right now, when she might only have a few more days left to spend with her father."

There was a stark reality beyond Aaron's gentle words. "You're dark," she whispered, realizing that he was right, and that Hunter might leave them any moment now. Today. Tomorrow. Soon. "You've seen too much death," she sighed, then brushed a rebel strand of hair off her husband's forehead.

"And you're a knight in shining armor," he replied, opening the door for her. They stepped inside, where the birds weren't trilling and the sun wasn't shining. "White armor," he added while she rushed to the windows to pull the blinds open and let some light in. "On a white horse, no less."

She chuckled and glanced at him lovingly.

"Rushing to save the world from all evil," he continued in the same lighthearted voice with deep, serious undertones.

She froze in place, hand caught in midair before reaching the lift cord for the blinds. "Are you saying I did something wrong by intervening?"

"You didn't intervene. Your actions didn't change the course of history. You wanted to find the truth for your protégé. People sometimes go their entire lives not knowing what happened to cause them to fail, to lose any chance in reaching their dreams." Aaron kissed her forehead. "Andi is lucky to have you." Grabbing his car keys from the table, he stopped in the doorway and added, "When the time is right, you might intervene, and there's no harm in that. But you have to let her come to you. She has to own her life and the consequences of her actions."

20

A Promise

It was still rush hour when Andi drove to the hospital to see her father. Mixed with fears for his health, memories of the night before stirred her up constantly. She and Craig had never argued before. Never had a real fight. And yet, although he'd tried his absolute best to hide his true feelings, she could sense he wasn't thrilled about her pregnancy. He didn't want the baby.

Maybe it took some getting used to the idea of becoming a father because he definitely hadn't thought of it as a priority. He wanted to be financially secure first, and the more she thought about it, the more she realized he was right. She couldn't get a job no matter how hard she tried. They had signed up for what seemed to be a crippling mortgage, although she'd never extracted any details from him.

It would be all right, she told herself time and time again, forcing herself to believe that statement a little bit more with every iteration. He might've wanted something else, and he might've been right about needing financial stability before having any children, but she was pregnant now, and that couldn't be helped. Yet, she felt guilty because she'd stopped taking birth control without thinking of the consequences. She thought she'd have to wait a long time after stopping the hormones before she could become pregnant . . . more than three weeks anyway.

The night before had ended badly, and she was almost entirely to blame. Emotionally exhausted after her father's heart attack and that endless party, saddened and shaken after seeing Craig's reaction to what she hoped was exciting news, the entire day had left her a ball of taut nerves.

And she'd snapped.

She said things to Craig he didn't deserve to hear, things that came from a deep, twisted, and dark recess of her mind, things she didn't know she was thinking. In a loud, grating voice, she accused him of using her, of not giving a crap about her feelings, about what she wanted in life. Prodding him with sharp, cutting words until he left the room slamming the door behind him, she poured onto him a torrent of accusations. He never shared his long-term plans with her. He didn't tell her he wanted to buy that house, and she still didn't know what they owed for it. How could she know what financial difficulties they were in, when he never shared anything with her, yet he bought Zegna outfits and Ferragamo shoes? White glove service for moving? What the hell happened to asking a few friends to help and renting a U-Haul truck?

That didn't change the sobering, disheartening fact that she was unable to earn a paycheck. She was nothing but an added expense, and now she had made it worse by getting herself pregnant.

For the first time in their lives together, he'd slept in the living room, on the bed turned lounge space, while she slept alone in the guest room, crying in her pillow until she finally fell asleep. By the time she woke up at seven the following day, he was already gone.

She'd found the blue pendant where she'd taken it off the night before, and put it on, a silent gesture to say how sorry she was for her outburst, a way to keep Craig close to her heart.

She'd called his cell to apologize, but it went straight to voicemail. Then she drove to the hospital, skipping the coffee and breakfast, aching to see her father.

Was he still alive? She'd checked her phone countless times overnight and had no messages. If anything had happened, they would've called, regardless of time, right? Pulling into the hospital parking lot, she filled her lungs with air and held it in for a few seconds, steadying herself. There was no reason and no excuse to let her father sense her anguish. It would only hurt him more, probably just as much as if she'd share with him the news about her pregnancy.

A tear crept down her cheek as she entered the building, heading for the elevators. Seemed that no one wanted this baby, but she did, desperately so, an instinct to protect it at all costs fueling her love for the unborn life growing inside her.

She rushed to room 307 and froze in the doorway, blood draining from her face. The bed was empty, the sheets changed, the monitors turned off. Feeling faint and nauseous, she faltered to the nurses' station.

"I'm looking for my father, Hunter Wilmore," she said to the young woman who was sifting through a pile of charts. "Please, where is he?"

She didn't raise her eyes from the paperwork. "Fifth floor. Five-ten, I believe." She finally looked up at Andi and smiled. "That's good news. He's out of intensive care."

Andi breathed, still holding on to the desk for balance, reluctant to let it go. Eventually, she did and found her way to the elevators, then to the fifth floor.

He was awake and reading a paper. A cannula delivered oxygen through his nostrils, and several wires came out of his gown, connected to one of the machines installed on a rack by the bedside. His left index finger was fitted with a pulse oximeter. The monitor above his head beeped silently in a steady, reassuring cadence.

"Dad," she whispered, then rushed to him.

He let the newspaper drop and opened his arms, and she burrowed her face against his chest, listening to his strong heartbeat, the way she used to when she was little.

"Don't cry, my sweet girl," he whispered, "there's nothing to cry about. I'll be fine, you'll see."

She wiped her eyes with her fingers and sat on the side of the bed. "You gave me one hell of a scare, Dad."

"Ha, you should've seen Mrs. Carson, the old lady with the poodle mix?" Andi nodded. It was one of the vet clinic patients she knew well. Mrs. Carson had been a patient since Andi was a little girl and hung out at the clinic to pet and feed the boarded animals. "I think she almost had a heart attack when I lay down on the floor and asked her to call Gabrielle." His voice was weak and out of breath, but there was humor in it. "It's always good to lie down on the floor when you feel these things coming, or you could crack your noggin." He tapped his skull with his finger and chuckled.

"Okay, Dad, great. I'll try to remember that the next time I have a heart attack." She laughed and touched the pendant.

"Always liked this pendant, although it looks a little rugged," he commented. "Craig might have some good taste on his side."

Her eyes were clouded by a quick frown. Maybe he was still confused from all the drugs they must've pumped into him. "Always? What do you mean? Craig gave it to me yesterday, before the party."

It was his turn to frown. "Did he now?" His voice was barely a whisper. "I must be confused then. Some of these medications are like Alzheimer's in a pill." A flicker of a smile touched his lips as his frown started to dissipate. "If I were a dog, and my owner," he pointed at her with a hand gesture, "said I'm acting confused right after having a heart attack, I'd say, 'What would you expect? He's going to be a little bit under the weather for a while. He needs rest, slow walks, a lean diet—'"

"Aha," she reacted, waving her finger at him. "So, you know what you have to do."

He shifted a little and pushed a button to raise the backrest, probably getting ready to mount a defense against his own arguments. The door to the room slid open, and a man wearing green hospital garb stepped inside. His surgical mask was undone, hanging from his neck.

"I'm Dr. Pontiff, your father's cardiologist," he said, extending his hand.

Andi refrained from smiling when she heard his name, appreciating the warm and confident handshake. It was surprising that doctors still shook patients' hands. It probably didn't matter to them because they washed their hands after each patient interaction anyway.

"Yes, everyone tends to snicker when I introduce myself," the doctor added with light humor in his eyes. "You can easily imagine what my high school nickname was, but I promise you, I won't be pontificating here today."

"Andi Wilmore," she replied, omitting her married name without knowing why. "I'm his daughter."

"I figured. The resemblance is there." He pulled out a four-legged stool and sat by the foot of the bed, flipping through the chart. His smile waned. When he looked up from the paperwork, his gaze was austere. "Your father suffered an NSTEMI or a non-ST-elevation myocardial infarction. That means the blockage was partial, not complete. We have him on ACE inhibitors and a combo of clot-dissolving meds and anticoagulants to prevent future clotting." He paused, probably waiting for Andi's questions, but she couldn't find the words. "Your father is out of immediate danger. He's what we call in serious but stable condition."

"Doctors always sound like undertakers," Dr. Wilmore said. "I know that. I do it too, but in my case, my patients can't understand a word I'm saying."

The cardiologist smiled, but that smile didn't take away the seriousness of his gaze. "You're a veterinarian, yes. Then you'll easily understand what I'm about to recommend."

Andi clasped her hands in her lap to keep them steady. Her breath caught, fearing every word that was about to come out of the man's mouth. Her father's jokes told her he was just as afraid, only didn't want to show it. She reached for his hand and squeezed it.

"You'll need to live in an assisted living facility for the next three to six months, at least," Dr. Pontiff announced.

"What? No," Andi reacted, standing but not letting go of her father's hand. "There's no need for that. I can take care of him."

"Andrea," Dr. Wilmore said softly, "let the man speak. He might know what he's talking about."

"Ms. Wilmore, your father cannot make any effort for a while. He'll need a nurse around the clock, and a doctor on-premises, to stabilize him if anything should happen. Meanwhile, we're considering several procedures to speed up his recovery. Angioplasty, to open up the arteries. Stem cell therapy, to help the damaged muscle recover faster. He will require medical assistance that you won't be able to provide in a home setting. No one could."

Tears streamed down her face, but she wasn't sobbing. It was as if her eyes overflowed with the pain inside her chest. She turned to her dad. "I'll take care of you, I promise. I'll be here every day, and we'll beat this. Together. You'll see."

"Dr. Wilmore," Dr. Pontiff said after allowing them a moment. "Please know we're doing everything in our power to return you to health as soon as possible. And, Ms. Wilmore, the worst is behind us now. With proper care and patience, your father might still make a full recovery."

She couldn't focus anymore. Odd thoughts came to her mind, unusual observations that didn't belong. The color of the window and how it refracted the sunlight with hues of greenish blue on the white walls. The warm dryness of Dr. Pontiff's hand when he squeezed hers again before leaving the room. The slight flicker in the overhead fluorescent light.

She sat on the side of the bed, struggling to gather her roaming thoughts. "I—I'll take you with me," she stammered. "As soon as they'll let you go home, I'll take you to live with us. That house is huge," she chuckled. "Plenty of room."

"My sweet girl," he whispered, taking her hand to his lips. He held it there for a while and closed his glistening eyes. "You know my presence there wouldn't be welcome."

"That's not true," she whispered. "You're wrong."

"He wouldn't want me there; I promise you that." Before she could push back again, he said, "You need to do something else for me."

"Anything." She held her breath. Her dad's request sounded so . . . final.

"Close the house. Our house, I mean. Empty the fridge, cut the water. Sell it if you want. It's been in your name for a while now. The deed is in my documents drawer, the middle one, in my desk."

"What? Sell our house?" She tried to stifle a sob but failed. "No way . . . You're coming out of this . . . You're coming back home." Her shoulders heaved as she broke down in bitter tears, her words turned into barely intelligible whimpers. "You're not leaving me alone here to deal with this stupid, unbelievably crazy world that makes no sense."

"Shh, Andrea, I'm not leaving you," he reassured her, forced humor tinging his voice again. "Not yet anyway. Not for a while. I'll even eat tofu or whatever if that will make you feel better. I'll dine on rabbit food stolen from the clinic. What do you say, huh?"

She looked at him as if it were the last time she might see him, wondering if he was still going to be there tomorrow. Would he be able to keep his promise? How many people had made the same promise on that same bed, only to break that promise along with their loved ones' hearts? All she had was now . . . those precious moments that still belonged to the two of them.

That and the new life growing inside her were her only certainties.

21

FAMILY

Craig cursed under his breath, stirring the pasta angrily while eyeing the simmering Alfredo in the saucepan. It was almost ready, and she hadn't called nor returned home yet. It was nearly nine.

He might've pushed things too far.

Storming out of the bedroom the night before, slamming the door, was a bad idea. Letting Andi cry alone all night after a complicated day like she'd had could prove a fatal mistake. Yes, she got bloody pregnant . . . but she was still his Andi, his perfectly beautiful and stunningly brilliant wife. The pregnancy was little more than a nuisance. Some of these things went away on their own, nothing but false alarms. But it could never happen again.

Earlier that day, he found himself hesitating before making the vasectomy appointment. What if, in twenty years or so, he'd like to have a kid after all? Someone to take over the business, maybe partner with Jude's kids if he had them. Someone to take care of him in his old age, to keep him company like Andi did her father. That's why he ended the call without scheduling the procedure. Were those surgeries reversible? Were there any men out there who had procreated after reversing their vasectomies?

He had time to figure all that out.

Until then, he had a wife out there, who knows where, and she wasn't speaking with him anymore. That was disheartening. He needed her by his side all the damn time. He relied on her; she was his foundation, his cornerstone, the steel in his structure. And she was nowhere to be found because he'd opened his big mouth, saying all the wrong things, when saying the right ones would've made such a big difference. Needing people . . . wasn't that a bitch?

The pasta was ready, boiled to al dente perfection. He pulled the pot to the side. The range fan still going, he didn't hear Andi come in.

"Hi," she said, standing in the middle of the kitchen, shifting her weight from one leg to the other. She was playing nervously with the blue pendant he'd given her, shooting apologetic glances at him, at the set table, at the stove.

She was wearing the pendant. That was a good sign.

"Oh, honey, I'm so sorry," he said, dropping everything and rushing to her. He folded her in his arms, kissing her lips hungrily, possessively. He would've liked to rip the clothes off her defiant body and take her right there, on the kitchen floor, until she forgot about anything and anyone else but him.

She responded passionately, whispering things he didn't understand.

"I was so worried," he murmured in her ear. "Don't do this to me again."

"I was at the hospital," she said, gently pulling away. "With Dad."

He frowned. "I figured. How is he?"

She pulled out a chair and sat at the table. He'd gone a little over the top that evening. The table was set with a white damask tablecloth, white candles ready to be lit, and the finest accoutrements. And yet, she didn't seem to notice. To her, it was probably just the same if she ate fried fish off a paper plate at the beach, licking her greasy fingers after each piece.

"He's in bad shape, Craig. He's going to need assistance, surgery, procedures." She wiped her eyes with a quick move of her fingers. She'd been crying for much longer than the few minutes they'd spent together since she'd returned. Her eyes were red and swollen.

He cut the heat under the saucepan and set it aside to rest. Then he turned to her and froze for a brief moment, feeling a surge of rage setting his gut on fire. She had sand on her shoes. She might've been at the hospital for a while but that wasn't the only place she'd visited while he was going crazy with worry, calling her over and over, only to get her voicemail.

Whenever she had a big decision to make or wanted to run away from something, Andi turned to the Gulf of Mexico like most people turn to friends and family for answers, for support and advice. She stared at the ocean for hours, barely moving, and that experience somehow recharged her, as if the sea itself was her fuel source. Since the wedding, she hadn't been there without him.

Until now.

Last night, he'd taken things too damn far.

He wasn't going to repeat last night's mistakes, that was for sure. His big mouth was going to stay closed unless he had the right words lined up, ready to be served with the proper intonation and the appropriate body language.

Opening the fridge, he fished out one of the better bottles of wine and grabbed the corkscrew on his way back to the table. With a few swift moves, he uncorked the bottle with a loud pop, then poured some burgundy into the two glasses. Remaining standing and holding one in his hand, he invited Andi to join him in taking a sip.

"Whatever might happen, whatever we might need to do to help him, I'm here for you." He clinked his glass against hers. She picked the glass up with pale, shaky fingers and barely tasted the wine before setting it down on the table. Her eyes remained lowered as if the kitchen tiles were by far more interesting than him.

What was she hiding?

"You've got sand on your shoes," he said, keeping his voice lighthearted.

She shot him a quick, apologetic glance. "They kicked me out of the hospital at seven. I—I wanted to see the ocean."

He managed to fake an encouraging smile. "How was it? Did you catch the sunset?"

A beat. "Yes, I did. Some turtle babies too." A faint smile stretched her lips.

"Turtle babies?" His voice was scratchy, his pitch higher than he would've wanted. That's why he'd been going insane with worry? For turtle babies?

"It's hatching season for sea turtles." She chuckled quietly, while a rebel tear rolled down her cheek. "I wanted to hear the waves, look at the sunset, watch the birds . . . You know, this is all the marine biology I get to do." Her voice was tinged with sadness and regret. "I wasn't going to be gone long. But then I had this idea, this irrational, magical thinking idea that if I saw a hatchling making its way to the ocean, I'd be fine. Dad would be fine. Our baby—"

He squeezed her shoulder, and she leaned against him. "I just wish I was there with you, that's all," he said gently. "I had no idea where you were. I was scared."

"I'm sorry," she whispered, lowering her eyes again. "I said things—"

"It's all right. I understand." He set the empty glass on the table and moved over to the counter to grate the Parmesan. "I'll walk you through all our financials tomorrow. I'll answer all your questions, I promise." He turned to her briefly, holding a piece of cheese with two fingers, gesturing with it. "Only if you promise you won't freak out."

She looked straight at him, concerned. "Is it that bad?"

He resumed grating the Parm. "Not that bad, no. Think of this as an investment in our future. Like with any business, at first, we only buy stuff. We build, we spend money, resources. Then we start making money, and lots of it. Money we wouldn't

stand a chance of making if we didn't invest in the beginning."
He finished grating and put the grater in the sink, then washed
his hands. "That's why I didn't want you to see the numbers for
now. They might seem scarier than they really are."

Seemingly absentminded, she was clasping and unclasping
her hands in her lap.

"The last thing I want to do is scare you or make you feel
even worse for not having a job."

She nodded, sniffling, her eyes still lowered. "Thanks for
making dinner," she whispered. "It smells delicious."

He grinned widely. "Your favorite. Pasta Alfredo with
herbs and spices, a little heavy on the spices, just how you like
it." He took a quick bow. "Anything else the chef might get for
you, Mrs. Brafford? Maybe a little bit more wine?"

She smiled and looked at him without saying a word.

"Anything at all?" He remained standing, potholder in
hand, taking his role as seriously as he could, wishing he knew
what to say or do to yank Andrea from wherever she was and
bring her into the here and now with him and that pasta.

She reached for his hand and clasped it in a silently
pleading gesture. "Could Dad come live with us if the assisted
living is too bad, or when they release him?"

He breathed. Great . . . *Then we'd be one clown short of a
fucking circus.*

Without skipping a beat, he replied, "Of course, he could.
He's family." He poured some more wine into his glass and
downed it thirstily. "I'm a little worried, to be honest. I know he
doesn't like me much. I'm concerned what his presence might
do to us, to our relationship."

"Thank you," she whispered. "I needed to hear you'd
welcome him into our home. I'm sure his presence wouldn't
damage what we have." Another tear moved down her face.
"All I've been thinking about lately is family. The people we
care about, and how easily we could lose them. How important
they are . . . more than anything else in the world."

He didn't like where the conversation was going but listened anyway. It always paid off to see where the train was coming from before stepping onto the tracks. Before entering the tunnel.

"Have you spoken with your mom and dad recently?" Andi asked.

He lowered his head to hide his frustration. "I told you, we're estranged. We had a falling out of sorts."

"They didn't come to the wedding. Did you invite them, like we discussed?"

He shook his head. "No. We went our separate ways a long time ago."

"But . . . don't you miss them?"

He touched her lips with his index finger, urging her to stop talking. "Trust me, it's better this way." He grabbed her hand and tugged at it until she stood. "You're my entire world, Ands." He kissed her lips quickly. "But you stink of hospital, and I say this with all my love. Do you think you can take a quick shower before the pasta gets cold?"

A few minutes later, when she returned from the shower wearing a pink terry bathrobe and fuzzy slippers, he'd filled their plates with fettuccine and Alfredo sauce, grated fresh Parmesan on top, and sprinkled just the right amount of fresh parsley, oregano, and basil.

22

SEARCH

Andi stared at the display in disbelief. It was late . . . past the wake-up time she'd set on the phone the night before. Her interview was in less than two hours, and it was all the way in downtown Houston.

She jumped out of bed and rushed into the bathroom, thirsty, a bitter taste in the back of her mouth. She was a little dizzy, weak even, instantly regretting the rush with which she'd left the comfort of her bed. Maybe she was coming down with something.

Making quick work of it, she rinsed her mouth and brushed her teeth. Then she started to get dressed, choosing her attire carefully. She was already overqualified for the customer service role she was interviewing for. She didn't want to add overdressed to their list of potential objections.

It had been a tough week since her dad's heart attack and that party. Her first-ever argument with Craig had been forgotten, at least she hoped so. He'd been sweeter than ever, calmer with her, more thoughtful, although she could tell he was under considerable stress. He continued to work long hours, some of the evening time from his home office, where he was constantly on the phone, trying to reach influential people and introduce himself to them. Andi could hear it through the walls; it wasn't easy.

With her father in cardiac rehab—that's what they called the short-term assisted living facility for people recovering from all sorts of heart problems—Andi had found herself unable to spend as much time with him as she wanted. His cardiologist, Dr. Pontiff, had explained to her in no uncertain terms that patients force themselves to stay awake and appear lively when they have loved ones visiting when, in fact, they should be resting. She could visit him every day, of course, but only for one hour.

The same doctor had reassured her that Dr. Wilmore's recovery was proceeding as expected and that the patient had been willing to do his part to get well sooner. The angioplasty procedures had been successfully performed, reducing future risk. Her dad was taking his meds, eating well, and resting well. Soon, in a few months at the latest, he could be released into her care.

Every day at about five in the afternoon, Andi showed up at the cardiac rehab center and wheeled her dad outside to spend their time together breathing fresh air and enjoying the mild setting sun of early fall. She hadn't told him about her pregnancy yet. Uncertain of how he'd react, given his unchanged feelings toward her husband, she thought it best to let more time pass before breaking the news.

Craig was right, as always, suggesting they waited another month or two before announcing it to their friends and her family in a cozy little party at the house. Perhaps they'd discharge her dad from cardiac rehab by then, or she could borrow him for one afternoon. Surrounded by friends who would be openly happy for her and Craig, maybe he'd mellow out, and the news of her pregnancy wouldn't upset him as much as Andi feared.

It was tough to say what would happen. Would it dismay him because it was Craig's baby? Or would the news instill joy in him because it was her child, his own grandchild? Could the tiny life growing inside her become the bridge between the two most important men in her life? She definitely hoped so. Her heart ached every time she thought about the rift between the two.

Almost completely dressed, she trotted barefooted through the house, collecting her things. The blue pendant was the last touch to her attire, and she clasped it on in a hurry, right before opening the fridge to swipe a slice of Swiss cheese on her way out.

A wave of sickness froze her in her tracks and sent her running to the bathroom sink instead. Morning sickness had been increasingly bad lately. Just like yesterday and the night before, the spasms were so fierce it felt as if the lining of her stomach wanted to come off. When she finally finished throwing up, she was breathless and faint from the effort, the taste in her mouth bitter and off somehow, although her stomach had been empty, except for a glass of water.

When she lifted her eyes from the sink, she saw herself in the mirror. She was pale, her lips barely pink, her face gaunt. She'd been sick every morning for the past few days, but it would soon end. Every bit of information she got from the internet spoke of the first trimester being the worst, then everything would settle nicely. Well, except for ridiculous food cravings for things like pickles and Chinese food and lemons.

Breathing slowly to curb her nausea, she thought of a slice of lemon, and that thought turned into mouthwatering cravings for something sour. A quick glance at the phone confirmed she still had the time to do what she'd set her mind to do that day.

It was time to meet Craig's parents.

The day before, she'd dug through Craig's personal documents and found his birth certificate. Their names were Louise and Murray Brafford. Craig's birth had been recorded at an Austin hospital. An internet search should give her their address.

Not that thrilled with her ghostly pallor after the bout of morning sickness, she applied makeup quickly and touched up her lip gloss. Then she moved to the kitchen, where she fired up her laptop and waited for it to load while she cut a lemon in half and started to lick the dripping juice, savoring how it refreshed her and staved off nausea.

A moment later, she gasped and threw the lemon flying into the trash while she rushed to the fridge. The juice was burning her stomach like never before. She pulled the lid off a yogurt container and swallowed a spoonful of it. As it reached her stomach, it soothed her pain.

The first trimester couldn't possibly go by fast enough.

Breathing with relief, she sat and started her search. A few moments later, she found a Mr. Murray Brafford registered in Smithville, Texas. The navigation app on her phone told her that it was less than two hours away if she took I-10. She thought of sending the Braffords' address from the laptop to her phone by text but then decided against it.

Craig could stumble on the message and get really angry with her for going to meet his parents against his express wishes. Both she and Craig used that laptop.

She memorized the address instead, wondering why she was doing something Craig shouldn't know about. She didn't keep any secrets from her husband . . . this was the only one. Was it wrong to reach out to his parents and introduce herself? How bad of a falling out did they have?

She was about to find out.

Deleting the search history from her browser, she powered down the laptop and closed the lid.

On the odd chance they didn't want anything to do with their son, Craig would never learn about her trip. No harm, no foul. But if her baby could have more grandparents, she wanted to do her part to make that happen. Grandparents made great childhoods awesome.

23

LEAD

There weren't any showings scheduled for that Thursday, and Craig had decided to work the phones instead. After the August 19 party, he'd signed up a couple of exclusive deals, listing the homes for sale with the agency but advertising them outside the realm Jeremy Hughes knew about. He placed the ads himself, paying out of pocket, and pushed the property to California and New York residents, wealthy Baby Boomers looking to retire someplace warm, even foreign nationals who wanted a foothold into the country.

It worked. It got him the interest, and one listing had a closing pending for over four hundred thousand more than the client had wanted to price it at. His off-the-books commission was 10 percent of that. Some of it, a little bit, would kick back to his boss, but at least the mortgage would be covered for a few months.

Yes, it worked. Not nearly fast enough. It could take months, if not years, before other properties would become available from the *first dozen*, as he called the attendees from the August 19 party. He needed another dozen and another after that.

He'd abandoned his suit jacket on the back of his chair and rolled up his sleeves. Still, it felt hot in the stuffy office. He loosened his tie and went to the kitchenette for a refill on his coffee. Then he topped the mug with a handful of ice cubes. Returning to his office, he nodded and smiled at Mary, then watched for a brief moment as her cheeks caught fire.

He had that effect on women, regardless of age. Maybe he could put it to work somehow. What if he called the wives of the first dozen, asking for referrals? Would their husbands mind? Argh . . . they probably would. Craig knew he would if some Realtor called Andi behind his back.

What if he asked Donati for some referrals? The man knew everyone, and he was willing to put capital behind Craig's business venture. Maybe he was willing to put more. Then, perhaps Jude's parents would be inclined to help? They didn't know too many people, but any referral was a good referral. Craig never held back on work, effort, and creativity when he was keen on a goal. One thing he lacked, though, was patience. He didn't want to give his business years and years to grow. He wanted it to spurt like Jack's beanstalk but on steroids.

Pencil in hand, he stared at a blank sheet of paper he'd titled, LIST, in caps, and underlined twice. No names had landed there since that morning when he'd started making calls. When his phone rang, he was startled and dropped the pencil. It rolled on the floor toward the wall and stopped when it reached a crease in the weathered carpet.

He didn't recognize the number. "This is Craig Brafford," he said instead of the usual hello. He loved being professional at the risk of appearing stuck up. It was much better than appearing superficial.

"Craig, Truman Haskett here." The raspy voice was familiar. He was one of the first dozen, the manufacturing tycoon with the stunning, way-too-young-for-him wife.

He grinned. Number three from the dozen probably had a house to buy or sell.

"Mr. Haskett, what a pleasure. Good to hear from you, sir. What can I do for you?"

A beat of silence got Craig's brow ruffled. That wasn't starting so well.

"I have a bit of a cash flow problem," Haskett eventually said after letting out a long sigh of frustration. His voice was low, muted as if he was trying to keep their conversation a secret on his end. "I need to unload this property I have, real quick if you know what I mean."

Craig's grin returned. "How quickly would you want it sold?"

"Ideally, by tomorrow."

"Oh," Craig reacted, recovering his favorite pencil from the floor.

"There's a huge opportunity for me to invest in some commodities and get a leg up on the market, but I have to move now."

"I understand. I'll be happy to help you. What's the address? Let's start there."

"It's in the Memorial Villages, right off Taylorcrest Road. Great neighborhood, excellent schools. Four thousand square feet of contemporary, top-notch living with all the improvements you can think of because my wife and I didn't spare a dime."

Craig hated when clients pitched real estate to him; it was a waste of time. All he needed was an address. Then he had a history of the property, what it was bought for, and everything else he needed to know.

"That's awesome. It will help sell it fast." Hesitating, he decided against asking for the address again but went after it a different way. "Can I see it?"

"It's on Timber Hill Court, number fifteen-oh-nine. It's sitting empty, ready to go. Drop by my office for the keys. I'll leave them with my assistant in case she can't pull me out of my meetings."

Craig typed the address quickly into his system. The house was impressive, with an estimated market value of almost three million dollars. Yet Mr. Haskett had bought it only four years ago for under two.

"So? What do you say?" Haskett asked, seeming more impatient than Craig would've expected. That question, voiced in that rushed tone, slashed another couple of thousand from what Craig was considering to offer.

He took a moment to think. "Well, sir, if I had a month or two, I could get you over three million for it. But if you want to close on this tomorrow, I'll need to put some feelers out and see what I can do. Don't worry, we'll get it sold; I'm sure about it. But you will take a loss."

"I will?" Haskett sounded as if he was about to change his mind. Craig couldn't let that happen.

"You probably wouldn't get for it less than you paid; just not full market value."

"I see."

He'd turned monosyllabic. Bad sign.

"Why don't I take this and run with it? If you sign an exclusive contract with me for the next twenty-four hours, I'll start making calls and get you the best anyone could get on such short notice, cash deals only."

"That's more like it," Haskett said, laughing with relief. "You had me worried for a while. Make me proud, son." Then, without any warning, he transferred him to his assistant, a woman with a pleasant, modulated voice who already knew about the contract Craig would send for signing and the keys he was going to pick up.

Efficiency.

He loved that about his wealthy clients. It was as if the richer they got, the better they understood the only irreplaceable commodity was time. That's why time should never be wasted.

In that vein, wearing a smile on his face worthy of a Cheshire cat, he called Jude.

"Are you ready for some action?" he asked the moment his friend picked up.

"As I'll ever be." He could discern the excitement in Jude's voice.

"Good, because we're on. Meet me at fifteen-oh-nine Timber Hill Court." He could hear Jude typing on his keyboard. "Is it too much? Can you make the financials work? I think I can get it for two mil, maybe two-two tops." Craig held his breath, hoping Jude could somehow make it happen. Then, in a year or so, when they resold it for above market value, they could make five hundred grand each. Or more.

"That would work. I can get the money. You just get me bottom dollar."

"Time to get rich, bro," he said, then ended the call and stormed out through the office door. "Tell Mr. Hughes I have a new client," he said to Mary as he passed by her on his way out.

In the corner of his eye, he caught her eyelash-batting smile. She was cute, a little too plump for his taste and her boobs were too large, but she was fuckable, nevertheless.

Life was starting to be really good.

24

CHANCE

Andi's interview didn't take long. It might've been the shortest she'd sat through. The interviewer, a morbidly obese woman who had given up on herself a long time ago, seemed pressed for time and otherwise preoccupied. Andi did her best to hide her disappointment and show the right amount of enthusiasm that would get her the job. She couldn't afford to waste a single opportunity if she was ever to earn a living.

Once outside, under the sun's piercing rays, she breathed with ease. She looked at the blue sky, staring at it until she felt she was floating, and the sky was drawing near, infinite blue endlessly surrounding her. Until she felt that everything was possible, and the endless sky was the limit. Then she put the top down on her Beetle and drove off toward Smithville.

Her first stop was one of the huge gas stations that Houston is famous for, a RaceWay, where she could find clean restrooms. She rushed inside and changed out of her interview attire, putting on stretch jeans, a V-neck T-shirt, and her favorite Reeboks. She hesitated for a moment, touching the blue center stone of her pendant. Should she take that off? Was that piece of jewelry a bit much for her sporty attire? Definitely, but, worn with her vintage wash T-shirt, the pendant looked like one of those dollar-store items that young girls often wear, fun and unpretentious. No one would be able to tell it was valuable, not by looking at her.

She loved wearing it . . . Except for the rather modest wedding ring he'd proposed with, Craig had never given her jewelry before. She didn't believe it was very valuable, and she didn't care. The pendant meant a lot to her because it was a gift from her husband, not because of its potential worth in the hands of a pawnbroker. Sapphires or rhinestones, to her it was all the same, but that wasn't something she would ever be able to tell Craig.

She drove off, west on I-10, the top down, music blaring in the car, welcoming the flow of air as waves of nausea hit her every now and then. She managed not to stop and throw up until she reached Smithville, although she had a couple of close calls along the way. Somehow, pulling over on the side of the road and retching in a ditch wasn't how she wanted to spend the day. Her stomach cramped, twisted, and revolted as if an alien creature was about to spawn from there, ripping it to shreds. She willed herself to resist the urge to vomit, breathing, turning on the air conditioning and aiming the vents at her face, and popping mints into her mouth one after the other.

Leaving I-10 in the rearview mirror, she took Highway 71 at Columbus and headed north. By the time she reached Smithville, it was about one in the afternoon. She considered lunch for a brief moment, then decided on black coffee instead; it carried less of a risk of a productive bout of sickness. Entering the Smithville downtown area, she looked for a Starbucks.

There wasn't one. The downtown area reminded Andi of the Western sets she'd seen at Universal Studios when she'd visited years ago with her father. Seeming forever frozen in time, she could bet the little town had not changed much, for at least fifty years. A quick search on Google Maps gave her directions to a local coffee shop aptly named, The Olde World Bakery and Café. The word bakery in the shop's name filled her mouth with water, anticipating warm baked goods and puffy pastries she could gladly sink her teeth into.

The small, cozy place smelled just as good as she'd imagined. An older woman was taking a tray of fresh croissants out of the oven, filling the place with the aroma of molten chocolate and butter-dipped pastry. Unable to take her eyes off that tray, she rushed toward the counter.

A freckled young man smiled at her from behind a large, old-style cash register. "What can I get you, miss?"

"Um, a large coffee, black, and one of those—no, make that two please, two warm croissants." She handed him her credit card and followed his direction to wait to the side until her order was complete. A minute later, she picked everything up and headed for the door, still eyeing the display of baked goods. Not paying much attention to where she was going in the narrow space, she carelessly brushed against a man and spilled her hot coffee on him.

"Oh, my goodness, I'm so sorry," she said, rushing to the counter to get fistfuls of paper napkins.

In his sixties, the man had a bit of a potbelly but still wore a traditional cowboy belt buckle and a wide-brimmed hat to go with it. He was staring at her intently, although Andi couldn't tell how mad he was. Two paper cups had fallen at his feet, spilling their contents on the mosaic floor.

"Please let me buy these for you," she said, then turned toward the freckled young man and said, "Please run his order again, on me. Mine too, I guess." Her croissants had scattered on the floor, getting soaked in spilled coffee.

She started patting the man's plaid shirt where coffee had stained it, then reached to pat a rather large spot on his jeans but hesitated. Instead, she handed him a few napkins and said, "Um, please, if you'd like to, um—"

"It's all right," he replied lightheartedly while she was crouched on the floor, picking up the croissants and the cups, and trying to contain the mess with napkins. He touched her shoulder. "Don't worry about it."

"We have your order, miss," the barista said. "No worries about that mess. I'll clean it in a jiffy. Happens all the time."

She paid for the coffees and handed two of the three cups to the man. Then she plucked a few more napkins from the holder and offered him those. He took them without a word, looking at her with smiling eyes.

A wave of nausea rose to her throat. She had to get out of there before she added fresh vomit to the décor job she'd done on the man's clothes. "Once again, I'm terribly sorry," she said. The man lifted two fingers at the brim of his hat and nodded, still smiling.

She rushed out of there, looking back for one brief moment as the door closed. Her foot caught a pebble and skidded to the side, rolling her ankle. She lost her balance and had to prop her hand against another customer's wrought iron table to regain her balance. Thankfully, no coffee was spilled on that occasion; the woman didn't have one.

Sheesh, she thought. I need a license to walk. Apparently, I'm not equipped to do that anymore.

The woman had a pleasant smile and kind eyes under long, chestnut bangs. Her hair, shiny as silk, was tied in a youthful ponytail, defying her sixty-ish age. Before Andi could apologize, she said, "Are you all right, my dear?"

"Y—yes," she stammered. "I'm so sorry." She straightened herself. Her ankle was a little sore. She tested it, putting weight on it gradually. It stung a little, but she could handle it.

"Why don't you take a seat for a moment?" she said, gesturing toward one of the chairs. Andi pulled out the one closest to her and sat.

"Thank you," she said, managing a smile loaded with embarrassment. "I don't want to impose—"

"Nonsense. Someone who manages to bump into things twice in two minutes should sit still for a while, catch her breath, and get her bearings before heading into traffic." Her smile was infectious, not in the least judgmental. "You know, before endangering yourself and others."

Andi's cheeks caught fire. "Oh, you saw that too?" She pointed toward the coffee shop where the man she'd bumped into was just coming out.

"Yes," she replied, then pulled her purse closer as if making room on the table. Or maybe she was a little wary of Andi.

The man approached the table and set his two coffees on it, then sat on the third chair.

"Well, hello again," he said, chuckling.

Andi covered her mouth with her hand and gasped. "Don't tell me, you're together?"

The man squeezed the woman's hand with arthritic fingers. "Since the day I set my eyes on this fine Texas filly," he replied.

Andi lowered her eyes, embarrassed. "You must think I'm some kind of loony. I'm just a little distracted, that's all."

They both looked at her with undisguised, genuine interest. "Why is that?" the woman asked. "We love a good story. As you can tell, there isn't much happening here in our little town."

"Right," the man added. "Spilling that coffee was the highlight of the year."

"You're too kind," Andi replied, hiding a wave of sickness under a grin and washing it down with a gulp of coffee. She wondered if there was any harm in sharing personal information with those strangers. She was aching to tell someone about her baby, someone who would be happy for her, even if they were strangers who didn't really care. "I'm pregnant," she added, her voice strangled with emotion.

The man was slack-jawed, speechless for a moment.

"Oh, my goodness gracious," the woman said, clapping her hands in surprise. Then she reached over the table and squeezed Andi's hand. "Congratulations, my dear. You must be thrilled."

She lit up. She needed their kindness like a breath of fresh air, to soothe her worries, her aching heart after Craig's cold reaction. "Yes, I am. I'm also constantly sick, but that's another story." She checked the time. It was getting much too late. She wanted to be done with Craig's parents and be home before he returned from work. "I should be going . . . it's getting late. I have someplace I have to be." She stood and collected her coffee cup and the paper bag with the two croissants, still warm. "Thank you both for your understanding and hospitality. It was nice meeting you."

"A pleasure meeting you, young lady," the man replied, holding his wife's hands in his tightly.

Andi managed to make it to the car, only slightly limping and without any further incident. From behind the wheel of her Beetle, she waved at the couple, then pulled out. Her first stop was on the side of the highway, where she crouched by the front wheel of the bug and retched. Not even a mouthful of bitter coffee soothed the burning in her stomach or washed the foul taste in the back of her throat. A few minutes later, panting from the effort, she rinsed her mouth with bottled water and climbed behind the wheel, waiting a while before resuming her drive to Craig's parents. Her hands felt weak, as if turning the wheel would prove too much of an effort for her to handle. She wanted to lie down, but she was several hours away from being able to do that.

It took her less than ten minutes to reach the Brafford residence. It was a small ranch on a quarter-acre lot with a white picket fence and a charming, old oak tree on the property's edge. A wave of anxiety swirling in her gut, she breathed a few times deeply while she straightened her tousled hair, then touched up her lip gloss. "As I'll ever be," she mumbled to herself before ringing the doorbell.

The door swung wide open. The man from the coffee shop smiled and invited her in with a hand gesture.

"You?" she asked in disbelief. "You're Craig's parents?" A wave of dizziness washed over her, and she reached for the doorsill for balance.

The two looked at each other, visibly excited. "Yup, that's who we are. Here, take a seat, my dear, and put those feet up on this ottoman," Mrs. Brafford said. "I'll bring you some ice for that ankle. How would you like some sweet tea?"

District Attorney Buscher: At which point did you realize who the young woman was?

Murray Brafford: I knew right from the start, when I ran into her at the café. When I recognized that pendant, I was so surprised, I dropped the coffee I had bought. Poor little thing, she thought she was to blame.

District Attorney Buscher: Did you tell her you recognized the pendant?

Murray Brafford: No. We gave her time to tell us herself who she was and why she was there. We assumed she came to town looking for us. We just waited.

25

VISIT

Rebecca had chosen that particular rainy day to pay Hunter a visit, marking a shift from her traditional morning routine that involved coffee served on the deck while Aaron dabbled in the garden, then some reading by the window. Rain was falling hard and heavy, restricting both of them to the covered portion of their deck, far from the edge where raindrops splattered against the banister.

Little was said between them after she'd announced her intention to visit Hunter that morning.

She'd been putting it off for a few days, still overwhelmed with guilt, despite her husband's scientific take on myocardial infarction causes and triggers. Regardless of how Aaron had tried to minimize it for her sake, she knew stress was a factor, and she'd delivered exactly that. Stress. Sudden and intense.

Aaron had offered to come with her if she waited until he cleared his schedule enough to step away for a couple of hours. After having given it some thought, she decided she wanted to visit her old friend alone. Then, maybe over the weekend, she could return with Aaron; she was confident Hunter wouldn't mind the company.

It was still raining when she pulled into the parking lot at the Cardiac Rehabilitation Center. She ran through the rain, splashing into small puddles and soaking her shoes, but felt invigorated by the time she reached the entrance. Maybe she needed that a little bit more in her life than she cared to admit, some energetic activity to push blood faster through her veins and jolt her with some adrenaline. Since she'd retired, she'd been content to read for hours each day, lost in a world of marvelous stories. She got all her exercise vicariously, like when traveling the Congo with Michael Crichton, chasing bad guys with Harlan Coben, going to battle with Sir Walter Scott's Ivanhoe, or escaping from prison with the Count of Monte Cristo. Aaron's explanation of how heart attacks came to happen hadn't been entirely lost on her; there were things she needed to change in her life or risk that someday the rehab center she'd just entered would become her home for a while. Gah.

She found Hunter still in bed, although it was almost ten. He was awake, looking at the white ceiling, his face a little tense and deathly pale. Whatever thoughts were festering in his mind, they weren't healthy.

"Good morning, sunshine," she greeted him cheerfully, hiding her concern.

"Ah," he reacted, and a big smile bloomed on his lips for a moment. "So good to see you."

She leaned over and placed a smooch on his cheek. He smelled of hospital and stale clothes. A three-day, mostly white stubble made him look older than he was, despondent, at the end of his wits.

He pushed a button on the side panel of his bed, and the back whirred into an elevated position. "There. Much better. Now we can talk." He gestured with his hand slicing through the air between them. "At the same eye level."

Noticing the tremble in his fingers and the increasing pallor on his face, Rebecca smiled and gave him the gift she'd carefully wrapped the night before and had managed to shield from the raindrops.

Beaming like a child on Christmas morning, he unwrapped the thin, rectangular package, shaky fingers tearing through the paper with difficulty. Sadness choked Rebecca and brought tears to her eyes, but she didn't help him.

"It's a notebook," Hunter said, running his fingers over the glossy, colorful cover, "and a pen too." His finger traced the contour of the smiling dolphin drawn on it.

"For journaling. It's helpful. Puts your thoughts in order."

He held the notebook to his chest with both hands, visibly appreciating the gift. "You know what I think?" His smile returned for a brief moment. "I believe you miss giving students writing assignments."

She chuckled. "Could be true, but perhaps I've seen the good it did them to write their way through some of the toughest challenges in their lives. Try it. You might find you like it."

"I promise I will," he replied, his voice instilled with the wondrous anticipation of a new activity, one that promised excitement, or at least an antidote to the endless boredom of looking at the ceiling. "It's not like I'm too busy around here. They won't let me do anything."

"So, how are you feeling?" she asked, taking the pen and notebook from his hands and setting them on the bedside table, within his reach. Then she sat on a stool she pulled closer to his bedside.

"Just as you'd expect, but I'm still here. Above ground, I mean."

She squeezed his hand, and he reciprocated, weakly and trembling, that slight tremor present in his fingers regardless of what he was trying to do. "Was it me?"

"Huh?"

"Was it what I said about Andi's interview at the university that triggered your heart attack?"

"No. Absolutely not," he said, his voice sounding like it used to for a moment, filled with stamina and determination. He propped himself higher against the pillows. "It was the cigar smoking, the twelve-year-old scotch, the steaks, the seven-day weeks at the clinic . . . I did everything wrong." He cleared his voice looking sheepish for a moment. "When it happened, I was surprised it hadn't happened sooner."

"I can take it," Rebecca said, looking at him squarely. "I'm a big girl. And If I did this to you, I can—"

"For three generations, men in my family have died of cardiovascular disease in some form or another. Women too, but not all of them; not like the men." He was silent for a beat, his eyes veering away at times toward the rain-battered window. "I've just given up, that's all. I haven't taken my walks. Instead, I put more hours at the clinic, eating junk food and not giving a damn."

"You're depressed," she added quickly.

"I'm the one with medical education. You're an English lit professor . . . what do you know about depression?" he quipped, glancing at her for a brief moment before looking away.

"From Hamlet to Holden Caulfield, I believe I've had a few opportunities to understand it, enough to recognize it when it's staring me in the face, lying through its cigar-stained teeth."

"Ha. I'm busted, am I not?"

"Yes, you are. One thing I don't understand. Why are you sad? Because of Andi?"

He didn't reply. Instead, he turned his head away from her, staring intently at the window, but she could still see the glistening of tears in his eyes. Silence overtook the room, the soft beeping of his heart monitor the only sound disturbing it.

"Hunter, Andrea got married and left the nest, but that's normal, and you know it. It's the way it should be." He didn't say anything, just kept his eyes turned away from her. "You wouldn't wish for her to stay with you forever, right?"

When he finally looked at her, his eyes were fiery, the pain in them unmistakable, but there was something else too. Angst, immense fear, and dread as if he were watching a train wreck about to happen, powerless to intervene and save the lives that were about to end in senseless slaughter.

"Absolutely, I wanted her to marry and start her own family and leave the nest. What kind of father would that make me, had I not?" He reached for the water glass and took a sip via the red, bendable straw, then cleared his throat quietly. "But I have always wished for her to find a good spouse, a true and honest partner. Not someone like . . . him."

That again. Whatever it was Hunter had against Andi's husband, it wasn't going away. "What's wrong with him?" she asked in a low, understanding voice. Perhaps she could get to the bottom of it because, to her, it made no sense. "The boy isn't sore on the eyes, quite the opposite. He could be taller, I'll give you that, but Andi doesn't seem to mind. He has a good job, good manners too, and seems to care deeply about Andi."

He grabbed her hand with both his, shifting on his side to face her without turning his head. His eyes drilled into hers with an unspoken plea for help. "There's something about him I can't place, something that scares me more than anything." He let go of her, then showed her a scar on his right hand at the root of his thumb, a white line about an inch long. "See this? A sweet, little spaniel gave me that with his baby teeth. He didn't want me to give him a rabies shot." Then he pointed at another scar on the inside of his ring finger. It ran about an inch and a half in length. "I could see the inside of the metacarpophalangeal joint when the Burmese cat opened it up with her claws during an ear exam. I was lucky she didn't sever the ligaments." He stopped talking for a beat. "Every time this happened—and it's happened more than twice—right before one of my patients became so pissed at me they had to pounce and draw blood, I felt my hackles rise. It was as if I knew it was going to happen before it did." He let a loud, shattered breath of air out of his lungs that sent a shiver down her spine. "It was as if I sensed their thoughts."

"What are you talking about?"

"Instinct," he bellowed, startling her. "Survival instinct. It's ancestral. It's what kept us alive when we used to live in caves," he added, lowering his tone to a normal pitch yet still passionate. He pressed his lips together for a moment. "Whenever I look at Craig Brafford, my hackles rise. To think that my daughter, my naïve, trusting little girl is alone with this man or sleeping by his side, is simply unbearable—"

She clasped his hand before speaking. "Are you sure you're not imagining things? We're getting up there in years, and age does weird things to our minds. That's how, in my uneducated opinion, we get to die completely batshit crazy. We gradually get there."

He scoffed. "What, like Alzheimer's or dementia? I tested negative for both before Andi's wedding. Then I had myself tested again last month when I saw it wasn't going away . . . the dread, the fear. Freddy did the eval; he would've told me if he saw anything wrong. He's never one to sugarcoat things."

A frown furrowed Rebecca's brow. She didn't know what else to say or do. She'd known Hunter for more than thirty years, and he'd never been delusional or obsessed the way she'd seen him when it came to his son-in-law. Perhaps he deserved the benefit of the doubt.

"I'm not going to say I understand any of this, Hunter. I'll just take your word for it and choose to believe you, regardless of how far-fetched it all seems."

"Thank you," he replied in a calm voice. "That's all I'm asking, really."

"What are you going to do?" she asked. Hunter looked at her inquisitively. "About Craig, I mean. If this is how you feel about the man, then—"

"Nothing," he said bitterly, slamming his hand down against the side of the bed. "My little girl is in love with this man and whatever I say or do would break her heart. You've seen it." He groaned in frustration. "But I won't stop looking for the truth this man is trying to hide. Not until I die, and even if my little girl won't hear it."

With those few words, she understood what was going on with her friend. "So, you turned to double cheeseburgers and vats of fries, alcohol, and whatnot, and I'm just guessing here."

"Ice cream too," he smiled with sadness. "Not the low-fat shit in the diet section of the grocery store, but the real deal. The stuff I denied myself all those years when . . . I had something to live for."

She stood and started pacing the room slowly, clasping and unclasping her hands, wringing them as she tried to think of the best way to reach Hunter beyond his famous wall of stubbornness. Then she stopped by the foot of his bed.

"If your daughter is to be happy with this man and you're wrong about your, um, hackles, you'd want to be there, by Andi's side, and witness that. Raise your grandchildren, even if they'd be his kids, and you'd have to figure out how to make that work for you." She bit her lip for a moment before continuing. "If you're right and this man is trouble, you have to be there for Andi when she needs you, because she will, when heartbreak comes calling; that's a given. Either way, cut the self-pity crap and get yourself back on track. She needs you."

Hunter's mouth gaped open for a moment. "I'm such a bloody fool," he muttered.

She'd reached him. Smiling, she said, "You're not that old, you're not dying, and I have thousands of dollars to win back from you at the poker table."

"I'll leave something in my will," he replied quickly with a quiet chuckle, lowering his eyes, seemingly ashamed.

"I want it much sooner than when you kick the bucket," she laughed, mock-punching him in the arm.

He raised his eyes and looked at her. They were brimming with tears. "Thank you, dear friend."

She smiled and nodded. "What are you going to do about Andi? About what I told you, with the university job?"

A brief frown clouded his eyes. "Nothing. Andi wouldn't do such a thing. She wouldn't keep such a secret from me. It has to be some kind of mistake. Maybe someone got the wrong name or something. I'm sure it's nothing."

On her drive home, Rebecca's thoughts dwelled about Andi's job interview with the marine biology department at the university and Hunter's statement, that it had to be a mistake, a clerical error of sorts. He had to be right; it made sense and was the only thing that did. They must've had Andi mistaken for someone else.

Yet something gnawed at her gut, something indescribable, a hint of uneasiness, an unseen threat. She felt a chill and turned the air conditioning in her car to a lower setting. As she put her hand back on the steering wheel, she noticed goosebumps on her skin. As a scary thought started to form, those goosebumps took over swaths of her arms and legs, traveling up her spine in an icy tingle until they reached the back of her head, tickling her nape with foreboding fingers.

Instinct.

Now she understood what Hunter was talking about.

District Attorney Buscher: Was there any other evidence found at the landfill?

Detective Barbara Otwell: Yes. We recovered a towel soaked with blood. We established it belonged to the victim.

District Attorney Buscher: How did you make that determination?

Detective Barbara Otwell: Our forensics team matched the DNA from the blood with hair collected from a hairbrush found at the victim's residence during the initial search and seizure.

District Attorney Buscher: Any other evidence recovered from the body dump site?

Defense Attorney Goodridge: Objection, Your Honor.

District Attorney Buscher: Withdrawn. Any other evidence recovered from the landfill?

Detective Barbara Otwell: A clump of the victim's hair and a wood splinter we matched to one of the kitchen chairs, all covered in blood.

26

MEMORIES

Andi sat comfortably on the sofa, her feet up on the weathered leather ottoman, a large photo album open in her lap. The sweet tea was forgotten on the coffee table, the cold, sweaty glass dripping water in a circle on the cardboard coaster bearing the Heineken logo.

Sitting right next to her on the edge of the sofa, Mrs. Brafford explained every photo with a lot of vivid detail. Sometimes, the Braffords didn't agree on the circumstances when some of the pictures were taken or recalled the same events but in a different sequence, seeding friendly, humorous quarrels between the two.

Lifting her eyes from a photo of Craig taken when he was about seven or eight years old, she looked at Mrs. Brafford, finding the resemblance easily, wondering how she'd missed it at the café. *The mind's eye sees what it wants to see*, she thought. *At the café, I saw strangers. Here, I see family.*

They seemed to have taken an instant liking to her, and she relished the feeling of warmth, of acceptance and love. The two were charming and would make absolutely loveable grandparents for her baby if Craig would let them become a closer part of their family. A passing frown ridged her brow for a fleeting moment. She'd find a way to make that happen. She had to.

"Here, he'd fallen and scraped his knee." Mrs. Brafford pointed at a photo showing Craig sitting on the ground in the middle of a playground, holding his knee. He had an expression of sheer horror on his little face. He was pale, slack-jawed, and whale-eyed, looking straight into the camera. "Craig has that, um, I forgot what it's called . . . he faints when he sees blood, within seconds, and he can't help it. He wakes up, sees the blood again, then faints again. Hematophobia, yes. In this photo, he'd just fainted, then recovered before I could wipe off the blood, but he covered it with his hands so he wouldn't see it anymore." She chuckled and ran her fingertips over the photograph where the little boy's face was. "His daddy was busy taking photos, and he was upset because we were laughing at him." She looked guilty for a moment. "He was hilarious, hiding the blood under his hands and shouting at his dad."

"He screamed at me that day, the first time he did," his father added. "I believe that's when we first witnessed his pride being injured." He whistled. "That boy, ten years old and four-foot-nothing, could stare anyone down if they so much as looked at him wrong."

As Andi turned the pages, the boy grew from one photo to the next, becoming more like the man she knew and loved, and at the same time, less. Teenage Craig had a deep frown joining his eyebrows together, a fiercely dark look in his eyes, an expression of acute determination, almost like an enraged form of ambition. Some of that still existed in the adult Craig, only softer, mellower, less intense. She knew he was working himself to the bone driven by the ambition that had bloomed many years ago, in that house, when he was a teenager. She wondered what had instilled it in that little boy.

Still, the photos depicted a happy family, loving parents taking good care of their child. "What happened? If I may ask, why aren't you a part of his life anymore?" Andi looked first at

Mrs. Brafford, who quickly lowered her eyes, then at her husband, who breathed loudly.

"He was ashamed of us, with—" Mr. Brafford started, but his wife cut him off.

"Murray, don't," she pleaded, wiping a tear with her fingertip. "Think what he'd say if he knew we were saying that."

Murray turned his gaze to his wife. "This girl married our son, Louise. Don't you think she has a right to know?"

Louise lowered her eyes, staring at her hands while she was wringing them. "All right," she eventually said. "But let me tell the story."

"Fine," Murray replied, leaving his armchair to grab himself a fresh beer from the fridge. He popped open the cap and sent it flying into the trash can, where it rattled for a brief moment before settling.

Louise turned to Andi, who was already feeling she'd overstepped. Yet, she was curious to find out what had caused such a deep rift between her husband and these seemingly nice people.

"Craig was always very, um, how do I put it, aware of how the world works," she said, her eyes darting left and right as if looking for a way to escape the room, the conversation. "We were not doing very well financially when he was growing up. We struggled—"

"We were dirt poor," Murray intervened. "I was a farmhand near Austin, and my wife was teaching first grade here, in town. Four hours a day. We barely made rent."

The small ranch house was telling part of that story. Even twenty years after Craig's youth, the furniture looked beat, the walls needed a fresh coat of paint, the fridge was old and noisy, rattling as if it was about to come apart each time the compressor kicked in.

"I still work some evenings and all weekends, but here in town, at the local hardware store. I stock the shelves, sometimes I work the registers. Louise retired after her bout of breast cancer."

Oh no . . . Andi looked at Louise, noticing things she hadn't earlier. Her shoulders poking through the thin fabric of her blouse, the gauntness of her face rendered almost unnoticeable by her warm smile.

"Don't worry, my dear," Louise said quickly, "I'm all right. I've beaten it."

"Whew," Andi sighed, the relief washing over her in a wave that brought tears to her eyes. "I'm so happy to hear that."

The woman reached out and squeezed her hand. "And my biggest wish is coming true. A grandchild."

"Yes," Andi said quickly, feeling she belonged. Then she remembered Craig, and her smile waned. "I'm hoping I can bring you and Craig back together. If you're up for it, of course."

Murray walked over to her with a heavy, almost stomped gait. "Nothing can be more heartbreaking than being shut out of your child's life. There's nothing I'd like more than for all of us to gather 'round a Thanksgiving table, or Sunday dinner, or whatever he'd be willing to do. But I don't think it's possible. He'll never accept us."

"Craig is very ambitious," Louise intervened. "He was that way since he was twelve. He discovered how other people lived when his father took him to the fair in Austin one fall. He saw the fancy cars and people with money who didn't smell of farm and straw and horses. He came back changed after that fair. Ashamed deeply of who he was, of who we were, my husband and I."

"He'll never forgive us for being poor," Murray stated simply, with disheartening acceptance. "He'd never have us cross his threshold because we would be an embarrassment to him, reminding him where he came from, how he grew up in poverty." He leaned over and touched her cheek with calloused fingers. "That's why we didn't attend your wedding, dearie, although we were thrilled to learn he was finally settling down with a nice girl."

"Yes, we would've loved to come, but he called us and warned us to stay away." Louise sniffled quietly.

Andi was shocked. Was that everything that was going on? Or had there been words between them, something that had happened years ago that couldn't be forgotten?

"After that fair," she continued in a soft, resigned voice, "he wouldn't have us show up anywhere. Not at school, to pick him up when we could. Not at summer camp. He wouldn't even come with us to church anymore."

Speechless, Andi turned a page in the photo album, irrationally hoping she'd find answers in there. A photo showed Craig looking at the camera with dark, almost threatening eyes. The other photo showed him laughing happily with another boy his age, running and holding hands, a textbook sample of a happy childhood. The other boy's head was turned, but she could still see he was laughing just as heartily.

"This was his best friend back then, the son of some rich folk from across the tracks," Murray said. "Craig became infatuated with that boy. He spent all his days at his house, where he didn't belong, tasting what that life was like, with servants and fine foods and all. That fueled his rage against us. Every day he went there, he came back home hating us more."

"Not hating us," Louise intervened. "I wouldn't go that far. Maybe just being more ashamed of us. Rejecting us."

"And don't think I didn't try to make more money," Murray said. "I took a second job, but it was still for minimal pay. I have no schooling." He pursed his lips and stared at the scratched hardwood floor for a moment. "But that boy, he, um, he and Craig got real close." He sighed and veered his eyes while his cheeks caught fire. "We thought he was gay, at least for a while, until his first girlfriend came around."

"He's not gay," Louise pushed back. "I told you a long time ago. He and that boy were just friends, that's all. You didn't believe me then, but you could believe me now when we're entertaining your son's lovely wife. Maybe that will tell you," she chuckled.

"It would've been all right if he were gay, you know," Murray added, lost in what seemed to be some painful thoughts. "We might be living in Texas, but we would've accepted him. We only wanted him to be happy."

"Craig isn't gay," Louise said with a determined voice. "Murray was just trying to make sense of the hold that boy had on our son, that's all. I think it wasn't the boy as much as his family, his big house, his wealth. Our son wanted that life so desperately he would've done anything to get it." She swallowed hard, holding back tears. "Then that girl . . . broke his heart."

"What happened?" Andi asked.

"He met a lovely girl, Julie was her name. He fell in love, head over heels, even forgetting about his best friend for a while. All he would talk about was her. We wanted to meet her, but he kept her away from us." She paused for a moment, choosing her words. "He got a bad cold that spring, and he was in bed for a couple of days. That's when Julie showed up at the door, with homework as an excuse." Another beat. "It was fate . . . him falling ill, that girl coming to visit."

"She took one look at us, at our home, went away and never looked back," Murray added coldly. "Seems she was rich too. He never forgave us for that. A few weeks later, he was gone."

Andi was at a loss for words. What could she say to the parents who had lost their child for such a senseless reason? The man they were describing was nothing like Craig, and at the same time, she recognized him in some photos, in some of the things his parents shared about him, in the fierce ambition they were describing.

She turned another page in the album and froze. The photo showed Craig at fourteen or so, wearing her pendant. Reflexively, she touched it with her fingers. "This was his?" she asked, unable to take her eyes off the photo. She had no idea the pendant used to be Craig's; she was led to believe he'd bought it for her before the party. Or had she assumed that, instead of asking? Sometimes she jumped to conclusions.

"Yes," Louise replied, smiling, a hint of sadness in her voice. "And there's a story that comes with it." She looked at Murray to ask him if he wanted to tell it, but he gestured with his hand, inviting her to share it. "It's about that friend of his again. When he turned fourteen, a few months before Craig did, he was accepted into some fancy country club in Austin. Lo and behold, all members received a ring. He met with Craig that day at his birthday party and showed him the ring." She shot Murray a quick look. Her husband nodded and plunged his hands into his pockets.

"What happened?" Andi asked, intrigued by the grim looks on their faces.

"Craig came back from that party heartbroken. You see, to him, that ring was a symbol of the class he didn't belong to. He cried his eyes out that night, sobbing into his pillow until the first light of dawn. Then he took out a horse and rode it until the poor thing was covered in sweat, foaming at the mouth. That day was the first time he didn't visit his friend. He didn't want to see him anymore."

"Yet somehow they talked," Murray added.

"Yes, you're right. Maybe over the phone."

"Why? What happened?" Andi asked.

"May I?" Louise reached for the pendant. Andi took it off and handed it to her. With delicate fingers, Louise turned the pendant on the other side and showed her two uneven lines on opposite sides of the pendant. "This was a ring before it became a pendant. This is where it used to be attached."

Andi gasped. "You mean, this is *the* ring? The one that—"

"Yes," Murray said grimly. "And they said it's very valuable, sapphires with topaz, I believe. Worth a fortune. That boy had his ring fitted with a chain, so Craig could wear it under his clothes and not get caught."

Louise smiled warmly as she handed Andi back the pendant. "He must love you a lot if he gave you this. To Craig, it represents access to the world he wasn't born into but would do anything to reach. He wore it religiously, his own version of the key to his personal Xanadu."

"Wow," Andi whispered. "I had no idea." Then a thought crossed her mind, and she looked at the two with humor in her eyes. "You recognized this when you first saw me, didn't you?"

"Yes, we did," Murray grinned sheepishly.

"Why not say something?"

"First off, we didn't know if you were coming to see us or not. If you wanted to meet us," Louise said. "And, mostly, because we were speechless. We couldn't believe our own eyes. Then you said you had someplace to be, and we rushed to get here before you did."

Andi laughed and shook her head. "What an awesome story to tell your grandkids," she said, turning another page in the album. A few more photos of Craig, sometimes smiling, but most times having that dark, steeled expression on his face. There were no photos of him and Julie.

Andi tapped her fingernail against one such photo and said, "This is not the Craig I married. He's gentle, helpful, always there for me. He's funny and sweet, a hard worker, an achiever. He's not that . . . angry at life."

"What does he do?" Louise asked.

"He's in real estate, an agent for expensive homes and business properties."

Louise and Murray exchanged a quick glance.

Then Louise smiled and said, "I'm happy he's changed. Maybe puberty was harder on him than we realized. Seems he was able to find his way, after all, make something of himself. I wish you both all the happiness in the world."

"Thank you," Andi replied, turning another page, but the rest of the album was empty. She looked up from its blank pages with an inquisitive expression on her face.

Murray scratched the roots of the thinning tuft of hair still clinging to the top of his head. "Well, a couple of weeks after

Julie left him, when he was about sixteen, Craig vanished, leaving us behind, his friend too."

"That boy was just as heartbroken as we were," Louise added.

"The night before he left, I'll never forget it," Murray said.

"Murray . . . no," Louise whispered pleadingly.

He pretended not to hear her. "Our son asked us, right at the dinner table, why we had kids. He shouted at us, called us irresponsible for having a kid when we were so poor. Then he proceeded to explain to us how much better off we would've been had we not had him. Had we not procreated, as he put it."

Andi listened to Murray's words with a heavy heart. That explained Craig's reaction to her pregnancy.

"He was gone the next day," Louise whispered.

"Our son just disappeared without a word. He simply discarded us like we were unworthy trash. It was years before we heard from him again. We even filed a police report; they did nothing with it, except stamp it *runaway* and ignore our calls."

"May I?" Andi asked, holding her phone and asking permission to take pictures of some of the photos in the album.

"By all means," Louise replied. "These will be yours one day, anyway."

She found it difficult to leave the hospitality of her in-laws but had to step on it if she was to reach home before Craig usually did, about seven. Both gave her long hugs, kissed her cheeks, and waved behind her departing Beetle until they disappeared from her rearview mirror. Yet there was a fear curled inside her, bothersome and heavy, that she was never going to see them again.

Defense Attorney Goodridge: Mrs. Brafford, what would you say is your son's most cherished possession?

Louise Brafford: I'm not sure about now, but for a very long time, it was that square, blue pendant on a silver chain.

Defense Attorney Goodridge: Have you seen that pendant recently?

Louise Brafford: Yes. His wife wears it.

27

HIRED

The entire week had been a dizzying high for Craig.

After the unexpected call from Truman Haskett about his house and his dire need for immediate cash, he figured out a plan to get a lowball offer signed. He needed Jude to do precisely what he told him when he told him, and things would work out just fine.

First thing on Friday, he invited Haskett to his home office to discuss options. Thankfully, Andi was gone that morning, another stupid job interview or visiting her father, like she did every day.

Haskett rumbled a little because he would've preferred to do everything remotely while he took care of his manufacturing business from his high-rise office. But his need for cash must've trumped that because he showed up at Craig's and had been patiently waiting since his arrival, sipping espresso and stinking up the place with his cigars.

Craig's strategy involved some waiting time, meant to stretch the seller's nerves taut, ready to snap as the weekend approached and the window of opportunity closed. During this time, he made some calls to some clients he knew wouldn't be interested in buying the house. Then, when Haskett was about to blow up, he called Jude.

As instructed, Jude showed a modicum of interest in the property. Craig shared the address and put the call on speaker, so Haskett could listen in. He used Jude's real name; once the sale went through, that name would be on record, public information for whoever was interested to learn it.

Jude, like the slick son of a bitch he was, seeded excitement in Haskett, saying the two-point-two million price was interesting enough to make him drop the day's agenda and close the sale. Then, like a hammer, came the final blow. He said he was about to sign another deal for a similar house, four hundred thousand cheaper, something Craig had carefully chosen for him from the available listings.

They started dancing on that phone call, Craig making a comparison between the two properties and showing how much better Haskett's house was and Jude playing hard to get. All that while Haskett was sweating profusely, angrily pacing the hardwood floors in Craig's home office.

Finally, Jude said he'd sign and close that day for four hundred thousand dollars less. Craig haggled a bit more until Jude threatened to end the call. Only then Haskett, muttering an oath, said, "Fine. Close the damn thing at one-point-eight."

Then paperwork started flying in and out of the fax machine, gathering signatures, making it all happen in less than an hour. Jude had done his part, having the money at the ready like Craig had instructed him. By the time the deal closed, it was almost four in the afternoon, when banks closed for the weekend, but they managed to get everything done in the nick of time.

After closing, Haskett left the law office with a firm handshake for Craig, followed by a pat on his shoulder. He even shook Jude's hand. Typically, Craig would've made sure the two men never met; it was a recommended best practice in the industry. But the time crunch had made it impossible to orchestrate.

Then the sucker went away, and Craig drove off too, not spending a moment more with Jude at the agency's law office or on the sidewalk in front of it.

He didn't stop smiling until he got home, a little after six. He found the house empty, stinking of cigar smoke and Haskett's cologne-tinged sweat, discernible still in his home office. But it was over. He turned on the air conditioning and lowered the setting a few degrees, then opened some screened windows to clean the air. Pouring himself a stiff drink, he hollered loudly enough to make the walls echo, "Whoo-hoo . . . Let the weekend begin. Yeah, 'cause we deserve it!"

Changed into jeans and a white T-shirt, skintight on his torso, he let himself drop into a large armchair in the living room and dialed Jude. When he picked up, he said, "Congratulations! You're the proud owner of fifteen-oh-nine Timber Hill Court."

"We are the proud owners, mate. We are," Jude replied, chuckling. "I formed a trust and put the house under it. You're on that trust."

Damn it. Leaving a paper trail was never a good thing. "We didn't discuss this. You should've asked me. We've bent a few rules with this deal, you know?"

"It's all right," Jude replied, seeming unfazed. "You'll see. Don't you want to write off the expenses we're going to incur on the house until it sells?"

"Yes, but—"

"Then, this is how it's done. Your turn to trust me."

"Fair enough. Next time, please tell me ahead of time. You could've left my name out of the trust; it would've been better. I know you wouldn't screw me over, even if we don't paper the agreement."

He ended the call, a little irritated with Jude. Was this trust going to cause any issues? Probably not. What were the chances that Haskett suspected any wrongdoing and started investigating the deal? Next to zero. But not really zero. *Fuck.*

And where the hell was Andi?

Lately, she appeared to spend more and more time away from home, doing who knows what, who knows where, instead of taking care of the house and figuring out the menu for the next party. He had a shit ton of work to do, work she could pick up and run with, leaving him time to focus on the important stuff only he could do. Why was she so damn restless?

He called her cell and cursed when he heard the muffled ringing, thinking she must've left it at home. That wasn't the case. As he started following the source of the distant sound, Andi came through the door, smiling, the ringing phone in her hand.

"I'm back." She met him in the middle of the living room and kissed his lips quickly, then pulled away. Kicking off her shoes, she asked, "Did you miss me?"

"I always do," he grinned, leaning against the table and crossing his arms. "Where were you?"

"Argh . . . just doing my usual," she replied, looking away for a moment. "Job interview, visit with Dad, running errands."

She was lying. He was sure about that.

"How was your day?" she asked quickly, seemingly eager to deflect attention from her.

"I made us a lot of money, babe." He walked over to her and wrapped his arms around her, drawing her close. She responded to his touch like she always did, with eyes half-closed and a passionate kiss.

"How much money did you make?" she asked. There was a glint of something in her gaze, something hidden, something he didn't understand.

"Um, about five hundred thousand," he announced proudly. "Signed the papers today."

Her jaw dropped. "Whoa . . . that much? Really?"

"Really. It won't be until next year when we sell the house, but it's there. Ours."

"What house?"

"Jude and I bought a house on the cheap today, a unique opportunity, too good to pass."

"But can we afford another mortgage?" She seemed worried, her joy long gone.

"Jude will take care of the money part. He's got plenty."

Something got her attention in what he'd just said because she tilted her head slightly, almost like a confused dog.

"Never mind that," he said, "let's celebrate. Why don't you wait for me on the veranda? I'll be right there."

He smiled encouragingly as she pulled open the patio door. There, she squealed with joy. "Oh, Craig, this is beautiful! I absolutely love it."

He'd bought a patio set in black wicker, lined with weather-resistant cushions. The set could be arranged as a round daybed or divided into various sections. Through the window, he saw Andi lounging on it and rolling on her side, then on her back, playfully trying different postures and arranging her pillows, delighted.

His beautiful, fantastic wife. She could make him so happy.

He grabbed a champagne bottle and a couple of glasses and joined her outside on the bed. Popping the cork with a loud noise, he poured the bubbly wine into the two glasses and handed her one. "Cheers, honey. Here's to many, many more days like this one."

She wriggled to the side of the bed and sat, then took the champagne glass hesitantly. "Babies and alcohol don't mix." She barely touched the fluid with her lips, then set it aside on the wrought iron table. "You drink all of it. I'll keep you company."

Just like that, all his good cheer vanished. She had to remind him of her pregnancy, of the betrayal he'd tried so hard to forgive and forget but couldn't. He'd achieved neither; how could he, when every day she made sure she mentioned it somehow? And how the hell could she be so proud of something he'd never wanted? Something she'd stolen from him?

His beautiful wife was far from being tame enough.

He ran his hand against the smooth surface of the cushion. "You like it?"

"Love it," she said, smiling widely and batting her eyelashes, flirting with him.

"Good. Now let's talk some business." His voice was a little cold, almost harsh.

"Oh," she said, turning wary, sad almost. "Okay."

"Let's plan for another party." She frowned and pulled away from him, not much, only a few inches, but the gesture was there, the message loud and clear. She loved the lifestyle but didn't want to do anything to earn it. Good thing it wasn't really her call. "We have to keep these things going."

"But we just had one," she argued. "Maybe give it some more time until we have another?" She bit her fingernail for a moment, looking straight at him, while he could see her wheels turning. "Let's have the baby party first."

A dash of anger rushed through his veins. He breathed it away, willing himself to stay calm. "I thought we agreed we were going to do that in a couple of months, right?"

"Yeah, we did. I just thought you wanted a party, and that would be more fun."

"I'm not looking for bloody fun, Andi," he snapped. "I'm looking to make money. These parties are how we make it happen. I've explained that to you before."

"You did," she replied, her voice tinged with sadness and compliance, pacifying. "I just didn't understand we'd have to have them that often, that's all."

"If we let too much time pass, you know what happens? The assholes list their houses with someone else. They buy someone else's properties." He cursed under his breath, irritated beyond words that he had to explain it to her all over again. Andi was no idiot . . . why was she behaving like one? "We have to do this all the time now. If we're in this game, we might as well play it like pros and win at the damn thing, right?" He forced himself to smile and ran his fingers through her short, tousled hair, tucking a strand behind her ear.

That hairstyle of hers maybe worked for sea turtles and dolphins, but not for the likes of Donati and Haskins. Their wives spent hundreds of dollars to have their hair done, and it showed.

"Are you my copilot?" he asked, still playing with her hair. "Will you work with me?"

She pressed her lips together for a moment. "Yeah . . . I guess I can." She chuckled bitterly. "It's not like I have any real choice, do I?"

"But is it so bad? To work with me?"

She sighed and looked away. "The passion you have for this," she gestured toward the house, "for real estate, for making boatloads of money, I have for the ocean and all its creatures. That's where I belong." Her voice turned brittle. "But it wasn't in the cards now, was it? Not that, not even a bank teller job or a dental receptionist. One thing I haven't tried is waiting tables. There has to be a cheap diner out there that would take me."

"Jeez, Andi! Draw the line somewhere and don't cross it."

She bit her lip. "So, yeah, you're the only employer in town who will have me. I guess I should be grateful. It makes me sad, though, that I can't be more than just your wife, helping with your stuff. I always dreamed I'd be more." She sniffled. "I can't even find the energy and drive to finish my doctorate. Why would I, right?"

He stared at her for a moment. She always had to say the worst possible things to make him feel like shit. But he needed her badly, and she'd grow to like it eventually. "Well, then, welcome aboard," he said, smiling and opening his arms. "This employer is thrilled to have you."

She cuddled at his chest and sighed. "I'll work for you, Mr. Brafford, sir. Does your employ come with maternity leave and benefits?"

He swallowed a curse, glad she couldn't see the expression on his face. She had to bring up the brat again. "Whatever you want. It will come with a BMW to replace that crappy car you're driving, and—"

"But I like my Beetle."

"Okay, keep the Beetle if you want, but could you please do me a big favor?"

She looked up at him. "What do you need?" She was all serious, not a hint of a smile on her lips.

"Why don't you let that hair of yours grow a little longer? Men have fantasies about women's hair." He smiled. "Lots of fantasies."

28

DISCOVERY

Plates were cast aside on their favorite table at Mille Ponti, still loaded with mouthwatering Italian food. Andi had ordered stuffed mushrooms but barely finished one of the two portabellas filled with ham and molten smoked cheese. Janelle had pushed aside her salmon Positano the moment Andi had asked, pointing at the skinny and lewd server, "How much do you think he's making?"

"All right, that's it," she said, and the plate grated in protest against the wrought iron surface of the table. "I can't stand it anymore, girl. You still don't have a job?" She pointed her rhinestone-encrusted fingernail at Andi accusingly.

Andi's eyes darted at Janelle for a moment before seeking patterns in the patio's maroon tiles. "I would've told you, right?"

"I was hoping you were an asshole," Janelle said, patting her lips with the napkin, then throwing it on the table as if it had offended her. "Way better than being unemployed after all this time."

She shrugged, wishing she had an answer. "Craig wants me to work with him, and I've said yes."

"To do what?"

Andi groaned. "Don't ask. Some sort of assistant for his real estate business. Superstar wife, host for his parties, glorified gofer. And cook. I forgot to mention, cook."

"A cook with a PhD," she added, going for the kill in typical Janelle style. "Are you kidding me?"

"I wish I was." Being there with Janelle, speaking her uncensored mind for the first time in weeks, brought her dangerously close to a crying spell. She gulped some ice water hastily to keep her tears in check and her nausea subdued.

Lately, her sickness had gotten worse, and every bout of retching burned her stomach as if she'd been eating glass shards. Sometimes, before an attack of nausea hit, she had cramps, violent to the point of leaving her breathless, curled up in a ball on the floor or keeled over, barely able to breathe. Only then the retching started. She'd grown to welcome it because it brought some relief from the cramping.

She'd wanted to see a doctor, but Craig had been putting it off while at the same time insisting he accompany her. He was right; doctors these days were nothing but cash-generating machines for the for-profit healthcare system, not because they wanted to, but because they didn't have much choice. As long as she could hold on and delay the expense, she would do it. Every bit of money helped. She'd looked it up on the internet, and all first trimester moms were complaining about the same thing, and it always went away on its own.

"You all right?" Janelle asked, squeezing her forearm. "You turned pale."

She wished she could share the news with Janelle, but she'd given Craig her word. She'd already spilled the beans with his parents; had he known, he'd be furious with her. "Just not feeling all that good today. Sorry for being such a pain lately." She forced a smile and looked at Janelle.

"Wait a minute, girl, you've got nothing to apologize for. If I were in your shoes, looking for work for all this time and still nothing, I'd be bonkers by now." She frowned and ran her hand through her mane of curly black hair. "I got an idea," she announced. "You know what I do for a living, right?"

"To some extent. You're at the Department of Labor. I know that much," Andi chuckled. "But I have no idea what color papers you push," she added with a wink.

"The right color," Janelle replied, raising her right eyebrow. "I sometimes investigate complaints of discrimination in the workplace and during the hiring process."

Andi looked at her with an unspoken question in her eyes. What did any of that have to do with her?

"If you happened to, say, file a complaint stating you were discriminated against during a job interview, that complaint would open a case, and I could snatch that case from the queue and work it myself."

"I wasn't discriminated against," Andi said.

Janelle scoffed. "Yes, you were. For being a woman. Trust me, you were."

"I was?"

Janelle nodded in a slow, exaggerated manner. "Now, please do me a favor and file a complaint against one of the schmucks who refused to hire you, stating you believe you were discriminated against on the basis of your gender. Send it to this address," she added, showing her an email address for the Department of Labor on her phone.

"Now?" Andi frowned, wondering if Janelle knew what she was doing.

"Yes, now. It doesn't have to be long. One line should do it. Dear so-and-so, during the interview for whatever role, I believe I was discriminated against because of my gender. Please help."

Andi typed the message as directed, then tapped send. A whoosh marked the successful transmittal of the message.

Janelle looked at the screen of her phone. "C'mon, c'mon," she mumbled. "Gotcha." She tapped on the screen a few times, then set the phone down. "Now your case is assigned to me, which means I can investigate without losing my job. I can ask questions. Whom should we call first? The university? What was that woman's name?"

"Marjorie," Andi replied, her eyes brimming with tears. She had no idea what she'd done to deserve a friend like Janelle. "Dr. Marjorie Hitchens, Department of Marine Biology."

"All right, here goes." Janelle dialed the number and put the call on speaker. Then, after asking for Dr. Hitchens by name a couple of times, she finally got her on the phone. "Dr. Hitchens," Janelle said, putting her index finger at her lips, urging Andi to stay quiet. "Thank you for taking my call. This is Janelle Larimer with the US Department of Labor."

"Yes, what can I do for you, Ms. Larimer?"

"We're investigating a complaint regarding a, um, Andrea Wilmore Brafford. She interviewed with you—"

"Yes, I remember her quite well. What's the question?"

"Was she qualified for the role?"

"Yes, she was. Ms. Wilmore was the best candidate for the job."

Andi's eyes burned with tears. She covered her mouth with both her hands to keep the sobs locked inside her chest.

"Did you extend her the offer?"

A moment of silence. "No. We were about to, but we received a call from the FBI, I believe it was. They notified us she was being investigated for contraband of rare and exotic species."

Andi's jaw dropped. Shaking her head, she mouthed, "No. It's not true."

Janelle held her hand up and said, "Thank you, Dr. Hitchens, that's all for today." She ended the call but didn't say anything. For a long moment, she stared at the phone, while Andi just sat there, shocked, speechless.

"Give me another," Janelle said coldly. "Another job you interviewed for."

The following call was the bank. The interviewer said they had received a call advising them Andrea Wilmore was being investigated for workplace theft.

A third place said Andrea Wilmore used them as a reference for a loan before she had actually started working there.

With each call she made, Janelle grew angrier and quieter, while Andi felt her entire world was spinning out of control. Resisting the urge to throw up with increasing difficulty, she sobbed quietly, letting Janelle work, making call after call.

The dental practice said they heard that Andrea was being investigated for credit card fraud. After that call, Janelle set the phone down and clasped Andi's hand. "Girl, look at me."

Andi tried to calm herself down but failed. She was sobbing hard, turning patrons' heads on the patio, making a complete fool of herself. "I didn't do any of these things—" she whimpered.

"I know you didn't."

"Who would want to hurt me so badly?" she asked, barely intelligible.

"No, Andi. The question is this: who *could* hurt you so badly? Who knew you were interviewing at all these places?"

Blood drained from Andi's face while her hands turned cold under the grip of unspeakable fear.

Only one person did.

29

SUSPICION

Andi couldn't recall how she got home after her lunch with Janelle. She must've driven without paying much attention, her instinct being to hide from the world until she could make sense of what was going on.

For a moment, she thought of going to her father's house instead, but it wasn't like her to run away. She'd have to face Craig anyway, and the fewer things she had to explain, the better.

She'd crawled inside the house and, the moment she set foot in the large living room, pain ripped through her abdomen, followed by a wave of nausea so intense she barely made it to the bathroom. She tried to remain standing as she heaved above the sink, but her legs were weak, shaky. Barely holding on to the counter, she let herself slide against the wall until she felt the cold marble under her butt. She dry-heaved a few more times, then everything went dark.

After a while, she came to, shivering from the coldness of the floor tiles. As she got her bearings and tried to stand, she remembered the events of earlier that day and the truths she'd learned. Gasping and wailing as reality hit again, she willed herself to stand and rinse her mouth, then faltered into the bedroom.

She didn't change; there wasn't any strength left in her weary body. Instead, she lay down on the bed, curled up on her side, eyes wide open.

The only one who knew about her interviews was her husband. No one else did, not about all of them. Her father and Janelle had known about the university one, the Ellefsons too, probably everyone at the poker table. But only Craig had known about the bank, about the dental clinic, about the many others. She'd been too embarrassed to share with anyone else how desperate she'd become, enduring failure after failure.

But Craig, doing that to her? It couldn't be.

He loved her.

She believed that with every fiber of her being. He'd become someone so intimately part of who she was, she couldn't conceive he would do anything to hurt her. It was just as unimaginable as the notion of her right hand stabbing her left.

He would never do that to her; he couldn't have. On the contrary, he'd offered to make calls and get her a job with his business contacts or clients or whatever those powerful men were. He'd offered to help her.

She thought of asking him if he was the one spreading lies to prospective employers and, for a moment, imagined how that conversation would take place. Asking him would be so insulting, it would cause irreparable damage and fracture their relationship. He'd feel betrayed, distrusted, and he'd shun her away from his loving heart. Forever.

Suspicion was something terrible. Horror scenarios woven by her overactive brain in layers of terror-instilling imagery, one after another, some logical, others plainly ridiculous, haunted her mind mercilessly. Suspicion, once seeded, could never be removed entirely, not until it met its deathly enemy, certitude.

She had to know. If she couldn't ask, what else could she do? How could she be sure?

Shudders rattled her body. She pulled the covers over her and tried to doze off, but the cramps were back, and soon another wave of sickness followed.

She was still throwing up when she felt Craig's hand on her forehead, holding her head. Startled, she tried to pull away.

"Shh, it's me," he said. Looking up from the sink, she met his warm, loving eyes in the mirror. For a brief moment, she didn't recognize him. The same suspicions that were poisoning her mind had cast a blanket of doubt and fear over everything they had, seeping everywhere and invading like the tides, unstoppable.

Retching turned to sobbing, her shoulders heaved spasmodically as Craig tried to hold her. She writhed free and pulled away. "No, no," she whimpered, holding her hand out to keep him from coming close to her.

Visibly dismayed, Craig stopped, letting his arms fall along his body in a gesture of desperation and abandonment. "What's wrong? This isn't normal. Let's get you to a doctor."

Weak and shivering, she crawled into bed. "No. I'm sure it's nothing, just a stomach bug." One lie inspired another. "You should stay away so you don't catch it."

He touched her feverish, throbbing forehead with a cold, refreshing hand, looking at her with worried eyes. "Let me get you something. Some soup? How's that sound?"

"Uh-uh. I can't hold anything down. I just . . . need to sleep." Closing her eyes, she pulled the covers to her chin and curled on her side.

He stood silently for a while, probably watching her, then dimmed the lights and walked out, closing the door gently behind him.

She opened her eyes.

That was her husband. Loving, gentle, considerate. Making soup, offering to take her to the doctor, saying and doing everything right, the totally awesome man she'd fallen in love with irreparably.

He wasn't some sociopath who would have her interview for jobs for months, only to sabotage her, so she'd—

She'd what? What could he possibly stand to gain from her lack of a career?

The answer to that question hit her in the solar plexus like a pugilist's fist.

"Would you be my copilot?" he'd asked her last Friday, and it wasn't the first time he'd asked her to work with him. No . . . it didn't make sense. Suspicion was a terrible thing. It created monsters that didn't exist, that weren't real. How did she know he didn't offer her to work with him out of pity because no one else would hire her?

Burying her face in her pillow, she let out a whimper. She could've had the job of her dreams, working with Marjorie at the university, finishing her doctoral degree. Only someone had screwed up her life, had robbed her of it.

It couldn't've been Craig. She'd just learned from his parents he liked money, so, if anything, he would've wanted to have more of it. Her salary would've helped the family earn more.

She closed her eyes, willing herself to fall asleep. Through the walls, she could hear Craig making client calls from his office phone, one after another, with superhuman patience. Against his distant voice, another appeared from memory, her father's, saying, "Who knows what your life would've been like if you hadn't met him?"

The memory shuddered her fully awake. Had her father really said those words? Could it be, all this time, he was right, and she was wrong?

If she were to live with that terrible suspicion weighing above her head, she'd lose her mind.

For a while, she breathed, willing waves of nausea away, touching her belly, thinking about her baby. Her pregnancy changed things more than she'd taken the time to acknowledge.

She needed to know. Absolutely, without a shred of a doubt.

And there was only one way she could find out.

In the dim light, she took her phone and did another search for a job in her field. She found one at the Downtown Aquarium. It was for a technician, requesting only two years of college, ideally four. With her advanced degree, she was more than qualified. More important, Craig knew nothing about that job.

She applied for the position quickly, using the résumé she had stored online. Then, with trembling fingers, she changed the passcode to her phone. She picked a random, six-digit code that had nothing to do with important dates in their lives.

A tear streaked her cheek as she set the phone on the nightstand. If the aquarium offered her the job, she'd know.

"I hope to God I'm wrong," she whispered in the silent darkness of the room. "Please, let me be wrong. I can't lose him."

Before she dozed off, the last visual that haunted the increasing darkness overtaking her mind was the image of two boys, running hand in hand, laughing.

30

DRESS

The mid-September day was as torrid as July, the air humid, dusty, and unbreathable. Cutting his workday short, Craig made a detour by the Galleria on his way home. He'd planned a stop at Neiman Marcus to find a dress for Andi. She was a size six, a four if she tried a little, but he was resigned to get a six for her. That belly of hers was swelling, sticking out like a sore thumb through any fabric stretched too tightly on her body. Such a shame.

He parked on the south side of the mall and stopped to grab a bite before shopping. Not necessarily enjoying fast-food chains, he opted for a late, sit-down lunch at The Cheesecake Factory. Their chicken piccata was decent.

He was still waiting for his check when he saw a tall blonde ambling toward the exit. She was everything he wanted Andi to become. Classy, refined, reeking of big bucks and expensive, well, everything. A tight little ass barely covered by a red stretch miniskirt. Perfect breasts poking through the delicate, semitransparent fabric of her white blouse.

Her stilettos were Louboutins, the exact model he wanted to get Andi for her birthday, black patent with red-accented open toes and red soles. They carried them at Neiman Marcus. He might as well pick those up too, as long as he was here.

The woman's hair was lusciously slick, mid-back length, with fine highlights and lowlights to give it dimension. It waved like strands of pure silk as she strolled by, swaying her hips on those four-inch heels, firing up his imagination. How would it feel to have that wave of silk touch his hard, naked body?

Something stirred below his belt. He cursed under his breath, then took a sip of ice-cold water, still looking at the woman's long legs as she was about to exit the mall. She was carrying a shopping bag with the Versace Medusa on it.

That's where he needed to shop for Andi's dress. Forget Neiman Marcus.

That was an inspired decision.

Versace had exactly what he was looking for. A black, sleeveless minidress with a generous, deep cleavage and gold accents. About thirty minutes later, he was home, happy to discover Andi was on her feet, looking a little better than the day before.

"Hey," she greeted him when he walked through the door. "You're early." She smiled from the kitchen sink, where she was loading the dishwasher.

"And I come bearing gifts for my beautiful wife," he announced, holding out the Versace shopping bag for her.

Wiping her hands in a hurry, she grabbed the bag and extracted the dress. "Oh, wow, Craig, this is . . . incredible." She shot him a long glance that made him frown a little. There was an unspoken question in her eyes, a wariness he didn't like one bit. "Shoes too," she added, pulling out the box bearing the cursive Louboutin logo.

"Would you try it on for me?" He sat in an armchair and rested his elbows on the sides, steepling his fingers.

Andi tilted her head playfully. "You'd like that, wouldn't you?"

"Very much," he whispered, his voice throaty, loaded with desire.

She disappeared into the bedroom with the dress and the shoes and left him waiting for a few long minutes. When she finally walked out of there, his breath caught.

Sexy as fuck. Bloody perfect.

Her phone chimed. She shot the screen a quick glance, then smiled for him, turning around slowly, making her long amethyst earrings jingle quietly. "What do you think?" She bit her lower lip deliberately, driving him insane. "Is this short enough for you? Or should I add a belt?"

"Uh-huh," he replied, struggling to stay put in his chair when he craved to take her with every heated fiber of his body. "A belt would be nice." Every single one of the eleven men who had RSVPed for the next party would have a hard-on, but that sensual prom queen was only his to fuck.

She raised her arms above her head in an elaborate pose, veering her eyes to the side, a hint of a strange smile on her lips. Her skirt lifted with her move, exposing a little bit more of her thighs.

"Turn around slowly," he whispered, licking his lips.

She obeyed, still looking away, seemingly lost in thought. Where was her mind wandering again? What was going on in that skull of hers? She'd managed to ruin the moment more effectively than an ice bucket challenge.

Frustrated, he let out a long sigh. "Who was that message from?" he asked, his voice normal, not a trace of arousal left.

Her arms dropped as if she were a puppet whose strings had been cut. "What message?"

"Just now. Your phone chimed."

"Ah . . . that was Janelle. She wants us to go on a girls' night out next week on Thursday."

The mention of that name had him clenching his jaws and grinding his teeth. Screw Janelle.

"Don't worry," she replied with sweetness in her voice. "I already told her I can't. That's when we have the next party, right?"

"Yes." He smiled widely. She was learning her priorities, her place. The hair would take a while to grow and fix to look just right, but he still wanted to have her on her knees, right there in front of the armchair, looking up at him as she undid his belt.

Reaching for her, he whispered, "Come here." She didn't move. She remained standing a few feet away, a strange expression on her face. "What's on your mind?"

She kicked off her heels and sat in another armchair, then crossed her legs quickly, not a *Basic Instinct* kind of move but rather a college-dorm vibe. Cold. Practical. Asexual. "If I get a job in my field at the San Diego Scripps Institution of Oceanography, would you consider relocating?"

He nearly choked. *Damn restlessness . . . What was it with this woman? When was it going to end?* "And start over with real estate in California?" He managed to sound normal, balanced, his voice conveying nothing of the rage he felt bubbling inside.

Andi smiled. "Bigger home values, bigger commissions."

"Huh . . . that's true." He frowned, considering the unexpected idea and failing to find much of a downside. First of all, that annoying little bitch, Janelle, and Andi's asshole father, would be left in the rearview mirror. Of course, he'd have to start all over again, find the California Donatis and Hasketts, but he'd done it once. Sure as hell, he could do it again. The only question was, would Jude consider moving? Because without him, nothing made sense. He definitely had the money to start them up on the West Coast, but would he?

He looked at Andi, studying her face. She didn't appear to have landed the San Diego job yet; her question didn't carry the urgency that would've come with that. She was calm and relaxed, yet also distant a little, almost apprehensive. That made no sense at all. Maybe it was all this pregnancy nonsense. Based on what he'd read on the internet about women in their first trimester, it was a miracle the human species had survived. Women turned into absolute zombies, a mess of hormones and mood swings and all sorts of unsightly things like drooping boobs, water retention, and weight gain. *Fuck.*

California. Might be a good idea.

He leaned forward, smiling. "If that would make you happy, I'd do it. I'd do anything for you." How the hell didn't he think of California and its soaring real estate market before? Jude would be so thrilled. But first, Craig had something else he wanted to do.

He stood and walked over to her slowly, undressing her with his eyes, watching her reactions to see if the fire he was starting was spreading out. She responded, a little slower than usual, but she took his hand and stood, welcoming his embrace, kissing his lips passionately, moaning with every breath. A rebel tear inexplicably found her cheek, but she didn't push him away, didn't stop kissing him, eagerly undoing his shirt buttons with cold, trembling fingers.

Gently, inch by inch, he pulled down the zipper at the back of her dress and peeled it off his gorgeous wife's body as he would've unwrapped an extravagant gift tied with a sumptuous silk bow.

District Attorney Buscher: When was the last time you saw your daughter?

Dr. Hunter Wilmore: On October seven. It was a Thursday.

District Attorney Buscher: And where was that?

Dr. Hunter Wilmore: At the Cardiac Rehabilitation Center, where I've been staying since my heart attack. She came to see me. She used to come almost every day.

District Attorney Buscher: Did Andrea Wilmore Brafford mention anything out of the ordinary?

Dr. Hunter Wilmore: No. She was feeling ill, though. She was pale; her hands were shaking.

31

CERTITUDE

About a week later, Andi heard back from the aquarium recruiter. She was invited to come in to sign her employment forms. If her background and credit checked out, she was hired. The offer was attached to the email, and they'd appreciate a signature in the following forty-eight hours.

At first, she read the message and didn't really comprehend it. She understood the words, their meaning, but not all that it meant for her. She got the job. They were excited to welcome her onboard and had every confidence she'd make a fine addition to the Downtown Aquarium team.

Then it sunk in, knocking the air out of her lungs. She let out disarticulate sounds then broke into heart-wrenching sobs. She got the job . . . the only job Craig had no idea she'd applied to.

She'd interviewed in complete secrecy, lying to him and telling him she was going shopping or to visit her father. All the emails from them she immediately archived into a folder she'd created, aptly named Coupons and Offers. Craig would've never looked in there. All the time that had passed since she'd applied for the aquarium job, every single day, she'd wished she'd fail the interview, knowing that if she got the job, it would bring the certitude she feared so much.

Her sobs subsided when a novel idea crossed her mind. Maybe the test she'd set up to find out if Craig was to blame for her failed job search wasn't that certain. Absence of evidence doesn't constitute evidence of absence. Andi remembered the aphorism she'd learned in school. The fact remained, she still didn't know for sure, one way or the other.

What if the aquarium job offer was nothing but a coincidence, destiny's way to mess with her, to pull a painful prank? All the articles she'd read about finding a job spoke of three to six months duration and how securing a job was an exercise in patience and a game of numbers. She'd been at it for months, but what if the aquarium was just meant to happen? The fact that Craig had no idea about it didn't absolutely mean he was the one who had been sabotaging her. Could be a coincidence.

She needed it to be a coincidence.

The unsettling email had found her rinsing her mouth after yet another bout of vomiting, so bad it had left her gasping for air and wondering why on earth was it called morning sickness when it was four in the afternoon, and it wasn't stopping already?

Now she washed her tear-streaked face, splashing cold water repeatedly to reduce the swelling and redness. It was Wednesday, the day before another one of Craig's parties, and she just couldn't bring herself to go through it anymore, when all she wanted to do was scream and ask him, once and for all, "Did you do this to me? Did you?"

In her imagination, she saw herself asking him that loaded question, but that's where it all stopped. She didn't see what he would answer or what came after the most-feared answer. Aimlessly wandering through the house, touching up details here and there in preparation for tomorrow's event, she abandoned herself to the thoughts that had been filling her nights with nightmares and her days with bitter anxiety.

How she wished she could ask someone what to do . . . but her father and all his friends were off limits. Her dad already hated Craig; telling him any of that would probably kill him. She considered calling Rebecca; she was like a mother to Andi and would've gladly helped. Phone in hand, she retrieved Rebecca's number but then cancelled the call and locked the screen. She couldn't bring herself to smear Craig's reputation with her suspicions . . . it wasn't something people easily forgot if she would be proven wrong.

Dusting off the corals on the mantle with a feather duster, an idea started to form, a plan that might just work to prove, beyond any trace of a doubt, if Craig had made those calls. For that, she needed to be what she never could be. A good actor. A politician, saying one thing when she meant another.

She'd always been annoyingly direct, her candor touching on bluntness without the malicious component, just a direct output of an honest, sincere, and uncensored mind. A little naïve, in her opinion, immature even. Lacking the refinement of career politicians, Andi knew she belonged with the world of scholars and researchers, where her communication skills were perceived as adequate and clean of any unnecessary fogginess. Now, she wished more than anything to be able to answer questions without saying anything, to deliver an entire evening of platitudes and small talk, to question Craig without actually doing it, to lie to him and act like nothing was wrong, at least until she could find the proof she was looking for.

She changed and applied a bit of makeup to hide her pallor and the black circles under her swollen eyes. She put on a light summer dress, one that Craig liked, and did her best not to think about what she would have to do if he was the one who had robbed her of her opportunities.

She'd lose him. She would have to leave. They, as a couple, would cease to exist.

Forcing some air into her lungs quickly to fight back the tears, she put on the blue pendant and looked at the stranger in the mirror. Perhaps she had it in her to play the part, to lie and deceive the man she loved. Most likely, all women did.

Looking straight into the reflection of her blue eyes, she steeled herself, second by second, until she was certain she was up for the task. It was just going to be for a few hours; it wasn't going to kill her.

Then she waited.

When Craig returned from work, he found her dusting off the bookshelves in the living room, dressed in that summer frock and wearing kitten-heel white sandals, projecting the image of the perfect wife, Stepford style. Craig's dream.

A wave of nausea hit her when he walked through the door, but she resisted it with a sharp breath and a smile. Then she made her way to the fridge and downed half a glass of cold, sparkling water. "How was your day?"

"Average," he replied, looking at her from head to toe with an appreciative smile. "Not every day I can pull off a whale of a deal, you know." He smiled awkwardly, almost apologetically. "Most days, I deal with undecided assholes who want too much house for the money they've got. Oh, and dealing with Hughes, the biggest asshole of them all."

"Is he still giving you crap?"

"Not lately," Craig replied, loosening the knot of his tie and removing it. She took it from his hand and waited for the rest of his attire to hang in the closet. The shirt came off next, then the pants. Andi stared at the familiar, athletic body and found it foreign, its nakedness obscene.

"Get me some shorts, babe, all right?" he asked, taking his shoes to the closet rack in his briefs.

"Sure," she replied without turning her head, right before entering the bathroom. She couldn't wait anymore; she had to know.

She emerged with a clean T-shirt and a pair of casual shorts a few moments later but hesitated before handing them over. "Why don't you take a shower first? You'd feel better. It's muggy out there." She tilted her head a little. "Take your time in there. You deserve it."

He looked at her for a moment. She held his gaze unflinchingly. Pasting a fake smile on her lips did the trick.

"Good idea." He took the clothes from her and disappeared into the bathroom. A moment later, she heard the water running in the shower.

She had about ten minutes, maybe longer. Sometimes he liked to spend a lot of time under the water jets, alternating cold and hot water until he felt refreshed.

His phone was on the counter, next to the keys to the Benz. She knew his passcode and unlocked it quickly, then went to check the list of recent calls. There were hundreds . . . Craig spent most of his time on the phone, dialing out, but she believed that somewhere in that endless list of numbers, there could be some that didn't belong. The number to the Department of Marine Biology at the university. The number from a bank where they didn't have any accounts, but Andi had interviewed for a teller job. The number from a dental practice they didn't use, the one that had interviewed her for a receptionist role.

There wasn't enough time to search. Instead, Andi started taking photos of his recent calls, one screen after another until she had scrolled to the end of the list, then locked his phone and put it back on the counter where she'd found it.

In the safety of the kitchen, while she kept her ear trained on the noises coming from the shower, she reviewed the images looking for numbers she recognized. She didn't find the number from the university, but the dental clinic was there, and so was the Brisbane Corporation, the company where she'd interviewed for a customer service role about a month ago.

It was there, staring her in the face, the killer of all suspicion.

Certainty.

The bringer of endless heartbreak.

She'd been held hostage, captive behind the brick walls of an oversized suburban mansion, to clean house and play high-end host for his business guests.

There was no denying it anymore, no matter how dearly she wished it wasn't true.

When Craig came out of the shower, his wet hair combed back but parting randomly under its own weight, he found her dressed in jeans and an old Bon Jovi T-shirt. The sandals were gone, in their stead her favorite Reeboks, and right next to her feet, a small go-bag filled with what little she really thought was hers.

The moment he saw her, he stopped in the doorway, frozen. "What's going on?"

She stood and placed the blue pendant in his hand.

"I want a divorce."

32

STAYING

Walking to the door took every bit of strength Andi had left. Each step had a finality to it, harder to take than the step before it as if she was tethered to Craig with an elastic band that refused to snap. Instead, it extended, taut, and the more it stretched, the harder it was to step forward.

"Andi," he called, and her step faltered. A few more, and she'd reach the garage. Then the car. Then, she'd finally leave. "Please don't go."

She wished she could block him out somehow, to not see or hear him until she'd had the stamina to complete the excruciating action she was about to.

Leaving Craig.

Only two weeks ago, it would have seemed impossible. No, completely insane. Earlier that morning, Andi still didn't believe it could be true. Captive in the merciless claws of anxiety, while waiting to find out for sure, she'd immersed herself in countless scenarios, trying to find excuses for him, ways in which he wasn't responsible.

Then, she'd moved on to invent ways in which she could diminish the importance of what he'd done. Fabricating excuses. Rationalizing the inconceivable. After all, it wasn't so bad to stay home and enjoy a carefree life, right? Well, maybe for other women, but not for her. She was a scientist, months away from becoming a doctor in marine biology, an expert in her field. He'd not only robbed her of a career, but of her self-esteem, and the fruit of all the years she'd spent studying for her profession. Her entire view of the world she lived in was tainted by what he'd done.

"Could you at least tell me why?" he called after her.

There was a tinge of deep sadness, of despair in his voice that froze her in her tracks. Her heart still resonated to the inflections in his voice.

She turned slowly, breathing heavily, afraid she was going to faint. A wave of weakness washed over her body the moment she stopped and looked at him. Still wet, wearing a towel around his hips and not minding the droplets pooling on the hardwood, he stood in the middle of the living room, vulnerable and defeated. An expression of complete confusion was written on his face, in the agape mouth, in the raised eyebrows, in his pleading gaze.

He deserved an explanation . . . or did he? Perhaps *she* deserved to know why, and that curiosity smoldered in every recess of her mind. It couldn't all have been about his stupid parties . . . it was impossible. Nonsensical.

Seeming too heavy to hold anymore, she let the go-bag hit the floor with a thud.

"I know what you've done, Craig."

"What are you talking about?" He took two steps toward her, but she put her hand up, and he stopped. "Please, baby, tell me what you think I've done."

"I'm not your baby anymore," she whispered, her voice tinged with sadness and anger. She would've slapped him across the face, shouting, "How could you?" But that wasn't who she was.

Her tears had dried, replaced by cold determination. She and Craig, they were over. The love story, the romance, the marriage—all gone. All that was left behind was scorched earth, scarred and contaminated, forever arid. How could she ever trust anyone again after that?

"What have I done? Would you please tell me?" he whispered. "I'll do anything—"

"There's nothing you can do, Craig. You've done enough." She scoffed bitterly. "More than your share."

"What are you talking about? You're scaring me."

Her lips quivered before she spoke. "I know you called all the places where I interviewed, spreading lies about me." She could barely stand looking at him. Her chest felt as if a heavy burden was crushing it. "The university, Craig? That place is like a home to me, like a second family. Can you imagine, all those people I know and respect and love, what they must be thinking about me now?" She sniffled and wiped a tear from the corner of her eyes with an angry gesture. "How could you? How will I ever show my face there again?" She breathed, shattered, shallow breaths that struggled to keep her rage locked inside. "You . . . *killed* me! All that I've worked for, all my dreams, you destroyed everything. Why?"

His shoulders hunched forward, he let his head hang low. "Yes, I did all that," he muttered. "I am so sorry . . . you have no idea how much I regret—"

"What? Getting caught?" She started pacing the room angrily, the adrenaline injecting some energy into her weakened body. "You were relentless, Craig. You didn't miss a single one of these places and told a different lie each time." Bile rose in the back of her throat, threatening her with another spell of sickness. "You're creative, I'll give you that, but in the most despicable way I thought possible."

"Please, forgive me," he whispered, looking at her with pleading eyes.

Not even then, he wasn't giving her a straight answer. Once a liar.

"I believe you wanted a hostess for your parties and, had I found a job, the role you had envisioned for me in your little real estate business would've been jeopardized."

He propped his hands on his hips and turned sideways in a gesture of frustration. "Is that what you think? *Screw* my real estate business," he shouted. "The hell with it all."

Andi stared at him in disbelief. It wasn't like him to raise his voice. But, then again, who was this man, and what did she really know about him? Did the Craig she'd fallen in love with even exist?

"I'll cancel Thursday," he said, taking another couple of steps toward her until she glared at him, making him keep his distance. "I'll change jobs. I'll go into whatever line of work you'd like me to, only don't leave me. Everything I've been trying to do has been for you."

She scoffed. "Are you kidding me?"

"This house, our life in the suburbs, the lifestyle, it's all been about you. For you."

Doubt, fueled by her wish to make it real and the love she believed she saw in his eyes, started to worm its way inside her mind. What if he was telling the truth?

"Think about it . . . when you met me, I was content to live in that apartment building with almost no furniture. I was no one, had nothing, and didn't care." He clasped his hands together, silently begging her to believe him. "Until I met you."

If she forced herself to believe him again and discovered it was all a lie, she'd never be the same. She'd never recover. And still, walking away from the love of her life was nearly impossible to do under the weight of all that doubt.

"If it was all about me, why keep me from working? Why sabotage my job at the university? And all the rest?"

He lowered his eyes. "I already told you . . . I was nothing, a nobody. You would've been immensely successful in anything you would've done. Then you would've discarded me at the curb, like old furniture no one needs anymore." He paused for a moment. "I didn't want to lose you . . . still don't. I'd do anything to make you stay."

Seemingly innocent words resounded badly in her mind. "*Make* me?" she said, raising her eyebrow.

"Convince you." He clenched his jaws for a brief moment. "Bad choice of words."

Or Freudian slip, she thought, but the ice she'd built around her heart to be able to leave him was still melting away.

"Let me whisk you away on vacation," he said, taking her by surprise. "Let's cancel Thursday and just go. Wherever you want. The Caribbean, Bahamas, wherever. Just say the word."

She let out a long sigh that melted whatever ice was left. Marriages needed work, lots of work. He wasn't the shouting or abusive type, he didn't drink, didn't cheat on her. He was just insecure, nothing more, and had made a mistake. Craig had run away from home at sixteen, and had struggled to make something of himself, while she had a family, a father who laid everything in front of her. A house and food on the table while she went to college, got her advanced degree, then started doctoral work. While he . . . had no one. Until her.

Maybe he deserved another chance.

"If you ever lie to me again, I'll be gone on the spot. Just gone. I won't explain it and won't talk to you anymore."

He took a step closer. "Yes, that's fair." He smiled shyly, his lower lip quivering slightly, his eyes glistening with tears. "Should I book us those plane tickets? Where would you like us to go?"

"I'm not done," she said, her voice still cold, factual. "We'll do the Thursday party, then we'll leave. On Saturday, so you have time for your follow-up calls. You've worked hard for it."

"Oh, Andi," he murmured, taking her hand to his lips. "You're the most incredible woman in the world. Will you ever forgive me?"

Her breath caught. It was a complicated question. Could she? Was it even possible? She didn't know . . . she hoped she could, but there was no telling what the passing of time would do to them. Their marriage was barely holding on, frail and unraveling, blown to shreds by the hurricane-strength winds of adversity and deceit. "I don't know. We'll work on that, one day at a time."

"That's all I need," he said softly, kissing her hand. "That and your preferred vacation destination, my wonderful lady."

Was she ready to spend a week alone with him? Lying in his arms, making love to him, while the ugliness of his lies, the uncertainty of her future still weighed so heavily in her heart? But successful marriages were hard work. Walking away was hard, complicated, heart-wrenching. Staying was much harder. The life growing inside her gave her little choice.

"The Caribbean," she replied calmly once her decision was made. "Montego Bay. One week, not longer. I'm starting a new job."

33

KEEPER

The entire week had been one of extremes, giving Craig whiplash from all the sudden turns and near disasters. Tired and feeling it in his bones, he rubbed the back of his neck while listening to the driveway chatter of one of his business guests.

He called it driveway chatter because that's when some guests seemed to become the most engaged, sharing one more story, one more joke, or remark before they finally left. That was an indication they had enjoyed the party and would remember him the following morning, when he was going to reach out and close whatever deal he could.

Thrilled with the party's success, he counted the wins in his mind while the chatty guest, a telecommunications CEO by the name of Virgil Eastland, talked and talked and talked. He pretended not to notice Eastland's libidinous gaze plunging deep into Andi's cleavage or running up and down her legs. Those were some fine legs . . . it wasn't the man's fault.

Eleven power couples had shown up. Three were Donati's referrals. Craig had been losing sleep lately, wondering what Donati was expecting from him in return. Did he want kickbacks? Highly unlikely . . . he had more money than he knew what to do with, and he would probably be insulted by any amount Craig could afford to give him. But Craig didn't know what he wanted, and that made him antsy, triggering his insecurities. He couldn't ask him either; it would be a terrible faux pas. At least that much he knew.

Out of the eleven, four had promised to make him the preferred Realtor for their companies, and that included access to all their employees living in the Houston area, if Craig were to shave one, maybe one-and-a-half percentage points off his commission. That meant a pipeline of deals just raining in his lap, effortlessly, for years to come. Of course, that was worth the discount.

Hughes was so thrilled with how the evening went, he offered Craig an upgrade to business class for their upcoming travel to the Caribbean. Andi would love that for sure. Who didn't?

The valet finally pulled Eastland's Land Rover onto the circular driveway. Regretting it visibly, Eastland peeled his eyeballs off Andi's legs and climbed behind the wheel. His wife, pale and tense and throwing hateful darts with her eyes, took the passenger seat without so much as a wave goodbye. That wasn't good. Andi might've made too much of an impression. After all, it was the wives who called the shots, and, by the looks of it, Mrs. Eastland would do anything in her power to make sure her husband never spoke with the Braffords again. With the Eastlands, he most probably had failed; he'd burned a damn good lead by pushing things too far.

Only Hughes was left, once the Land Rover drove off, and he had mouthfuls of excitement to share. Andi apologized and went inside, and Hughes watched her swaying hips until she disappeared from sight. The Versace dress barely covered her butt. He didn't remember it being so short, but she'd been fabulous all night, making him proud. Wearing the Louboutins, she was at least two inches taller than him, but he didn't mind. Many successful people married supermodels who dwarfed them. But Andi was more than her looks. She knew how to work a room, spreading smiles and banalities and delicious hors d'oeuvres to all the guests, making everyone feel welcome. His girl had style, something extremely rare. She had breeding, just like Jude. It was in her blood, the way she related to wealthy people as an equal. One could tell she came from money.

"She's a keeper, this one," Hughes said, still looking at Andi's departing behind. "Not like the other one, if you don't mind me saying."

"The other one?"

"I met your former girlfriend at the Christmas party a couple of years ago. The tall, skinny brunette?"

"Ah, yes." He grinned and winked. "I've already forgotten about her."

"I can understand why." Hughes grinned and patted his breast pocket as if to make sure the thick envelope Craig had given him earlier was still there. "Keep doing what you're doing, son. You got the goods." He squeezed his shoulder, then climbed into his SUV and drove off, with Mrs. Hughes by his side. In her case, things had gone much better, Mrs. Hughes had been eager to help Andi with serving the guests and offering enough unsolicited advice to make him want to shoot her.

Drained, he paid the neighbor's kid generously and sent him on his way, then went inside, closing the door behind him and locking it with the deadbolt.

With the clunking lock, his face dropped. He'd managed to survive the evening, although he'd been tense, worried that Andi might snap, still raw after their conversation the day before. None of that bullshit still lingered . . . she'd been wonderful.

But . . . divorce? That still lingered with him. What the heck? Was she bloody insane?

That would mean the end of him, of everything he was and could ever be. She'd get half of everything he owned, their house, even half of his share of the Timber Hill property because Jude had been an immense idiot and had put it in both their names. Two million dollars . . . a quarter of that, what she stood to get, was five hundred thousand, and that was only one house. He could take her to court, in theory, with money he didn't have, and risk exposing their shady deal just to avoid that. Or Jude could sell the property right away, raising all sorts of red flags with Haskett and losing a ton of dough.

Hell no . . . no way she was going to divorce him. He had to make sure of that.

For now, he could breathe with a little bit of ease. The difficult evening was finally over, and on Saturday, they were leaving for a week's worth of beach time and making her fall in love with him all over again. He could definitely do that.

Yes, Hughes was right. She was a keeper.

Forever.

District Attorney Buscher: What do you think was the victim's role at the defendant's business parties?

Janelle Larimer: He was dangling her in front of his clients like a piece of meat. He liked how everyone looked at him when she took his arm, when they showed up together somewhere.

District Attorney Buscher: To your knowledge, was Andrea Wilmore Brafford aware of it?

Janelle Larimer: Yes. She was sad about it. She thought Craig was strong enough professionally not to need such tactics. She desperately wished she could become more than a wife people envied Craig for. More than his possession, his arm candy. She felt used. Pimped out to make those people use his services.

Defense Attorney Goodridge: Objection, Your Honor. Hearsay.

34

PARADISE

It was a north-facing beach with shimmering white sands and slow-moving waves. Everything about that place was peaceful, relaxing. The smell of the ocean was so fragrant Andi had abandoned the tall virgin Margarita on the side table by her white wicker lounge chair and had immersed herself in the surrounding nature, one lungful of salty sea air at a time.

Somewhere behind the tall palm trees lining the beach, the rising moon was starting to show, its weak rays getting stronger, peeking between the leaves. Listening intently, she followed the sound of the rustling palm leaves for a moment, her eyes closed, knowing she wanted to hold on to that sound forever.

Craig had rented them a cabin right on the water. From the bedroom door, she could climb down a few steps straight into the warm Caribbean waters. Since they'd arrived on Saturday night, she'd loved every moment of her time there. She even felt better, her nausea almost completely gone, the searing pain that sometimes ripped through her belly forgotten. She'd probably needed some rest.

Reaching out for the sweaty Margarita glass, she took a sip, noticing the ice cubes had long time melted. The virgin version of the drink was tasty but lacked the alcohol buzz. She didn't regret it, though; her baby's health came first. She just didn't find herself all that into virgin cocktails.

"Let's get you another one," Craig offered, raising his hand and snapping his fingers to get the server's attention. Within seconds, a young girl wearing a red bikini top and a short, ruffled white skirt that didn't completely cover her butt appeared by their side.

"What can I get you?"

"Another virgin Margarita for my—"

"Actually, let's switch to apple juice if you have it," Andi said, smiling as she looked at the girl. She couldn't've been more than twenty years old. Her long hair, tied in a loose ponytail, hung over her right shoulder. A white hibiscus flower adorned her left ear, Hawaiian style.

"Just . . . apple juice?"

Andi's smile widened. She was craving it, cold and sweaty. "Make that on the rocks, please."

The girl nodded and turned to Craig.

"And another beer for me, as cold as you can find it."

"You got it." She headed toward the tiki bar with a playful sway in her hips. She looked at Craig, but he wasn't looking at the girl; he'd turned his attention to the sea.

Every moment of every day since they'd left Houston, he'd been incredible. The trip felt like a second honeymoon, soothing her wounded heart, appeasing her fears. She loved him enough to desperately want to forgive and forget. Although she was usually rational about everything in her life, deciding with her brain rather than her feelings, she found herself shying away from the memory of what Craig had done, like fingers jolting back after touching a burning stove.

Thinking about what he'd done was unbearable.

Being next to him was also unbearable, and at the same time, intoxicating.

The night they arrived, she had pointed at the small couch in their cabin living room and had chosen to sleep alone in the lush linens of the king-size bed. He accepted it without argument, just a tinge of sadness in his subdued smile and a lowered glance.

She felt as if she was kicking a wounded dog. Guilty. Ashamed. Vindictive.

Somehow, for three exquisite days, she'd turned into the bad guy, while Craig had been nothing short of a wonderful, loving, and patient man, the man she remembered from before her life had been turned into hell.

She was falling in love with him all over again. She wanted to believe in a future with him. Maybe wanting it hard enough would make it real.

Eyes half-closed, she took the glass filled to the brim with crystalline apple juice from the server's hand and thanked her. Shaking it gently, she listened to the ice cubes sloshing in the fluid, clinking softly as they hit the glass.

"This is my paradise, you know," she whispered, looking at the stars reflected in the calm ocean surface. "Lower case P, that is."

Craig took a sip of beer and looked at her inquisitively. "What do you mean?"

"I mean, paradise, but not in a biblical sense. Not *the* Paradise, but a similar place, here on earth, where you get to visit without having to die first."

"I see what you mean." He smiled.

For a moment, she imagined his lips touching her heated skin, lighting a fire deep inside her body. Her cheeks flushed, and she looked away. Craig's time sleeping on the sofa was over.

"Of course, I'd probably have a real Margarita in my hand if I had a choice." She chuckled. "Yeah . . . that's my own personal paradise. The Caribbean, lounging by the sea, Margarita in hand. So many times, I've dreamed of it, and it looked just like this. White sands, moonlight, green waves lapping the shores. Paradise."

He shifted in the lounge chair so he could face her without turning his head. "What's with you and words? Lowercase letters, word games, puns—"

"That comes from Rebecca." She took a sip of refreshing juice. It was perfect, fragrant, and sweet. "She instilled the love of language in me."

"Then, why not go for an English lit degree?"

"I love the ocean more." The simple statement made her chest swell. "Turtles and dolphins and whales and all. You have to admit, it sounds just a little bit more interesting than English lit."

"I bet it does," he chuckled. "I'll make sure you get to visit it as many times as you'd like."

A cloud washed over her face. His words had snapped her right back into reality, too soon, before she was strong enough for it. A chill touched her skin, raising goosebumps. She rubbed her arms with her hands. "Yes, about that," she said, straightening herself on the chair. "We need to set some terms if we are to have any future together."

He abandoned his beer and sat on the edge of the lounge chair, steepling his hands in his lap. "I'm listening."

"I'm proposing a new alliance," she added, softening the tone of her voice. "I get whatever job I like, and if I don't have the time to cook for your parties, we'll hire caterers and housekeepers."

"Done," he said quickly.

"Even if that job is in San Diego. I always wanted to work with sea lions."

He didn't flinch. "Just say the word, and I'll get us moved over there."

She nodded, appreciative of his enthusiasm. A distant, unwanted thought made her wonder if that was real, the enthusiasm, his determination to make a change in their lives. She was about to find out. "I'd like your parents to become a part of our lives."

"Andi . . ."

"Please," she insisted, her hand touching her belly. "Our baby deserves all the grandparents we have available, don't you think?" She was almost two months into her pregnancy; soon it would start to show.

"But we're not speaking anymore. We—"

"It's important for me, Craig. Please try. It would make me happy, and I'm sure it will eventually make you feel better too."

She could almost hear him grinding his teeth.

He lowered his eyes to hide the glint of frustration in them. "Okay, you got it." His voice was tense, raspy. "Anything else?"

"And a girls' night out every week, for Janelle and me." She'd instilled humor in her voice, hoping it would soothe Craig's ego.

A lopsided smile tugged at the corners of his lips. "Okay, just as long as you don't bring some handsome guy home with you." The smile didn't touch his eyes. Those bloody insecurities of his were surfacing again.

"I already have a handsome guy. Don't need another one."

"Then we're set. You and Janelle will go out for a fun night in town while I'll stay home and work. Or endlessly argue with my parents to make you happy."

She chuckled. The first was probably true; he would work.

A long moment of silence captured the tense space between them. The rhythmical sound of waves washing the shore resonated with her heartbeat. Upheaval. Restlessness. Danger lurking beyond the surface.

"Do you think we still have a chance?" she asked, playing with her pendant. "You and me?"

His lips tensed for a brief moment. "I hope we do. I'll do my part and root for us with every fiber of my being." He took a swig of beer and swallowed it thirstily with a loud breath. "What do you want to do tomorrow?"

She lit up. "You have to ask?"

He rolled his eyes jokingly. "Smell some turtle gunk somewhere?"

"Let's go scuba diving tomorrow. I found a place that would take us on a boat out to the coral banks. I'm hoping to see some seahorses. Maybe I can show you a lionfish." She made a hissing sound and a hand gesture. "Right before we kill it with a spear." He stared at her in disbelief. "They're invasive and venomous. We're supposed to kill them."

"Okay," he replied cautiously. "Got me worried there for a moment. Thought you might've become a killer or something." She laughed. "Can I stay in the boat this time?"

"Sure, no problem," she replied lightheartedly, hiding the sadness she felt. He wasn't interested in exploring her world with her, in accepting what she had to offer as a gift. Seeing the ocean landscape below the surface was a transformational experience, the beauty and serenity of it unique and memorable, a real fantasy world. Yet he'd said no, and she would go alone. Her excitement waned.

She listened to the waves for another moment, then looked at Craig and asked, touching her pendant, "Where did you get this from?"

35

NORMAL

Visiting her dad was the first priority after returning from the Caribbean, yet Andi had struggled to leave the house. Her morning sickness was back with a vengeance, bouts of nausea preceded by searing pain ripping through her stomach, leaving her breathless, a shapeless clump on whatever floor the attack happened to find her. It was as if Houston was bad for her baby somehow. Maybe it was the stress that inevitably came with her returning home, the realities of their marriage still haunting her. Craig had suggested her scuba diving could've been a factor, but she knew that wasn't the case. She'd been careful; only dove to about ten feet, moved slowly, carefully watching her oxygen mix.

Soon it would be over with the stupid barfing, she told herself as she pulled into the parking lot at the Cardiac Rehabilitation Center. She was coming up on two months; two-thirds of the dreaded first trimester were already gone. *I'll have to tell Dad one of these days.*

Thinking of his reaction brought a heavy weight to her chest. He wasn't going to take it well, his dislike for Craig getting in the way of him enjoying his first grandchild. But could she really blame her father, now that she knew what Craig had done? Perhaps older folk were wiser after all, seeing things she didn't see, not then, when she'd fallen for him, not even now, when she was supposed to be smarter about all things Craig. She was still blinded by her feelings for him.

She signed the visitors' log at the main entrance. "Good morning," she greeted the receptionist, a tall and scrawny blonde who barely took her eyes off her phone to see who was entering the building. Good thing people were generally honest, and rarely anyone visited rehab centers with malicious intent.

"Good morning, Ms. Wilmore," the blonde replied, surprising her a little. She'd visited her father almost every day since the three-story rehab center had become his temporary residence, but she didn't expect to be recognized. The woman lowered her eyes to the phone in her hand and said, "He'll be out back at this hour, trying to sneak a cigar puff past the orderlies. But you can wait here, and I'll send someone—"

Andi chuckled. "Thank you. I'll go find him." It seemed the receptionist was paying more attention to what was going on than Andi had given her credit for.

Crossing the gleaming tile floor to the back exit, Andi noticed in passing several other residents looking out the window from the comfort of their chairs. It was a beautiful October morning. The air was crisp and filled with the promise of fall foliage turning and just a touch of dew that clung to grass blades and low shrubs. The perfect time to spend out there, on the sun-filled patio, yet they chose to remain indoors, defeated, lifeless.

Not her father. He was a fighter. He wasn't ready to give it all up and wait for death's call in a wheelchair behind a window. He made her proud.

The patio was large, overlooking a three-acre yard that was landscaped to perfection. Narrow, smooth asphalt paths followed the shape of the landscaping, the occasional bench under the crown of a secular tree the perfect spot to stop and rest in the shade.

Her father had chosen a different area, though. He'd withdrawn to the far right of the yard, between two rows of four-foot-tall shrubs, where only his white hair was visible to any passing orderly. Not the hand that held the cigar responsible for the bluish clouds of smoke that seemed to emanate from the foliage, barely discernable before disintegrating into the morning breeze. From where he was, the yard backed into a stretch of forest, part of a large park; at least from that side, no one could surprise him and take away his smokes.

Andi approached with a spring in her step. "You cheater," she said, keeping her voice low. Cheater or not, she wasn't going to draw the orderlies' attention to him.

His face beamed when he saw her, then a frown set a couple of lines across his brow. "I'm not cheating," he said quickly, hiding the cigar behind his back like a schoolchild. "It's my right, you know."

"But should you be smoking, really?" She raised an eyebrow and looked straight into his eyes.

"I'm not inhaling, just playing with the smoke," he said, then quickly demonstrated as if she had no idea how cigars were meant to be smoked. "See? It's all gone. Poof."

She reached down and hugged him, then placed a smooch on his cheek. A notebook slid from his lap and fell to the ground. Flustered, Hunter dropped the cigar and tried to stand.

"Don't worry," she stopped him, "I'll get it for you." She crushed the cigar under her foot, then sent it under the shrub with a quick swipe of her shoe. "Let's not start a fire here."

Reaching out for the notebook, she looked at the colorful cover. A smiling dolphin . . . just what she would've chosen. Several loose papers were about to fall out of it, but he was holding his hands out, eager to get it back. "What's this?" she asked, placing it carefully on his lap.

"Ah, just Rebecca being Rebecca." His eyes veered away from hers. "The woman shouldn't have retired; she misses ordering people around and giving them writing assignments."

"Oh, so you write?" She was thrilled. His stamina was returning, driving him to engage in activities. He was getting better, and Rebecca was a godsend like always, knowing just what to do.

"I dabble," he mumbled, carefully shifting the loose papers between the notebook's cover but without opening it as if he was hiding something from her. "Don't expect a book to be coming out of my convalescence. Not going to happen."

"When are you coming home, Dad?" The threat of tears made her voice sound choppy, strangled.

"Soon. Another month at the most. I can't wait to get out of here. I want my life back." He smiled, his blue eyes watery, but it felt good to see him smile like that, his face lit by the sun.

She tousled his white hair and crouched in front of his wheelchair. "I've got good news, Dad. I got a job. I'm starting on Monday."

"That's fantastic," he reacted, sliding the notebook under his legs. "I'm so happy for you. Where is it, at the university?"

It was her turn to look away. "No, at the Downtown Aquarium."

"I didn't know they had a research facility there."

She kept staring at the tree line. "They don't. I'm . . . going to be a technician. Feed the stingrays and the dolphins, clean the pools. I'll do technician stuff for now. Then, we'll see."

"Andi, why? Why settle for a technician job?"

Just as he said the words, pain ripped through her abdomen. She gasped, putting her knees down and grabbing her belly with both her hands. The retching came with viciousness as if the lining of her stomach was about to come out. Holding on to her father's wheelchair for support, she heaved while he held her forehead as best as he could, with trembling hands.

When it was finally over, she wiped her mouth with a tissue. "You wouldn't happen to have any water, would you?"

"Always prepared," he announced, fishing a bottle of Dasani from the side pocket. His voice was forced cheerful, but his worried eyes stared at the puddle of vomit she'd deposited by his chair. "Are you pregnant?"

Oh, how she wished she could tell him the truth. She'd promised Craig another month before telling people, and she was afraid the news of her pregnancy would make her dad sick again. He didn't seem strong enough to handle an emotional shock. The irony of hiding the truth from her father because she wanted to keep a promise to her lying, betraying husband wasn't wasted on her. Had the situation been any different and her father healthier, she would've shared the good news despite the promise she'd made to Craig.

"I—I don't believe so," she stammered, deeply uncomfortable lying to him. He didn't deserve her lies . . . only the truth.

His warm, trembling fingers touched her face, then pulled her lower eyelid gently. "Look up for me, sweetie." He squinted while focusing. "You're a tad jaundiced. You're going to see a doctor."

"No, I don't think it's that serious—"

"Today. You're pale, gaunt, thinner than I remember."

"I swam a lot in the Caribbean." She tried to smile, but the reassurance she was trying to convey wasn't fooling anyone.

"At night?"

She chuckled. "No. I'm a strong believer in SPF seventy."

"Then you have to remember to supplement with Vitamin D." He took out a pen from his chest pocket, then extracted the notebook from under his legs and tore a piece of paper from the last page. He scribbled a quick note then handed her the paper, folded in half. "You'll see this man, Dr. Bruce Hanfield. He's the head of internal medicine at Memorial Hermann. Show him this. He'll make time for you today."

"Dad, you're freaking me out. I just threw up, that's all. It's happened before."

"That's not exactly reassuring." He took her hand and squeezed it softly while a pair of vertical lines flanked the bridge of his nose. "If you had a dog that was throwing up like that, and it wasn't the first time either, what would you do?" He caressed her short hair with an unspoken plea in his eyes. "Wouldn't you take poor Fido to the vet?"

She sighed. "Okay, I'll go."

"Today. Now."

She nodded, then leaned over and placed a kiss on his forehead. "Now. I promise."

Because he'd mentioned the doctor, fear had started churning in her gut. Was there something wrong with her baby?

Walking toward the rehab center, she took a few deep breaths and felt better. Her father had reacted the way he had because she'd given him wrong information. She'd lied to him. Had she told him she was pregnant, he would've probably sent her shopping for pickles instead.

Right before entering the building, she turned and noticed a puff of bluish smoke coming up from the bushes where she'd left her father moments ago. Shaking her head and hiding a smile, she decided the least she could do was see that doctor. Throwing up like that couldn't be too good for the baby. Back in Montego Bay, she thought her sickness was over.

It clearly wasn't.

36

DOCTOR VISIT

The gown was clean and smelled of antibacterial laundry detergent. It felt raspy on her skin. The hospital's laundry process must've not included fabric softeners.

Restless, she paced the exam room, waiting for Dr. Hanfield to show up. She was surprised he'd agreed to see her without an appointment; her dad's name must've carried a lot of weight with the internist.

Wishing Craig was there with her, she reread the text messages she'd sent him, telling him where she was and why. He still hadn't responded yet.

Eventually settling on the side of the bed, she stared at the ceiling for a moment. Some of the white ceiling tiles had been replaced with a piece of glass or plastic depicting a landscape, a field of colorful wildflowers backlit by several light bulbs. It was most probably intended to soothe the minds of patients lying down on that bed for procedures.

The door opened, and a man walked in quickly, holding a chart. "Ms. Wilmore?"

"Yes, I'm Andrea Wilmore Brafford." She shook his hand, repressing a smile. He was younger than she'd expected for the chief of internal medicine in a hospital of that size. He had large ears that stood out like Dumbo's, the lobes refusing to stick close to the skull. A pair of black-rimmed glasses settled on a long, aquiline nose, intelligent, inquisitive, lively eyes behind them.

He sat on a stool and opened her chart. "We have your test results back," he said in a reassuring voice tinged with concern.

Her breath caught. "Already?"

He shrugged as if apologizing. "We're a teaching hospital. Things happen pretty quickly here."

She swallowed the knot growing in her throat. "I'm listening."

"I see a few out-of-normal ranges, and some of these things raise concerns." It was interesting to notice how he used the passive voice. He didn't say he was concerned, just that concerns were raised.

He stood and pulled the ultrasound machine cart closer to the bed. "Lie down for me, please." She obeyed without saying a word. "I assume you know you're pregnant?"

"Yes."

"How far along?"

"Almost eight weeks." She smiled. It felt great to talk about her baby.

"Did you see your OB-GYN yet?"

She looked at the wildflowers on the ceiling. "Not yet. I was going to do that next week."

"Do you have someone in mind?"

"N—no. Not really." She laughed softly, a little embarrassed. She'd been putting off the task, not sure who to trust with the health of her unborn baby. She needed her father's advice . . . she'd been stalling, waiting for him to feel better.

"I can recommend someone," he said, staring at the screen while driving the ultrasound's transducer over her abdomen, stopping in various spots and pressing down gently. The gel felt warm on her skin, soothing. "I think you should see an OB-GYN as soon as possible."

Fear ripped through her heart. "Is there something wrong with my baby?"

"I don't believe so, but I'd like to be sure. By week six or seven, we can usually detect fetal heartbeats. I'm not picking that up. It could be too soon." He glanced at her reassuringly. "Don't panic. We doctors like to be sure, that's all."

"Uh-huh." She tried to swallow, but her throat was dry. "I've been throwing up a lot. Sometimes I have pain, right before—"

"Pain? Where?"

"In my stomach, here." She took her hand to her abdomen but ran into the ultrasound and the doctor's hand and pulled away quickly.

She breathed shallowly the entire time Dr. Hanfield took to examine her. Silent tears emerged from the corners of her eyes and headed for her temples.

After what seemed like forever, Dr. Hanfield placed the transducer back into its cradle and handed her a small towel. "You can use this to clean off the gel."

She made quick work of it, although she believed the doctor expected her to do that on her own after he'd gone. But he seemed patient, understanding, not in the least judgmental, and she wasn't too modest. "Ready," she announced, sitting on the side of the bed, anticipating his words with the heavy heart of a condemned prisoner awaiting sentencing.

"All right," he said, opening her chart. "I see elevated—"

A quick rap against the door as it opened tentatively, and Craig's head appeared. He seemed out of breath. His hair was tousled, falling forward over his ruffled brow. "I've been looking all over for you." He rushed inside and closed the door, then stopped by her side and took her hand. His presence weakened her as if she could now lean on him for strength, no longer needing to summon hers. Once his arm wrapped around her shoulders, she started sobbing, covering her mouth with her hand to keep the wails locked inside.

"There's no heartbeat, Craig. The baby—"

"What's wrong with the baby?" Craig asked, looking at the doctor with a strange intensity in his eyes, rage-like almost.

"Could be nothing," Dr. Hanfield replied, "or it could be your wife's rather severe symptoms are an early indication of complications. I'm recommending an OB-GYN consult at the earliest." He noted something on her chart. "I've taken ectopic pregnancy off the list of potential issues, but I'm concerned with some blood values I'm seeing."

"What values?" Andi asked. Her voice was broken, her breathing shallow.

"Some of the liver values are a bit higher than normal. On the ultrasound, the liver appears a bit enlarged. Not much, but for someone your age and otherwise fit, it's a red flag." She stared at him, waiting for more information, while Craig clasped her hand tightly. "Your ALT is over the limit. Let's put you on a low-fat diet for a while and check back in two weeks. Platelets are relatively low, and you're a little anemic, but we'll build those numbers up with iron supplementation. Then calcium is abnormally high, and I can't account for that based on what I'm seeing. We could be looking at hyperparathyroidism, and we'll test for that before you leave here today."

A heavy moment of silence engulfed the small exam room. Andi searched Dr. Hanfield's eyes, looking for an unspoken promise that everything was going to be all right. His voice had been reassuring, his body language matched it, but his eyes told a different story.

"Worst-case scenario, Doctor. What am I looking at?" She heard herself speak and didn't recognize her own voice.

He pressed his lips together for a brief moment before replying. "Your calcium level should be below ten-point-five. Yours is eleven-point-eight. At twelve, there's a high risk of fetal death."

A whimper came out of her chest. Craig's arm around her shoulders tightened, supportive, reassuring. "Shh . . ." Craig whispered, "we'll sort this out. You'll see."

She looked at Dr. Hanfield through a blur of tears. "Do you believe that, Doctor? Does my baby still have a chance?" A shudder ran through her entire body. "What would you do if I were your daughter?"

"I'd recommend bedrest, immediate OB-GYN consult, full thyroid and parathyroid panel, and checkups every couple of weeks. A low-fat diet high in healthy protein and fruit." He stood and looked at her with warmth. "It's not over yet, Ms. Wilmore. There's hope."

She lowered her head. A teardrop fell on her gown. She stared at that stain for a long moment, watching it grow, engulfing the tiny pink flowers in the gown's pattern and turning them red, bloodlike. "All right," she eventually said. "Let's do all you said we should."

"I'm sending a prescription for antiemetics. That should help a little with the symptoms. Front desk will give you the first appointment available for the OB-GYN I recommended; I've already sent them a message. It's most likely going to be tomorrow. Let's check back in two weeks, shall we?"

She nodded.

"Yes, Doctor, we will," Craig replied. He seemed grim, angry even. He had every right to be.

Dr. Hanfield said goodbye and left the room, closing the door behind him, leaving them in silence.

She cried softly, her face buried against Craig's shoulder, while he caressed her hair with rhythmic movements. "It will be all right, Ands," he whispered. "You'll see."

Moments later, a phlebotomist showed up and took a few vials of her blood, quickly, professionally, barely looking at Andi. To her, she was just another patient. Anonymous. A work task, not a real person, not a mother whose heart was breaking.

By the time they reached the front desk, she was numb, going through the motions as if it was all happening to someone else, not her.

The earliest appointment with the OB-GYN was on Friday. The doctor took Wednesdays and Thursdays off, and she was gone already; there was nothing anyone could do. Andi would have to endure through two endless days of worrying and waiting.

"Damn," Craig said as they were leaving the hospital hand in hand. "I have the Miami conference on Thursday. I was supposed to leave tomorrow afternoon. I'll cancel."

It was the Realtors Annual Conference, and Craig had been talking about it for months. Hughes had arranged to make him a speaker, and he'd been obsessing over the speech he was about to give.

"No," she replied. "Go . . . I'll be fine on my own. If I need help, Janelle can take care of me, or one of Dad's assistants. Don't worry about me."

He stopped and looked at her with that intensity he sometimes had. It was fiery yet chilling. "Are you sure, baby?"

She nodded. "Uh-huh. Of course, I'm sure." She secretly wished he'd still cancel and tell her she and their baby were more important than a stupid conference.

He squeezed her hand tightly, then took it to his lips. "You're the best," he whispered. She felt his warm breath on her frozen fingers. "You okay to drive?"

"Yes," she replied, surprised she felt a bit eager to be alone.

They walked in silence to her car, still holding hands. When the red hood of her Beetle came into sight, he asked, "Is this doctor a friend of your dad's?"

"More like an acquaintance. Why?"

"He called you Ms. Wilmore, and I was right there, by your side, wearing the same wedding band as you do." His voice was dark, loaded with frustration.

"I don't know why he did that. I introduced myself with both last names." She clicked the remote, and the car flashed and beeped.

He held the door open for her. "Why did you keep the Wilmore name, anyway?"

Tears choked her and streamed down her face. She sat behind the wheel and started the engine.

"I'm so sorry, my love," he whispered, reaching for her hand. She pulled away from his touch, looking straight at the car parked in front of the Beetle. "I'm a tactless, selfish little prick."

She didn't flinch, didn't rush to forgive him like she'd normally do.

He stood straight by her car, silently glaring at her, his shift from remorseful to angry, mercurial and dizzying. She shut the door and shifted in reverse, then pulled out of the parking lot and drove off.

The entire time she drove home, he followed her at a close distance, but she barely noticed and didn't care. Alone with her thoughts at last, she wept bitter tears for her baby, for the happy future she had envisioned for herself as a young mother. Touching her belly, she whispered, over and over, "Please, little one, don't leave me," her voice fraught with tears. "Stay with me. Stay awhile."

In the distance, the sun was setting, leaving behind a wonderfully blue sky tinged with shades of purple and violet. A dark cloud, looming over the horizon, took chunks from the majestic celestial show, casting blackness over the setting sun's rays, menacing, like the promise of a fearful tomorrow.

District Attorney Buscher: Did you order a blood test for Vitamin D levels?

Dr. Bruce Hanfield: Not at first, no.

District Attorney Buscher: Any reason why you didn't?

Dr. Bruce Hanfield: It's not what we typically test for in pregnant patients presenting with nausea, vomiting, and cramps.

District Attorney Buscher: But you later reconsidered?

Dr. Bruce Hanfield: After seeing her elevated blood calcium levels, yes. I ordered the test as part of a comprehensive hormonal and metabolic panel.

District Attorney Buscher: What did you suspect at the time, Doctor?

Dr. Bruce Hanfield: Primary hyperparathyroidism.

District Attorney Buscher: Did you discuss the findings with your patient, Andrea Wilmore Brafford?

Dr. Bruce Hanfield: I left her a voicemail on Thursday morning to come see me, another one the following day. She never returned my calls. Since then, I've learned that on that same Thursday night she was killed.

Defense Attorney Goodridge: Objection, Your Honor.

37

ARGUMENT

The sound of the door closing behind Craig, when he'd left for the airport a couple of hours earlier, still resounded in Andi's mind. Numb and more scared than she'd ever thought possible, she hadn't moved from the large armchair where she sat with her legs folded underneath her body.

She'd welcomed the silence of his absence for a while because she could think. She could abandon herself to the all-consuming panic that ripped through her while the hours passed much too slowly. Her OB-GYN appointment was on Friday morning, at ten. Not a moment too soon. She was happy Craig was away . . . she was torn about him, doubtful, anguished. Every time she tested him, he passed. She'd asked about the pendant, and he'd told her the truth, just as his parents had shared, the heartwarming story about his wealthy childhood friend who didn't want him to feel excluded. He'd been an absolute sweetheart all the time, except for a few minutes of unleashed insecurities that made him behave absurdly about her last name.

She'd forgiven him about that too . . . a little too soon like she always did, not able to bear seeing him upset. His lips were adorable when he smiled, his eyes lit up, his face beamed, while she stood by in awe, watching him soak up happiness every chance he got. She made most of those chances possible for him, although he wasn't too quick to give her credit for them.

But when it came to her baby, she was still torn about him. The day she'd told him about the pregnancy reverberated in her memory, aching and throbbing, the wound cast by his reaction feeling fresh, painful. Did he really want that baby? Or was he secretly rooting she'd miscarry?

Well, on the odd, heartbreaking chance that was the case, he was way better off at the Realtors convention, giving his precious speech. It might take a little persuading, but maybe he could be convinced to go to work on Friday morning, instead of accompanying her to the doctor.

For a fleeting moment, a deeply troubling question swirled through her mind. Why was she still staying with him if she couldn't even trust that he wanted to have a child with her? What was she still thinking she could do, when their marriage was frail and torn and stuck together with Band-Aids and duct tape? What was she holding on to?

A knock on the door shattered the disturbing thought. "Come right in," she called, knowing it was Janelle. Her friend walked right in with a spring in her step and a beaming grin on her face, then froze in the middle of the living room. Her smile waned, leaving a surprised grimace in its wake.

"Girl, what the hell is going on with you?" she asked, dropping her purse on the floor and propping her hands on her thighs. She wore tight, ripped, stretch jeans and a white top. Thin bracelets and long earrings jingled and tinkled softly with every move.

"Good to see you too," Andi replied, smiling shyly. "It can't be that bad."

"It can't?" Janelle replied, taking Andi's hand and tugging with determination. "Come, let's have a look at you in the mirror."

She followed her to the wall mirror in the foyer, squinting a little when Janelle turned on all the lights. Then, pushed by her determined friend, she approached the mirror and studied her face carefully.

She'd cried, yes, for hours, and it was showing. Her eyes were puffy and red, bloodshot as if she'd spent her nights drinking.

"You're pale as shit, Ands," Janelle said. "You just came back from a vacation in the Caribbean, and you look like this? I wonder what you looked like before you left."

Her skin was yellowish-pale, with dark circles under her eyes. Her lips were discolored, stained in places as if she'd eaten blueberries. "Okay, you're right," she admitted. "I'm having a hard time with the pregnancy, that's all—"

"Pregnancy?" Janelle's voice climbed a notch or two with excitement. In the heat of the moment, Andi had forgotten she wasn't supposed to say anything about it. But those were Craig's rules, not hers, and she was growing tired of Craig's endless rules.

"Yes," she replied shyly, just as Janelle was wrapping her in her strong arms. "Nothing to celebrate yet," she added, and Janelle pulled away, looking at her with worried eyes. "I'm not doing that well, Jan. I've been throwing up, and the baby—" She couldn't bring herself to say it. "We don't know yet. They don't know. I have to go back the day after tomorrow for more tests."

Janelle covered her mouth with her well-manicured hand. "Oh, my goodness, hon, I didn't know. You didn't tell me. Why barf in silence and solitude when you could've had me by your side, bringing you pickles and ice cream and whatever else preggies crave these days?"

"Craig and I were planning a party for all our friends. But I got sick—"

"Yeah . . . Craig and you," she said, speaking slowly, her tone loaded with unfiltered contempt. "So sorry to be telling this to a pregnant woman, but are you fucking insane?"

Taken aback, Andi withdrew from the mirror and found her way back to her favorite armchair. She curled up in it and hugged her knees. "What do you mean?" she asked, although she believed she already knew the answer.

"I can't believe you forgave him, after that shit he pulled. No way, I told myself, that can't be my smart, independent Andi. That can't be my girl."

Andi nodded, her eyes riveted on the armchair's fine leather upholstery, where two perfectly parallel stitch lines ran along the edges of the soft cushions. She'd never visited a furniture factory; she had no idea how armchairs were made. It was something she wanted to do one day. With Craig. "Yes, Janelle, I forgave him."

"Why?" The jingling of Janelle's earrings underlined the shaking of her head in dismay.

"It's . . . complicated." Andi shot her friend a quick glance. Janelle's eyes were fiercely determined, judgmental. She hated that . . . why couldn't Janelle be more understanding? "I'm pregnant, and I—"

"Oh, so you're staying with him just because you're pregnant?"

She bit her lip and lowered her eyes, tracing the stiches again with her fingernail. "No. I'd be lying if I said that was the only reason. Truth is, I'm still in love with him." Once the words came out, she felt better. It was the truth. "I can't picture myself *out* of love with him. I don't know what that looks like."

Janelle scoffed. "Sure, he's insanely handsome and totally fuckable, I get that. But still, that was some nasty shit he pulled."

Andi looked at Janelle in disbelief. Even out of her blunt friend's mouth, those words were a bit unexpected.

"Well, I hope you'll enjoy your new job cleaning fish caca from pool walls and doing menial work when you could've worked as a researcher at your alma mater. Have you ever wondered, how you are going to face those people again? People *you* care about?"

Andi stood, a wave of rage coursing through her veins. "By all means, Janelle, don't pull any punches." Her nostrils flared, but she stopped short of calling Janelle a couple of names in the heat of the moment. She wasn't upset with her friend as much as she was embarrassed under her barrage of valid, logical questions that made her doubt her own sanity. Was she a self-deluded fool? Again? Forgiving the man she loved sounded like a no-brainer . . . Marriages need work.

Playing with the pendant, she wondered, for the twentieth time that day, if she should stay. If she should continue to cling to their marriage, tooth and nail, and fight for it until the last breath of air left her chest. It sounded romantic, chivalrous even, but was it the smart thing to do? Did she actually know the man she'd married?

But her new job was starting on Monday, and she hoped the OB-GYN wouldn't sentence her to bed rest for the duration of her pregnancy. She was still excited about working in her field, even if at the lowest level, cleaning . . . what was it Janelle had said, fish caca?

She burst into laughter.

Janelle stared at her. "Okay . . . now I get it. You've completely lost your mind."

"Fish caca . . . that was awesome."

Janelle joined her in laughter. "I—I really don't know if fish pee or poop or whatever. I improvised."

Andi chuckled. "You're awesome, you know that?"

Janelle's smile waned. She sat on the arm of Andi's chair. "He could be a narcissist, Ands," she said softly.

Andi didn't reply. The chilling thought had crossed her mind, only to be quickly shunned away by rushed rationalizations and evidence of the contrary in his behavior, evidence she never bothered to validate, wishing it to be true so much it was scary to check.

"You know I always envied the shit out of your relationship with this man," Janelle insisted.

Andi pulled away from her. Envied her? That was news to her . . . disappointing news. "Is that so?"

"Yes, it's so, but that ended with the terrible stuff he pulled on you as if he'd poured a bucket full of ice water over my head." She paused for a beat, but Andi listened, her jaws clenched, her soul frozen. "I see him clearly now, girl. He wants to use you, show you off to his friends." Janelle arranged Andi's crooked collar, but she pulled away and stood, eager to put more distance between them. "You're just a piece of property to him, Ands."

"Shut up, Janelle," she whispered in a low, menacing voice. "You should've shut up before telling me you envied me."

Janelle raised her arms in the air in frustration. Her bracelets jingled. "It's me, Andi. Remember me? I'm Janelle, your best friend since forever. Do you know who this man really is?"

"Right now, I don't know who *you* are," Andi replied coldly. "Maybe you're too envious to see things clearly."

"Andi, that's not what I—"

"Tell me, are you in love with my husband, Janelle? If that's the case, I think you should leave."

Her mouth gaped open for a moment while she struggled to find her words. "Jeez, woman, you're insane. I think he screwed with your brain so badly it's beyond repair."

Grabbing her purse on the way, she reached the door in a few determined steps, then left, slamming the door behind her.

Silence fell heavy, leaving Andi alone with her dark thoughts and unanswered questions, one more bothersome and chilling than all the rest.

How well did she really know Craig?

Defense Attorney Goodridge: Have you had arguments with Andrea Wilmore Brafford before?

Janelle Larimer: No. That was the only time we argued.

Defense Attorney Goodridge: What was the argument about?

Janelle Larimer: She wasn't making much sense. Nothing, really.

Defense Attorney Goodridge: Humor us, nevertheless. You're still under oath.

Janelle Larimer: She accused me, out of the blue, of having a crush on her husband. Considering what he'd done, I would've had to be—

Defense Attorney Goodridge: Were you? In love with the defendant?

Janelle Larimer: Absolutely not. The things she said didn't make much sense at first, until I realized what she was going through. Until I found out what had happened.

Defense Attorney Goodridge: What are you referring to? What exactly had happened?

Janelle Larimer: He killed her, right?

Defense Attorney Goodridge: Can you testify, under oath, that Craig Brafford killed his wife? Did you witness the murder yourself?

Janelle Larimer: No.

Defense Attorney Goodridge: In fact, you just admitted you were the last person to see her alive, and you argued with Andrea Wilmore Brafford on Wednesday night. Is that correct, Ms. Larimer?

Janelle Larimer: Yes.

Defense Attorney Goodridge: Did you kill Andrea Wilmore Brafford, Ms. Larimer?

38

THE FIND

The entire night, Andi sat in that armchair, eyes wide open, hand on the phone. She wanted to call Janelle and apologize, ask her to come back, tell her she was right and that she'd lost her mind. Yet she'd postponed that into the early morning hours, then gave it up for a while. Waking her up in the middle of the night with a call made even less sense than everything else she'd done recently.

What an idiotic thing to ask her best friend if she was in love with Craig. Realizing she'd become obsessed with the man she loved to the point where she couldn't think straight anymore, a night of introspection brought her closer to a decision. Thankfully, there were a few people in her life she could trust. Her father, Rebecca, Janelle. If she didn't trust her own judgment, maybe she needed to surrender her decision-making to them, like an on-demand intervention of sorts.

There was no real need for that, though. Janelle, the only one who knew what Craig had done to her, had been quite direct about it. Her father and Rebecca would probably say and do much worse. Her father wouldn't stop short of getting the authorities involved, and that would rip her life apart, expose her, turn her into the town's latest gossip bit, the butt of every joke, crowning her the most gullible and idiotic wife who ever lived.

Was that much worse than having the people she respected the most at the Department of Marine Biology believe she was a smuggler of exotic species, the most despicable human being a biologist could think of? At least that part of her reputation would be cleansed, but she'd always be branded Craig's victim. People never forgot anything anymore; Google didn't allow that to happen, not in the United States, where people had lost their right to privacy eons ago.

She blinked away tears, irritated by them. There was no time for crying, not before she could answer another big question.

Why was she there? Why was she staying?

Of course, because she loved Craig. The immediate, superficial answer was easy to find, even easier to hide behind. Who did she love, exactly? A charming, endearing man who took care of her every whim, spoke to her like men only did in romance novels, and made love to her like Patrick Swayze made love to Demi Moore in *Ghost,* always there for her, behind her, supporting her, yearning to love her with every fiber of his body?

Or had she fallen hard for a con artist, a controlling manipulator and a narcissistic sociopath, a man who lied to her and everyone else to entrap her behind the brick walls of a suburban Texas mansion to serve at his pleasure, while he stopped at nothing to alienate her from everything that brought meaning to her life? Had it not been for Janelle's willingness to make those calls, she would've gone on living a life trapped, enslaved, her flight stopped short when she'd been captured in the carefully constructed web of lies, slowly learning to accept that no one wanted her, that she was a pitiful, worthless creature who couldn't earn her own keep. Another year or two and she would've given up, becoming more and more grateful to the man who loved her despite her shortcomings, knowing that without him, she couldn't survive.

Bile rose in the back of her throat. She got up from her chair and headed to the kitchen in the gray light of early dawn. She reached to get a glass from the cabinet when something tickled her nose. Pulling a tissue from the box on the counter, she wiped her nose and found blood in the tissue.

It wasn't the first time she'd had nosebleeds recently. They were minor issues compared to nausea and cramps and didn't bother her that much. She pinched the bridge of her nose until it stopped, then grabbed the glass and filled it with ice water from the fridge dispenser.

After a couple of sips, a wave of nausea churned her stomach. It was as if the water had triggered it. She sat at the breakfast table, setting the glass on a coaster and leaning her forehead into her hand.

Struggling to keep her stomach from heaving, she breathed deeply while tears flooded her eyes. She'd fallen in love with the love story, with the idea of them living the dream. She'd been desperately trying to ignore the facts clearly displayed in front of her, the little signs, just to keep the dream from unraveling.

The signs had been there all along. Her father's obsession with him; maybe he had reasons for that obsession. Craig's reluctance to have any of her friends around, not even Janelle. She could only visit when he was away on business. His reaction to her pregnancy. His contempt for her passion for marine biology, for the corals on the fireplace mantle and the turtles she loved to watch on the shore. For everything that mattered to her, including her unborn baby.

The sun's first rays cut through the gloom and started to fill the house with a yellowish light, promising a perfect fall day. She had until the evening to reach a decision and act on it. Craig wasn't returning from Miami until about seven.

Another sip of water washed the bad taste in her mouth but churned her stomach as it reached down. A pang of pain cut through her abdomen, so sharp it left her breathless. Grabbing the edge of the table for support and bending over in an attempt to ease the pain, she stood up shakily.

She felt a gushing of warm fluid between her legs, spreading on the inside of her thighs, coloring her jeans with the deathly hues of blood. Another strong cramp sent her keeling on her side, gasping for air.

"No . . . no . . . my baby," she wailed, holding her belly with both her hands. "Oh, please, no."

She stayed on the floor in the growing pool of blood, unable to stand, while cramps came and went, each slightly weaker than the one before. Sobbing, then crying softly when she'd run out of strength to sob anymore, she couldn't bring herself to reach for the phone and call 911. What for? Her baby was gone. That much she knew . . . she'd known since Dr. Hanfield had said there was no discernible fetal heartbeat but had refused to accept it like she seemed to do with all disasters in her life. Now she wanted to mourn in peace, not be poked and probed and touched by people for whom she was nothing but a work task. A bar code.

Time passed as the shadows of sunlit furniture shifted and danced on the bloodstained floor. She must've dozed off for a while on the cold marble, the chill traveling through her blood, because she woke up shaking, weak, afraid she wasn't strong enough to stand.

Slowly, carefully planning her moves, she grabbed onto a chair for support and leaned against it, then lifted herself from the floor. Her soaked jeans were sticky and had hardened in places, sticking to the floor. As she finally stood, another wave of nausea had her rushing for the sink.

In passing, she accidentally swiped the glass of water, sending it flying to the floor. It exploded into tiny shards as it hit the floor, just as she leaned over the sink, retching.

The following couple of hours were a blur. She'd managed to get herself cleaned up. She'd showered for what seemed like a long time, sobbing and squeezing her eyes shut to not see the blood coming off her body and swirling around the drain.

Then, slowly, as she mourned the life that had left her body, she got dressed and steeled herself at the thought of cleaning the mess she'd made on the kitchen floor.

The blood had congealed on the white tiles, the color contrast stark, disheartening. Still in shock, she stood by the kitchen island, staring at the garnet stains littered with glass shards, her mouth agape and covered with her hand.

One by one, the details of what she needed to do started coming into her mind as half-baked thoughts, glimpses of ideas, glimmers of images. There was hydrogen peroxide in the bathroom, in her cabinet. There was a broom in the hallway closet. There used to be a dustpan under the sink. Craig never let her do the dirty work, as he called it. The taking out of garbage, the sweeping of floors. He always did that himself. He . . . wasn't there.

Leaving the broom leaning against the wall, she chose her footsteps carefully, avoiding the glass shards and the bloodstains as best she could. Crouching in front of the sink cabinets, she opened the doors.

The trash can was there, with a fresh liner in it and otherwise empty, just like Craig had left it on Tuesday night. Behind it, she could see the dustpan handle. Sliding the trash can out of the way, she froze, her hand caught in midair, inches away from the dustpan she was reaching for.

A bottle of rat poison, almost half empty, had been hidden behind the trash can.

Staring at the colorful label promising immediate, durable results, Andi gasped, air refusing to fill her lungs. The sound of her heart thumping against her chest was the only thing she could hear for a while, her breath caught, her mind frozen.

This wasn't happening. It couldn't be true.

Yet the inconceivable truth was right there, under the kitchen sink, staring her in the face in green, bold lettering above the image of a chubby rat munching on some green-colored grains.

District Attorney Buscher: Please explain to the court how rat poison kills.

Dr. Aaron Ellefson: The specific poison used in this case was a mix of two powerful chemicals. One, cholecalciferol, increases the concentration of calcium in one's blood until it compromises organ function. The second, bromadiolone, is known as a superwarfarin, a powerful anticoagulant with cumulative effects.

District Attorney Buscher: In your practice as medical examiner for Harris County, Texas, how often do you encounter poisoning with rodenticides?

Dr. Aaron Ellefson: Not very often. This is the first case I've had in about five years. People know not to touch that; it's a terribly slow and painful death.

District Attorney Buscher: Why do you think people have stopped using it for criminal activities?

Dr. Aaron Ellefson: Rat poison kills very slowly. It's not an effective murder weapon.

District Attorney Buscher: Kills slowly? Isn't that contrary to what is sought in an effective pest poison? Quick and effective elimination of rodents?

Dr. Aaron Ellefson: Rats have evolved over thousands of years as pests that humans have always wanted to eradicate. Consequently, the rats developed a defense mechanism against poisons. Only a few rats in the colony will ingest new, unknown food, and very little of it. The rest wait and see if the food is safe enough to be eaten. Quite surprising, if you think about it. That's why modern rodenticides have combined, cumulative effects.

District Attorney Buscher: No more questions, Your Honor.

39

REALITY

Andi felt her blood draining from her face, leaving icicles behind, cold, merciless, depleting her willingness to fight as if suddenly faced with an enemy too powerful and cruel, invincible. With every piece of the puzzle slowly falling into place, the truth was more irrefutable, starker, deadlier.

Her elevated blood calcium. The cholecalciferol identified on the label was to blame for that. It had been slowly killing her for a while, damaging her heart, calcifying her kidneys. Her nosebleeds, the low platelets in her test results, the miscarriage, the sharp pain in her stomach, all those symptoms pointed to the second ingredient in the poison, bromadiolone, a strong anticoagulant.

Her poor baby never stood a chance.

Tears streamed down her face, silent, shocked, bitter. Breathing shallowly, she remembered how nausea and vomiting had started, how painful it had been from the beginning, the bad taste in her mouth in the mornings, a faint chemical taste, something she couldn't identify.

The fairy tale was over, the deceiving fabric of it forever torn, shredded, unraveling with the wool over her eyes, leaving behind nothing but the cold reality of truth.

"You killed my baby," she spoke loudly as if Craig was there to hear her words. Her voice sounded distant, factual as if the words had been uttered by a distant, clinical stranger stating the obvious.

And still, worming its way into her weary mind, doubt reared its ugly head. Could the bottle of poison have been there when they moved in? Was there any chance it wasn't Craig who had been poisoning her?

No one else had access to the house but the two of them. Through a haze, she recalled the day she'd first seen the property. Craig had given her the tour, pretending he was a Realtor selling her the house, while she was deliriously happy. Showing her the upgraded countertops. The new cabinets. Opening a few of them, including the one under the sink.

It used to be empty.

Soon after they'd moved in, he'd started wanting to be the only one who took the trash out. "Spoiling you rotten with little gestures," he'd said. What better way to hide the poison from her? She was too sick to handle the chores he was offering to do and grateful to be allowed to rest more. To keep looking for work.

Eyes still riveted on the bottle of poison, she felt the table surface for her phone and dialed 911. Her trembling finger hovered over the green button for a long moment but then she canceled the call and abandoned the phone back on the table.

If the cops came, they'd investigate. They'd probably charge him with something or other for poisoning her, possibly even with attempted murder, but he'd never pay for the life he'd taken. Her unborn child, under the law, was not a real person until born alive.

Her dear husband had made sure that would never happen.

Just like she would have to make sure he paid dearly for the life he'd taken.

Wiping her tears with the back of her hand, she checked the time. It was almost noon; she had six, maybe seven hours until Craig returned.

Careful not to leave any evidence behind, she cleaned the blood pool from the floor with paper towels and broke the larger shards of glass into smaller ones using a small frying pan. Soaking the bloodstains with hydrogen peroxide, she carefully removed every trace of blood, burning it with peroxide until the floor was gleaming white, including the grout between the tiles. Then she dumped the blood-soaked wads of paper towels into the toilet in small quantities, flushing after each one, until all evidence of her baby's death was removed from the house. She poured the rest of the peroxide down the kitchen sink drain and scrubbed the toilet thoroughly.

Then, weak on her feet but driven by the rage burning in her chest, she went shopping.

A hardware store on the other side of town carried the same rat poison. Andi parked across the street from the store, paid for the poison in cash, and kept her head low. Wearing a ball cap and oversized shades, she made sure no one could recognize her.

The following stop was an obscure gas station, where she picked up a disposable burner phone, also paid for in cash.

Then she drove over to her father's house. Rummaging through his top desk drawer, she found his wallet with all his ID cards right where she'd put it after he'd been admitted to the hospital. She extracted his vet license card, issued by the Texas Board of Veterinary Medical Examiners. It bore Dr. Wilmore's license number. Fido couldn't go to the vet just yet, but there were other means to the same end. She could take care of herself, at least for a while.

Holding her breath, Andi dialed the Texas Poison Center Network from the burner phone. "I'm calling from Dr. Hunter Wilmore's office, license ID five six four four two five. What's the latest protocol for cholecalciferol and bromadiolone poisoning?" she asked after the operator had validated the credentials.

"For the anticoagulant, it's intravenous vitamin K1, daily, for up to one hundred and sixty-eight days. Platelet count and clotting factor will indicate when you can stop administering it." Andi nearly choked when she heard the operator's words. Almost six months of daily intravenous shots? Bloody hell. "For hypercalcemia control, it's calcium gluconate IV daily until blood levels normalize."

"Anything else?"

"Gastric lavage if the ingestion is recent."

She ended the call and closed her eyes, trying to remember when she last ate something that had been prepared or served by Craig. Fresh tears choked her. Their romantic, candlelit dinners, Craig making all her favorite foods extra spicy, just like she liked it. Nothing but a ruse to poison her. Nothing more. No fairy tale.

"I'm such a bloody idiot," she muttered, going through her father's drug supply. Dr. Wilmore kept a home office ready for most veterinary emergencies, and, thankfully, the two drugs recommended were among those he had stocked up plentifully.

Using one of her father's ties for a tourniquet and wondering how all the junkies in the street or in movies seemed so adept at finding their own veins while she struggled badly, she eventually administered herself the first dose of vitamin K1 and calcium gluconate. She had no idea if she'd given herself enough of the drugs or too much, but whatever the case, it had to be better than doing nothing.

Mumbling an oath as she checked the time, Andi grabbed a couple of surgical gloves from her father's home office, and a few things from the pantry, and rushed out the door.

On the short drive home, she carefully planned every step of what she wanted to do next. With less than an hour left until Craig's flight from Miami touched down in Houston, she had little time to spare.

As soon as she arrived home, she slid on a pair of nitrile gloves and grabbed the bottle of poison from underneath the sink. She sniffed the content; it didn't smell of anything too pervasive, just a faint, bitter-sourish odor she recognized. Then she made a mental note of the level of the liquid in the bottle. It was up to where the rat's tail reached the edge of the label.

She set that bottle aside on a piece of paper towel, then retrieved the one she'd bought earlier that day and emptied it in the kitchen sink. Then she rinsed it thoroughly, lathering the inside with dish detergent then rinsing it clean a few times until every trace of poison was gone. Thankfully, the label was heat-shrunk plastic and didn't curl or become loose.

Taking her time, she dried the bottle's exterior thoroughly, making sure not even a single drop of water was trapped under the label. Then she started mixing the items she'd brought back from her father's house in a small bowl filled with water. Citric acid. Salt. Food coloring until the shade of the liquid in the bowl came close to the color of the poison.

The spoon clinked as she mixed the fluid in the bowl, listening intently for the soft noises made by dissolving grains of citric acid. All that time, she knew she should've just walked away, leaving that madness behind and never looking back, but she had to look Craig in the eye as he poisoned her again. She had to see what had most likely been there before, and she somehow missed noticing. The evil intent. The hatred, glimmering in the eyes of the apparently loving and funny and charming man, while he was dousing her food with poison. His beautiful eyes, locked with hers, watching every bite she ate and smiling, knowing it was only pushing her closer to a painful and slow death.

She loved salty foods; she enjoyed sour-tasting ones too; she liked her fried fish drenched in lemon juice. This time, no matter how little poison he would add to her meal, she would sense it. She would taste it, and she would instantly know, above all shred of a doubt, that the man who looked at her lovingly while lighting candles and offering her dessert was a killer.

Only then could she leave, and his penance could begin.

Still mixing the solution, adding small increments of food coloring until the match was near perfect, she envisioned herself sitting across from him at the dinner table. Chatting, asking him about his trip, about the speech he'd given, while her mouth tasted the salty and sour proof of his murderous intent she was looking for.

What would he say? What would she see in his eyes at that precise moment?

He deserved a chance to—

No. He didn't deserve any more chances. She did. It was her turn now.

He only deserved to pay for the unborn life he'd ripped out of her womb.

When Craig arrived home that night, the bottle under the sink was filled with the salty-sour mixture to the right level, while the real poison bottle with Craig's fingerprints on it was stashed inside the HVAC unit in the garage.

And she was waiting.

Defense Attorney Goodridge: You testified that the symptoms Andrea Wilmore Brafford presented with were consistent with the ingestion of rat poison. Is that correct?

Dr. Bruce Hanfield: Yes.

Defense Attorney Goodridge: Yet you didn't treat Andrea Wilmore Brafford for poisoning.

Dr. Bruce Hanfield: There was no reason to suspect that. The symptoms she presented with are relatively common, with other ailments being more likely culprits than poisoning, especially in a pregnant woman.

Defense Attorney Goodridge: So, you did not believe her life to be at risk?

Dr. Bruce Hanfield: Not at first, no. But after seeing her extended metabolic panel, then—

Defense Attorney Goodridge: No more questions for this witness.

40

DECISIONS

When Craig pulled into the garage, it was almost ten. He was supposed to make it home much earlier, but his plane was held back on the tarmac for hours while he suffocated and broke into sweats countless times, angry as hell, trapped inside a plane filled with stinking people. It was *his* time they were wasting, and to him, time meant money. And for what? A banal thunderstorm, some stupid lightning strikes that didn't even fall close to the damn airport but had all the planes stopped short of their respective jetways, while strobes went on and a strange, pulsating alarm sounded for almost three hours.

He'd expressed his frustration to the flight attendants vocally, repeatedly, not relenting until they threatened him with an arrest at the time of deplaning if he continued. That shut him up, but anger was bubbling inside him.

The rest of his trip had gone swimmingly, totally worth the anguish of traveling economy. Now he wanted to shower and relax at the dinner table, telling Andi how it went, then planning the following week. She was starting her new job. The thought of it had him grinding his teeth and cursing under his breath. Just when he and Jude were getting ready to incorporate, they needed support with paperwork, the website, the first round of marketing materials. But what did the bitch want instead? To feed fucking fish for nothing an hour, that's what she wanted. That's why she was abandoning him.

Thinking of her defiance ignited a craving for her rebellious body he could barely wait to quench. He wanted her subdued, moaning and wanting more, begging him to take her. But there was a chill curled in his gut, a foreboding. He'd been gone for two days, and she hadn't called him once. No more messages in his voicemail, no more texts filled with hearts and hugs and kisses.

Just silence.

He'd called her repeatedly from the tarmac and she'd eventually picked up, just to tell him coldly she was waiting for him to return so they could talk. He asked why, but she was tightlipped about it.

"Damn that woman," he muttered, cutting the engine and closing the garage door. He thought the Caribbean had taken care of her ruffled feathers and then some. Otherwise, he would've never wasted an entire week killing time on the beach or hanging out on a stinky boat with a half-drunk Jamaican while she was busy diving and taking pictures of every piece of underwater slime she could find. The only gain from the trip, other than shutting Andi up and having her settled down again, was a quick assessment of the real estate opportunities in Montego Bay. He had yet to speak with Jude about it, but they could make some serious money with the right investment strategy.

Craig found the living room shrouded in darkness, except for a faint light coming from one of the bathrooms. Feeling for the switch, he turned on the light and squinted, blinking a couple of times until his eyes adjusted.

"Hey, babe," Andi said, without rushing to meet him. She sat in her favorite armchair, the one by the fireplace, her legs folded underneath her, dressed in a plain, white, terrycloth bathrobe.

He was about to walk over and scoop her in his arms, eager to feel her body writhing under his weight, but he noticed folded sheets, a blanket, and a couple of pillows stacked neatly on the sofa. That froze him in his tracks. "Did someone stay here while I was gone?" He tried to keep his voice friendly, unthreatening, but he wasn't sure he'd managed that.

Andi chuckled. "No, don't worry, no one stayed here. I'll explain." She smiled at him, tilting her head slightly.

She was in a good mood, even looked a little better. That meant she was still pregnant. Otherwise, she would've been pale, resting in bed, and bawling like a scalded cat. *Damn it to hell. Why did it take so long to get that shit done?*

"How did it go?" Andi asked. "At the conference. Did you give your speech?"

"Yeah, I did," he replied excitedly. "It was so well-received that Hughes offered me a partnership right after the talks ended." He came to her and took her hands in his. They were cold to the touch, unwelcoming. She was letting him touch her but wasn't responding her usual way. "Sure, there will be terms, and we have to deliver a certain amount of business to the firm during the qualifying period, but . . . partner! Can you believe it?"

Her smile widened, briefly touching her eyes. "We . . . That means more money, yes?"

He nodded vigorously. "Yes, and lots of it. My share of every deal I bring in will change, plus I'll make a little money out of every deal the firm closes, even if I didn't bring it in myself. It's a real partnership, not just a paper title."

"How much is enough, Craig?" she asked calmly, her smile gone. "You'll make partner, and you have this other side deal with Jude . . . will this be enough?"

He let go of her hands and started pacing the floor angrily. "Never! It's never enough money." He shoved his hands into his pockets to keep himself from punching something. "I wish you'd understand."

"Oh, but I do." She spoke softly, dispassionately. She wasn't arguing or pleading with him. "I'm just not the right girl for you, Craig, that's all. I want a divorce."

So, they were back to the divorce again. All his efforts had been for nothing. She was ready to walk right out of his life, leaving him behind without any concern for his feelings, for what that did to him.

He could find other women, sure, but Andi had class and came from money. Not loads of money, but enough to make her passable to the people he wanted to impress. He'd invested time and resources into making her who she was today. Taught her how to properly wear a dress, how to make herself the center of attention, how to sell that body of hers. If it were up to her, she wouldn't ever get out of ripped jeans, old T-shirts, and worn-out sneakers sprinkling beach sand with every step.

She was one ungrateful little bitch, wasn't she?

After scheming to get herself pregnant, she just wanted to leave him, knowing he'd be on the hook to pay child support and alimony for two decades, a hefty percentage of everything he earned. Or maybe it was a fixed amount, he didn't know for sure. Nevertheless, he'd been scammed. Trapped. Soon to be laughed at by Houston's entire business community. Yet another sucker, thrown to the curb by some skirt.

She wasn't going any-fucking-where.

Craig wasn't thinking straight, and he knew it. He'd been enraged like that before. Later, when the clouds of anger had dissipated, he'd lived to regret some of his actions. But the rage was there, raw, aching, demanding blood to be spilled. Justice to be had for the insult he'd been dealt.

This time though, it was more than rage. It was necessity. Whatever a judge would order him to pay in the divorce settlement, he simply didn't have it. And these things, like his inability to pay the settlement, had the nasty habit of making it in the news, on people's lips, in social media circles, a tasty morsel of gossip passed around from one bored Karen to another until his reputation would be finished. His life would be over.

Because people forgave many things, indiscretions, judgment errors, even business fails, but there is one thing no one ever forgives, nor forgets.

Poverty.

Insolvency.

That's where it all ends. Friendships, careers, opportunities, everything.

But it wasn't over yet. His betraying wife was still curled up in the armchair, dressed in a bathrobe, seemingly not planning to go anywhere, at least not that night. He could still win this.

"What pushed you away from me while I was gone?" He resumed his pacing but slowly, looking at her, studying her reactions. He forced himself to breathe, still enraged, and if that rage seeped into his voice, she'd be gone in an instant. "Was it your father?" He chuckled bitterly. "The old son of a bitch never liked me."

A lopsided smile fluttered on Andi's lips for a brief moment. "No, it's not him, and calling my father names isn't helping, Craig."

He stopped in front of her chair, his head bowed, his eyes riveted to the floor. "You're right, and I'm sorry. It's just that my heart is breaking, Ands. I can't lose you. I wouldn't know how to go on without you." That statement rang true and got her attention. Her gaze softened, the lines ridging her brow almost disappeared.

"It's my fault, Craig." She clasped her hands nervously and looked away for a moment. He thought he saw tears in her eyes. "It's me . . . I can't get over what happened. I thought I could, but I just can't." Her breath was shaky, shallow. "I was crying in your arms over the marine biology research job, after I got the letter. We were in our old apartment, remember?"

"Of course, I remember. You have no idea how I felt—"

"You held me and comforted me when it was *you* who made the call that ended my chances with them. How does one move past that?" She wrung her hands in her lap nervously, staring at the floor. "I just don't know how. I can't."

"In the Caribbean, you were fine," he argued weakly. The same foreboding chill strangled his voice. "You were starting to forgive me. You were still in love with me." He smiled shyly and reached for her hand. She didn't pull away but didn't seem to welcome his touch either. "I will never forget that night—"

She chuckled bitterly. "I *am* still in love with you, Craig, and I'm a hopeless idiot in such matters, because I should've never gone to the islands with you." She sniffled quietly. "What kind of paradise is that, if it's based on betrayal, on lies and deceit?" A flicker of a sad smile stretched her lips as she glanced at him quickly, then looked away. "If I ever go back to my paradise, I would be alone there, always missing you, but alone. I can't bring myself to trust you again, no matter how hard I try." When she looked up at him, the tears were gone, and her mouth was a firm line. "I'm sorry, Craig. We're over."

The jacket felt insufferably warm and clingy, and his Armani tie choked him. With rushed gestures, he peeled off the jacket and yanked off the tie, then threw both items on the sofa before he dropped to his knees in front of her. "Andi . . ." He reached out to touch her hair, but she pulled away. His hand froze in mid-air for a moment, then he withdrew. "I can't live with the thought of you in another man's arms, of you abandoning me, of leaving me behind. Of discarding me like I'm a bucket of garbage."

For a beat, she stared at him intently as if gauging if he was truthful. "If you're concerned about money, about this house, don't be. I didn't bring anything into our marriage; I won't take anything out either. I'll sign a full release." She pressed her lips together for a moment. "I don't want anything from you. Not a single dime."

The relief he felt was so intense he couldn't help but let out a long breath of air, contained as much as he could. She shook her head only so slightly, her movement barely noticeable. She saw right through him and thought less and less of him with each moment. A nothing, a nobody, looked at him with unspeakable contempt before her eyes glistened, and she veered her gaze toward the fireplace mantle.

"What about the baby?" he asked, getting up from the floor and walking slowly toward the sofa.

"What about it?" she asked calmly, her coolness worrisome, dangerous, the stillness of a snake before pouncing. "I don't believe you want to be a part of its life, do you?" He shrugged. "I figured as much. So, no, I don't want any child support or alimony. This baby is no longer your concern."

His jaws were clenched so tightly his teeth hurt. He couldn't take her word for it. No way. First thing the following day, he had to consult a lawyer. She said she didn't want child support or alimony now, but the threat of it would be looming over his head for years and years.

Perhaps there was still a way out of this mess. A way that took care of the unwanted kid and the woman who'd entrapped him, both at the same time. People wouldn't be thinking he was some idiot whose wife left him, but someone whose perfect happiness was brutally cut short by a criminal hand, a villain who was never caught, striking while he was held back on a plane with about two hundred witnesses. Sympathy would be pouring for the charming, heartbroken widower from all directions, and with it, heaps of new deals.

I'm sorry, Andi, I tried everything I could think of, but you really want this to happen. You're leaving me no other alternative. It's all your fault.

"All right," he conceded with a heavy sigh. "But it doesn't have to happen tonight, right? Can we still have dinner together?" She raised her hand in protest and unfolded her legs, getting ready to stand. "I promise, I won't insist anymore. I respect your decision, even if it breaks my heart. You're my whole life, Andi, and I don't know how I'll be able to survive your absence, but we can still have tonight."

"Not tonight," she said, speaking softly. "Just dinner." She wiped a tear quickly with the tip of her finger.

He smiled wholeheartedly. "Thank you. Why don't I make us some Chinese stir-fry with steamed rice while you take a shower?"

Hesitating for a moment, then smiling briefly, she said, "Sure. Thank you for doing that." For a beat, she looked into his eyes with indecipherable intensity. Anguish, sadness, determination too. She was gone. Her mind was already made up.

And so was his.

Defense Attorney Goodridge: In your experience with poisoning, did you encounter cases where too little poison had been given to a victim?

Dr. Aaron Ellefson: No. Usually, the victims are given too much poison, not too little.

Defense Attorney Goodridge: Could it be possible that Andrea Wilmore Brafford had ingested these amounts of poison by accident?

Dr. Aaron Ellefson: I don't see how that would've been possible, no.

Defense Attorney Goodridge: But if the intention were to kill Andrea Wilmore Brafford, wouldn't the killer have used a larger quantity? To make sure she died?

District Attorney Buscher: Objection, Your Honor. Calls for speculation.

Judge Barry Cromwell: I'll allow it.

Dr. Aaron Ellefson: It's difficult to say. If the goal were to take her life quickly, then yes, I would've expected more poison to have been used. If the goal was to torture or—

Defense Attorney Goodridge: No more questions for this witness.

District Attorney Buscher: Redirect, Your Honor?

41

WILLPOWER

As soon as the bathroom door closed behind her, Andi leaned against it and breathed, letting the mask drop. The face staring back at her in the mirror was that of a shocked, heartbroken woman whose grief was almost too much to bear, loud and pounding against her chest in the rhythm of her weary heartbeats.

Every few moments, her mind careened into the land of doubt again, the painful reality too much to bear. What if she'd been wrong about the poison? What if Craig really loved her and was just someone who'd made a mistake, afraid of losing her? What if she—

No. The poison was there. Her blood tests, her miscarriage, the excruciating pain in her abdomen, everything pointed in the same direction, at the same man, the stark, pale finger of death that had touched her life.

But how could she have been so gullible, so deluded? "We see what we want to see," she whispered in a broken, tearful voice as she turned on the water and let it run. Those words were the feeble way her analytical, sound mind fought against the weakness in her heart.

She *was* weak; that was a fact. More fragile than she'd ever thought possible, so vulnerable she was ashamed of herself.

Perhaps her thinking was impaired by the poison, or so she wanted to believe, an excuse for her own fickleness when she wasn't busy still making excuses for Craig.

As the bathroom slowly filled with steam from the running shower, the image reflected in the mirror turned blurry, unrecognizable. Why was she still there? Why wasn't she picking up the burner cell in her bathrobe pocket to call Aaron and Rebecca? Dr. Ellefson would show up at the door within minutes with half a police precinct in tow.

Grabbing a small towel from a shelf, she buried her face in it and wailed, pressing it against her open, agonizing mouth until the suffocating burn in her chest relented a little, and she could think straight again. She knew he was going to try to kill her that night. Despite all logic and going against her screaming instincts, she wanted to look him in the eye as she ate the tainted food.

It was ridiculous. A senseless risk she took with her own life. Yet she couldn't walk away. Mesmerized, trapped like an unsuspecting fly caught in a spider's web, she was unable to free herself from his grip. Where had all her grit gone? Her willpower? She was acting like a naïve child, so in love with the stalker she'd met online she couldn't bring herself to understand she was falling for a predator, a dangerous animal ready to pounce.

Still, as if watching a train wreck in slow motion, she was unable to walk away until she believed with every fiber of her body that Craig was her baby's killer. She wished she could save herself, put herself first instead of eating dinner with him. She bitterly and desperately wanted the mental fortitude to run. Walk away. Call someone. Call Dr. Ellefson. Do something that made a modicum of sense.

Then she thought of her father. What would he say if he knew what she was planning to do? Over the years, he had been her litmus test. If she didn't tell him something, if she kept a secret from him, she knew that she was doing something intrinsically wrong. Yet, she still wanted to go through with it. And she would've never told him what she was planning to do.

Leaning her head against the wall, she bit her fist until sharp pain awakened her senses. "Why?" she whispered. "Why do I want to do this?"

Because I loved him more than life itself. Because when my heart aches like it's been stabbed with a thousand blades, I'll have to remember who he is.

The answer, surfacing from her subconscious and layering soothing calmness onto her anguished mind, instilled her with the willpower she so desperately needed.

She'd have the dinner.

Then she'd drive away and spend the night at her father's place.

Once decided, she cut the water in the shower and ran the blow dryer a little, leaving some moisture in her short hair. Then she changed into fresh jeans and a clean T-shirt, feeling chilly without reason. Car keys in one pocket and burner phone in the other, she had one last item she wanted to add.

With shaky, hesitant fingers, she put on the blue pendant Craig had given her. It was suitable for the occasion, a symbol of the chasm between her husband and her.

It was going to be the last time she wore it.

District Attorney Buscher: Dr. Ellefson, considering the relatively small amounts of poison the victim had ingested, what do you believe the perpetrator's goal could've been, if not to take her life?

Dr. Aaron Ellefson: Considering that Andrea Wilmore Brafford was also pregnant at the time of the poisoning, I believe it's safe to assume the perpetrator could've potentially wanted to terminate her pregnancy chemically.

District Attorney Buscher: Based on the forensic analysis of the victim's hair, over what period had she been given the rodenticide?

Dr. Aaron Ellefson: Normal hair growth in humans is about a half to three-quarters of an inch per month. We found poison in the victim's hair fibers in a section of about an inch from the root, so I'd have to say a month, maybe five weeks, not more.

District Attorney Buscher: Based on Dr. Hanfield's testimony, we know the victim was about eight weeks pregnant at the time of the consult. Is it safe to assume the perpetrator had started poisoning her immediately after learning she was pregnant?

Defense Attorney Goodridge: Objection, Your Honor. Calls for speculation.

District Attorney Buscher: Withdrawn. No more questions for this witness.

Defense Attorney Goodridge: Recross, Your Honor?

42

DINNER

With every step that brought her closer to the kitchen, Andi's blood chilled. A shudder rattled her as she took a seat at the table while Craig held her chair like the gentleman he was. Uneasy with him standing behind her, she turned her head and looked at him. Fear unfurled in her gut while her instincts screamed. What if he wasn't going to poison her this time? What if he did something else, something she wasn't prepared for?

Craig smiled warmly while offering her a napkin she unfolded with frozen fingers and laid on her knee. He'd set the table with a single, silver candlestick to the side, holding a tapered white candle waiting to be lit.

"Are you ready, my love?" he asked, turning to the stove, where their plates awaited keeping warm, already stacked with generous servings of Chinese stir-fry with a side of steamed rice. The smells of soy-lathered veggies and shrimp sauce were mouthwatering, yet nausea held her stomach in a vise.

"Don't call me that," she reacted, his words tugging at her heart more than she cared to admit. She wanted to scream at him, shout until the windows rattled, slap him across the face and ask him how he dared call her that after what he'd done.

He turned briefly to look at her over his shoulder, a sad smile fluttering on his lips. "You might leave me tonight, and you might file for divorce tomorrow, but you'll always be my love. My one and only love. My Andrea."

She swallowed hard, breathing away tears that didn't belong. He turned and set one plate in front of her and another in front of his empty seat. He moved smoothly, naturally, completely relaxed. There was no tension in his shoulders, no furtive glances loaded with guilt. Nothing. Just a charming, loving husband serving his wife a home-cooked meal.

She looked at him intently, keen on seeing anything that could've been an indication of his real intentions. There was nothing. Clinging to unreasonable hope like a drowning person to a straw, she picked up the fork and took a small bite of beef.

The moment she put it in her mouth, she knew. It was intensely salty and sour, as if the food had been cooked in the citric acid mix. This time, he meant business. He wanted her dead.

Chewing the unpalatable food slowly, she watched him take his seat across from her and light the candle. His eyes were candid and warm. His demeanor was completely relaxed and guilt-free.

She was staring at a sociopath.

The thought chilled her blood and raised goosebumps on her skin. At the same time, it redeemed her from her own guilt. She wasn't to blame for not noticing something was wrong with Craig, all those times he'd poisoned her in the past. There wasn't anything to notice.

"How is it?" he asked as he always did when he cooked. "Do you like it?"

She managed a weak smile. "A lot. Thank you for doing this. You know, you didn't have to," she added, finding it soothing to play double entendre games with a killer, dancing on the brink of the abyss. She took another mouthful of food and chewed it faster. The sour taste relieved her nausea a little, but the saltiness was too much to bear. "Could you please give me some sour cream? I think you might've overdone the soy sauce a bit."

Not a flicker of worry. Not the tiniest reaction in his pupils. "Sure," he replied, then pushed himself away from the table, the legs of his chair scraping loudly against the tiles. Grabbing a spoon from the cutlery drawer, he opened the sour cream and set it in front of her with the spoon in it, ready to serve. "Here you go."

Taking a spoonful, she spread it on her rice, then took a bite, mixed with meat and vegetables. Better. "I appreciate you letting me go." She couldn't resist the double-meaning word games as if taunting a killer was the smartest thing she could do. Another bite went down her throat easily. "I know it must be very difficult for you."

He reached across the table and squeezed her left hand. "You have no idea. Letting you go is the hardest thing I've ever had to do. I will never be the same after you've gone."

For a brief, scary moment, she thought maybe he was playing double entendre with her too. What if he'd found out she'd changed the poison? What if he was still killing her, right then, right there, only a different way, one she didn't see coming?

She'd eaten more than half of the food. And she had no idea what was in it.

Panic spread through her body like wildfire. Her heart thumping against her chest, she felt dizzy, her head spinning, while a disturbing thought surfaced in her unnerved mind. What was it her father had said? Something about dizziness and the noggin. Lying down before it comes . . . before what comes?

She couldn't remember. Grabbing at the edges of the table with shaky, weak fingers, she tried to stand, but nausea had her stomach in a twist. She managed to get up on her feet, heaving, gasping for air, knowing she had to run away from there as fast as she could. But her body was betraying her.

She looked at Craig and whimpered, but he sat calmly in his seat, watching her. "Is there something you need, honey?" he asked. His voice was that of a stranger, of a man she'd never known, cold, uncaring, impatiently waiting for her to die.

Her entire world started turning darker, slowly at first, while she tried to understand what was happening. Then the floor rushed toward her in a whirling, dizzying move, and she couldn't do anything to escape it.

On her way down, she hit her head against the edge of her chair. Stars burst wild and green in her skull before she could feel any pain. Before everything went dark.

43

BLOOD

Craig watched his wife falter and whimper without flinching, hoping it would be over soon. His dear wife wasn't going to leave him now. He'd poured enough poison in her food to take down a horse. But he hadn't planned for her hitting that chair and bleeding all over the floor.

"Oh, shit . . . blood!" Gasping for air frantically, Craig rushed to the sink and stared at the drain intently, focusing on the stainless-steel circle, forcing himself to notice details. The embossed letters of the manufacturer's brand. The touch of rust, defying the stainless-steel claim, making him wonder what it was really made of. Anything worked as long as he didn't look at the growing pool of blood staining the floor near Andi's head.

What was he going to do? This wasn't supposed to happen.

If he'd been able to stand the sight of blood for mere seconds, Andi would've been gone already. There were easier ways to handle such matters; unfortunately, most of them involved the spilling of blood. He'd considered such options in the Caribbean, where the place was ripe with opportunities. The dive boat, for example, would've been a great place for Andi to "slip and fall," and hit her head against the gunwale when the drunk Jamaican wasn't looking. But then what? He'd faint right there by her side, unable to handle things, and he'd wake up in jail. Not an option.

His thoughts raced and his heart thumped in a frenzy inside his chest. If he looked at Andi, he would faint. He'd come to at some point, then faint again as soon as he opened his eyes and saw the pool of blood. He was already feeling weak, about to pass out just from the metallic smell of the damn thing.

He needed to think, come up with a solution, and fast.

"Numb my senses," he muttered, opening kitchen cabinets mindlessly, looking for a solution. "C'mon, c'mon," he said, careful not to turn his head by mistake and see the body.

Nothing in the cabinets worked for his purpose. Walking sideways, he reached the fridge and opened the door. Grabbing the bottle of vodka from one of the door bins, he took a couple of swigs and breathed loudly, feeling the burn of the alcohol traveling down his throat. He put the vodka back and continued to look.

"This should do it," he mumbled, opening a bottle of balsamic vinaigrette and rubbing some under his nostrils. He promptly choked and coughed, but he couldn't smell the blood anymore.

Closing the fridge door, he braced himself, breathing slowly and deeply, trying to subdue the panic racing through his veins. His entire plan depended on him getting rid of her body quickly, so his alibi would work. But how was he going to remove her body from the house, if he couldn't look at blood without fainting?

"Damn it to fucking hell," he shouted, slamming his fist angrily against the granite counter. "This can't be the end. Not like this."

Another swig of vodka from the fridge gave him a new idea. All he had to do was cover the blood. That was going to be enough. Not seeing it. Not feeling it against his skin either. Gloves would take care of that. Andi kept some in a drawer somewhere.

He found a pair of blue nitrile gloves in a drawer by the stove and slid them on. Keeping his eyes trained on the wall, he left the kitchen and stormed into the bathroom. A dark blue towel hung from the bar next to the sink. He grabbed that and went back into the kitchen. Forcing himself to breathe deep, calming breaths, he threw the towel over Andi's body without looking, more guessing than seeing where the blood had pooled.

Grabbing the edge of the counter, he dropped to his knees and slowly, one inch at a time, he steered his eyes toward Andi's body. She lay in an unnatural position, her legs twisted under her body, her arms spread out. A chair was knocked over on the floor. The towel was soaking quickly, and with the sight of that, he felt a wave of heat rush through his body. Even if the liquid appeared dark purple on the towel instead of red, he still *knew* it was blood. "Oh, no, no, no . . ." He looked away and breathed until the heat waned. Then he looked at her again.

Was she really dead?

By the amount of blood soaking that towel, she had to be. But her eyes were slightly open, haunting. Looking sideways, he felt for her pulse but didn't feel anything. Closing his eyes, he listened for her breath. Nothing. He couldn't hear a sound, just the whooshing of his own blood rushing through his veins in a hectic rhythm.

"Think, think, damn it," he mumbled. He couldn't carry her to the car if that meant her blood spilling all over the place. He'd never be able to clean it up. He'd never make it past the kitchen door before passing out. Just visualizing that was too much for him. He barely made it to the fridge for another touch of balsamic under his nose.

His eyes veered away and stopped on the dining room rug. It was supposed to be waterproof, to protect the hardwood from potential spills. He reached it with a few large steps. Pushing the table and chairs out of the way, he grabbed the rug and took it into the kitchen, where he let the edge of it cover Andi's body. Then, looking elsewhere, he rolled her inert body into the rug. Just as he was about done, he remembered the pendant she had been wearing at dinner.

"Oh, shit," he whispered. Keeping his eyes on the ceiling fixture, he sneaked his hand inside the rug, feeling for her throat. Gloved fingers struggled to sense the chain, but eventually he grabbed hold of the chain, then the pendant, and yanked forcefully. It came out with the clasp broken. A few of Andi's hairs still clung to it, and blood stained the pendant and parts of the chain.

Panting heavily, he rushed to the sink and turned on the water, rinsing it quickly as his legs turned too weak to hold him. With the disappearing traces of blood off the pendant and his own gloves, his strength returned. He abandoned the pendant on the counter, then turned to look at the rolled rug.

One end of it was soaked in blood. One tiny glimpse of it was all he could handle before he had to look away. He was just about to give it up, to leave the body as it was and make a run for it, maybe drive all the way across the Mexico border, when a crazy idea came to his mind.

He could only see the blood if the light was on.

In the dark, he would have to move slowly and feel his way around furniture, but he'd be able to get the job done.

With a sigh of relief, he rushed into the bathroom, where he snatched the plastic shower curtain and took it into the garage, where he used it to line the inside of his SUV's trunk. He considered Andi's Beetle for a moment, but it was too small.

Carefully turning off all the lights, he went into the kitchen and grabbed the rolled carpet, holding it from the middle, where it was clean of blood. Then slowly, one step at a time and careful not to touch anything with his load, he carried it into the garage, then put it inside the trunk of the Benz. It took some pushing and struggling until it fit. When he was able to pull the cargo cover over it, he was covered in sweat.

Later, he'd have to clean up one hell of a mess. But he could do it, in the dark, using lots of bleach and paper towels he could later burn in the backyard, together with his Armani shirt and Brooks Brothers pants.

Still keeping the lights off, he found the laundry room sink and rinsed his gloved hands thoroughly in it. Then he went back to the garage, ready to leave.

Jumping behind the wheel of his car, he pressed the garage door opener and drove off, keeping his lights off until he left the neighborhood. Only a few miles to the landfill; at almost two in the morning, no one would be there to see him dump the body.

44

SURVIVOR

It was the most unbearable stench Andi had ever smelled, and still, she drew air forcefully, desperately trying to fill her lungs. She couldn't move much, although she writhed with every ounce of strength she had left, trying to free herself. It was dark, pitch blackness all around her. A throbbing ache in her left temple sent flashes of green inside her skull, worse with every move she made.

She pushed herself against whatever it was that had her immobilized, clawing at it, pushing her feet against it, until a wisp of colder air rushed through her hair and touched her face. With it, the stench grew much worse, unbearable, but her lungs were filling with air thirstily. Gasping with every breath, she opened her eyes and stared intently into the darkness. For a panicked moment, she wondered if she'd gone blind. But then faint shadows started to form in the distance. A star, a tiny little beacon of light, right above her head. Others more like it, smaller, fainter, a welcome sight, nevertheless. There were probably more, but her eyes were partly covered still.

Rolling to her side, she managed to squeeze her arm between her body and whatever was wrapped around her and reached above her head to where the air was coming from. Once she freed that one hand, she felt around for something she could grab onto but found nothing but squishy plastic bags and small, loose pieces of debris. Something crawled over her fingers, and she screamed, the piercing sound of her voice unanswered in the eerily silent darkness.

Understanding brought a chill down her spine. She was at the landfill somewhere, buried alive in trash. Willing her mind to be rid of the intense panic, she breathed deeply, counting the seconds between breaths to lower her heart rate and think logically. Feeling for whatever was wrapped around her body with the hand she'd freed, she felt a fringy edge, silky to the touch on one side, raspy and rubbery on the other. She was rolled inside a rug. There was something else around her neck, a different texture, soaked in something sticky. It felt like a towel.

She tried rolling herself out of the rug, going in the opposite direction from the edge of the rug, but nothing happened. Her knees felt tightly bound, and there was something tight running over her stomach. Feeling over the rug with her free hand, she quickly identified what that was.

Duct tape.

Out of alternatives, she wormed herself free, one agonizing inch at a time until she was able to pull her legs out, one at a time, and pull away from the rug, panting from the effort and whimpering.

She stood, faltering at times, her legs feeling weak and unstable, the mountain of trash under her feet an uneven, treacherous surface. Falling to her knees every couple of steps, she eventually gave up trying to stand and crawled her way out of the immense sea of refuse, heading toward the dim light she saw in the distance.

When she reached firm land under her feet, she stood, forcing her eyes to distinguish something in the darkness. Scattered pieces of paper blew in the wind, faintly lit by the residual light coming from the spotty low cloud cover, tiny ghosts chasing one another and never settling. Not a single soul anywhere. Nearby, a couple of compactors and a bulldozer were eerily silent and threatening in the dark as if they could suddenly come alive and chase her back into the refuse, then level her into the ground never to see the light of day.

For a moment, she felt a wave of shame washing over her. Shame and guilt. She should've never stayed. She should've run when she had the chance. But she was there now, still alive. There was no time for regrets.

The sky was beginning to turn gray to her right, and that helped Andi get oriented. If that was east, then the lit area to her left had to be the interstate going into Houston. She was about fifteen minutes away from her father's house.

Driving time.

She started walking, every step fueling the throbbing pain in her temple. Tentatively and painfully aware of how dirty her hands were, she felt the area gently with the tips of her fingers. It was clogged in blood and dirt, her hair a matted mess. She felt a lump under the lacerated skin; that was bad news. She could've had a concussion. Closing one eye at a time, she focused on the distant lights of the interstate, checking herself for blurry vision. There was none.

And pain she could handle.

Apparently, she was a glutton for it. For punishment and unnecessary risk taking too.

A burning sensation tingled her nape. She felt her skin with her fingers, and it smarted under her touch, right where the chain of her pendant used to be. It was gone. Craig must've snatched it from her neck, too precious of an item to discard with her body.

Reaching inside her pocket, she found the burner phone. She flipped it open and found it was still charged. Cops and an ambulance were a quick phone call away, yet she still hesitated. Craig deserved so much more than an attempted murder charge for what he'd done to her. He'd taken not one life, but two, even if, through some touch of fate, she was still alive. As far as she was concerned, Craig had killed her.

With every step she took, the stench subsided a little. Walking as fast as she could bear with the pounding ache in her head, she soon reached the edge of the landfill. An eight-foot-high chain-link fence kept her from getting to the street. She walked alongside the fence until she found a hole in it, probably from a car running into the nearby bent post by accident. She crawled through the hole with difficulty, then climbed onto the asphalt and smiled weakly.

She was going to be okay.

The burner didn't have GPS or maps, but she kept turning onto streets, always choosing the wider road at each turn until she reached a street she recognized. The sun was almost up by then, and traffic was starting to pick up.

Whenever a car drove by, she hid, either behind a tree or someone's trash can or by dropping to the ground in a ditch so that she wouldn't be spotted. Chances were, anyone who saw her covered in blood and dirt would call the cops, and she didn't want that. It was better not to have witnesses to what she was about to do.

As it got later, traffic became heavier and almost impossible to avoid. But she was close enough; she recognized the Clear Creek meanders and the nearby Walter Hall Park and chose to leave the street and walk alongside the riverbed for the remainder of the way, cutting straight through the woods behind the fire department training site and the water treatment plant.

It was almost nine when she made it to her father's house. Instinctively, she reached inside her pocket for the keys but only found those for the Beetle. Inside her car's glove compartment were the keys to the house, out of reach, inside the garage of what used to be her home.

She circled to the back of the house and tried the back door, but she'd locked it the last time she was there. Out of options, she took a rock and broke one of the small panes in the door, the one closest to the lock. Then she reached inside and turned the deadbolt to unlock it.

Once inside, she breathed a sigh of relief, but didn't take a moment to rest. Instead, she went straight to the bathroom, eager to get the landfill stench off her body. She turned on the faucet and, while waiting for hot water to come down the spout, she studied the gash in her temple.

It was deep, covered in debris and congealed blood clumping her hair, and would probably need stitches. Definitely a tetanus shot. Antibiotics too.

Water running down her head made her wound smart, increasingly so as it cleared the clumps of blood and dirt away. As gently as she could, she washed her hair a couple of times, unsure if she'd removed the stench of landfill from her hair. It didn't feel like she did, but the stench had become so engrained in her skin and her nostrils, the only thing she could smell was the foul odor of refuse.

When she was done, she stepped onto the cold tiles and wrapped a towel around her body. Clearing steam off the mirror with the palm of her hand, she stared at her image and didn't recognize the woman staring back.

Her wound was bleeding again, running streaks down her cheek, her neck, and turning the white towel red where it dripped onto it. As through a haze, she remembered the poison had an anticoagulant component; if she didn't control that bleeding soon, she could be at risk of losing her life.

Still wearing the towel, she left wet footprints everywhere, gathering the things she needed. Surgical needle and thread from her father's emergency kit. Hydrogen peroxide, a fresh bottle. Local anesthetics in a small syringe fitted with a subdermal needle. Band-Aids. Her father's razor.

Then she returned to the bathroom.

Tilting her head to the right above the sink, she poured hydrogen peroxide over her wound, grinding her teeth and panting while the liquid sizzled and cleaned the wound. She shaved her scalp carefully around the wound, then rinsed it with water, thoroughly.

Then the real pain began when she had to sew the gash in her scalp. Even with the local anesthetic she'd injected clumsily in various spots along the laceration, she could still feel the pain, the pulling of the thread.

"I'm no Rambo, that's for sure," she said to herself in a weak attempt at self-deprecating humor, only to break the heavy silence and hear something besides her shattered breath. Sewing her own skin was much more difficult than she'd anticipated. The scalp was thick, and even the slightest touch sent flashes of pain through her irritated nerves. Yet she was thankful for the labwork she'd done in San Diego and the few times she'd watched her father stitch up his patients.

The anguish seemed to last forever, but several excruciating minutes later, she was ready to apply a large Band-Aid.

The wound was visible, right above her ear and into her temple, the lump large and painful to the touch. Nothing some ice couldn't handle, and a ball cap couldn't hide from her father's eyes. She had to see him that morning, not a moment later. She couldn't afford to let him find out she was missing or presumed dead from the cops and risk him having another heart attack.

Right before turning off the light in the bathroom, she looked at herself again. The stranger in the mirror had steeled willpower, seeping from every pore of her skin. Her eyes were dry. She hadn't shed a single tear since awakening at the landfill. She'd paid dearly for her insanity, for wanting to be sure about Craig's intentions, when she should've already been sure a long time ago. She'd learned her lesson. The Craig she'd fallen in love with had never existed; there was nothing to cry about. But he would soon pay dearly for what he'd done.

Heading into the kitchen for a quick bite to eat before leaving to see her father, she noticed the pile of mail she'd brought from the mailbox the last time she was there. With a spark of mischief in her eye, she sifted through the envelopes until she found one that would serve her needs. It was a thank you letter from one of Dr. Wilmore's patients, stamped with a forever stamp depicting the Liberty Bell and bearing a wavy, USPS mark showing the date and location from where it was mailed.

Then, grateful she never got to clearing her father's fridge, she took a small pot from the cabinet and started boiling some eggs.

Defense Attorney Goodridge: Dr. Ellefson, were you surprised to hear about Andrea Wilmore Brafford's pregnancy?

Dr. Aaron Ellefson: No.

Defense Attorney Goodridge: Were you not, in fact, as a close friend of the Wilmores, expecting to hear about her pregnancy firsthand, from Andrea herself, not from the tabloids?

Dr. Aaron Ellefson: People have various reasons—

Defense Attorney Goodridge: Is it not true you should've recused yourself from testifying in this trial as an expert witness, considering your personal relationship with Andrea Wilmore Brafford?

45

LIES

It was early in the afternoon on Friday when Andi reached the cardiac rehab center. She drove her father's truck to the park that was adjacent to the center's backyard, then walked the distance across the park using a handheld GPS she and her father used to take along when hiking. It was a beautiful fall day, the air crisp and fresh, the leaves just starting to turn. The sky was the purest shade of California blue, probably helped by a low humidity index, a rare occurrence for Houston.

Slowing down as she approached the property's boundary, she put on the ball cap she'd brought along, wincing as the band ran over the Band-Aid covering the laceration on her temple. When she reached the fence, she stopped, crouching behind a shrub and taking stock of what was going on in the facility's yard.

A handful of patients were still outside, even fewer staff. The culprit was lunch. They served the meal between twelve and two, and most residents wanted to be among the first to take a seat at a table. Thankfully, her father wasn't one of them.

Barely visible between the two parallel hedges, a wisp of blue smoke appeared briefly, then vanished. Andi's heart swelled, then a frown ridged her brow. Who was supplying his cigars? At that rate, he must've already smoked his way through an entire box.

Lurching behind bushes while keeping her eyes on the few patients and staff who strolled through the yard, she reached a point where she could climb over the fence without much risk of being seen. A few moments later, she emerged from the hedges by her father's wheelchair.

The cigar now gone, he was absorbed in his work, jotting notes in his new notebook, something that looked like a bulleted list. Probably not what Rebecca had in mind when she'd recommended writing.

He seemed a little stronger. There was firmness in his jaw, in the way his eyebrows ruffled as he wrote. His white hair needed a trim; the edges exceeded the collar of his shirt by almost an inch.

She took off her sunglasses, wincing when the left temple scraped against her wound. She turned sideways, so he wouldn't notice the Band-Aid.

"Hey, Dad." The instant the words came off her lips, tears flooded her eyes. She crouched by his side and wrapped her arms around his neck.

"Ah, what a wonderful surprise," he said, quickly closing the notebook in his lap and sliding it under his leg. Then he put his arms around her shoulders and sighed, a long sigh of relief. "I miss you. Did you know that? Uh-huh . . . I miss you all the time. That's what I do all day. I sit out here and miss you."

Those few words unlocked the floodgates. She cried with her face buried at his chest, their conversation going nothing as she'd planned.

"Sweet girl, what's wrong?" he asked, his voice tinged with worry. "Tell me what happened." Gently, he pushed her away, searching her eyes. She kept them lowered, hiding. With two fingers, he lifted her chin. "You look pale. Are you eating well? What did that doctor say?"

"I'll be all right, Dad, I promise," she said, wiping her tears and letting out a long breath of air. "But I need your help."

"Anything," he whispered, drawing her close to his chest again. He smelled of aftershave and the rehab center's scent of laundry detergent. Her cheek flush against him, she could hear his heart beating in a steady, calming rhythm.

"Do you trust me?" she asked, her voice barely a whisper.

"More than anyone in this world." Worry came across clearly in the way he spoke. The cadence of his words had turned clinical, rushed yet calm at the same time. Perceptive. Ready.

"Would you lie for me?" She raised her blue eyes and looked into his for a brief moment, then hid her face again, ashamed.

"My dear child, I would die for you." He rocked her gently back and forth, soothing her the way he used to do when she was little. "Please tell me what's wrong. I can feel it. Parents are like that, you know. They sense when things go wrong with their offspring."

She chuckled with sadness. "You were right, Dad." She drew air sharply. "About Craig."

He didn't say anything. The rocking faltered for a moment, then resumed. "Tell me what I can do."

Andi relished his closeness for a long moment. It fueled her, making her stronger. But she wasn't able to stay long. With each passing minute, she risked someone passing by or some remote camera catching a glimpse of her face. Filling her lungs with air, she pulled away a little and looked into her father's eyes.

"Don't tell anyone I was here. Promise me you won't. If anyone asks, the last time you saw me was right after I returned from the Caribbean, on Monday. Last time we spoke on the phone was yesterday morning."

Hesitating just a bit while his brow furrowed, he replied, "You got it. What else?" He seemed more alert, invigorated, ready to spring to his feet and fight by her side.

"Promise me that whatever you hear, you'll know I'm all right."

His frown deepened. "You're scaring me, Andrea. What's going on? Are you in some kind of danger?"

She shook her head. "No, Dad. Not anymore. I need you to believe this. Whatever people come and tell you, just know I'm at your house, lying low, and people can't know I'm there."

"Who's looking for you?" He sounded panicked. She sensed his muscles tensing. "I can help you. I'm recovered. I sit in this chair because it's easier, and because they didn't think of putting a bench here, where no one can see me smoke, but I can function. You and I can run out of here right now."

"No need for any of that, Dad," she said, kissing his hand then nestling her cheek against it. "I need you to stay here, rest, get better, so when all of this is over, you can come home. And we can learn to live and be happy again. Both of us." She swallowed hard. It could take a while before that happened, before she would be free. "Just remember you said you trusted me."

He exhaled. "I do trust you."

"Then let me lead on this, Dad."

"Whatever you say. Only be very careful with Craig. He's . . . there's something about him that makes my hackles stand on their ends. I already told you that, didn't I? These meds are really bad for my memory." He seemed to try to recall what he'd said to her about Craig. "I don't know what it is yet but promise me you'll be careful. He scares me." The last few words faltered coming out of his mouth, as if they'd made it out without his intention to speak them.

"I know. I believe you now." She squeezed his hand. "Remember: whatever they say about me isn't true."

"Like what?" he asked, shifting in his chair. "What exactly should I be expecting?"

She wasn't ready to share that, mostly because she didn't know it herself. "I'm not sure yet. You'll just have to trust that I'm okay, and we'll see each other soon."

"Good grief, Andi. What the hell happened?"

"Nothing, Dad." Her voice climbed a little, frustrated. "As you can see, I'm okay."

"Yes, you are. I believe that because you're lying to me just like you used to when you were little and up to no good."

A tear clung to the corner of her eye. "Please, believe me. There's no other way. I have to do this on my own."

He stared at her for a long time, then eventually nodded, pressing his lips together. "Okay."

She looked around, checking to see if anyone was coming. Even fewer people were outside than before. Then she looked at him and clasped both his hands in hers. "Whatever they ask you, just say you don't know. You're ill, still recovering; it will make sense."

"Anything you need." He was clinical again. He'd probably decided to trust her and was acting accordingly.

"Do you still have the key to my house?"

"To *your* house?" His eyebrows shot up, ruffled. "Sure. It's in my desk, the top drawer on the left side."

"How about some cash?"

His eyebrows remained up, creasing his forehead. "Same side, the second drawer from the top, in an old cigar case."

"Thank you," she whispered, lowering her eyes, embarrassed she had to ask for money. She should've had her own. "Now, let's work on some hypothetical questions, all right?"

His frown returned, and his eyes darkened with worry. "Fire away."

"If someone should theoretically have a tetanus shot, how much can they delay the administration of said shot without risk?"

"Jeez, Andi . . ." Seemingly stunned, he shook his head. "The hypothetical someone shouldn't wait more than twenty-four hours from the time of injury, or risk dying. If not from tetanus, then at my own hand," he added, his attempt at humor bringing tears to her eyes.

"Dogs don't need tetanus shots, do they?"

"No, they don't, and neither do cats," he replied, clenching his jaws. "But if the someone waits here for about twenty minutes after we're done talking, I might get that someone a vial. If this center has one, I'll snatch it. I know where they keep their goodies, and how to get to them. Then that someone can self-administer the shot deep into the thigh muscle."

"Thank you." She blinked back tears. "How about a general antibiotic, something that would work just as well for dogs and people too?"

"Andi . . ." He shook his head again, lowering his gaze. He seemed saddened she didn't trust him with her problems. He deserved to know what was going on, but how would he react if he'd known the truth? He'd call the cops in a heartbeat. "Doxycycline, one hundred milligrams, twice daily. Ten days minimum. It's in my home office." His voice was low, riddled with undertones of sadness, defeated. He lifted his gaze and looked at her with unspeakable anguish. "Just walk away from the bastard, Andi. Whatever this is you're doing, it's not worth it. It's dangerous. Walk away, go to the hospital, get proper care."

She nodded. "I will. But it's not that simple, Dad." *Not after he killed me,* she added in her thoughts, afraid to speak the words out loud.

District Attorney Buscher: Do you remember the name of Craig's childhood friend? The one who gave him the pendant?

Louise Brafford: I do. His name was—is Jude Drennon.

District Attorney Buscher: At the time of her visit with you or at any time after that, did you share this information with Andrea Wilmore Brafford?

Louise Brafford: No. She didn't ask. I didn't volunteer it. I saw no reason to. Until now, I honestly believed Craig had left Jude behind, just as he'd left us.

46

EVIDENCE

The weekend had been a long and complicated one, even if Andi had anticipated it would be uneventful. She didn't dare leave the house, afraid she'd be seen. Instead, she'd pulled all the curtains shut and didn't turn on the lights after dark. Instead, she rested, regaining her strength, at least physically.

The emotional part lagged, more challenging to handle, especially after the sun disappeared over the top of the trees behind the house and darkness started to fall in the evenings. For a while, she grieved, not sure at times what she was grieving for the most. The loss of her baby, of her life, as she thought she knew it, of all her hopes and dreams. Or Craig, the one she thought she had married. Grief came and went in waves, renewed after each instance when she'd dozed off or she'd kept herself busy with something else, briefly forgetting what had happened. Then it all came crashing back, and she reeled, going through the shock, the senseless loss once more.

On Sunday, she cleaned up carefully the mess she'd made in the bathroom, where she'd taken that first shower after escaping from the landfill. She ran her clothes through the washer twice, only to have them dried, folded, then thrown at the bottom of her closet, sealed in a shopping bag tied with a knot and ready to dispose of at the first opportunity to take the trash out. It wasn't as if she would ever again want to wear the clothes she wore when her husband tried to murder her and dumped her body.

Replacing the small windowpane on the back door took some creative doing, but she couldn't call the store and order a replacement. Instead, she took a glass pane, slightly larger than what she needed, from a kitchen cabinet and, with the infinite patience of the woman with a purpose, filed away at it with her old diamond nail file until it fit the spot.

The mindless filing that took hours while she stood over the sink left her mind free to wander and deal with problems she'd been putting off. How would she restore people's trust in her after the lies Craig had spread about her all over town? How would she rebuild her life after he'd gone, short of leaving her dear Lone Star State behind?

The answer came when she was a tenth of an inch short of being done filing. She needed to purge herself of the filth he'd smeared all over her, to emerge like a butterfly from the chrysalis, leaving the smeared shell behind her to wither in the sunlight. And for that, she needed the burning, seething power of media defending her, set on Craig like a starving pack of wolves with foaming, blood-smeared snouts.

As soon as she replaced the windowpane, she fired up her father's laptop inside a windowless room and started typing an article. She reread her work a couple of times, making edits here and there until it looked just right. Until it felt inflammatory enough to get journalists to investigate and publish.

A while ago, she'd read somewhere that journalists welcomed contributions that were well-written, saving them the time they'd have to spend rewriting. They also liked short articles with concise information and verifiable facts. She'd done just that, she believed, after reading it once more, this time aloud.

After she finished, she created a new ProtonMail secure email account and sent the article to all the local media contacts she could find. Then she went to bed, glad the weekend was over.

On the cool, gloomy Monday morning, Andi waited at a safe distance from Craig's house, eager to see him leaving for work. She'd checked the headlines over the weekend; not a single peep about Craig or her. The neighborhood app didn't mention her disappearance, which meant Craig hadn't had the guts to report her missing yet.

She flinched when the garage door opened in the distance, letting herself slide lower in the seat of her father's truck. She wore large shades and a cap and still feared she'd be recognized from over a hundred yards away. But the black Mercedes-Benz turned left and disappeared at the usual time, a little after nine.

Giving it a few more minutes, just to make sure he didn't return, she walked over to the house, then sneaked inside the yard, lurching after checking to see if anyone noticed her. There was no traffic on the cul-de-sac, and the tall hedges provided some cover.

The key in her hand opened both the front and back doors, a touch of genius from the builder. She opted for the back door and unlocked it with ease, then entered the house and closed the door silently behind her.

The house felt strange, foreign, as if it hadn't been hers for two months. As if she'd never lived there. That didn't surprise her, though. Even if she'd chosen the rugs and a couple of pieces of furniture, the house was all Craig. It smelled of him, of his cologne. His presence filled the air, chilling her to the bone.

"Okay, let's do this," she whispered, sliding a pair of gloves on her hands, eager to be done with the visit.

The first stop was the kitchen cabinet under the sink. She opened it widely and removed the trash can after taking note of its position and how it was oriented. The bottle of citric acid mix was gone, just as she'd anticipated. Of course, Craig had disposed of it, covering his tracks.

She went into the garage, where she gave her abandoned Beetle a sad glance, then opened the HVAC door and retrieved the bottle of poison, handling it carefully with two fingers to not compromise Craig's fingerprints. Then she placed it under the sink, in the cabinet, where she'd found it Wednesday night. The trash can was last, placed precisely how she'd found it. Garbage collection day wasn't until Thursday; Craig had no reason to look behind that can until Wednesday night.

Then she found her old phone in the bedroom, on the dresser, plugged into the wall, exactly how she'd left it. She copied several key numbers into her burner phone, then locked it and put it back on the dresser.

The bathroom came next. She found her hairbrush on the counter and picked it clean of hairs, then disposed of those hairs in the toilet and flushed. Then she brushed her hair for a few moments, keeping clear of her left side, until a few new strands attached to it. They came off quite easily; probably hair loss came with the territory of being poisoned.

Leaving the bathroom, she froze. Someone was at the door. Was that Craig?

She held her breath, wondering where she could hide. There was enough room inside the walk-in closet, behind the dresses and in the far corner, behind the large suitcase. Holding her breath, she listened. The person rang the doorbell, then dropped something on the mat. A moment later, a truck door slammed shut, and a revved engine faded away.

It must've been a delivery.

Breathing deeply, she steadied her trembling hands, then started looking for the necklace. It was the final piece of evidence she needed. Almost thirty minutes later, she was still searching for it, opening drawers, reaching inside Craig's pockets. Where on earth was it?

She stopped in the middle of the bedroom, wondering where he might've put it. He'd thrown out the poison to cover his tracks. Would he put the pendant with his things, when everyone knew she was the one who wore it?

She smiled, opening the drawer where she kept her jewelry. It was there, the chain neatly coiled under the pendant, the clasp broken.

Now she could leave.

District Attorney Buscher: At which point did you realize you had been scammed?

Truman Haskett: It wasn't until I saw my Realtor, the defendant, having dinner with the client, Jude Drennon, at a downtown steakhouse. They seemed really chummy. Way closer than Craig Brafford had disclosed during the undervalued sale of my property.

District Attorney Buscher: Did you take any action?

Truman Haskett: No one forced me to sell, although this wasn't an arm's length transaction. I don't believe there's much I can do at this point. An attorney might feel differently though.

47

ANONYMOUS

The precinct stank of Mexican food, although it wasn't even eleven yet. Someone had warmed up something greasy and mouthwatering in the microwave, and now everyone had to live with the odor for the rest of the day. It was chilly outside, and the air conditioning had no reason to kick in any time soon to clear the air.

That someone was her partner.

Feeling hungry, Detective Otwell slammed her hands against the file folder open in front of her. She wasn't going to troll the kitchen at eleven in the morning just because she craved Mexican now. No. She was going to be an adult about it. Drink more coffee, swear between her teeth, and pop a breath mint or two. Otherwise, she'd soon be just as fat as Alonzo, the three-hundred-pound detective who was stuffing his face with a quesadilla covered in mouthwatering guac while reading the news on his desktop computer.

"Gee, thanks, Alonzo," Otwell commented, unable to refrain. "Now my stomach is growling."

"Want some?" Alonzo offered, speaking with his mouth full.

"Oh, hell, no." It wasn't clear in her mind if she craved the food or was repulsed by it. "But thanks. Next time, please let me leave the building first." A couple of uniformed cops giggled behind their screens.

"Shut up, you two," Alonzo ordered, and the laughter flared instead of subsiding.

He chewed in silence for a while, while Otwell reviewed the file for the umpteenth time since the case had been officially closed. There was something about Nikki Edwards that didn't sit well with her, more like a gut feeling than hard evidence or a lead she could follow. A twenty-five-year-old girl from an upper-middle-class family with a neat apartment, a good job, and a decent car doesn't just overdose one day. And where was the boyfriend or the man who'd gotten her pregnant? He was nowhere in her social media, and she'd wasted tens of hours of her personal time digging through endless strings of useless crap for the tiniest reference to a name, a hint, anything. Fetal DNA had returned zero hits in CODIS. She had nothing. Even the medical examiner had ruled it an accidental overdose. No signs of struggle, no forced entry, only her fingerprints on the syringe. Witnesses placing her with a small-time dealer buying dope.

She had nothing, but it was a certain flavor of nothing.

In Otwell's experience, that particular set of circumstances happened if the victim had been raped. That would've explained the girl's sudden descent into the world of opiates, abandoning a perfectly good life for fleeting moments of forgetfulness. With Nikki gone, she could never collar the bastard who'd ruined that young girl's life.

Still, she didn't close the file. Instead, she turned another page, rereading the medical examiner's findings slowly, wondering what she could've missed.

"Oh, crap . . . come read this, Otwell," Alonzo called, laughing out loud while pointing at the screen. "How stupid can you get? All we have to do is show up and collar this sorry-ass son of a bitch."

Intrigued, she rose from her worn-out chair and approached Alonzo's desk, leaning over to read the screen. It was an article published that morning by *The Morning Journal,* a Houston digital and print media. Alonzo pointed at the title, cackling so hard his abdomen rippled from it. "Can't believe it."

She skimmed over it quickly at first, but then something caught her attention, and she read it again, word by word.

Husband Tarnishes Wife's Reputation, Compromising Her Ability to Secure Employment

In this modern-day version of the tale with the wife locked inside the castle, Craig Brafford, 29, of Brookhaven, has turned to lies and deceit to thwart his wife Andrea's efforts to score a job. Posing as law enforcement, he made countless calls to his wife's prospective employers, spreading lies and putting human resource departments on notice that she was a wanted fugitive. Or a smuggler of rare and exotic species. Or a suspect in a credit card fraud scheme.

Our publication has investigated several of these calls and has established, beyond any doubt, that Brafford made said calls, some from his mobile phone, others from the landline in his real estate office. Sources who prefer to remain anonymous have provided the information necessary to piece together this bewildering puzzle. As to the reason why Brafford decided to act in this manner, we can only speculate. Mr. Brafford remains unavailable for comment.

"I know these people," Otwell mumbled, while Alonzo and a uniformed cop, attracted by the detective's laughter, still commented loudly. Otwell's words silenced them.

"How do you know them?" Alonzo said.

"Run a quick check for me, will you? See if Brafford's old address wasn't in Nikki Edwards's building. I think I met this woman, his wife."

Alonzo's chubby fingers danced above the keyboard, typing fast. "Yup, you're spot on. You and your Nikki Edwards file. You're spooky." He took another mouthful of quesadilla.

"I'll finish this in a few, then let's pick this bastard up. After all, he impersonated law enforcement, right?"

The other cop laughed. "Damn right."

Otwell was already back at her desk when a chime alerted her to new email. She didn't recognize the sender; it showed as a string of numbers. When she opened it and clicked the sender's address, it was a ProtonMail address, completely untraceable. Not only was it hosted in Switzerland, where American law enforcement didn't reach, but it was world-famous for its encryption and security. It was the type of email account that people sent tips to cops and media from.

The email subject line drove an icicle through her gut. She read the message with her mouth agape and her right hand covering it.

Have You Seen Andrea Wilmore Brafford?

You might want to look into the whereabouts of Andrea Wilmore Brafford. She was last seen on Thursday, October 7. If her husband has her locked up inside the house, it's not with her consent. She's pregnant and in need of medical attention.

The email message wasn't signed.

"Hey, partner," Otwell called, beckoning Alonzo. "We gotta go now. Forget that quesadilla. Shit is getting real." She turned to the uniformed cop. "Let's get some warrants ready. An arrest warrant for this guy, Craig Brafford. Search warrants for his house, his car, his office. I want everything. Then ping his phone and let me know where he's at."

Pulling her drawer open, she grabbed her service weapon and checked the magazine, then holstered it, the image of Andrea Wilmore Brafford still fresh in her mind. Her happiness, her newlywed glow, her trusting, youthful naivete. The way she'd reacted when Otwell had handed her the letter she'd found on the hallway floor, her face an open book, her heart on her sleeve. The voice of her husband, making phone calls in the other room. Stacks of boxes, ready for the move scheduled for the following day. A life just starting, with its ups and downs.

What was it about Andrea Wilmore Brafford that had seared the memory of her inside Detective Otwell's mind?

District Attorney Buscher: What was your perception of Craig's solvency?

Jude Drennon: I had no idea Craig was broke. Had I known, I would've posted his bail, got him a better lawyer.

48

ARRESTED

Craig had spent his entire morning on the golf course, at Wildcat Golf Club, with Bill Parsons. He was a big name in oil distribution and someone who'd attended his parties a couple of times. Yet, until that day, Parsons had remained unreachable whenever Craig had tried to call him to talk business.

Until that morning.

Out of the blue, Parsons had summoned him to the golf course with a seven a.m. call that found him still asleep. He dressed in a hurry, grabbed his clubs, and rushed out, barely able to make it to the club by eight.

Parsons, like all people with money, took his sweet time. He wanted breakfast and coffee first. He endlessly commented on oil production, price rigging, distribution, and the role of cryptocurrencies in the growing threat of ransomware attacks on pipeline companies. The man was in love with his voice and could talk forever, nothing of what he said of any real interest to Craig.

To make matters worse, the entire morning, Craig's phone had been chiming with missed calls, voicemails, and texts as if the world couldn't turn without him. After a few chimes and a couple of raised eyebrows on Parsons's smug face, he'd switched the phone to silent but still felt the vibrations in his pocket every few minutes.

What the heck was going on?

He couldn't break free from Parsons for one moment to find out and it drove him crazy. When the guy finally propped his hands on his thighs and said, "Time for a visit to the john," that was an invitation, not an announcement. Parsons didn't move toward the building until Craig followed, leaving their clubs with the caddy next to the eleventh hole. While in the can, he went on and on, even at the urinal, when he asked Craig, "Do you know why I golf on a public course, instead of a country club? It's the people," he immediately answered, not waiting for Craig's reply. "I like to see new faces, study them."

Then he wanted to have lunch while the caddy sat under a tree, shielded from the sunlight. Monday's gloom had vanished, leaving behind a clear blue sky and northerly winds to bring a crisp chill to the air. And it wasn't until the eighteenth hole, when he finally stopped talking for a moment, then said, "I have a mansion in Galveston I'd like you to sell for me. It's worth about seven million, maybe more. Then, my wife and I would like you to find us another one, someplace where the beaches are nicer and the ocean is blue and clear, not like here, murky. Maybe in Tampa or in Naples. We'd have to fly there anyway."

"Absolutely," Craig said, grinning. It was starting to happen. His carefully laid-out plan was beginning to show some results. Terrified of the idea of spending another half day listening to Parsons talk, he said, "Mr. Parsons, I have some paperwork in the car with me, if you're ready to sign."

"Call me Bill," he replied, giving him a meaningful stare as if to warn him that his friendship came with strings attached.

About half an hour later, they were signing the contract on the hood of his Benz, when two unmarked police cars approached with red and blue flashers on. Craig's gut twisted into a knot but then relaxed. It couldn't've been about him. Then he remembered the endless missed phone calls and froze.

"Craig Brafford?" a woman asked, flashing her badge. She was a tall blonde dressed in cheap, brown polyester slacks and a blue cotton shirt. Some women really tried to look like crap. No sense of style whatsoever.

"Yes," he replied, smiling. "How can I help you?"

She didn't smile back. Instead, she yanked Craig's arm and turned him around, then slapped a handcuff on his wrist. The touch of the cold metal jolted him. He tried to pull away, but her fingers were like steeled claws digging into his flesh, unyielding. "You're under arrest for impersonating law enforcement. You have the right to remain silent."

"What?" Craig tried to turn around and face her, but she slammed him against the hood of his car, then grabbed his other wrist and cinched the cuff around it. "What are you talking about?"

"Anything you say can and will be used against you in a court of law—"

But Craig wasn't listening anymore. He was watching Parsons as he fished the contract he'd just signed out of Craig's open briefcase and tore it to pieces.

"Waste of my time," he said, calmly looking Craig in the eye with disappointment while he threw the pieces of paper in the air. Then he climbed behind the wheel of his Maybach and drove off.

"We should fine his ass for littering," Alonzo said.

"Let's settle for this scumbag today," Otwell replied. Then, grabbing Craig's arm, she turned him around and looked straight into his eyes. "Where's your wife, Mr. Brafford?" She patted him down, searched his pockets, and took his phone.

Craig froze. His mind started spinning, going through scenarios. Had they found her body at the landfill? Maybe he didn't bury her deep enough. No . . . if they had, they would've charged him with murder, not this impersonation bullshit. He decided to stay calm and remain silent, then see what happened. He might need to hire that lawyer he'd found, just to be on the safe side.

It felt as if it wasn't happening to him. The arrest, the dragging away in handcuffs, the ride in the police car. His mind was stuck on Parsons's face, and the thought of that smug son of a bitch calling all his friends, Donati included, to tell them the news of his arrest. He was finished. People rarely came back from shit like that. Not unless they were Martha Stewart or Lindsay Lohan.

Hours later, chained to a crooked, filthy stainless-steel table inside a small, gray room, he was still waiting for someone to speak with him. To question him. When the door finally opened and the tall, blonde cop from earlier came through the door, he sighed with relief.

"Finally," he said. "Let's sort this out, because it's just a big misunderstanding."

"Is it now?" The cop pulled out a chair, its legs grating on the uneven floor. She threw a small evidence pouch on the table with his phone inside. "You should've taken your calls, Mr. Brafford." Through the plastic, she touched the screen, and it lit up. "Seventeen missed calls. Twenty-three new messages. Almost fifty unread emails."

"I'm a busy man," he replied calmly. "Now, can I go, please?"

She shook her head. "You won't be going anywhere for three-to-five, Mr. Brafford, and that's just for starters." She pushed his phone across the table to him. "People were trying to reach you. Warn you. The newspapers were looking for comments."

"The newspapers? Comments about what?" Nothing made any sense anymore, as in one of those surreal nightmares he sometimes had.

"Where's your wife, Mr. Brafford?"

"I—I don't know," he said, just as he'd rehearsed in his mind countless times. "She was angry with me for being gone at this conference in Miami. When I got home, she wasn't there. I assumed she ran off to her dad's house. He's in the hospital, and she has the place to herself."

"She's not at her father's house. We checked."

When did they have the time to check Wilmore's place? They were a step ahead of him, and that wasn't the way it was supposed to happen. He was supposed to be the victim here, the poor schmuck whose wife had disappeared.

"Has it happened before, Mr. Brafford?"

"Has what happened before?"

"For your wife to disappear like that, for days, without a word." Silence. He didn't know what to say. It was a trick question. "Without her car, her phone. Has it happened before, sir?"

What a good joke. She was calling him sir and Mr. Brafford but wanted to lock him up and throw away the key.

"No," he eventually said. It was better not to lie about that when countless witnesses could've testified to the contrary. "It's the first time."

"You didn't report her missing. Weren't you worried that something might've happened to your wife?"

"Of course, I was. I still am. But she'll come to her senses and come back home. All she needs is some cooling-off time."

"Why? What happened?"

He wasn't about to tell her.

"You might not know this, Mr. Brafford, but I met your wife, when you and she were about to move into a new house, I believe. I spoke to her about a girl who overdosed in your building."

"Ah, you're that cop," he replied. "Andi told me you came and asked questions. She showed me your card. But I'd forgotten your name. Sorry."

Otwell glared at him. "Two months ago, your wife was very happy, Mr. Brafford. What happened to make her need cooling-off time away from you?"

He shrugged. Maybe it was better to remain silent after all. "Let's get me a lawyer if it's not too much to ask. I have someone you could call. His name is Lamar Goodridge." He'd done his homework, specifically for a scenario such as this. He hadn't met Goodridge yet, but he hoped the man wouldn't turn him away in his hour of need.

"Sure," Otwell replied, standing. Right then, the door opened, and the other cop came in, carrying a bunch of evidence bags in a box. "What do you have for me?" Otwell asked her colleague.

Craig held his breath.

"They found this under the kitchen sink," the man said, lifting a plastic bag with the bottle of rat poison sealed in it.

What the hell? That wasn't happening. He wasn't insane. He knew exactly what he'd done. He'd emptied it at the sink, then taken the empty bottle and thrown it in a Dumpster near a construction site all across town.

"Rat poison? In Brookhaven?" Otwell said. "Isn't that interesting?"

"You bet," the other cop replied, visibly entertained. "It's got his fingerprints on it too. Real smart." They both chuckled at his expense.

He slammed his chained fists against the table. "No. This isn't true. This isn't happening. I'm telling you, this can't be real. It couldn't be." Craig's voice sounded strangled, high-pitched, riddled with hues of desperation. He was losing his mind.

"We got her hairbrush. It's got hairs in it. Where do you want this?" The cop lifted the bag holding Andi's hairbrush in the air, dangling it in front of Otwell. They were acting as if they hadn't even heard him.

"The ME's office," Otwell replied.

"Hey, will you listen to me?" Craig shouted. "I'm telling you, this shit ain't real. It can't be."

Otwell turned to him, frowning. "Are you waiving your right to an attorney, sir?"

Taken aback, he hesitated. "No."

"Then we cannot talk to you. I'm sorry." Smiling wickedly, she turned to her partner. "Anything else interesting?"

"Big time. The shower curtain in the bathroom was ripped off. They did a luminol test in the kitchen, and the floor lit up like a Christmas tree. A chair too. I think he killed her."

"And dumped her somewhere?"

"They're going over the GPS in his car as we speak." The overweight cop rubbed his belly, as if he'd just had a big lunch, and licked his lips. "Should we charge him with murder?"

"Let's try to find the body first," Otwell replied. Her eyes had turned dark, enraged. "The DA likes his cases neatly packed."

"You got it," the detective replied, then took the box of evidence and left, leaving Otwell alone in the room with Craig.

She waited until the door was closed and leaned over the table until he could feel her breath on his face. "If you killed that beautiful, young wife of yours, Mr. Brafford, I swear to God, I'll throw you in a hole so deep you will never see the light of day again. You'll wish you were dead every hour of every single day, and that's my promise to you, sir." Then she stood and grabbed the door handle, about to leave.

"Please, you don't understand. I didn't kill my wife, I swear. She was gone when I got back from the conference. Ask the airlines, we were held back on the tarmac until ten or something. When I got back, she was gone already. Please, you have to believe me."

"For the record, Mr. Brafford, I cannot speak with you without your attorney present. That was on your request. Please remain silent. I'll be back when we can locate him for you."

The sound of the door closing reverberated in his mind for endless moments. Did he dream he got rid of the bottle? He remembered it clearly or at least he thought he did. He'd smashed it against the Dumpster, and it broke into a million pieces. Or was he losing his mind?

It was a nightmare, one from which there was no awakening.

District Attorney Buscher: Please state your name and title for the record.

Arthur Flanagan: Arthur Flanagan. I'm an estate attorney in Houston.

District Attorney Buscher: People's exhibit number fourteen, Your Honor. Mr. Flanagan, do you recognize this envelope?

Arthur Flanagan: Yes, I do.

District Attorney Buscher: Please tell the court how you got possession of this envelope.

Arthur Flanagan: The envelope and its contents, sealed, was mailed to me by Andrea Wilmore Brafford, with the request that, in the event of her death, I hand-deliver it to her husband, Craig Brafford. Her request included her credit card authorization form for our fees, as our office had previously instructed her to proceed.

District Attorney Buscher: When did you receive the envelope and the instructions?

Arthur Flanagan: I received it on Friday, October eight. The envelope was postmarked October four. That was a Monday.

District Attorney Buscher: Did you deliver the envelope as instructed?

Arthur Flanagan: Yes, I did, as soon as I learned from the media that my client was deceased, and her husband was charged with her murder and remanded. I located Mr. Brafford and delivered the envelope the next day.

District Attorney Buscher: No further questions for this witness, Your Honor.

Present Day

49

STRATEGY

Mornings started early in jail. Inmates were startled out of their restless sleep at six by a loud, buzzing sound that Craig had learned to hate since he'd first stepped inside Houston Southeast Jail.

He wasn't due in court until ten. It was the third day in his murder trial. With every piece of evidence presented, every witness testimony, and every legal argument brought by the blood-thirsty District Attorney Isaac Buscher, he felt the noose around his neck tightening.

Having lost all control over his existence was driving him insane every minute of his caged life. It wasn't something Craig was capable of accepting, even when circumstances dictated it. More and more, he found himself wishing he was dead but clinging to the hope that he'd soon be set free by a jury of his peers.

That hope had disintegrated the night before when he'd read Andi's letter and had touched the center stone of the blue pendant.

Somehow, she'd survived. He hadn't killed her after all. Struggling to understand how that was possible, he relived every moment of that Thursday night, playing it in slow motion inside his head, trying to figure out where he'd gone wrong. It must've been his damn fear of blood that played the trick on him. He couldn't check if she was dead, not well enough, it seemed. Maybe she'd still had a pulse, but in his elevated state of phobia, he couldn't sense it. He'd just assumed.

It was fate, snarling at him before it ended him, laughing as he agonized in a cold prison cell.

And now, Andi was playing a vicious and spiteful game of cat and mouse with him, with his life. He'd snatched the pendant off Andi's neck before he dumped her body at the landfill. Yet it was delivered to him in a letter supposedly given by Andi to that estate lawyer when she was still alive. How the heck did she pull that off?

Was he losing his mind? Was any of this real?

If he told the truth, he'd self-incriminate himself as a killer, while at the same time, he would cast enough reasonable doubt over the validity of the murder charge to hope for a—what exactly? They weren't going to pat him on the shoulder, wish him a good life, and let him go. No. They'd reduce the charges to attempted murder and find him guilty. Less time behind bars, but he wouldn't last a month more. He couldn't.

There was no way he could walk. The vengeful hand that was weaving the noose around his neck was skilled and cunning and evil. It tore him apart to not know for sure if it was Andi after all. Was she still alive?

If not Andi, who else could hate him so much? Who could know so much detail about what had happened, other than Andi herself? But he'd buried her body with his own hands in that landfill. She'd bled on the kitchen floor, so much it soaked a rug. He didn't imagine things; just thinking of all that blood made him queasy and weak.

Sitting on the side of his bunk with his head in his hands, he didn't notice Chavez approaching.

"Hands, seven-one-nine," he said, startling Craig. "Your attorney is back."

Putting his hands through the opening and bracing for the cold metal of the handcuffs to snap around his wrists, Craig thought of asking which lawyer had returned. But he was going to find out in a moment anyway.

Chavez unlocked the cell and grabbed him by the arm, leading him along. "Are you going to throw another spaz attack like you did last night?"

"No," Craig replied quickly. "I—I'm really sorry about last night. It was unexpected to hear from my wife after—" He stuttered, not knowing how much damage he was doing to himself with every word. "After she'd gone. She just disappeared," he said, trying his hand at what was emerging in his mind as a possible new line of defense. "They never found a body. There's no autopsy, nothing, but they still charged me with her murder. She's setting me up. Now I know."

Chavez shrugged as he opened the door to a small interview room that stunk of bleach and urine. "Sorry, seven-one-nine, nothing I can do for you. Life ain't fair, you know."

Lamar Goodridge sat at the small stainless-steel table, dressed for court in a charcoal suit, white shirt, and gray tie. His lips were pressed tightly into a thin line, his hands clasped in front of him, his glare searing. Craig nodded and took his seat across from him at the small, dented table while Chavez withdrew near the door, leaning against the wall.

"I don't appreciate having to rush down here at this ungodly hour on a court day," he hissed, "because my client found it necessary to throw a shitfit over some stupid letter." He drew air sharply. "What is this letter about?"

"They didn't give it to you?"

"Not yet. The DA will give me a copy later today, probably after court, but I don't like surprises."

Craig looked sideways, wondering how much to say. Goodridge hadn't been interested to know if he was guilty or not. The stupid letter complicated things more than he cared to admit.

"I'm waiting," Goodridge said, bouncing his foot impatiently, the sound of the sole of his shoe hitting the floor a rhythmic, unnerving rap.

"It's, um, a letter from my wife. She gave it to some estate attorney to be brought to me in the event of her death."

"That's fabulous," Goodridge snapped, grinding his teeth. "What's in it?"

"Essentially, she said something along the lines of, 'The girl you killed is watching from paradise with a drink in her hand,' some cheesy shit like that. And she said I was the one."

Goodridge's jaw slacked a little. His eyebrows ruffled, creasing his forehead. "I believe it's time for me to ask you this question, and I'm warning you to speak the truth. Or else." Craig nodded. "Did you kill your wife, Mr. Brafford?"

He didn't expect that question. He wasn't ready for it yet. "I thought you didn't care about any of that. You said you believed all clients deserve the best defense their money could buy."

"That was before I started to doubt that I'm the best attorney for your case. I'm growing tired of dancing around you, Mr. Brafford. Seems to me you can't speak the truth no matter what, and that makes you a liability." He glared at Craig over the small table until he lowered his gaze. "You're lying to me, Mr. Brafford, every time your lips move. And I'm not being paid nearly enough to lose a case."

"What are you saying?" Craig's throat went parchment dry in an instant. He tried but couldn't swallow. If Goodridge left him, he was as good as condemned to life behind bars. He didn't have any money left to secure a decent defense attorney. He'd die in jail at the incompetent hand of a public defender.

"I'm saying you're lying to me, and this was one of my conditions to take your case, Mr. Brafford. Even if you didn't have the decency to see me before summoning me here as your attorney, I took your case. Even if I have reasons to believe you're insolvent, I'm here. Still, you lie to me."

"I won't," Craig blurted, pleading, his breath shaky under the threat of tears. "Not anymore, I swear. Fire away, and I'll only tell you the truth."

Goodridge leaned back against his chair and crossed his arms at his chest. "Did you kill your wife?"

"No, I didn't," Craig replied, believing it more and more. It was the only scenario that made any sense. They would've found her body.

"And you're not lying to me?"

"No, I swear." He looked Goodridge straight in the eye until the attorney relaxed a little. The tension in his shoulders waned as he settled his hands on the table. "But we're losing. I can feel it. I can feel the noose tightening around my neck."

"We're not losing. All they have is circumstantial. I'm surprised they filed the charge without a body. Do you know how rarely prosecution wins a murder trial in the absence of the victim's body? It almost never happens."

"It doesn't feel like that from where I'm sitting," Craig said, lowering his head and staring at the scratched, stained concrete floor for a long moment.

"In a day or two, they'll come up with a plea offer, and then we'll know how strong they believe their case is. Give it time, Mr. Brafford. Your wife's pregnancy and that poison evidence in her hair are tough to dismantle."

"Put me on the stand," Craig said, excitement coursing through his veins as he saw an opportunity to clear everything up.

"When they offer you that plea deal, and after I negotiate it as low as it would go, I suggest you take that offer, Mr. Brafford," Goodridge replied as if he hadn't heard a word Craig had said.

"No, I can't do time," he said, desperation seeping thick in his voice. "I can't. I would die in here. I have to take my chance with a verdict if that means I have even the slightest chance to walk out of here a free man." He leaned forward over the table, reaching to Goodridge's hand, but he withdrew. "Put me on the stand. I can explain a lot of things, even what's written in that letter."

"What else was in the damn letter?"

"Just references to paradise and how she's watching me from there. She mentioned our life together, how we fell in love, that kind of stuff."

"But then she says something about the girl you killed? That's how she refers to herself in that letter?"

Craig lowered his head, swallowing hard. "Yes."

"Were you poisoning her, Mr. Brafford?"

A beat. "Yes."

Goodridge crossed his arms again. "Whatever plea deal they offer, you should take. That letter could be seriously damaging. People tend to listen to voices from beyond the grave, and forensic evidence has you trying to poison her for quite a while. They placed you at the landfill, dumping a bloody rug, for crying out loud." He frowned and lowered his head without breaking eye contact with Craig. "You seem like a smart man to me, Mr. Brafford. Why not shoot her or something?" His voice was a mere whisper. "Why the stupid rat poison? It's slow and messy."

Craig pressed his lips together for a moment. "I have hematophobia. If I see any amount of blood, I faint."

"Got to be kidding me," he snapped, raising his arms in the air for a brief moment.

"I wish," Craig smiled bitterly. "Put me on the stand, Mr. Goodridge, please. It's my only chance. I can twist everything around."

The attorney stood and started pacing the room slowly. "If you waive your Fifth Amendment rights, you'll be forced to answer any questions the prosecutor might ask. Do you understand that?"

"Yes." He looked Goodridge firmly in the eye.

He stopped pacing and leaned over the table, his palms against the scratched surface. "Help me understand, why risk it? Why are you willing to chance a guilty verdict in a murder trial?"

"Because of what's in the letter," he said quickly, knowing it was his last chance to persuade Goodridge. The attorney had worked hard his entire career to have an almost impeccable win rate, and his hourly rate depended on his continued success. He wasn't willing to risk a loss in court, but Craig had to try to talk him into it. It was his life, after all.

"What do you mean?"

"It's the paradise thing. It's with a lowercase P, and that's the Caribbean for my wife. That's Montego Bay, not the biblical place where people go after they die. She's playing games with me."

Goodridge's head tilted slightly, while his gaze turned doubtful, incredulous as if doubting his client's sanity. "What are you saying, Mr. Brafford?"

"She's alive and well, and fucking with me, that's what I'm saying," he exclaimed, a little scared of how Goodridge would react, but also relieved he was finally getting to tell the truth to someone who could help him. "She's setting me up, making me pay."

"For what?"

"For killing her. Because, technically, I did."

"Are you insane?" Goodridge ran his hand over his agape mouth, then scratched the roots of his trim hair. "I'm thinking we should change our plea to not guilty by reason of insanity, although it hasn't been working so well in recent years as it used to in the eighties."

"I'm not insane," he replied bitterly. "I wish I was."

"Th—then tell me what happened," Goodridge stammered. "Step by step. Then we'll figure out how to put you on the stand, if you want to risk it." He checked the time and muttered an oath. "I have to leave in five minutes, and you won't be far behind. We're due in court, so make it quick."

Craig leaned against his chair and breathed. He only needed one minute of the five, maybe two. Then Goodridge would have no choice but to put him on the stand.

50

Testimony

The courtroom was already stuffy, and it was barely ten. Every seat was taken, the front rows mainly by people close to the proceedings. Craig's parents were there, huddled together and holding hands. Since Mrs. Brafford had testified, they hadn't missed a single session.

Dr. Wilmore was seated right behind the prosecutor, with Rebecca Ellefson by his side. Dr. Blass and Dr. DeMaria were also in attendance, seated on the second row behind Hunter Wilmore.

There was a persistent, tense hum fueled by the low-pitched chatter, a little louder toward the back of the courtroom, where media, law students, and the usual courtroom trolls were seated, eager to follow the most talked about trial of the year as it neared its conclusion. Excited gossip went in circles, dissecting every aspect of Andrea Wilmore Brafford's life, and the things the media had published about her, about her husband.

Opinions were as polarized in the courtroom as they had become in the entire nation, the case's notoriety propagating like wildfire. While everyone agreed Craig did wrong when he sabotaged his wife's job search, some people believed it wasn't really that big of a deal to be a homemaker, living a good life in a wealthy neighborhood and residing in a house of the kind most never even dreamed of. While others, the feminists, the women's rights voices, spoke of imprisonment, of slavery, of a hard-earned professional life being ripped away from a loving and unsuspecting young wife. These voices demanded a strong punishment.

That was only on the subject of Andrea's job situation.

Adding the murder charge to that undercurrent of gossip had stoked the fire as if the new charge had rained jet fuel on top of it.

Was Craig guilty? He had to be. He was a domineering asshole, a selfish bastard who only wanted to further his career at the expense of his wife's. He had to be a control freak. His narcissistic and conniving nature, exposed, scrutinized, and seared under the laser of public opprobrium, served as incriminating evidence in the streets, in lieu of what the prosecution couldn't bring in front of the jury. In the court of public opinion, Craig Brafford had long been tried and found guilty. Some voices even called for the death penalty, an impossible feat when the victim's body had not been found. Other voices, fewer and much weaker, spoke of a mistrial.

"All rise," the bailiff called, and the simmer of low-voiced chatter subsided as all in attendance stood. The shuffling of feet against the wooden floor, of seat bottoms tilting and squeaking surged, then ebbed into silence. "The court is now in session, the Honorable Justice Cromwell presiding."

Judge Cromwell was tall and slender, walking with an oddly rigid and slightly crooked gait, probably the sign of chronic lower back pain. Well into his sixties, the judge wore thin, metallic frame glasses with perfectly round lenses that gave a library mouse look to the otherwise distinguished, elegant countenance. A neatly trimmed white beard and buzz-cut hair complemented the tall forehead and imposing stature.

District Attorney Isaac Buscher was already at the prosecution table, flanked by his right hand, Assistant District Attorney Kendra Coben. Buscher, a glutton for white-collar cases in the financial and oil industry, an insatiable carnivore for the flesh of magnates and billionaires, was a rare appearance at a murder trial. Had it not been for the overnight notoriety of the defendant and the career-making potential of the case, Coben would've been trusted to handle the case by herself. But Buscher had been there every day, his beady eyes glinting with satisfaction whenever he made a point for the prosecution or drove home an argument.

At the defense table, Lamar Goodridge sat next to his client, seeming a little nervous. He'd dropped his pen on the floor twice, the second time cursing under his breath as he retrieved it, loudly enough for Buscher to bare his teeth in a mock grin and ask, "Feeling all right this morning, Counselor?"

Craig Brafford was dressed in one of his better suits and sat calmly on his seat, his hands clasped together neatly in front of him. He looked straight ahead at the empty witness stand, seeming completely withdrawn, dissociated from what was going on around him. Prison had not been kind to him; a swollen bruise marked his left cheek and seeped around his eye in hues of black and blue. Recently, his lip had been split open right in the middle, a thin, vertical scar marking the spot.

Rumor had it his best friend had posted his bail yesterday, but the system was taking its sweet time to process. Otherwise, he should've been released the day before. The two back rows were still abuzz with low-pitched chatter, and there was a pool starting to gain traction, with three-to-one odds for a guilty verdict. Seated on the last row by the aisle, a tall and rather pale redhead captured a lot of attention, but remained focused on the jury, the defendant's table, the front of the courtroom. She wore large, reflective shades that covered a significant part of her face. Her sleek, long hair wove down her shoulders, some of it brought to the front, worn like an accessory to her elegant garb, a white silk blouse and black slacks.

"Order," the judge said, slamming the gavel forcefully a couple of times until the courtroom was silent enough to hear a pin drop. "Please be seated," he said, and the shuffling and squeaking resumed for a moment while everyone complied. The jurors took their usual seats and fidgeted a while until they settled. "Calling the case of the People of the State of Texas versus Craig Brafford." He had a deep, pleasant voice that commanded respect. "Is the defense ready to proceed with their next witness?"

Lamar Goodridge stood and buttoned his charcoal jacket. "Yes, Your Honor. The defense calls Craig Brafford to the stand."

The courtroom reacted to the announcement like a single living organism gasping. Breaths caught in countless chests, low murmurs, astonished glances.

The defendant stood and was quickly sworn in. He took his seat on the witness stand, seeming calm, composed, well-prepared.

Goodridge walked toward the stand, taking the opportunity to nod a few greetings to the jury. He was always keen on paying attention to the jurors and making every one of them feel important, connected. Then he stopped by the witness stand and looked straight at Craig with an encouraging look in his eyes.

"Mr. Brafford, you have decided to waive your Fifth Amendment rights for the opportunity to clear your name, is that correct?"

"Yes." The defendant's voice was strong, unfaltering.

"Let's start with the disappearance of your wife. When was the last time you saw Andrea Wilmore Brafford?"

"The morning before I left for my conference in Miami. On Wednesday, October six."

"How were things between the two of you that day?"

A moment of hesitation, then Craig cleared his throat. "Not good. We had been running into issues, mostly because of her pregnancy and, well, the job situation."

"Please clarify what you mean by that."

Craig lowered his head, seemingly embarrassed. "It's already public knowledge I have made a grave error in judgment and have intentionally sabotaged my wife's career aspirations. She never forgave me for that."

"You also mentioned her pregnancy."

"Yes. It wasn't planned . . . It made matters worse. I was thrilled to have a baby with her, but she was livid about it. All because of what I'd done with the job thing. In all fairness, I had manipulated her and caused her a great deal of hardship, of unwarranted disappointment. That's all on me. I understand why she feels this way about our baby."

"What happened on Thursday, when you returned from the conference?"

"The plane was stuck on the runway because of a thunderstorm. We were not allowed to deplane for hours. Andi got angry, especially after she cut herself peeling some onions for the stir-fry she was making for dinner. When I called her from the plane, she was crying, hysterical, saying I was never there, and she was hurt and alone, and that wasn't a life for her. She said she wanted a divorce, and that she was leaving."

"What did you do next?"

"I pleaded with the flight attendants to let me deplane. I insisted until they threatened to place me under arrest if I didn't settle down. I had to wait until the storm was over. When I got home, she was gone. I assumed she might've gone to be with her father. He's recovering from a heart attack at a cardiac rehab center. They are very close. She was going to bring him to live with us."

"She left to see her father without her car?"

Craig lowered his head for a moment, then looked at Goodridge calmly. "I could only assume at the time that the cut on her hand she'd mentioned was serious enough to prevent her from driving. The amount of blood spilled on the floor was scary. For a while, I feared she might've hurt herself on purpose."

"What do you mean by that?" Goodridge's voice remained friendly, supportive.

"There was a lot of blood on the kitchen floor. Too much for a simple kitchen accident. I was afraid she might've slashed her wrists. She was desperate about her pregnancy, not thinking straight."

"Yet you didn't call her after you arrived home. Phone records show that."

"Her phone was still plugged into the bedroom wall. I saw it when I was in there looking for her. I had no way to reach her."

"During your interview with the police, before they honored your request to have counsel present, you stated, and I quote, 'All she needs is some cooling-off time.' Is that true?"

"That's what I thought I was doing when I refrained from calling her father or from driving to his house to speak with her." He paused for a moment as if collecting his thoughts. "I pushed her too far with the job situation. I knew that. I hoped we still had a future together after she'd had some time on her own to think, to remember how much she loved me. I still cling to that hope, even now, against all odds."

"What did you do next that Thursday night?"

He pressed his lips tightly together for a moment. "I fainted." The courtroom reacted to his words with a collective gasp. "More than once, actually."

"Why did that happen?"

"I have severe hematophobia. I've had it since I was a child. The sight of blood, any amount of it, makes me faint."

Chatter rose like a tidal wave from the audience, flooding the room.

"Order," Judge Cromwell said, slamming his gavel a couple of times. "Order, or I'll have the courtroom cleared." The threat brought instant silence.

"What did you do, then, with the blood on the floor?"

Craig stared at his hands for a while, wringing them. "Between fainting spells, I was able to see the blood was mainly on the kitchen rug. Looking away, I rolled it and tied it up, then took it to the landfill."

"At two in the morning?"

A sad smile tugged at the man's lips. "If it's dark and I can't see the blood, it's better. Not by much, but it's slightly better."

"Some people might think you had something to hide, and you chose to drive to the landfill in the dead of the night for that specific reason. To keep your actions hidden from view."

"I was frantic about the blood I found, about her being gone without her car and her phone. I wanted to do something, anything, to bring some normality into our house while waiting for her to come back." He cleared his voice and continued calmly. "It might sound suspicious to some people, but they didn't find a body with that rug, did they?"

"No, they didn't. What did you use the shower curtain for?"

"To keep the bloody carpet from staining everything else in the house and my car."

"Let's move on to the bottle of rat poison. The one the crime scene technicians retrieved from under the sink. It had your fingerprints on it. Please explain."

"We have rats in the backyard, by the shed. Or mice, I don't really know. I found droppings. I bought the poison, then my wife said not to use it, because it would kill the squirrels she loves so much. I never used it."

"But forensics found traces of poison in your wife's hair fibers going back for about a month. She had been ingesting that particular brand of poison for a while. How do you explain that?"

Craig wiped a tear, real or feigned, with the tip of his finger and veered his eyes for a moment. "I can't. All I know is she was furious about her pregnancy, didn't want the child of a lying son of a bitch growing inside her. Andi's words, not mine," he added bitterly, touching his forehead for a brief moment, sadness and shame clear in his voice. "The only thing I can do is assume she didn't get an abortion because of her father and his convictions, but she might've tried to provoke that abortion by ingesting small amounts—"

"This man's a liar!" Dr. Wilmore bellowed, standing abruptly and pointing his finger at the defendant. "My daughter would've never done that to herself. Never!"

The redhaired woman on the back row almost sprung to her feet but then settled back into her seat, holding on to the armrests with white-knuckled fingers. By Dr. Wilmore's side, Rebecca Ellefson held his arm, whispering something in his ear.

The judge's gavel fell. "Dr. Wilmore, one parent to another, I can understand how you must feel. It's the reason why you're not already held in contempt. But this is your final warning."

"I apologize, Your Honor," Dr. Wilmore said, his voice brittle, shaky. "It won't happen again." He took his seat with difficulty while Rebecca held his arm tightly, still whispering in his ear.

Goodridge looked at the jury, probably assessing the level of damage Dr. Wilmore's outburst might've caused. "You're making a disturbing accusation, Mr. Brafford. You're saying that your wife, a highly educated professional in the field of biology, had found no better way to rid herself of an unwanted pregnancy than swallowing rat poison?"

The sadness on Brafford's face remained. "How else can you explain she hadn't told anyone about her pregnancy? Not her father, not her family friends, not even her best friend, Janelle Larimer? No one knew about it except me." He paused for a brief moment. "Maybe everything that happened was too much for her. Her father's heart attack, the job situation I caused, the unwanted pregnancy . . . I offered to take her to a psychiatrist, but she was livid with me, hysterical. She slept in the living room that night and I—I never brought it up again."

Goodridge paced slowly for a while, rubbing his chin, allowing Craig's words to be digested. "Last night, you were deeply upset by a letter you received. Tell the court about that letter."

"My wife wrote that letter and gave it to an estate lawyer to be given to me in the event of her death."

"Why were you frantic about it?"

"In the letter, she calls me a killer. But I didn't kill her. I couldn't have. I'm still in love with my wife." His voice shattered. "I'm still waiting for her to come back to me. To forgive me."

"So, then, what do you think is going on, Mr. Brafford?"

Craig hesitated for a moment. With him, the entire courtroom held its breath. "I believe she is framing me to punish me for screwing up her career. I think it's that simple and twisted at the same time. I ruined her career, now she's ruining mine, my life with it. One of these days, she'll show up and prove me right."

"What are you saying, Mr. Brafford?" Goodridge insisted, a smart way of underlining the conclusion for the jury to remember.

"I'm saying she's alive and well somewhere, lying low." He swallowed and briefly hid his face in his hands. "I know it seems nearly impossible to believe but think about it. Had I poisoned my wife, would I have left the poison bottle for the police to find?" He paused for a moment, probably for dramatic effect. "I would've discarded it already, together with her phone, maybe even her car, because that's what a guilty person would do." He clasped and unclasped his hands a couple of times. "If for no other reason, I couldn't've stabbed or shot or killed her in any way that would justify the pool of blood on the kitchen floor because I would've fainted, over and over, right there by her side." He shook his head, seeming at the end of his wits. Then he looked straight at the jury and said, "I didn't kill my wife. I swear to God I didn't. Time will prove me right."

Goodridge nodded calmly, then turned to the judge and said, "No more questions for this witness, Your Honor."

"We'll recess for lunch and reconvene at two." Cromwell's gavel sealed his statement.

From the back row, the redheaded woman was the first to leave the courtroom, unnoticed, while everyone was staring at Craig Brafford. The odds were now two-to-one in his favor.

51

APPEARANCE

District Attorney Buscher didn't follow the crowds to the cafeteria downstairs. Instead, he took a left turn after exiting the courtroom and walked another hundred feet on an empty corridor with ADA Coben in tow, then stopped, his shoulder leaning against the wall. He was fuming. His nostrils flared, his eyes glinted with rage, his fist pounded against the wall repeatedly.

He was losing. And that never happened to him. Never.

"This is what happens when you bend the rules," he said in a low, tense voice to his assistant. Kendra Coben listened, nodding slightly, probably knowing not to interrupt him until he was done ranting. "You never, *never ever* prosecute murder one without a body. Without an autopsy report and solid forensics."

"Are you saying you believe Brafford?"

His jaws clenched for a moment while he drilled his eyes into Coben's until she lowered her gaze. "I don't believe him. The bastard is guilty as sin and a lying sack of shit, but my opinion doesn't matter. It's the jury that matters, and they were lapping up his tearjerker story." He pounded his fist against the wall several more times, discreetly, shielding his gesture with his own body. "It's about proving beyond any reasonable doubt.

Remember that part? They taught it to us in the first year of law school." Coben didn't deserve to be on the receiving end of his bitter outburst. She'd been the voice of reason, repeatedly cautioning him against taking the Brafford case.

Coben nodded, seeming defeated, just as he felt. He was used to the taste of victory, not failure. He hated it with every fiber of his body. It made him feel small, insignificant. Replaceable. Ridiculous.

"One by one, he dismantled all our circumstantial evidence, tearing it to shreds. All he had to do was create reasonable doubt, and he's done just that with his pathetic revenge story." He closed his eyes and breathed slowly in a futile effort to regain his cool. In about an hour, he'd have to cross examine that lying asshole into incriminating himself somehow. He'd never be able to do that if he was still fuming, enraged beyond his ability to reason.

Silence overtook the hallway, almost empty now while the last of the courtroom spectators made their way toward the café downstairs.

Inhaling sharply, Buscher reminded himself it wasn't over yet. "We can't prove mens rea. Not beyond any reasonable doubt. Not even after what he'd done with the woman's job, not with his fingerprints on the poison bottle, because that bastard is not stupid enough not to have disposed of the poison bottle if he indeed killed her." His lips, pressed into a thin line, kept words from pouring out for a long moment, especially the ones he knew he had to speak. "We have to talk deal and hope he'll be scared enough to take it."

Coben shook her head slightly. "I don't think—"

"Well, I don't think he'll take it either," Buscher said, his voice a shouting whisper. "But if you see any other option, do let me know. We're about to become the laughingstock of the entire justice system. Prosecuting murder one without a body and losing like an idiot." He bit his lip, then mumbled a detailed, colorful oath. He was finished; his career was over. Come election time next year, people would read his name on the ballot and have a good laugh, then put the checkmark next to the other person's name. "That's the risk with high-profile cases. When you step into the limelight, any screwup is visible from miles away. Memorable. It lives on and on in people's minds, on the internet, in social media, fueling gossip at every dinner table in the state."

Coben looked at him with understanding. "Do you want to try—"

He let out a long, heavy breath of air, cutting her off again. "We need to salvage what we can. Offer him murder two. Fifteen years, not a day more. Remind him his fingerprints were on the poison bottle; milk it for all it's got." Another long breath. "If they make a counteroffer, take anything, even manslaughter. Involuntary, if we can't get anything better than that. There's something vile and twisted about this man, and I want him behind bars."

Coben shrugged, then looked at Buscher with a frown on her face. "I'll see what I can do. Chances are they'll laugh in my face."

Better in your face than mine, Buscher thought. "Do what you can. Save this case. Come year-end, I'll make you smile at bonus time."

The clacking of approaching heels distracted Buscher for a moment, but he lowered his voice further and continued speaking. "In your heart, do you believe he's guilty? Do you think he murdered that beautiful wife of his? What does your gut say?"

Coben nodded vigorously. "Totally. Hundred percent he did it."

"Exactly," Buscher replied. "He's guilty. I know a killer when I see one, but this particular slimeball is about to walk."

"You could try challenging the hematophobia argument regarding the cleanup he managed to do. If he managed that much with the blood-soaked rug, he could've also disposed of the body. And I didn't believe him for a moment when he said he was waiting for her to come back. No. He knew she wasn't going to come back and went on with his life. Didn't even bother to report her missing, to fake it."

Buscher ran his hand through his hair a couple of times. "Do you think this was his strategy from the beginning? Building these arguments for his defense? All the logical things he would've done if he had killed her, but didn't do, hence he's innocent?"

A moment of silence. "It's a risky strategy," Coben replied, "but he might've pulled it off like a pro."

"Damn it to hell, the prick played us for fools," Buscher whispered between grinding teeth. "I should've never prosecuted this case. Not without a body. We should've prosecuted the law enforcement impersonation while the cops found us the body. It's out there somewhere, for crying out loud. It has to be."

"He's going to walk, isn't he?"

The question startled both Buscher and his assistant. Turning on his heels, he recognized a red-haired woman he'd noticed a few times in the back of the courtroom. She was stunning, her body a ten-plus, but he glared at her. Last thing he needed was an eavesdropper. "I'm sorry, ma'am, we can't discuss this matter with—"

"But you *are* losing the case, aren't you?" she continued unfazed, looking at him through oversized, reflective sunglasses.

"Ma'am—"

"It's all right. Your eyes have already answered my question." She smiled briefly, apologetically. "I have a solution for you."

Buscher crossed his arms at his chest. She must've been another one of those courtroom lunatics. Every few trials he ran into one. Some were psychics; others were long-forgotten relatives of the victims or defendants, people who'd lived in another state but claimed they knew everything. "And what would that be?" he asked, his voice dipped in unfiltered sarcasm.

"Put me on the stand."

A lopsided grin stretched Buscher's lips. "I apologize, but you'll have to excuse us. We have work to do." He grabbed Coben's arm and started walking away, but the rushed clattering of heels behind him told him it was useless. The stranger was following them, unabated. Irritated, he stopped and faced her. "Listen, we can't—"

"I'm terribly sorry I didn't come forward until today," the woman said, speaking softly and calmly. "I was afraid for my life, still in shock after what happened. I wasn't thinking straight. I'm so sorry." She swallowed hard, then cleared her throat. "But I'm willing to take the stand."

An uneasy feeling unfurled in Buscher's gut, apprehension mixed with an uneasiness, a sense of foreboding. Could his day get any worse? "Who are you?" he asked, feeling his throat dry.

The woman removed her sunglasses, then tugged at her long, luscious hair. The wig came off, revealing the short, highlighted strands he recognized from the photos he'd seen in the case file.

"I'm Andrea Wilmore Brafford."

His jaw slacked for a brief moment.

"Oh, fuck me."

52

LETTER

After the recess, Craig Brafford was seated at the defense table. From the prosecutor's side of the aisle, DA Buscher threw him a couple of annoyed glances, keeping his jaws tightly clenched. He could've sworn that man had killed his wife. For the second time since he'd laid eyes on this case, he'd been wrong.

Goodridge stared at Buscher inquisitively, then shrugged off his client's unspoken concern.

"All rise," the bailiff called, and everyone stood. It was a little after two in the afternoon, and the faint smell of fast food had accompanied some of the attendants into the courtroom, clinging to their clothes and their hair like burrs to a stray dog's matted coat.

Judge Cromwell took his seat, then dropped the gavel quickly. "The court is now in session. Mr. Buscher, are you ready for cross?"

He wasn't. Not by a long shot. Inhaling sharply, he stood, bracing himself for the shitstorm his words were about to unleash. "Your Honor, at this time, the state moves to dismiss the murder charges. New evidence has come to our attention—" He paused for a moment, his words swallowed by the commotion in the courtroom.

"Order," Judge Cromwell shouted, banging his gavel angrily a few times. "Order. This is the last warning I will give. One more disruption to these proceedings, and we will continue behind closed doors." One more gavel strike sealed his threat, and the commotion duly subsided. The muted sound of people shifting in their seats and a few whispers still disturbed the peace for a moment, but Cromwell glared from the bench until he was satisfied. "Please proceed, Mr. Buscher."

The DA cleared his throat quietly, then he instinctively tugged at the knot of his tie, feeling he couldn't breathe. "New evidence has come to our attention," he repeated. "In light of said evidence, the state would like to proceed with new charges." A beat of tense silence. "Attempted murder in the first degree."

The frustration that had replaced Cromwell's initial surprise was unmistakable. "Mr. Buscher," he said calmly, in a low, threatening voice. "You're turning my courtroom into a circus, and I won't have it. I'm past the age when I care to see clowns doing sleights of hand for the show." He seemed to consider his options for a while, glaring at Buscher, who held his gaze unflinching. There wasn't anything else he could do. "Counselors, approach," he called.

Buscher waited for Goodridge to catch up, then approached the bench.

Cromwell covered his microphone. "What's this about, Mr. Buscher?"

"We have discovered that the defendant's wife is alive. She's willing to testify. I'm planning to call her next."

"Your Honor," Goodridge said, his tone inflamed just as Buscher's would've been if he were in the defense counsel's place. "This is ridiculous. My client is clearly innocent, and the state is on a fishing expedition, nothing else. I move to have all charges dismissed."

Cromwell frowned at Goodridge. In his enthusiasm, the defense had made a critical mistake. "Not so fast, Counselor. There's a charge your client admitted guilt to, and that charge stands." He steepled his hands on the shiny surface of the bench and pressed his lips together. "I, for one, want to hear what the defendant's wife has to say about this entire mess."

Goodridge held his hands up in a pacifying gesture. "But, Your Honor, we're not prepared for cross—"

"Ask for a continuance, Mr. Goodridge. I'll grant it. After direct."

Goodridge looked at Cromwell as if to gauge if it was worth pleading with him some more, then he ceded and said, "Understood. Thank you, Your Honor."

Buscher returned to the prosecution table and remained standing, while Goodridge took his seat next to Craig Brafford and grabbed his forearm, then whispered something in his ear.

Clearing his throat again, Buscher said, "The state calls Andrea Wilmore Brafford."

Despite the many gavel strikes by Cromwell's impatient hand, whispered comments and interjections of surprise rushed through the spectators, rising like an ocean surge during a storm.

"That didn't take long now, did it?" Craig Brafford shouted, his voice distinguishable over the crowd noise. "I told you she's alive."

"Order in the courtroom," Cromwell repeated, his eyebrows ruffled. He leaned over the bench as if he were about to step down from there and discipline the disobedient public himself.

The entrance of the defendant's wife brought silence and stupor to the public. She raised her hand and repeated the words of the oath, then took her seat on the witness stand. Pale, gaunt, deathly thin, and seeming overwhelmed, she locked eyes with her father, whose barely contained, tearful joy told Buscher her appearance was a surprise to him too. How interesting.

Buscher approached the stand, still thinking of the best strategy for the direct examination of the witness no one had expected to see on the stand. "Andrea Wilmore Brafford, let me start by saying how happy we all are to see you're alive."

"Thank you." She leaned forward when she spoke to be closer to the mic.

"Let's start from the beginning, with the evening of October seven, the Thursday when your husband returned from the conference in Miami. Do you recall the events of that night?"

"Yes," she replied calmly, her voice somber, riddled with sadness. "I'll never forget that night. It was the night my husband killed me."

The defendant sprung to his feet, leaning over the defense table. "You set me up! You're still bloody alive."

"Mr. Goodridge, control your client," Cromwell ordered.

Goodridge grabbed Brafford's arm with both his hands and pulled him down into his seat. Based on the angry whispers and cutting gestures he observed from a distance, Buscher could tell Goodridge was threatening his client into behaving appropriately.

Unperturbed, the witness continued. "It was the night he killed me, or at least he thought he did." She paused for a moment, seeming at a loss for words. "From all perspectives, he did kill me, just as he killed my unborn baby. I woke up covered in blood, wrapped in a rug, and buried in trash at a South Houston landfill. I barely survived."

Dr. Wilmore gasped and covered his mouth with trembling hands while tears streamed down his face. Looking at him, Andrea started crying too, softly, without making a noise. She pressed her hands to her chest in an unspoken message to her father.

"What did you do after you woke up at the landfill?"

She shook her head and lowered her eyes. "I barely made it to my father's house. There, I spent countless days slipping in and out of consciousness. I lost my baby," she added, her voice shaky, choked.

"Did you call nine-one-one?"

"No."

"Why?" Buscher asked, curious to hear her explanation. "You're a scientist, a biologist a few months short of earning her PhD, and still, you didn't seek medical attention."

"It wasn't until very recently that I realized I had been poisoned. I thought I was in shock after what had happened, nothing more. I was afraid for my life, grieving for the loss of my unborn baby." She looked at her father again. "I wasn't making sense . . . maybe I still can't. It might be the poison's effect on my brain; I don't know."

"The police looked for you at your father's house, and you weren't there. The following Tuesday, October twelve, after an anonymous email called attention to your disappearance. Where were you on that day?"

Andrea looked at her father again with a faint smile on her lips. "There's a small cabin by the river. It's not even a cabin, just a cover over a hammock and some mosquito netting, something my father built. That's where I was, the entire time I wasn't in the house."

"Didn't you hear when police came and searched the premises?"

"During the first couple of weeks, I was slipping in and out of consciousness. I don't recall them being there."

Buscher paced the space in front of the witness stand anxiously. There was something about her testimony that didn't add up. What did she eat all that time? She was pale and thin, so maybe not that much. Why didn't she at least call her father? "A highly educated scientist doesn't call for help after suffering a head wound and losing a lot of blood. How do you explain that?"

"I . . . don't," she replied candidly. "I believe I was still in shock after what happened on Thursday night."

"What did happen on Thursday night, after your husband returned from his trip to Miami?"

She shifted in her seat slightly and breathed. Maybe it was Buscher's imagination, but it seemed she turned deathly pale, a whiter shade than she already was.

"I waited for Craig to return from his trip and told him I wanted a divorce. He wasn't happy about it, but it wasn't the first time we were discussing it. I reassured him I didn't want any money or part of the house or anything. He seemed to agree, then offered to eat dinner together while we ironed out the details. I was going to leave that night and move back into my father's place."

"Then, what happened?"

"I was eating the stir-fry he'd cooked while I was packing my bag. The food seemed a little off, but I ate some of it. Then I felt dizzy and nauseous. I got sick, and I fainted." She paused for a moment, her eyes staring into emptiness. "Right before I fell, I remember him staring at me indifferently and asking, 'Is there something you need, honey?' He watched me as I fell and didn't lift a finger. I must've hit my head on something because the last thing I remember was seeing stars. Then I woke up at the landfill, hours later."

"What a traumatic experience. Still, after waking up, you didn't seek justice for yourself." He glanced at the defendant, noticing the pure hatred in his eyes as he stared at his wife.

"I was, and still am, in shock," she replied, her voice faint, broken. "I don't know how one can come back from this. I thought we were happy. Then, especially after I told him I was pregnant, I feared that something was terribly wrong. I confronted Craig a few times, but he denied it. That's when I wrote the letter." She sniffled. "I was afraid for my life, but I couldn't walk away." She smiled with sadness and looked briefly at the jury before bowing her head. "I was desperately in love with my husband. In a stupid, childish way, I chose this manner of telling him I knew what he was going to do, instead of leaving him, instead of protecting my own life and my child's." She paused for a brief moment. "I'll have to live with the consequences of my actions for the rest of my life."

Buscher looked at the jury. There wasn't a single dry eye among them. Andrea's explanations didn't account for the time she'd spent watching the proceedings wearing a disguise, but his job was to get a conviction for the hateful, conniving son of a bitch sitting next to the defense counsel. He wasn't going to bring any incongruities up. Let Goodridge ask all those questions during cross.

"Speaking of that letter, would you mind reading it to the court?" Buscher stopped by his desk, swiped a copy of the letter, then handed another copy to the judge. "People's exhibit fifteen, Your Honor."

Andrea took the letter with trembling hands while the audience held their breaths. Her voice, frail and shaky at first, gained a little strength as she read, but ended choked in tears.

My dearest Craig,

I thought the day I met you was special for me, giving me a reason to celebrate our love over the years, a date to circle in our calendars. A day after my birthday, as fate had it, I'd received a belated gift I appreciated more than anything in the world.

I was lucky, immensely grateful for the way the gods smiled on my life. I had everything a woman could wish for. A husband who loved her, family and friends, the promise of a successful career, and now, a child. Who could ask for more?

Yet, as if the gods had changed their minds, with their latest gift came my biggest sorrow. You weren't ready to become a parent. You chose to lie to me, to hide the truth behind transparent excuses and feigned enthusiasm. I would've appreciated your honesty instead.

Like with all fairy tales, it all unraveled from there. Soon after that, I learned you didn't ask me to give up my career to help with yours; you just snatched it away from me, leaving me struggling with disappointment, rejection, and failure I didn't understand or deserve. While you held me in your arms at night when I was crying, offering me support. That betrayal hurt the most.

Still, I forgave you. I tried to understand your reasons and chose to believe you were genuinely sorry for what you had done.

With every passing day, things had turned for the worst. Trusting you became impossible while loving you tore my heart open. How could I leave you if I was still in love with you? But then, how could I live by your side if I couldn't trust you? How could I raise our child with you if I knew, deep down inside, you didn't want that child to see the light of day?

And knowing you, I was sure you'd do anything in your power to keep that from happening. Only I didn't know what you'd do. Paralyzed, a deer caught in your powerful headlights, I waited for you to strike while wishing with all my heart you'd choose not to.

And now you have.

The girl you killed is watching over you from paradise, lounging on cloud number nine with a Margarita in her hand, hoping you'll have everything you deserve in this life after she's gone. Goodbye, my love. You were the one.

After Andrea finished reading, Buscher allowed one long moment of heavy silence while the jury reeled from the reading of the letter, then said, "No more questions, Your Honor."

53

THE CALL

It had been weeks since Craig's sentencing, but Andi's eyes still teared up when she recalled the judge's blistering comments. While she cleared the dinner table and loaded the dishwasher, those words resounded in her head clearly, hurting her just as much as they had that day.

"Every now and then in a judge's career, there's a case that is both puzzling and unforgettable," he'd said. "The jury has spoken, and the defendant, Craig Brafford, has been found guilty of attempted murder in the first degree. The victim's testimony, as difficult to believe as it was, is supported by evidence retrieved by the police. Multiple surveillance videos show the victim crawling her way out of the landfill and trudging along deserted streets, making her way home. Blood tests performed at the hospital found levels of poison high enough to cause the mental impairment that could explain why the victim didn't reach out for assistance." He'd stopped speaking for a moment and rubbed his forehead. "Yet I can't help but wonder if what we've witnessed here wasn't some form of sick, twisted, psychological BDSM. We have slavery and bondage. A victim who endures humiliation and never fights back. A young, educated woman who doesn't defend her life when clearly threatened. We have torture and sadism in a domineering and reckless man who took pleasure in prolonging his victim's suffering. Or should I say, his partner's?"

He raised his eyes and stared at Craig first, then at Andi through the round lenses of his glasses. "Fortunately, the law is very clear in such cases. BDSM or not, a sickening game or not, poisoning someone, attempting to kill them, then dumping their body is illegal and punishable by long years behind bars. However, failing to ask for help after having been victimized is not a crime." He closed the case file set in front of him and placed his hand above it. "Mr. Brafford, you will serve fifteen years in a state penitentiary." Then he'd turned to her, ignoring Craig's protests. "Ms. Wilmore, as a father to a young woman about your age, I strongly recommend you seek help from a reputable psychologist or psychiatrist. All human life is precious, and that includes yours. The fact that you didn't realize that is deeply troublesome for me. I hope you will receive the help you need."

Closing the dishwasher door, Andi pressed a couple of buttons, and the machine started taking water. She leaned against the edge of the counter, trying to shake the memory of Cromwell's voice from her mind. She wiped her tears, hiding them from her father, but it was too late. His arms were wrapping around her shoulders.

"Shh, it's over, my sweet girl. He's not going to hurt you again. You're safe."

Her face buried at his chest, she wept for a moment, allowing herself to feel protected and loved. "I know," she whimpered. "It's what that judge said at sentencing. He was right, you know. No sane person would've done what I did. And he doesn't know the half of it."

"Dr. Ellefson said the levels of poison in your blood stream accounted for impaired judgment. You heard him; he was bewildered you survived."

"I didn't feel impaired, Dad. I felt a lot of other things, but I didn't feel crazy. I made some awful choices, yes, but they seemed logical at the time."

He guided her to the table and pulled out a chair for her, then sat next to her, holding her hands in his. "I'll tell you what it is, and you're right, it's not just the poison." He smiled, but his blue eyes were glistening. "When you're being psychologically abused, you soon learn that you don't matter, that your suffering has no meaning, and that there's no escape." His eyes darkened as they strayed down to her arm, where needle pricks marked her veins. "I wanted to kill him, you know." He frowned and lowered his head. "Just like you put down a rabid animal. Seeing you like this, knowing what you've been through, I wish I had, even if that meant I'd be serving time now instead of him."

A shudder ran through her body. "I'm glad you didn't," she whispered. "I would've lost you too and would've never forgiven myself. I brought this evil among us, Dad." She breathed deeply, willing herself free of tears and sorrow for one evening. "We're here now, we have everything we need, and we could watch a movie together and eat some ice cream. What do you say?"

"Sounds like a great idea," he replied. "Let's take that ice cream on the patio. Can I *pretend* to smoke a cigar?" She frowned jokingly. "Half of a cigar then?"

Grinning, she turned to the freezer and took out a pint of diet chocolate ice cream, grabbed two spoons, and went out on the patio. Her father was already seated on one of the wicker armchairs, puffing smoke. They sat silently for a while, indulging in their respective treats and watching the deep purple hues of the late twilight.

"I still can't believe what you've done," he said after a while, "but I'm proud of you. More than you'll ever know."

She smiled, fighting back a knot in her throat.

"How things change," he said, "and also stay the same. You still boil eggs, don't you?"

Her smile waned.

"I'd forgotten, but it just came to me. You were about six years old when I taught you how to steal a postmark with a hard-boiled egg. Remember that one?"

Silence was her only response.

"A couple of years later, you put it to the test. Do you remember that? You didn't want your mother to attend the PTA meeting one time; you were in second grade, I believe, right?" She nodded, wiping a rebel tear with her fingertip. "You typed this notification advising residents to be home for a gas line inspection and stamped it and all. I don't know where you copied the text from, but it was perfect. Your mother stayed home that evening." He chuckled silently. "We didn't have the heart to tell you the date on the notice was wrong."

"What?" She turned to face him, her mouth agape. "I can't believe it. Then, why didn't she go to the meeting?"

"We knew about that C already," he replied, tucking a strand of her hair behind her ear. "We figured you might try harder if you thought you got away with it, that's all."

"Ah, you manipulated me," she said, pointing a finger at him.

"It was all you. Before faking an official notice, check your dates, missy." They laughed, their voices harmoniously joined in the shared moment of joy. "Then it hit me, a moment ago, sitting here. That's how you pulled it off. The letter. I was wondering, because I heard that lawyer testify he'd received the letter postmarked four days prior to your, um—You must've boiled some eggs and—"

She took her finger to his lips, and he fell silent. For a while, they listened to the hubbub of the creekside woods, with toads croaking, crickets chirping, and the occasional owl hooting.

"You will love again," Hunter said, out of the blue. "I promise, you will."

Her hand froze halfway to her mouth. She couldn't see herself with another man, dating, sleeping with him, being alone with him. She shivered and abandoned the spoon in the ice cream, then set it aside.

"Freddy wants to talk to you," he said, staring at the tip of his cigar, his brow ruffled as if the incandescent circle had offended him somehow. "He believes he can help."

Her head hung under the threat of tears.

"It's better to speak with a friend than a stranger," her father added softly. "Freddy won't judge. He's a great shrink." He chuckled and puffed some cigar smoke. "I had myself checked for dementia, when I started having those gut feelings about Craig." She looked at him, surprised. "Twice. I did, yes. I didn't trust myself. I thought I might've," he made a twisting gesture with his open hand near his temple, "you know, gone cuckoo."

She breathed deeply, and the humid, chilly evening breeze gave her the strength she needed. "Ask Freddy when I can see him."

He threw a couple of smoke circles into the night air. "Ask him yourself," he replied softly.

She smiled and squeezed his hand. It was time for the healing to begin.

After he'd gone to bed, she cleared the table of the remaining items, then went through the day's stack of mail. The Texas A&M University logo on a white envelope got her attention, sending shivers down her spine as she remembered the last time she received a letter like that.

She opened it quickly, tearing the envelope, eager to read its content. As she perused the short paragraph, a wide grin blossomed on her lips. They were offering her the research scientist job after all. Dr. Marjorie Hitchens was signing the letter with a personal note welcoming her aboard, if she was still interested.

Still grinning, she snuck in her father's bedroom to share the news. He was sleeping soundly, snoring softly. Her news could wait until morning.

It was quite late, after midnight, but she couldn't sleep. Deciding in favor of a movie, she sat on the couch and reached toward the coffee table for the remote. Under the table, on the wooden shelf, her father had abandoned his smiling dolphin notebook, the pen still attached to its cover. Hesitating for a moment, she reached out for it and opened it slowly, painfully aware of how carefully he'd kept it hidden from her. It felt like an invasion of privacy her father didn't deserve.

Her fingers turned ice cold when she saw the loose papers stacked inside. The first one, a screenshot of Dr. Wilmore's vet clinic software, was the patient profile image for Nikki Edwards and her cat. The practice took a series of photos of new pet owners with their pets and placed them in the system, so that anniversary cards and reminder notes could be personalized to them.

In the photo, Nikki Edwards was wearing the blue pendant.

Feeling the blood draining from her face, Andi stared at the photo in disbelief. A scribbled arrow pointed at the pendant, and a handwritten note above it said, "Is this a widely available commercial item? A coincidence?"

With trembling fingers, she turned the page. The second image was another screenshot from Nikki Edwards's vet clinic system profile, her contact information. The page listed two phone numbers. Nikki's own, validated by a note from her father, who remembered calling her with test results on various occasions. A second number, surrounded by a scratchy circle Andi's father had drawn in hard-pressed blue ballpoint, and the words, "Whose number is this?"

She read the phone number twice, digit by digit, afraid she was making a mistake. Her father had never used it, but she had, numerous times. It was Craig's office number at the real estate firm.

"Oh, God," she whispered, icicles running through her blood.

The third page was part of the same system, a record of one of Nikki Edwards's visits at the clinic, the consult findings, the total amount billed, and some other pieces of information that clogged the screen space. Yet the date of that consult stood out, easily recognizable. It was Andi's birthday last year, the day before she met Craig. Her father's obsessive underlining had almost torn the page under the time of the visit: 5:25 p.m. When she was there, eating cat-whiskered cake and celebrating her day with her father and his staff.

Feeling dizzy and weak, she pushed herself to turn another page. It was a grainy surveillance video with a date and time stamp. It showed her Beetle, parked at the university campus in Galveston, a day after her birthday. Crouched by the left rear wheel, a man was doing something to her tire. The time stamp read 4:45. The photo was too grainy to figure out, but she recognized the wavy hair of the man, the way it curled above his ear, even from a profile view. "Who is he?" her father had jotted down and underlined at least twice. He'd met him once, at her wedding, but had no reason to remember him after all that time or recognize him from such a grainy, distant photo.

But she was sure she knew who that man was.

Jude.

Setting her up. Deflating her tire, so that Craig could rescue her.

Craig must've seen her on her birthday at the clinic and decided to prey on her. Why her? Her mouth agape, she covered it with her hand, stifling a sob.

That was the last detached page inserted at the beginning of her father's notebook. She set it aside, then turned to reading her father's notes. Her own conclusions, echoed by her father's suspicions. Pieces of a deeply troubling puzzle falling into place to form a nightmarish image.

Shocked, she sat there, staring at her worst fears, bullet listed in her father's handwriting, unable to move. Why her? What did Craig see in her to make him want to entrap her like that?

It was daylight already, and Andi hadn't moved, the open notebook still in her lap, scattered photos on the couch. She'd never know why. No matter what she did. Even if she went to see Craig in prison, he'd never tell her the truth; the man was incapable of honesty.

Why her? She'd never know.

Then she thought of Nikki. Beautiful, successful, coming from a good family.

And pregnant.

Her death, completely bloodless.

The needle she'd used was a subdermal one, the kind Dr. Wilmore gave his patients to use for insulin shots in diabetic cats. The kind Craig knew Nikki had.

"Andi," she heard her father's voice from the doorway. Dressed in wrinkled pajamas, he stared at the open notebook in her lap with worried eyes. "You shouldn't've read this. It's too soon—"

She looked at him with an unspoken plea in her eyes, then reached for her phone. She was ready to do what needed to be done. Recalling a number from the phone's memory, she listened to it ring twice before a familiar voice picked up.

"Detective Otwell, Houston PD."

~~ The End ~~

If *The Girl They Took* had you totally immersed and gasping at every twist and turn, then you have to read more unputdownable page-turners by Leslie Wolfe!

Read on for a preview from:

Dawn Girl

A short-fused FBI Agent who hides a terrible secret. A serial killer you won't see coming. A heart-stopping race to catch him.

THANK YOU!

A big, heartfelt thank you for choosing to read my book. If you enjoyed it, please take a moment to leave me a four or five-star review; I would be very grateful. It doesn't need to be more than a couple of words, and it makes a huge difference.

Join my mailing list to receive special offers, exclusive bonus content, and news about upcoming new releases. Use the button below, visit www.LeslieWolfe.com to sign up, or email me at LW@WolfeNovels.com.

Did you enjoy *The Girl You Killed*? Would you like to see some of these characters return? Which ones? Your thoughts and feedback are very valuable to me. Please contact me directly through one of the channels listed below. Email works best: <u>LW@WolfeNovels.com</u> or use the button below:

If you haven't already, check out *Dawn Girl*, a gripping, heart stopping crime thriller and the first book in the Tess Winnett series. If you enjoyed *Criminal Minds*, you'll enjoy *Dawn Girl*. Or, if you're in a mood for something lighter, try *Las Vegas Girl*; you'll love it!

Connect with Me!

Email: LW@WolfeNovels.com

Facebook: https://www.facebook.com/wolfenovels

Follow Leslie on Amazon: http://bit.ly/WolfeAuthor

Follow Leslie on BookBub: http://bit.ly/wolfebb

Website: www.LeslieWolfe.com

Visit Leslie's Amazon store: http://bit.ly/WolfeAll

PREVIEW: *DAWN GIRL*

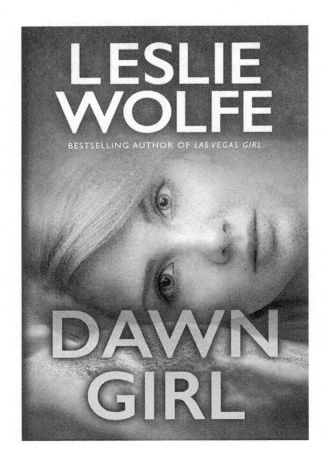

Chapter One
READY

She made an effort to open her eyes, compelling her heavy eyelids to obey. She swallowed hard, her throat raw and dry, as she urged the wave of nausea to subside. Dizzy and confused, she struggled to gain awareness. Where was she? She felt numb and shaky, unable to move, as if awakening from a deep sleep or a coma. She tried to move her arms, but couldn't. Something kept her immobilized, but didn't hurt her. Or maybe she couldn't feel the pain, not anymore.

Her eyes started to adjust to the darkness, enough to distinguish the man moving quietly in the room. His silhouette flooded her foggy brain with a wave of memories. She gasped, feeling her throat constrict and burning tears rolling down her swollen cheeks.

Her increased awareness sent waves of adrenaline through her body, and she tried desperately to free herself from her restraints. With each useless effort, she panted harder, gasping for air, forcing it into her lungs. Fear put a strong chokehold on her throat and was gaining ground, as she rattled her restraints helplessly, growing weaker with every second. She felt a wave of darkness engulf her, this time the darkness coming from within her weary brain. She fought against that darkness, and battled her own betraying body.

The noises she made got the man's attention.

"I see you're awake. Excellent," the man said, without turning.

She watched him place a syringe on a small, metallic tray. Its handle clinked, followed by another sound, this time the raspy, telling sound of a file cutting through the neck of a glass vial. Then a pop when the man opened the vial. He grabbed the syringe and loaded the liquid from the vial, then carefully removed any air, pushing the piston until several droplets of fluid came out.

Dizziness overtook her, and she closed her eyes for a second.

"Shit," the man mumbled, then opened a drawer and went through it in a hurry.

She felt the needle poke deeply in her thigh, like it was happening to another person. She felt it, but distantly. She perceived a subdued burning sensation where he pushed the fluid into her muscle, then that went away when he pulled the needle out. She closed her weary eyes again, listless against her restraints.

The man cracked open ammonia salts under her nose, and she bounced back into reality at the speed of a lightning strike, aware, alert, and angry. For a second she fought to free herself, but froze when her eyes focused on the man in front of her.

He held a scalpel, close to her face. In itself, the small, shiny, silver object was capable of bringing formidable healing, as well as immense pain. The difference stood in the hand wielding it. She knew no healing was coming her way; only pain.

"No, no, please…" she pleaded, tears falling freely from her puffy eyes, burning as they rolled down her cheeks. "Please, no. I… I'll do anything."

"I am ready," the man said. He seemed calm, composed, and dispassionate. "Are you ready?"

"No, no, please…" she whimpered.

"Yeah," he said softly, almost whispering, inches away from her face. "Please say no to me. I love that."

She fell quiet, scared out of her mind. This time was different. *He* was different.

CHAPTER TWO
DAWN

"What if we get caught?" the girl whispered, trailing behind the boy.

They walked briskly on the small residential street engulfed in darkness, keeping to the middle of the road. There were no sidewalks. High-end homes lined up both sides, most likely equipped with sensor floodlights they didn't want to trip.

She tugged at his hand, but he didn't stop. "You never care about these things, Carl, but I do. If we get caught, I'll be grounded, like, forever!"

The boy kept going, his hand firmly clasping hers.

"Carl!" she raised the pitch in her whisper, letting her anxiety show more.

He stopped and turned, facing her. He frowned a little, seeing her anguish, but then smiled and caressed a loose strand of hair rebelling from under her sweatshirt's hood.

"There's no one, Kris. No one's going to see us. See? No lights are on, nothing. Everyone's asleep. Zee-zee-zee. It's five in the morning."

"I know," she sighed, "but—"

He kissed her pouted lips gently, a little boyish hesitation and awkwardness in his move.

"We'll be okay, I promise," he said, then grabbed her hand again. "We're almost there, come on. You'll love it."

A few more steps and the small street ended into the paved parking lot of what was going to be a future development of sorts, maybe a shopping center. From there, they had to cross Highway 1. They crouched down near the road, waiting for the light traffic to be completely clear. They couldn't afford to be seen, not even from a distance. At the right moment, they crossed the highway, hand in hand, and cut across the field toward the beach. Crossing Ocean Drive was next, then cutting through a few yards of shrubbery and trees to get to the sandy beach.

"Jeez, Carl," Kris protested, stopping in her tracks at the tree line. "Who knows what creatures live here? There could be snakes. Lizards. Gah…"

"There could be, but there aren't," Carl replied, seemingly sure of himself. "Trust me."

She held her breath and lowered her head, then clasped Carl's hand tightly. He turned on the flashlight on his phone and led the way without hesitation. A few seconds later, they reached the beach, and Kris let out a tense, long breath.

The light of the waning gibbous Moon reflected against the calm ocean waves, sending flickers of light everywhere and covering the beach in silver shadows. They were completely alone. The only creatures keeping them company were pale crabs that took bellicose stances when Kris and Carl stomped the sand around them, giggling.

"See? Told you," Carl said, "no one's going to see us out here. We can do whatever we want," he said playfully.

Kris squealed and ran toward the lifeguard tower. In daylight, the tower showed its bright yellow and orange, a splash of joyful colors on the tourist-abundant stretch of sand. At night, the structure appeared gloomy, resembling a menacing creature on tall, insect-like legs.

"It looks like one of those aliens from *War of the Worlds*," Kris said, then promptly started running, waving her arms up in the air, pretending she was flying.

Carl chased Kris, laughing and squealing with her, running in circles around the tower, and weaving footstep patterns between the solid wood posts.

"Phew," Carl said, stopping his chase and taking some distance. "Stinks of piss. Let's get out of here."

"Eww..." Kris replied, following him. "Why do men do that?"

"What? Pee?"

"Everybody pees, genius," Kris replied, still panting from the run. "Peeing where it stinks and bothers people, that's what I meant. Women pee in the bushes. Men should pee in the water if they don't like the bushes."

"Really? That's gross."

"Where do you think fish pee? At least the waves would wash away the pee and it wouldn't stink, to mess up our sunrise."

"Fish pee?" Carl pushed back, incredulous.

"They don't?"

They walked holding hands, putting a few more yards of distance between them and the tower. Then Carl suddenly dropped to the ground, dragging Kris with him. She squealed again, and laughed.

"Let's sit here," he said. "The show's on. Let's see if we get a good one."

The sky was starting to light up toward the east. They watched silently, hand in hand, as the dark shades of blue and gray gradually turned ablaze, mixing in dark reds and orange hues. The horizon line was clear, a sharp edge marking where ocean met sky.

"It's going to be great," Carl said. "No clouds, no haze." He kissed her lips quickly, and then turned his attention back to the celestial light show.

"You're a strange boy, Carl."

"Yeah? Why?"

"Other boys would have asked me to sneak out in the middle of the night to make out. With you, it's a sunrise, period. Should I worry?"

Carl smiled widely, then tickled Kris until she begged for mercy between gasps of air and bouts of uncontrollable laughter.

"Stop! Stop it already. I can't breathe!"

"I might want to get on with that make out, you know," Carl laughed.

"Nah, it's getting light. Someone could see us," Kris pushed back, unconvinced. "Someone could come by."

Carl shrugged and turned his attention to the sunrise. He grabbed her hand and held it gently, playing with her fingers.

Almost half the sky had caught fire, challenging the moonlight, and obliterating most of its reflected light against the blissful, serene, ocean waves.

Carl checked the time on his phone.

"A few more minutes until it comes out," he announced, sounding serious, as if predicting a rare and significant event. He took a few pictures of the sky, then suddenly snapped one of Kris.

"Ah… no," she reacted, "give that to me right this second, Carl." She grabbed the phone from his hand and looked at the picture he'd taken. The image showed a young girl with messy, golden brown hair, partially covering a scrunched, tense face with deep ridges on her brow. The snapshot revealed Kris biting her index fingernail, totally absorbed by the process, slobbering her sleeve cuff while at it.

"God-awful," she reacted, then pressed the option to delete.

"No!" Carl said, pulling the phone from her hands. "I like it!"

"There's nothing to like. There," she said, relaxing a little, and arranging her hair briefly with her long, thin fingers. "I'll pose for you." She smiled.

Carl took a few pictures. She looked gorgeous, against the backdrop of fiery skies, pink sand, and turquoise water. He took image after image, as she got into it and made faces, danced, and swirled in front of him, laughing.

The sun's first piercing ray shot out of the sea, just as Kris shrieked, a blood-curdling scream that got Carl to spring to his feet and run to her.

Speechless, Kris pointed a trembling hand at the lifeguard tower. Underneath the tower, between the wooden posts supporting the elevated structure, was the naked body of a young woman. She appeared to be kneeling, as if praying to the rising sun. Her hands were clasped together in front of her in the universal, unmistakable gesture of silent pleading.

Holding their breaths, they approached carefully, curious and yet afraid of what they stood to discover. The growing light of the new morning revealed more details with each step they took. Her back, covered in bruises and small cuts, stained in smudged, dried blood. Her blue eyes wide open, glossed over. A few specks of sand clung to her long, dark lashes. Her beautiful face, immobile, covered in sparkling flecks of sand. Her lips slightly parted, as if to let a last breath escape. Long, blonde hair, wet from sea spray, almost managed to disguise the deep cut in her neck.

No blood dripped from the wound; her heart had stopped beating for some time. Yet she held upright, unyielding in her praying posture, her knees stuck firmly in the sand covered in their footprints, and her eyes fixed on the beautiful sunrise they came to enjoy.

~~~End Preview~~~

Like *Dawn Girl*?

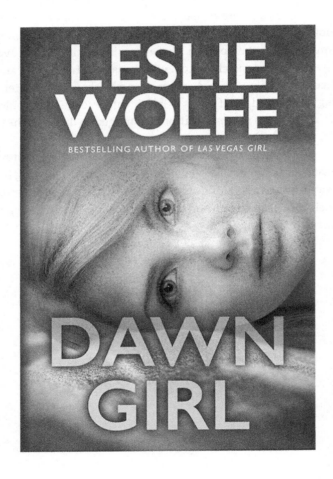

Buy It now!

ABOUT THE AUTHOR

Meet Leslie Wolfe, bestselling author and mastermind behind gripping thrillers that have won the hearts of over a million readers worldwide. She brings a fresh and invigorating touch to the thriller genre, crafting compelling narratives around unforgettable, powerhouse women.

Her books are not only an adrenaline-packed ride, but they're also sprinkled with psychological insights, offering readers an immersive, authentic experience that goes beyond conventional suspense.

You might know her from the Detective Kay Sharp series or have been hooked by Tess Winnett's relentless pursuit of justice. Maybe you've followed the dynamic duo Baxter & Holt through the gritty streets of Las Vegas or plunged into political intrigue with Alex Hoffmann.

Recently, Leslie published *The Girl You Killed*, a psychological thriller that's pure, unputdownable suspense. This standalone novel will have fans of *The Undoing, The Silent Patient,* and *Little Fires Everywhere* on the edge of their seats.

Whether you're into the mind games of Criminal Minds, love crime thrillers like James Patterson's, or enjoy the heart-pounding tension in Kendra Elliot and Robert Dugoni's mysteries, Leslie's got a thriller series for you. Fans of action-packed writers like Tom Clancy or Lee Child will find plenty to love in her Alex Hoffmann series.

Wolfe's latest psychological thriller, *The Surgeon*, will have you racing through the pages gasping for breath until the final jaw-dropping twist, delighting fans of *Gone Girl* and *The Girl on the Train*.

Discover all of Leslie's works on her Amazon store, at Amazon.com/LeslieWolfe. Want a sneak peek at what's next? Become an insider for early access to previews of her new novels, each a thrilling ride you won't want to miss.

- Email: LW@WolfeNovels.com
- Facebook: https://www.facebook.com/wolfenovels
- Follow Leslie on Amazon: http://bit.ly/WolfeAuthor
- Follow Leslie on BookBub: http://bit.ly/wolfebb
- Website: www.LeslieWolfe.com
- Visit Leslie's Amazon store: Amazon.com/LeslieWolfe

BOOKS BY LESLIE WOLFE

TESS WINNETT SERIES

Dawn Girl
The Watson Girl
Glimpse of Death
Taker of Lives
Not Really Dead
Girl With A Rose
Mile High Death
The Girl They Took
The Girl Hunter

STANDALONE TITLES

The Surgeon
The Girl You Killed
Stories Untold
Love, Lies and Murder

DETECTIVE KAY SHARP SERIES

The Girl From Silent Lake
Beneath Blackwater River
The Angel Creek Girls
The Girl on Wildfire Ridge
Missing Girl at Frozen Falls

BAXTER & HOLT SERIES

Las Vegas Girl
Casino Girl
Las Vegas Crime

ALEX HOFFMANN SERIES

Executive
Devil's Move
The Backup Asset
The Ghost Pattern
Operation Sunset

For the complete list of books in all available formats, visit:

Amazon.com/LeslieWolfe

Made in the USA
Monee, IL
04 April 2024